Content Warnings

*Abuse/Trauma (physical, emotional, sexual)

*Drinking/Drug use

*PTSD

*Rape

*Suicide/Suicidal thoughts

*Miscarriage/Infertility

*Depression/Anxiety/Mental Illness

*Panic Attacks

Dedication

To my husband Nick, who has told me for years to get a hobby and stop
bugging him.

Acknowledgments

I just wanted to take a moment to say thank you to the many wonderful people in my life who have supported me in all different ways that lead to me publishing my book. Including those that were taken from me too soon.

Thank you to my family. While there are many of them, I wanted to thank my husband Nicholas Jensen who has supported me in rekindling my passion for my writing. My sons Quinten and Dominik Jensen for just being them and filling my life with love. Also, to my older sister Stephanie VanDoorn-Kazyak for setting up my website and guiding me through marketing. And my younger sister Nikki Fewless for reading every single draft and talking to me through them all.

A special thank you to Marla Taviano, my amazing editor, to whom me making it this far would not have been possible.

Thank you to the amazing writing community that I have found on social media. You all inspire me every day! But again, a special thank you to Kaithlin Shepherd for taking the time to walk me through the entire self-publishing ordeal, and for designing my amazing cover and social media graphics! (Please check out her amazing romance novels).

Thank you to all that supported me by reading my book before i released and gave me feedback. But especially to my co-work Wendy Zeigler-Hesche, who read multiple drafts of my book, has been incredibly supportive to me and my writing.

Thank you to Panera Bread in Grandville for giving me a spac work away from my crazy household, and for their great food amazing customer service.

Prologue

The mundane act of eating dinner and scrolling through his phone did nothing to lessen the severity of Ben's look—neither did his black suit. Though he was known to most for his charm and a smile that could break hearts, *I* was the one that got to experience the full spectrum of emotions he was capable of.

I stopped fidgeting with my food and took a bite while he continued with his silence.

I didn't take it personally. He was a busy man—always working—always stressed. Which I would be, too, if I had to juggle a job, a wife, a son, *and* a mistress.

But I couldn't complain, seeing how I *was* the side piece.

"So, I, uh, wanted to talk to you about something," I began.

"Okay."

"Could you put your phone down?"

He complied and looked up, waiting for me to continue.

"I, uh, took a pregnancy test. And, I'm pregnant. Well, *we're* pregnant."

I hadn't expected tears of joy or overwhelming excitement, but the silence that fell back over the room was deafening.

He continued to stare—motionless, so I picked up my plate and emptied the rest into the trash. I had lost my appetite anyway.

"I don't understand," he began.

I smirked. "You don't understand how we got pregnant?"

But I could tell even from across the room he wasn't amused.

I took a deep breath. "The shot isn't a hundred percent effective," I said, rinsing off my plate. Then I continued to try and fill the silence. "I didn't think—"

"That's the problem, isn't it, Harper?" he interjected while shaking his head. "You didn't *think.*"

My chest tightened. I attempted to yell *fuck you* to him, but the words never left my mouth.

"Hey, I didn't do this alone," I replied. "Listen, I get this isn't an ideal situation and all, but you can't be pissed at *me.*"

"You're the one who said you were on birth control."

I crossed my arms, and my face got warm. "I *am* on birth control."

"Yeah? Well, I'm starting to wonder."

I rolled my eyes.

"Don't," he snapped. "You know I hate that."

"Oh, so you can be a prick, but God forbid I *roll my eyes*!"

Ben sprung from his seat. "I'm not being a prick. I'm just trying to understand how your birth control conveniently stopped working a week after you find out I didn't leave Mia."

"I took the pregnancy test *a few weeks ago*!" I shouted in defense of myself. "Why the fuck do you think I stayed when I found out?"

"Oh, so you've been lying?"

My eyes rolled once more.

"Damn it, Harper, knock that shit off. You're a grown-ass woman," he said as he took a step toward me. "You don't need to roll your eyes like a bitchy teenager."

"Fuck you," I replied. It was all my brain could think to respond with.

His lips curled into a smile. "Yeah? Is that the best you got?" he asked. "So, what, did you talk to Mia? Find out how she got me to stay around all these years?" He paused and shook his head. "I'll be damned if I get trapped into another eighteen years of child support because *you* don't know how to use contraception."

"Is that all you care about? The *money*?"

"Of course I care about the money. The fact that you *don't* tells me all I need to know about you raising a child," he continued. "Kids are *expensive,* Harper. They rely on you for everything. They ruin your body; you can't hang out with friends, go to the bar…"

"You don't seem to have any issues leaving your son to spend time with a woman who *isn't* his mother."

His eyes grew dark as they seared into mine. I was getting to him.

I couldn't believe how unbearable he was being. I had stayed with him when I found out he was still with his wife. He had promised he was leaving her and was waiting for the right time. I didn't necessarily believe him, but I had also just found out I was pregnant, so I wanted to take time to decide what I wanted to do about him— *and* about the baby.

"Jesus, Harper, could you concentrate for two fucking seconds?"

My thoughts broke away, and I looked at him. "Sorry," I said out of habit, then wanted to kick myself for doing so.

He exhaled. "Yeah, you're always sorry."

"What the hell does that mean?"

"I just don't understand how you could be so stupid."

"*I'm* stupid? God, you are such an *asshole*!" I replied as my nails dug into the palms of my hands. "And you know what? I don't have to put up with this."

I stepped past him and headed into the living room.

"Stop being so dramatic, Harper," he replied, following behind.

"I deserve better than you. Better than someone who cheats on his wife."

"Yeah? Says the home-wrecker herself."

"*I* didn't know you were still *with* her!"

"Bullshit. You can't lie to me," he said with a snicker. "You *knew*. You might be stupid, but you're not *that* stupid. You knew when I wouldn't stay here, it was because I was going home to her," he continued. "You just want to be the innocent victim in this, but you're *not*. You're just some crazy *bitch* who got knocked up trying to keep a guy from leaving."

My fist connected with his face before I had time to think it through.

Time slowed as his eyes narrowed—searing into mine.

I turned around, making a run for my room.

He followed, but I was faster.

I slammed my door shut and locked it. The wood flexed from the weight of his body.

My heart pounded in my ears. I was going to throw up.

I took a few deep breaths as Ben hit the door once more.

"Glad to see all your boxing lessons came in handy," he said.

"Ben, you need to leave."

"Oh, so, you can throw a punch, but you can't take one, huh?" he asked. "This is *assault,* Harper. I could have you arrested."

It was true; he could.

I swallowed the lump in my throat.

He was silent for a moment before I heard glass shatter.

"Whoops!" he said, his voice unnervingly calm.

I put my ear to the door and heard his footsteps recede.

I let out another deep breath as a pain started to form in my side.

Breaking glass echoed down the hall.

He was acting like a psycho. That's what I was telling myself anyway. The judgmental voice in my head disagreed.

The only psycho here is you, It said.

I looked at my throbbing hand. Disagreeing with my own head was pointless. I couldn't dispute the fact that he hadn't hit me. He hadn't assaulted me. I *was* the crazy one.

The front door slammed, and everything went silent.

I climbed up on my bed and watched out my window as he got into his car and peeled out of the driveway.

I stepped out of the bedroom, tiptoed around the remnants of a picture frame, and hurried to the front door, securing the deadbolt. I took a deep breath, leaning my back up against the wall for support.

I examined my living room, taking note of the damage. There wasn't much sentimental value to anything I owned, so the broken pieces from my belongings on the ground caused me little pain. However, the fact that I had just chased off the only person left in my life generated an all-too-familiar sense of abandonment. With another deep breath, I walked to the dining room, picked up my phone, and pressed Caleb's name.

As it rang, I stared at Ben's half-finished plate of food. My adrenaline slowed, accentuating the pain that was pulsating in my hand.

Caleb's soothing voice came over my speaker. My heart dropped as the recorded message said he wasn't available.

Neither was Ben, but that didn't stop you, The Voice commented.

A rush of nausea swept in again. My deep breathing wasn't strong enough that time to keep my dinner in place. I ran to the kitchen, and my undigested meal met the sink. As the contents of my stomach swirled down the drain, I glanced up at my reflection in the window.

Alone again. This time with a baby, The Voice began. *With no father* and *a shitty mother, this thing is going to be just as fucked up as you.*

Chapter One

A little over a month later

"Do you want to talk about what happened?" Sarah asked.

I glanced over at her as she looked at me with a smile. But while her lips showed warmth, her eyes displayed concern—a look that aggravated me to my core.

"There is nothing to talk about."

"Harper... you've been coming here for two weeks now, and we haven't gotten anywhere."

I shrugged. I hated talking about my past; I didn't see the point in it. Bad things happen. People eventually move on—the end.

"Your mother said..."

"I'm sure whatever she said was only *partially* true."

"Well, I would know your side of things if you would talk to me."

"What is it that you want me to say?!" I asked, taking her by surprise. "I'm twenty-eight, I live alone, I enjoy a nice glass of wine every night with dinner, I probably have more mommy issues than daddy ones, and a month ago, I had a miscarriage, and lost a fallopian tube."

Her eyes stayed on me while mine drifted away. She wasn't impressed by my child-like outburst. I wasn't either. But she had asked for it. She was the one prying into my past—asking questions that didn't concern her.

Shrink or not, if I didn't want to share, I shouldn't have to.

"Well, there's a lot in there to unpack."

"If you say so."

While I said it casually, I also couldn't deny my life got dark the day I was released from the hospital. Up until that point, I was used to my dark days, used to the endless chatter of the unrelenting voice in my head poking at my insecurities. Typically, it wouldn't have been a problem; it wouldn't have been out of my control. But something felt different that day. Something that hadn't scared me like that in quite some time.

Sarah narrowed her eyes as if she was thinking.

She got up and rifled through her filing cabinet. "I don't know if you like to write or not. But it can help to write things down. For instance, you could write about the people in your life, events that have happened—maybe you could even start by telling me a little bit about yourself. You know, so I could get to know you." She held a notebook in her hand as she turned around to face me. "I know it's hard to talk to a stranger about things, but I do want to help you. I just need you to let me."

The idea of my thoughts written permanently on a piece of paper didn't thrill me, but maybe what she said was true, and writing things down could help.

Not knowing what my intentions were exactly, I told her what I knew she wanted to hear. I told her I would give it a shot.

***

I took a deep breath, letting my exhausted body ease up from the tension I had been holding in. My phone pinged as I moved it to the passenger seat. Shutting my eyes, I let out a heavy sigh at the thought of dealing with anyone or anything else that day. But as I glanced at the screen, I couldn't ignore the name that appeared. If I did, she would just start calling.

Serena: Hey girl

I was confident I didn't have the energy to deal with anyone, even my best friend, Serena. Which caused guilt to emerge, knowing I should be excited to hear from her—to hear from *anyone*. But the guilt grew twofold when I realized I was so wrapped up in my own world I had forgotten she would be in town.

Although we didn't see each other often, we were there for each other when it mattered. Well, when I allowed her to be around for it anyway. I couldn't blame her for her absence when I didn't let her in on everything that was occurring in my life. It was a common thread in my relationships that my therapist was bound to pull on soon.

Harper: On my way home now!

I was sure she was aware I had forgotten. I didn't know if it was genetics pulling the strings of a shitty memory or if it was my narcissistic tendencies that came out at inopportune moments. But likely, it was a combination of both.

***

"Forgot I was coming, huh?" Serena asked as I unlocked the door to let us in.

"I'm sorry; it's been a crazy week."

It was more than that, but I didn't want to dive into any of it with her—well, with anyone.

"It's fine," she commented. "You didn't make any other plans for tonight, did ya?"

"No, just trying to catch up on some of my shows."

"Good. I don't want to go alone."

I walked back into the living room, where she was already looking my way. Undoubtedly waiting for whatever excuse I was going to give.

"I really don't feel like…"

"I don't care. We're going."

With her pushy attitude, I knew in the long run that rejecting an invitation was pointless.

"Alright… can I at least know where we're going?" I asked.

She smirked and looked away.

My stomach did a small somersault. "Oh jeez, I'm not going to be like the third wheel on a Tinder date, am I?"

Her brows furrowed as her gaze reconnected with mine. "I thought you were kidding," she replied with a heavy sigh. "You really do have like the shittiest memory, don't you?"

I flopped down in the recliner across from her. "What do you mean?"

"We just talked about it at your birthday party."

"I don't remember much from that night," I laughed. But a familiar rush of guilt ran through my body.

"Clearly," she replied, shaking her head. "The ten-year reunion is tonight. I didn't think you'd need a reminder for something like that." She raised her eyebrow at me. "I assume then you didn't RSVP to their Facebook invite."

"No, when they sent it out, I thought it would be easier just not to respond either way. I didn't want people giving their fake ass responses of, *oh, you should come… we miss you.*"

"Bold of you to assume they would care," she retorted.

Though bitchy, she wasn't wrong.

But her apathetic response showed me an open door to deny the invitation. "Good. Then I don't have to go.".

Her eyes flew up from her phone. "Dude, *I'm* going, which means *you're* going."

"But what if Ben's there?"

"Then I'll punch him in his fucking face, and we can continue to have a good night."

I glanced at her, unamused.

"Come on, Harper, you can't hide out forever. You're going to run into him at some point. Besides, you shouldn't be the one hiding. He's the one that should be ashamed."

I stayed silent while my fingers fidgeted in my lap.

For that one instance, I regretted having left out any details from my fallout with Ben. I had meant to tell her everything. But as usual, keeping my world a secret got easier with each passing day.

"Just come for a little bit," she said. "If he's there and you can't handle it, we'll come home."

My mouth felt dry as I tried to feel reassured by her words.

"Alright," I said with a sigh. "I'll go."

***

The steam rolled out from behind the curtain as I slipped my clothes off onto the tiled floor.

The intense heat from the water scalded my skin, but with the pain came relief.

My stiff body began to relax while the troubling thoughts that had been burrowing a hole in my stomach subsided.

My mind was put to ease, knowing that there was an open bar in my near future.

Yeah, God forbid you don't drink for one night, The Voice said.

The irony of my own head telling me I drank too much was that I drank too much *because* of my own head. The Voice was only known to shut up once enough alcohol had entered my system. A problematic solution to some, but a welcomed one to me.

I tried to make the argument that it was a social event. But who was I fooling? I was doing what I always did—justifying my need to drink.

***

I was startled by a creak from the door as Serena's voice echoed throughout the small room.

"What are you gonna wear tonight?" she asked but gave me no time to respond. "I brought something, but I don't know about it now."

I shifted the shower curtain enough so I could see her. "I'll just wear whatever. You can look through my closet if you need something."

She nodded, closing the door—the breeze from which sent a chill up my spine.

I pulled the towel off the bar and hugged the fabric tight to my skin.

Moments later, the door opened once more as the cold from the central air flowed around her, depleting the steam I had built up.

"That was quick," I responded with a smile.

"You good with me wearing these?" she asked as she straightened out the top.

I nodded.

She clearly had already had that in mind when going to look. But I didn't care; my closet was full of clothes that hadn't seen the daylight in months.

Ben had a habit of critiquing everything I wore. And while our time together may have been short, I had difficulty not hearing those comments every time I put something on.

Besides, they looked better on her anyway. She had clearly been hitting the gym in her free time.

She stepped aside and then followed me as I walked to my room. I flipped through my closet to the most risqué dress I owned, determined to show Ben—or *anyone*—that I didn't care what they thought.

I pulled it off the hanger as my phone pinged from the bed.

By the time I looked, Serena was already holding it, grinning ear to ear.

"I didn't know you and Caleb were talking again," she said.

"We're not. I mean, we haven't been," I responded, snatching the phone out of her hand and reading the message.

Caleb: Hey

I exhaled as I tossed the phone back on the bed.

What did you expect? The Voice asked.

"Are you still pissed at him?" she asked.

"I'm not anything; we just haven't talked. I'll message him later."

I walked back into my bathroom, hoping to drop the conversation, but instead, she followed.

"I know you guys were taking some time apart because of Ben, but since that's over, I figured things might have started up again between the two of you."

I stayed silent. I wish she would read the room.

"I mean, you're not back with Ben, are you?"

I raised my eyebrows.

"Sorry, that was stupid of me to ask," she said.

I wanted to agree, but given my track record, it really wasn't. I had a habit of making bad decisions, so I felt like I couldn't just leave it at that. "I haven't talked to Ben in over a month."

"And Caleb?" she asked, raising her eyebrows even higher than mine.

Caleb was a whole different story.

After a moment of continued silence on my end, she took the hint and let the conversation dry up.

The conversation's dry spell led her to the kitchen to wet her whistle while I finished getting ready.

A ping from my phone rang through the bathroom as I touched up my makeup.

My stomach twisted into knots while I messed with my hair. Caleb's sudden reappearance in my life hadn't been on my agenda for the evening. Well, none of it had.

But I would be lying if I said his return didn't elevate my mood; although, his awful timing did stop it short of being able to fully take over.

When I got down to it, my procrastination was the obstacle to my enthusiasm. I had plenty of time to figure out how I wanted to handle him—handle *us*. It was always a matter of time before our worlds would collide once again, and we would end up right back where we always did—in one of our beds.

I sighed, trying to push him away from my thoughts. I let the towel fall to the ground as I stared at myself in the mirror. My fingers trailed over the almost-healed scar on my lower abdomen. While the physical wound would disappear in time, the emotional one was sure to linger year after year like all the other ones I had suffered in my life.

I was glad it wasn't sore anymore and that regular sexual activity could resume. Whether I was ready for those activities was a whole other discussion. While the thought of taking off my dress in front of another human didn't thrill me, I knew it wasn't a must when having sex.

I put on my bra and underwear, then slid the dress over my head—covering the parts of my body I desperately wanted to hide.

I kept messing with my hair as my anxiety continued to pump throughout my body like blood in my veins. As usual, my mind began pestering me about my looks. But I knew my natural hair color was fine. It was suitable for me and my complexion. I had given the dye job some thought, months before when I was amid my relationship with Ben. I'd wanted to make sense of the girl I saw in the mirror.

"Harper, I poured you one!" Serena called out. "But you have to hurry up. The Uber will be here in 10!"

I grabbed my heels off the floor and slid them on as I walked to the kitchen.

"Ugh, I love that dress on you," she said as I approached her.

"Thanks," I replied, picking up my drink.

I lifted the bottom of it into the air and let the bite from the vodka run past my tongue and down my throat. After a moment, the glassware clinked against the counter as I set the cup of deserted ice cubes back down.

I smiled at the sensation that cascaded throughout my body.

"Are you sure you're good?" she asked.

"Yup," I replied, her worry pulling me from the first small amount of bliss I had been able to experience that day. "Sorry. You said the Uber was coming."

She eased up on her uneasy expression and took a sip of her drink. "Yeah—well, we still have like five minutes." She paused and then continued as if my mental health was still weighing on her mind.

"I promise, if anything happens tonight, I have your back. I doubt Ben will even show. He's stupid if he does."

My stomach knotted once again.

I reached for the bottle, and instead of pouring myself another, I pressed it to my lips.

He was stupid; that was what I was worried about.

Chapter Two

The streets of Grand Rapids were littered with cars and people. All of whom were downtown for either the bars, sports, or concerts. Our event was being held at one of the largest hotels in the city. It was a classier feel than what you would expect from people who spent their teenage years drinking by a large bonfire and smoking weed in the cornfields.

As the Uber pulled to a stop under the main door's bright lights, I started to get nervous thinking of all the people I would run into—all the small talk I would have to endure.

Why had I let Serena talk me into coming?

As we walked through the doors, the table to check-in at sat just past a small crowd. I went towards it to find the bar, while Serena had already been swept up in a warm embrace by an old friend.

"Excuse me…who are you?" a woman asked as I tried walking past her into the large banquet room.

She looked vaguely familiar, but I didn't care enough to inquire who she was.

"Harper Jones."

She glanced down at her sheet. "I don't see you on the list."

"I didn't RSVP," I replied as I tried peering inside the room to spot the bar.

When I looked back, I caught the end of an eye roll.

"Since you didn't RSVP, we don't have a name tag for you. You'll have to write your name on here," she said, handing me the glossy sticker and a marker.

"Do I *have* to have a name tag?" I asked.

"Yes."

I filled out my name and ripped it off the paper.

"It's forty dollars at the door since you didn't pay ahead of time," she added.

I reached into my purse and handed her the money. At least I would be getting my money's worth from the open bar.

"Serena!" The greeter girl yelled.

"Dana!"

I left them to exchange their pleasantries and headed to the area where I planned on spending most of my night.

"Vodka cranberry please," I said to the bartender.

He made my drink and slid it over to me.

While the vodka passed my lips, I felt my purse vibrate. I had already ignored four text messages.

My last night with Ben had resulted in an unanswered call to Caleb. By the time he returned it, I had come to my senses and let it go to voicemail. I didn't even know what I would have said to him that night, what I would say to him when we did talk. I wasn't sure if we had had enough time apart for us to continue as we had before. I wasn't confident that any amount of time would make that possible.

I needed more alcohol.

"Can I get two shots of vodka?" I asked, pulling my lips from my drink.

Wouldn't it be easier to just ask for the bottle? The Voice questioned.

The bartender's eyes briefly met mine, but I quickly looked away. I didn't need his judgment. However, it wasn't like his feelings on the subject would change my drinking habits. If my own overly critical mind didn't get me to stop, a contemptuous look from the man pouring the shots would certainly have no pull.

"It's for me and my friend," I commented.

Why did I always defend myself? I had every right to drink what I wanted. Wear what I wanted. *Do* what I wanted. Why did I care what he thought?

Because you care what everyone thinks, The Voice said.

He had probably sensed as soon as I had walked up that he would be seeing a lot of me that night. But whether his Spidey sense was tingling that the woman in front of him liked to indulge herself with liquor, he exhibited no signs of actual judgment while he tended to my need and poured the shots.

I tossed one back and carried the other one toward Serena, still caring for some dumb reason what he—or anyone possibly watching—thought about me.

I waited for him to help another guest before the other one disappeared down the hatch. As soon as it had, I knew it would do the trick. I just needed to wait a few more minutes for the alcohol to snuff out the wretched voice that seemed to do more damage to my mind than the alcohol did to my liver.

"Already starting without me?" Serena asked.

"Yeah, sorry, didn't feel like chatting it up with Dana."

God, you're petty, The Voice said.

It was right. My experience in high school wasn't the least bit traumatizing; these people hadn't left a lasting impact on my life. I spent the first half of my high school experience being invisible and the second half consumed by my relationship with Jacob. No wonder no one noticed me. I did what I could to blend in and be left alone. Only alcohol could make me an extrovert.

Serena walked up to the bar with me trailing behind. She ordered her drink as I finished mine.

She smiled in my direction. "Also, another Vodka Cranberry."

***

As my former classmates continued to fill the room, I only recognized a few of them. Serena, on the other hand, had a knack for remembering almost every person she met. She moved quickly around the room—networking as she called it—with anyone she could. She didn't care so much for the small talk either, but she was all for expanding her network of people.

My phone vibrated against the tablecloth.

It was probably as good of a time as any to hand it over. The last thing I needed was to get drunk and send stupid shit to people I shouldn't. I picked it up and looked at the screen—two more texts from Caleb and one from an unknown number.

"Can you take my phone?" I asked Serena, interrupting one of her many conversations.

She laughed and tucked my phone into her purse as she carried on.

***

Most of the night was unmemorable. I guess I should have planned for that possibility. I spoke to a few people I hadn't seen in years. I even got hit on at the bar by a few guys who didn't know I had been in their class. But even the alcohol couldn't make me charming.

My sultry, moody behavior didn't seem to have the same effect on the men there as it typically did at bars. Maybe the odds were better there. Or maybe my bitterness was just reaching harsher levels.

Part of me had wanted to be there to be spiteful when seeing Ben—showing him I could ignore him in person too. Although that plan seemed a little undercooked and possibly fueled by the alcohol because realistically, I was glad he hadn't come. I was still so angry at him. But while the relationship proved nearly fatal to my self-worth, there were moments—many in fact—where it felt better than being alone.

When Ben had come back into my life, less than a year before, I was committed to making it work. I had said *fuck it* to my feelings for Caleb, along with my clearly unstable tendencies, and flew towards the light.

I knew it wasn't love, but it was better than loneliness. In an attempt to save myself from drowning in that sea of solitude, I had headed straight into the sun. But the prolonged exposure to his true self only left me burned.

***

By 11:00, I had stopped counting the drinks. The world around me had started to spin while my body stood still, so I rested my head on the table. Serena was still immersed in conversation with a guy she had been chatting with all night. I only lifted for sips of water from the cup she had brought me earlier.

"Harper?"

Lifting my head required too much effort.

"Thanks for coming," Serena said with a slight chuckle. "I wasn't ready to go yet, but she clearly is."

Had she forgotten who had talked me into going? I wanted to remind her, but that seemed like a lot of work.

"Babe, you gotta get up."

I could feel his hand graze the small of my back. The touch felt intimate—familiar. I tried to focus my energy on listening to his voice, but my concentration kept slipping.

"Maybe you should carry her," Serena said. "She hasn't stood up in a while. She might not be able to."

"Why did you let her drink this much?"

Serena exhaled loudly. "It was an open bar. Besides, you know I have no control over that."

She wasn't wrong. *I* didn't even have control over my own drinking.

"Harper, I'm going to pick you up."

I smiled as I finally recognized the soothing voice. Then I frowned. What was he doing there?

I lifted my head. "No, I can walk."

I propped myself up against the table and willed my vision to adjust. Caleb's eyes met mine. I could feel my pulse rise as his lips curved into a smile.

God, I had missed him. It had been months since I had seen him last and almost a year since we had talked.

Something seemed different about him. It wasn't his hair, or even his build, though he certainly didn't look to be skipping any time at the gym either. I wanted to ask him what it was but then realized what a weird and stupid question that would have been.

What a sight I must've been, and not in a good way. That was not how I wanted him to see me, not after what seemed like forever apart. I was probably just reinforcing why he should be with Cassy— *if* he was still with Cassy.

"Harper." Serena waved her hand in front of my face. "Jesus girl, even wasted you go in your own damn world," she said with a laugh as the others at the table followed suit.

My face flushed. At least my blood still knew where to rush to.

Caleb appeared agitated by Serena's comment, but she didn't seem to notice.

I stepped towards him, immediately feeling the whole building shift.

"Whoa…" he said as he grabbed my stomach to catch me.

I turned my head and looked into his eyes.

What was he doing?

I savored the feeling of his touch for a moment before pulling away.

"Here's her phone and her purse," Serena began as Caleb let go. "I was supposed to stay at her house tonight, but I'll probably crash somewhere else. Can you make sure she's good before you leave?"

"Yeah," Caleb responded.

***

I opened the door to his truck as he stood behind me. I climbed in while he reached for the seatbelt.

"I can buckle myself."

He rolled his eyes and shut the door while I struggled to do what I said I could.

He climbed into the driver seat and turned the key. I let the faint melody of R & B calm me.

I put my head against the headrest and closed my eyes, wanting to give in to the depressant and fall asleep. But instead, I turned and looked at Caleb while my mind drifted.

Serena and I had been close since graduating high school. She was my best friend. But Caleb—he was my person. And he had been for the better part of the eight years we had known each other.

What had started as young love turned to devastating heartbreak. A dark period that was followed by an agreement to be fuck friends, which subsequently blossomed into a very strange but meaningful friendship.

He became the person I could be angry in front of and could say whatever to without fear of him thinking I was a terrible person. Because after everything that had happened, I wasn't trying to make him love me, and I wasn't trying to impress him. I knew he was just another boy who would eventually move on, another person who would leave. And I had convinced myself that I was okay with that.

Then a few years in, he met a girl named Alyssa. At first, I gave him shit about her. He would take her out on dates and then would finish his night with me. But then that became less and less frequent, and the overnights started with her instead. Then promptly followed weekend trips away and holidays with her family. Soon, I found myself terrified at the thought of losing him.

So, I stopped telling him what I was thinking and the anxiety that went along with it. I stopped letting him see me at my lowest and would lie and say I was out so he wouldn't come over, even when I needed him the most. I stopped letting him take care of me with the hope that he wouldn't think I was too much to be around and wouldn't eventually leave like I had thought before.

But with the distancing of the only person that I felt ever really knew me came with a whole new slew of problems. A new kind of self-loathing that attached to my insides like a tumor that fed off my insecurities. I was the creator of my own dystopian reality, and I was bound and determined to keep him in my life—even if it was just as a friend.

The times I stopped seeing him were for our own good. He saw it as cruel and vindictive. I saw it as a break from our stupidity of boundary crossing and borderline infidelity. A friendship couldn't survive a future wife finding out we were together. And being the jealous person that I was, I couldn't blame anyone for having that stance.

While my plan had worked to keep him in my life, it also served as a catalyst for our fighting—something that pushed our passion into a whole other segment of our relationship. It happened without impacting our time spent in the bedroom, as that was the most consistent thing about us.

All of that started after things ended with Alyssa, but I always knew there would be more. So, when Cassy came along, I braced myself again for the possibility of her being his future wife. While she might not know about Caleb's and my history exactly—she wasn't stupid. She could see the way he looked at me. But I needed him to stop. I needed him to do better, to see past his intense passion for me. I did it all so that, in the end, I didn't lose him. So, in the end, I got to keep my person—my best friend.

He turned and looked at me, his eyes briefly meeting mine.

"What?" he asked as his brows furrowed.

"Where's Cassy?"

He shrugged.

"Some boyfriend you are," I replied.

"We aren't together anymore."

I hated that I was relieved to hear that. As much as it pained me to see them together, I wanted that for him. I hated her purely out of jealousy. She seemed good for him, and he deserved a good woman. He deserved someone who didn't drive him crazy.

"What about you? You still seeing that guy?" he asked.

I glanced out the window, watching a streetlight flicker as we drove past. I had to close my eyes to readjust my vision once more, almost losing my train of thought on giving him an answer.

My drunken thoughts drifted about. Wondering what would happen if I said no. Would we end up in my bed? Would everything be like it was before? Was our arrangement still intact? If it was, for how long would he be with me before he met someone else? Could I handle his absence again?

On the other hand, if I said yes, could I handle not having him again at all?

"No," I answered but then allowed my anxiety to get the best of me. "Not really, anyway."

He looked as unsatisfied with that answer as I had been with saying it.

I needed to stop making it so complicated. It was a no. It was a hell no.

"Why didn't you return my call?" he asked. "I've been worried about you."

His brief glance my way showed his sincerity, not that I ever needed to question it.

I hid a smile and shrugged, trying to buy myself time to come up with an answer. But as we turned down my street, the sight of a familiar car in my driveway muted my thoughts in a way that no vodka could.

Chapter Three

Caleb pulled in front of my house. My chest tightened, making it hard to breathe.

"Looks like your *boyfriend's* here," Caleb said.

I wanted to roll my eyes, make a comment—something. But my body and brain seemed paralyzed.

I was nowhere near ready or sober enough to deal with Ben. Where was Serena when I needed her?

Ben's eyes met mine as he leaned onto the back of his car. My anxiety clung tighter causing me to release my gaze from his and peer down at my fingers while they picked away at the small amount of nails I had left.

"Are you okay?" Caleb asked.

His hand moved to mine, interfering with my nervous habit.

"Uh, yeah. Yeah. I'm fine." I tried to prove it with a forced smile, but the nerves didn't allow for it to stay long.

"Do you want me to stay?" he asked.

Yes, was what my head shouted, but I needed to be realistic about what Caleb staying could do to us both. Confusingly enough, everything—yet nothing, had changed since the last time we had seen each other.

"Uh, no. It's fine," I responded.

My feet unsteadily hit the ground as my recently intoxicated mind tried to will itself sober.

I approached Ben expecting to hear Caleb's truck pull away, but the hum of the engine lingering in the air told me he wasn't ready to leave.

"So, is *he* why you've been ignoring me?" Ben asked.

He was as pleasant as always. I resisted the urge to give him my famous cross look and instead tried to concentrate on appearing sober. "No, he was just giving me a ride home," I answered.

I didn't know what I was expecting him to look like when I saw him again. It had only been a little over a month, but a lot had happened in that time. I knew I looked worse for the wear. Maybe I was expecting the same of him. But as he stepped into the light, he looked like his typical handsome self.

While the severity was still apparent, his charming grin hung flawlessly on his perfectly symmetrical face. While it no longer fooled me into thinking any kindness he showed was sincere, I preferred his manipulation tactics to his spiteful ones.

"You look really beautiful," he said, reaching for my hand.

I stepped back, almost losing my footing, and crossed my arms.

"Thank you."

I could sense his annoyance by my brush-off, but he continued calmly. "I've been calling since…well since the last time I was here."

We both fell silent. The crickets, along with Caleb's engine, gave a weird ambiance to our conversation. I thought about inviting him in to talk, but that was just the alcohol talking. Sober me wrestled with the idiocy of the thought.

The question Serena had asked me earlier was all too on point for the way I lived my life. I had a bad habit of backsliding, and he had the persistence of a door salesman.

"Earth to Harper."

"Sorry. Uh, I've been busy."

He smirked. "So that's all I get? You've been *busy*?"

I looked up at him and caught his glance, his eyes returning to their rigid state.

"Why weren't you at the reunion tonight?"

He wasn't known for passing up an opportunity to be doted on by others, especially women.

"Why would I want to see any of those people?" he questioned, using a tone that sucker-punched the stupidity he clearly thought I was showing.

"What is it you want? Why are you here?" I asked.

"I wanted to say I'm sorry. I've been trying to apologize for weeks," he replied, as his eyes grew softer once again.

I looked away. I wasn't going to fall prey to his manipulative strategies.

While I tried to come up with a reason for dodging his attempts—even contemplating trying the truth—my eyes shifted to Caleb's truck briefly before I looked back at Ben.

"I know things got…crazy," he said. "But things are different now. We can be different."

Again, he took a small step towards me. The delayed reaction I had from the alcohol allowed him to rest his hand on my hip. His other hand moved up to stroke my cheek with his thumb as he leaned in for his lips to meet mine.

Unfortunately for him, I had anticipated his last move and turned my head, causing his lips to graze my cheek.

He immediately pulled back. "Seriously?"

The sound of Caleb's truck door opening caused Ben's expression to grow more intense.

"Everything okay?" Caleb asked.

I took a deep breath. "Yeah, everything's fine." My voice cracked.

My intimidated tone bothered Ben, which was almost laughable, as before, it always seemed to serve as a boost to his ego. But I had a feeling his ego was searching for a little more than that with Caleb around.

The truck door shut, and he approached us.

"She said she's fine," Ben said. "You can take off."

Caleb stopped next to me and lightly touched my back. "You good?" he asked.

"She's fine," Ben replied. "We're just talking."

Caleb turned towards Ben, his eyes narrowing.

It was like two dogs fighting over a piece of meat.

I touched Caleb's forearm. "I'm fine," I managed to say.

"See, so you can leave," Ben commented as if my answer allowed him to lay claim to the meat.

"Harper…" Caleb looked right into my eyes.

"It's fine. You can go," I said, returning his gaze.

But he knew me better than that. However, how much of my not being okay was from me fearing Ben, and how much of it was because of the inevitable conversation I knew I needed to have with each of them?

To avoid any secrets being exposed on my front lawn, I needed to get rid of them both. "Ben, you can leave, too," I said, swallowing hard.

The smug look fell from his face, and his vexed expression returned.

"Why? So, you can just ignore me again?"

In the brief moment that my pupils shifted to the corner of my eyes, I realized my mistake.

"Are you fucking kidding me with that shit?"

The hair on my arms stood up, and Caleb stepped between us. "Okay, now you really need to leave," he said to Ben.

But the step only fueled Ben's anger and need to show his dominance, both over the situation and, surely, over me.

"She asked you to leave, too," Ben said, inches from Caleb's face.

I had asked them both to leave, yet there we were.

But there was little time for snark. I was going to need to deescalate the situation before someone got hurt.

I shifted myself, rather ungracefully, so that I could see them both. "Caleb, back off. I'm fine. And, Ben, I'll answer next time you call, okay? We can set up a time to talk." Noting to myself that it would be in a public setting. Away from my house—away from Caleb.

Neither of them budged.

"Caleb."

He exhaled and took a step back.

"That's all I wanted," Ben replied, his expression softened once again as his eyes met mine. The way his moods shifted with such ease made me shudder.

He gave me a smile and leaned in, that time with the intention of kissing my cheek.

I wanted to punch him. But we had been down that road before. So, I allowed his lips to make contact, watching as Caleb shook his head in disgust.

The fact that my fist connecting with his face a month prior didn't cause him to run in the other direction just furthered my belief that he was crazy. Unfortunately, it also revealed just how equally crazy I was every time I had to relive it.

The weight from my chest shifted as Ben's car disappeared down the street.

The feeling of relief only exacerbated the pain in my temple. A single tear rolled down my cheek.

Caleb's hand moved to my lower back. "For real. Are you okay?"

I nodded, avoiding eye contact.

I pulled my keys from my purse, wiping my cheek as Caleb followed me to my front door.

It had been a while since he had been at my house. It felt like a lifetime had passed since then.

As I stepped inside, I turned around to say thank you, to say goodnight, to say anything that would let him know our night was ending right then and there. But the words got caught somewhere between my logical and foolish thoughts.

He leaned his body against the frame of the door, crossing his arms, with eyes full of concern.

Resisting the urge to trigger the fight response to the look, I took a deep breath. "I'll be fine. Seriously. I'll deal with him later."

"If he's a problem, I can help you."

I forced a small grin knowing no one could help me with my Ben situation—not even Caleb.

"No, I can handle him. Don't worry." While neither of us actually believed that, we both knew that was a problem for another day.

"Did you want to come in?" I asked.

His smile touched his eyes as I stepped aside to let him pass.

I took off my jacket and brought my purse with me into the kitchen. Caleb leaned up against the dining room table as I pulled out my phone. I had two missed calls from an unknown number, along with a few texts.

I set it on the counter, closed my eyes, and began to massage the side of my head.

What was I going to say to Ben when I saw him again? Did he really want to get back together? Why? Surely there were better women out there than me.

Better, but not as stupid, The Voice said. *You're easy for the picking. A damaged girl like you doesn't have better options.*

As I tried to think of a defense against my own debilitating thoughts, Caleb's hand grazed my hip, causing me to jump.

He stepped back with a shy smile crossing his face. "Sorry," he commented and then took a step toward me once more.

I forced another grin as my pulse slowed back down.

"Thanks for bringing me home," I said.

He nodded as I nervously tucked a stray hair behind my ear.

"Anytime," he replied, putting his hand on my hip once more. "I'm glad Serena called, but you really should pick better friends."

In Serena's defense, that was our friendship. She wasn't my keeper, and she knew Caleb would get me home safely.

I took a deep breath. "She's fine."

While the silence built around us, I knew I needed to say goodnight—to show resistance for once in my life.

But Caleb looked good in the glow of my small kitchen light. He looked good in *any* light. It was clear that he *had* been spending his free time at the gym. And while the results sent an ache through my stomach, his reason for being there was a cause for concern.

I inadvertently placed my hand on his biceps and followed it up to his shoulder.

"I really missed you," he said softly.

I averted his glance, and I looked down at my feet.

"I missed you, too," I replied, trying to disengage myself from all emotions.

Seven years before, when Caleb and I had ended our relationship. I was in a bad place, mentally, emotionally—you name it. However, it wasn't the ending of the relationship that caused it.

But it had fueled the already bitter woman I had become. After a couple of months and some failed attempts to put myself back out there, I approached him about hooking up with nothing more to it. It was a way of taking control of my life—something I desperately needed at the time.

The pattern seemed to be repeating itself once again.

If I got into bed with him, Caleb would be the person getting me back in the saddle—helping me regain control. Even though inevitably, over time, I knew he would be the reason I would lose it all over again.

I didn't know how long I had been standing there silently staring at the floor. My face got hot as I started to pull away.

But Caleb stopped me. He tipped my chin toward him, lightly pressing his lips to mine.

I brought my arms up and around his neck, my body fitting perfectly against his.

At that moment, I was weak. But when it came to him, I was always weak. My emotionally stunted mind would take a brief pause, allowing for a moment like that to feel perfect—permitting the feelings of possibilities to flow in. But the dreadful bitch that was reality would inevitably hit, causing me to do whatever I could to keep him at arm's length.

The thoughts of our past mistakes tugged at my anxiety. But I did my best to ignore any thoughts that pushed for me to stop. Instead, I upped the ante by taking his hand and leading him to my room.

His hands glided across my skin as he slipped off my underwear and kissed my neck.

I brought his face up to mine and pushed my lips hard against his. He pulled my body close, and with one smooth motion, moved me to be on top.

I reached my hands to my back, unhooked my bra, and pulled it off without removing my dress.

His heart pounded. His eyes closed as he moaned. I followed suit with audible sounds from the ecstasy that was erupting throughout my body.

With his body grinding beneath mine, I focused my thoughts on one thing—him. I shut my eyes tightly as I let out another moan. My nails that routinely dug into my palms dug into his back instead. I inhaled breathlessly—my entire body riding an orgasmic high.

***

Caleb rolled off the bed and headed down the hallway to the bathroom. The rush of thoughts I had successfully held off long enough to orgasm came flooding in as the dam gave way.

Our arrangement had been put on hold as he explored the possibilities of a future with Cassy, a girl he had met at the gym. At first, I had been jealous because that was *our* place. Well, I was jealous for plenty of reasons. But it was no one's fault other than my own that I had no claim on him or the space we had shared.

While I was never a fan of Cassy's, I had tried in the beginning to be friends with the two of them. She was a down-to-earth woman with a good job, a nice house and seemed to have her life together. She was looking to settle down, something I knew he eventually wanted to. And above all else, he seemed happy when he was with her.

Caleb and I tried to hang out as friends when we got into relationships with other people, but our passion always got in the way. We tried hard to fight any urge we might have had to be together—or I guess *I* was fighting it; he was just fighting *me*. Overtime I just found it easier to not see each other at all. I had little self-control in general, but even more so when it came to him—a feeling I knew was mutual.

Everything would have been easier if I hadn't known that Caleb loved me—that was what I tried to tell myself anyway. I had suspected that was how he had felt for a while, but I had ignored it since he had never brought it up. But, about eight months before, I had told him I needed to stop seeing him for a while, even as a friend.

He was becoming more serious with Cassy, and it was getting hard for me to watch. But I told him it was because I needed to focus on finding my own friends and boyfriend, which was hard to do with him around.

As per usual, he got upset, and we fought. Amid the yelling and chaos, he told me he loved me. I responded that he shouldn't.

That was the last time we had talked. We had seen each other around a few times once I started dating Ben. But we were stubborn humans, and neither of us would budge to approach the other.

I heard the bathroom door and then his footsteps in the hall, so I shut my eyes and pretended to be asleep. I didn't know if he would want to talk—if he would want to hold each other. Or even more alarming, if he would tell me he loved me, again.

Chapter Four

The next morning wasn't as bad as I had expected. I wasn't sure whether to thank the rolls Serena had made me eat around hour three or if it was the dopamine that had coursed through my veins after the much-needed sex. Either way, my hangover wasn't the hell on earth I had been expecting.

It was 9:00 in the morning. Food and a shower sounded heavenly. Since Caleb was still sleeping, I decided to shower first, hoping to gain some clarity on the situation that I found myself in.

The edgy yet soothing tone of my alternative rock playlist expelled from the speaker as my mind drifted back to the previous night. Caleb coming to my rescue; Ben being in my driveway. I myself once again, being too intoxicated to handle—well, anything.

I knew I was going to have to meet with Ben. As much as I didn't want to keep my word on talking to him, I didn't want him showing up at my place again.

I was so relieved he didn't say more in front of Caleb. I was relieved that Caleb had been there to keep me from slipping back to Ben. But I guess, either way, I had slipped. But if I was going to put my life into reverse for even a moment, Caleb was the better direction to head in.

Things won't work out with Caleb either, The Voice said maliciously. *You've been down this road before.*

I wanted to argue with myself that it was different before. But that was only because I was different, and although he had said he loved me, I couldn't help but think he only loved the girl he thought I was. The girl I had pretended to be. Because how could he love someone he didn't really know?

***

I had expected a conversation to ensue at breakfast over what had happened. I had expected him to talk about the next steps. What I hadn't expected was for everything to be as casual as it had been before. Like the last year hadn't occurred, as if he had never told me how he actually felt.

After arriving back at my place from the diner, Caleb had dropped me off with no mention of coming in. However, it wasn't like I had offered up an invitation either.

Maybe he had had a change of heart. Maybe he agreed we weren't meant for the dating thing. Or maybe things had ended worse with Cassy than I had thought.

But with no discussion on the topic, it seemed we were back to our original agreement of friends with benefits tied tightly with emotionally hidden strings.

It is *what you wanted,* The Voice said.

I took a deep breath.

I hated that I felt disappointed. I hated that I was never satisfied.

***

Serena returned to my place in the late morning. She skipped the lecture on my drinking and had gone straight for a shower. When she got out, she plopped down on the other end of the couch.

I had noticed her glance over a few different times. I didn't know if she was waiting for me to start a conversation about the night before or if she was working up the courage to ask how things had gone. But when I finally went to say something and put an end to the awkward silence, she beat me to it.

"I hope you're not mad about last night," she said, taking me by surprise.

"Mad? Why would I be mad at you?"

"That I had Caleb come get you."

I exhaled, letting a grin form. "Oh. No, I'm not mad. You knew he would take care of me..."

He always has to take care of you, The Voice said.

I ignored the intrusive comment as Serena hurled a follow-up question.

"Did he...take care of you?"

"He did."

She smiled proudly.

"But I don't know what it means."

"What are you talking about? I thought you guys had an *arrangement.*"

"I mean, we do. We *did*. But I don't know. After he told me he loved me—"

"I *knew* it!" she replied.

"Oh… yeah. It happened before I started seeing Ben."

"You live in a romantic comedy," she mocked, giving a slight eye roll.

"I wish."

My life couldn't have been further from anything deemed romantic—or a comedy for that matter. Romantic comedies typically had happy endings. I had a feeling that wasn't how it was going to end for us.

She shook her head. "I get the whole friends with benefits thing, but it's been going on a long time."

"Yeah, seven years. Not including the year that we dated," I responded as my eyes stayed glued to the floor.

"Jesus. I mean, you guys might as well make it official. What's stopping you? Do you not love him back?"

"Even if I do, that isn't always enough."

"Well, it beats the crummy one-night stands *I've* been having," she retorted in disgust. "From where I stand, your situation looks pretty good."

"Hey, I still have crappy one-night stands."

Although, it had been roughly nine months since I had partaken in that particular activity.

I had never told Serena what had happened between Caleb and me—why we had broken up in the first place. Even if she had known the circumstances of everything, I wasn't confident she would have agreed with my decision.

Caleb himself didn't understand because I had never been completely honest with him either. He used to question me about it. But he had stopped a while back. Well, until our last fight, when it all seemed to come back up again. He didn't fully grasp the cons that came with us being together. I, on the other hand, didn't seem to understand the pros—or so he said. Silly of him to think that an overthinker like myself hadn't weighed every possible outcome.

"Are you okay?" Serena asked softly.

I glanced over at her. I could tell she had been staring. The look of concern I hated so much lingered in her eyes.

Brushing everything off as I usually did, I diverted the topic to something else. "Yeah, uh, did you want to catch a movie or something tonight?"

"No, there's nothing good out," she paused. "But Drew just texted me," she began. "He's still in town and said a few people are getting together downtown later."

I had thought the "excitement" from the night before was over.

But at least it wasn't a room full of our graduating class—I could handle a few of them. Maybe I could try for a crappy one-night stand. Maybe I just needed to get my head on Caleb's level—get us back to where we were before.

***

When we arrived at the bar, Drew and other former classmates were already inside. Serena hugged Drew, but I opted for a slight head nod as I slid into a booth.

The waitress was quick to take our orders and return with the hair of the dog that had bitten me the night before.

While Serena carried her drink to mingle with those around us, I pulled out my phone.

You would think that, after years of spending my free time in similar places, I would handle the environment better. That small talk wouldn't make me cringe or lead to an awkward silence; that I wouldn't need to use my phone as a crutch for my social anxiety.

I opened my Facebook and saw a picture of Ben. In the picture, his skin had yet to see any ramification of age, though I was certain he would never receive even one crease from laugh lines.

His eyes held a sadness I hadn't noticed at the time. It was a sadness I wouldn't learn about until years later—years after we had stopped talking—years after he had broken my heart.

I couldn't help but wonder if he had posted it to get my attention.

And you think he's the narcissistic one? The Voice asked.

The photo wasn't just any picture from our youth, but one that I had taken. One taken in our many days spent together in the formative years of our childhood.

Ben had called me over Christmas break and told me to meet him at the old elementary school playground. An opportunity to be alone with him that I didn't miss out on.

I had told my mom I was going to take pictures of the scenery, forgetting she would be the one getting the photos developed. At the time, the memories had been worth the scolding I got for it.

I continued to stare at the picture. His eyes grew darker the longer I stayed fixated on it. At some point in our journey of growing into full-fledged adults, his sadness had cascaded down a rabbit hole of hostility. Something I was fairly confident he only revealed to me. While I had seen the progression of his tormented soul over the years, I hadn't allowed it to serve as a warning to myself.

Because, while our damage wasn't cultivated in the same way, it was the kind of devastation that was woven deeply into both of us. Unlike other people in my life that had suffered a similar amount of destruction, Ben and I had chosen anger and resentment over everything else.

"Hey…Harper…right?" a handsome man said, sliding into the booth beside me. "I'm Ian. Drew's friend."

I looked over at Drew, who was talking with Serena.

They glanced back, Serena winking at me before going on with her conversation.

"Hi," I replied.

"Did you get dragged here too?"

"As always," I replied with a grin that was surprisingly not forced.

Ian was my type from what I could tell—tall, clean-cut, nice build, and most likely just looking for a hookup. Coincidentally, I was in the market for that exact thing.

I was hoping he was a better conversationalist than what I was known for. But at the end of the night, a good dialog between the two of us had little to do with what I was aiming to accomplish.

Serena and Drew slid into the booth across from us while Ian made himself comfortable at my side. "So, Harper, I haven't seen you in years… I wanted to talk to you last night, but you were pretty hammered," Drew began.

"Yeah, sorry," I replied, embarrassment sweeping across my face.

"It looked like you were having fun on the dance floor, though," he continued, although I wished he didn't.

"Yeah, well, alcohol will have that effect on you."

They laughed as I felt Ian's body shift closer to mine.

But the all-eyes-on-me feeling made my mouth dry, causing me to move the straw in my drink aside to allow a faster and smoother transition into my body.

I hadn't intended on drinking to excess like I had the previous night. I typically didn't have two big nights of drinking in a row. In my recent years of alcohol consumption, I was known to ride the high of a couple of glasses of wine each night with—or for, dinner.

It was a way of padding the walls of my brain from the critical Voice and putting a straitjacket around my anxiety. Preventing them both from escaping the confines of their lobe, which would cause me to think, feel, or express emotions that I had proven ill-equipped to handle.

But with the conversation that was starting to flow from Ian and The Voice chiming in at my lack of charm and personality, the need for a quilted interior in my brain caused me to finish my first drink of the night and immediately order another one.

***

I was three drinks in, which was a good pace for me over the course of an hour and a half. With the ease up from The Voice, I was able to have a good buzz going and begin to enjoy the conversation with Ian. While the discussion itself was nothing special, it was a needed change from the intense emotion that Ben and Caleb had exhausted me with the night before.

Serena nodded her head towards the bathroom while Ian sat close to me, discussing the most recent season of *The Walking Dead.* A show I had yet to see all the way through but at least knew enough of to follow most of the exchange.

Ian slid out from the booth, allowing me to comply with Serena's gesture. The small amount of space he had given me to get by caused my body to brush up against his. I grinned flirtatiously, letting my eyes meet his for a second before I casually looked away.

Serena's eyes indicated she had a pretty good buzz going as well. Although, unlike me, she was good at knowing when to rein it in and cut herself off.

"Ian's cute," she commented.

"Yeah. He is."

I stepped into a stall as it became available.

"You guys heading back to your place?"

I grew annoyed at her yelling through the stall, or maybe it was the question she had asked. I hated girl talk in the bathroom.

"So? Are you?" she asked a minute or so later as we approached the sink.

"I don't know, kind of early in the night to tell," I answered. However, I wasn't sure why I felt the need to hide my intent, especially with Serena.

As I walked back to the table, Ian stood up, once again leaving little room for me to pass. I appeased his flirtatious behavior by pressing my body up against his, moving slowly to my side of the booth. He looked pleased as he took his seat beside me and rested his hand on my thigh.

I picked up my drink, trying to look as casual as possible as I finished the rest of it.

I set my glass down and quickly scanned the bar while Ian started the conversation up where we had left off. My concentration was redirected as I watched Cassy walk through the door and head in the opposite direction.

And even though I had been relieved for a moment, I knew it would be almost impossible to dodge her the entire night. I knew that at some point, our paths would cross, and I would be forced to small talk Caleb's ex. A situation that already sounded atrocious, but so much more so with the happenings of the previous night still fresh in my inebriated mind.

While I had allowed myself to dive back into the topic of shows being binged, my absorption of the conversation was obliterated with the appearance of Caleb through the front door. I moved closer to Ian, trying to make myself blend into the crowd as Caleb looked around. Ian took it as an opportunity to up his advances and moved his hand further up my thigh.

But his smooth voice and cool demeanor were going to be no match for the distraction that would be plaguing my brain for the entirety of the evening. Even more so, once I noticed Caleb's intent wasn't to meet friends, it wasn't for some reason to locate me, but rather, he had come there to see *her*.

I picked up my drink right as the waitress set it down, pressing it to my lips with the immediate need to tighten the restraints that were holding my anxiety captive.

"Girl, you need to pace yourself," Serena joked.

But I was too distracted by everything else to even acknowledge her comment.

My anxious thoughts began to break free in a bitter reveal of their strength against the alcohol's confinement.

Of course he lied to you, The Voice said. *Maybe if you didn't make it so easy.*

I felt Ian's hand rubbing smoothly on my upper thigh. A movement that caused a brief shift in my focus, returning it to him.

"Do you want another drink?" he asked seductively in my ear.

It wasn't particularly loud in there, so I assumed the close proximity was another advance being made to assure his night would end the way he was hoping it would. A round on him was probably just another method to seal the deal.

"Uh, yeah. That'd be great."

I think you've had enough, The Voice said.

But with Ian's hand grazing my thigh and Caleb sitting twenty feet away with a woman who was supposed to be his ex, I knew my fight or flight response was going to kick in.

A response that, to almost any sane person, would be to sneak out and carry on the night somewhere else. But I never claimed to be sane. So, I would choose the third option they didn't teach in school—the response of getting plastered.

Chapter Five

When Ian got up to get us another round, Caleb caught my stare. He looked surprised and then nervous. He had to have known that I had seen Cassy.

We kept our eyes on one another as Ian slid back beside me.

"She's bringing the round over," he said, placing his hand back onto my thigh.

Caleb's nervous look changed to annoyance as he broke his gaze away from mine.

"Thanks," I responded, sliding closer to fill the minuscule amount of space that had been left between us.

While Serena and Drew tried to involve us in their conversation, Ian seemed more invested in the next steps with me to keep up. I, on the other hand, was dividing my thoughts between the placement of Ian's hand and Caleb's unwelcome intrusion into my night out.

Cassy seemed too immersed in whatever she was talking about to notice Caleb shifting his eyes between hers and mine. I didn't know if the look on his face was from jealousy or if he was just annoyed to see me out again so soon after our night together.

The alcohol did little to repress the rage that was bubbling inside of me.

My mind had skipped rapidly from anxious thoughts of what we had done to resentful ones of what name he was helping me create for myself. If he was still with Cassy, I had not only helped wreck one home but had easily set fire to a second.

I wanted to think that Caleb's sudden appearance had nothing to do with my hand shifting to Ian's lap or allowing for his tongue to be in my mouth. But I felt an aggressive push on my part the moment The Voice started laying into me, which caused my typical response of allowing my anger to fuel my decision-making.

Horrifyingly enough, for once, The Voice didn't sound like my mother, but instead, like *Ben*. It was telling me I was only relevant to Caleb when he needed to get laid. That I was a wild ride that one takes when they need a break from the mundane life they lived. A life that, no matter what, they will go back to. Because you don't *marry* the girl full of chaos—you only *fuck* her.

The main lights dimmed as the dance floor lit up. Ian pulled me close and leaned his face toward my neck. "Wanna dance?" he asked.

"I'm going to need a shot or two before I can do that," I replied with a laugh. Though my brain—possibly my liver—was contesting my need for more alcohol.

Drew ordered a round of shots as the waitress dropped off our drinks.

I watched Serena scan the bar. I could tell she had noticed Caleb. Her expression briefly shifted, first to concern, then to that of willful ignorance.

She downed the rest of her drink, then looked my way. "Harper, come with me to pee," she said, as more of a statement than a question.

I shrugged and pulled my hand from Ian's lap.

I could sense his disappointment, but the wheel in his head seemed to spin a benefit to my departure. "There's enough room for you to get around me," he commented, giving me the same flirtatious grin he had been sporting the entire evening.

I smiled mischievously, putting my leg on the other side of him so that I was straddling his lower half. I pushed my body against his and gave him a soft kiss on the lips, lingering for a moment as I tasted the smoothness of the Jack in his Coke. Then, while leaving him wanting more, I brought my legs together on the other side and stood up.

"Well, that answers my question," Serena said as we walked away.

I glanced at Caleb's table. A flashing strobe light lit up his eyes as they seared into mine. The anger that had briefly subsided while distracted by Ian's body beneath mine came rushing back.

Unfortunately, with my game of one-sided sexual chicken, I hadn't noticed Cassy had left their table.

"Harper!" Cassy shouted with a smile as she stepped out of the bathroom.

She put her hand on my arm as if we were close friends.

"Hey," I responded with a forced smile, taking a quick glance over at Caleb to see his nervous expression.

By the time my focus shifted back to Cassy, Serena had exited the conversation and disappeared into the bathroom.

"So, how are you?" she asked.

"Fine, and you?" I replied, feigning interest.

"I'm good," she answered with more enthusiasm than I would expect from a girl who had supposedly broken up with her boyfriend of almost a year.

And like clockwork with situations such as those, the awkward silence began to loom over us.

"So, we were just getting ready to take off," I said, motioning toward Serena, who had finally returned from the bathroom.

But as she joined us, so did Caleb, catching me off guard from the other side. I imagined he had been contemplating whether it would be worse to let us talk amongst ourselves or for him to be present.

If he had been, I felt he had chosen wrong. I could sense the tension he was giving off. I wondered if it was just as obvious to the others as it was to me.

"Hey," Caleb said, not making direct eye contact with me but instead looking at Serena.

"Hey."

Oh yeah, it was obvious.

"You guys should stay. At least for a little bit," Cassy exclaimed with a smile.

"We're not leaving," Serena replied, looking perplexed in my direction.

Either she was clueless, or for some reason, had decided to punish me.

"Good!" Cassy replied with an annoying amount of excitement.

I noted to myself that a signal needed to be made. How had we been best friends that long and not had one?

I tried to communicate with her using my eyes. But my communication was just a death stare that seemed to go unnoticed by her. However, it wasn't as inconspicuous to Caleb, who had finally decided to make eye contact with me.

"Is it just the two of you?" Cassy asked.

I looked over at our table as the guys started walking over to us carrying our shots.

"Nope," I responded, ready to boost my confidence level.

But my confidence took a drastic dip as I watched Cassy intertwine her fingers with Caleb's. I took the shot from Ian and tipped it back, feeling a slight burn as it hit the back of my throat. My eyes met Caleb's while I savored the rush of straight alcohol that would soon make me numb to the chaos I had found myself in.

I broke away from his gaze and turned towards Ian. "Ready to dance?"

Mid nod, I took his hand and led him to the dance floor with Drew and Serena following closely behind. It was the perfect music to get my body closer to his—to make Caleb regret his misstep the night before.

I would like to say I was better than that, that I wasn't the type of person to use someone to piss someone else off. But I wasn't, especially when it came to Caleb. One of the biggest cons on our list was our stubbornness—our bullheaded reasoning. It didn't mix well with our inability to just walk away.

Ian's hands were placed firmly on my hips, pulling me closer so our bodies could grind against one another's.

Caleb wasn't known to partake in dancing, but after what looked like his failure to protest doing such, he followed Cassy onto the dance floor and quickly formulated the same dance moves as Ian and I had. I turned my back towards Ian as I continued to move my body in unison to his. Caleb's eyes again seared into mine, becoming dark and intense.

I realized that was what had looked different about him the night before—his eyes.

Over the years, when I had looked at him, he always had a tortured, passionate, intense look in them. But when I had seen him the day before, he had looked calm, relaxed—carefree. Even drunk, I could see the difference in what not being around me had done for him. It was like he had gotten clean of me and, in one night, I had pulled him back in.

He continued to look at me until Cassy put her hands on his jawline and led his lips to hers. He pulled her close as they continued to move to the music.

Was he trying to beat me at my own game?

For a moment, I felt stupid to assume it was about me. Maybe he had just wanted to kiss his girlfriend. Maybe he wanted to forget about the night before and move on. Maybe he was angry at the mistake he had made with me. Maybe he realized I was the mistake.

My mind started to race as my chest tightened up. Was Caleb's calm and collected look Cassy's doing? Did it really only take one night with me, and then it was back to being tortured, intense, angry even? Did I push him? Did I make him cheat?

I shook my head at the absurd thought. I couldn't make someone do something they didn't want to do.

"I need a drink!" I shouted to Ian as the song changed.

No, you need water, The Voice said.

I tried to give him a smile so he wouldn't think anything was up. But who was I kidding? He was too drunk to notice—and surely too drunk to care.

Ian stayed on the dance floor with everyone else as I headed towards the bar.

My heart continued to race as I felt a sudden pain set into my chest, causing me to change course and head for the door.

The brisk springtime air caressed my skin, dispersing goosebumps all over my body.

I leaned up against the building, shut my eyes, and took a deep breath—realizing how stuffy it had been inside.

I curled my hands tightly into fists to try and stop the trembling.

"You okay?" Caleb's voice rang through my ears.

I took another breath, trying to calm everything inside of me.

"What are you doing here?" I asked.

He seemed to be searching for an answer. But when he didn't speak, I continued. "You told me that you two broke up."

"We did," he replied anxiously, "or I *thought* we did."

His petty excuse caused my eyes to glare into his. He didn't look away as I had expected him to. Instead, he continued, giving only a sliver more of information to help make his case.

"We had a fight last weekend, I left, and we hadn't talked since." He paused long enough to sigh and run his hand through his hair. "I really thought we were done. But Cassy's saying it was just a fight and said she just gave me time to cool off."

As much as I wished the stuff he was saying was making me feel better, it wasn't. How did I end up in this situation again? At what point had I gotten on karma's bad side?

"So, what happens now?" he asked.

I shifted myself upright off the wall.

"Are you still with Cassy?"

He shrugged and then nodded reluctantly.

"Okay… and I'm here with Ian."

Caleb sighed, looking annoyed, which just irritated me in return.

He didn't deserve to have an opinion on that.

"Alright, so that's what happens," I began. "Everything continues like before."

And, without another word, I walked back into the bar, needing that drink more than ever.

Chapter Six

The bartender poured my vodka cranberry and then placed two shots of vodka next to it.

I glanced at Serena on the dance floor with Drew, then spotted Ian dancing with another woman next to them.

So much for a random hookup.

Caleb's eyes were on me as Cassy was talking to some girl next to them. His expression was riddled with apprehension. I continued to stare at him as I downed the first shot. I grabbed my drink off the bar and held it up to cheer him from across the way. I thought it was funny, but he didn't seem to share in my amusement.

I watched as Serena and Drew went back to our booth and sat down. Shortly after, Cassy followed as she took Caleb's hand. Serena's expression made me laugh as she looked unimpressed; I knew she didn't like the idea of sitting with them. Cassy had never been very social with me—or my friends. Not until that night anyway.

Maybe she knew something. At the very least, it was possible she suspected something; she did seem more territorial than she had in the past. But maybe that was because they had been together longer at that point, and I was just overthinking everything.

I took a sip of my drink, trying to get back on pace with quieting the words that struck internally.

Ian noticed me from the dance floor, leaving the other woman to dance with her friends as he approached me. I downed the second shot as his eyes focused on mine.

I knew I couldn't wait for the shots to sink in, so while throwing my impulsivity into the mix, I pressed my lips to his. I could tell I had caught him off guard, but he quickly got his bearings, moving me closer to him.

He placed one hand on my hip and the other on the back of my head. I let our tongues feel one another's for a moment before pulling away. I left my hand on him to steady myself as the shots sank in along with a lightheaded feeling.

I smiled mischievously as my eyes left his, meeting the ones at our booth. I was greeted with amused expressions from three of the four. I guess my blatant PDA wasn't for everyone.

I could tell Ian wanted to continue what I had started, but I had made my point—for the moment anyway. I took his hand and led him to our audience.

Cassy started to stand up, attempting to give us back our seats.

"No, you're good," I said, looking at her, then at Caleb. I held my drink in my hand as Ian put his arms around the front of me and nuzzled closely to my back. I brought the glass to my lips and took a sip.

The vodka's bite was dissipating as my body became numb.

"Girl, you might want to pace yourself. You don't want to end up like last night," Serena stated.

My eyes narrowed as I grinned again. "Why? I enjoyed myself last night."

Her face twisted into an uneasy look but then crept back to a smile. She knew what I was doing, but I wasn't sure if she approved.

I glanced at Caleb. I knew he felt guilty. But I also knew he was masking it with his anger and concern for me—yet another con for us. We rarely showed the appropriate emotions.

***

As the alcohol finally started doing the job I had given it, the next hour became a blur. My brain switched modes, not remembering anything past the current moment. I thought I was at a good place to coast, but apparently, somewhere in there, I had said yes to taking another shot—possibly two. I hadn't even fully recovered from the previous night, and there I was, drinking vodka like it was water all over again.

Time became fluid. One minute I would be talking to everyone in the booth, and the next, I would be back on the dance floor. From what little I could comprehend, it seemed Caleb was sticking around to make sure I was okay. Maybe even to remind himself why he was with Cassy. Though I was certain that, either way, he wasn't impressed by me. And I knew I wouldn't be either when I woke up the next morning. But at that moment, I had zero fucks to give to either of us.

Well, almost zero. I was greatly perturbed by his perfect girlfriend and her ability to heavily nurse her drinks.

Thoughts of her nearly flawless behavior only made my judgment get more clouded. It made me go harder at the pursuit of seduction with Ian, something that didn't require much—if any—effort on my part.

As I tried to concentrate on my next moves with him, atrocious thoughts of the two of them in bed crossed my mind. They just continued to get worse as Cassy snuggled up to Caleb in the booth. I watched as she ran her hand across his cheek in an intimate manner. As their lips locked, it felt like time slowed. The music quieted, sounding almost distant to my ears. I tried to take a deep breath while I continued to dance, trying to ignore his blissful love life.

Ian pressed his body against mine as I put my arms around his neck. Usually, the alcohol and distractions were enough to help me become numb to the overwhelming emotions. But as the thoughts of them together spread like wildfire through my mind, I felt my chest tighten, and every breath I could manage felt shallow. The air around me increased in temperature as a bead of sweat ran down my neck.

Ian pressed his lips to mine, putting his hand behind my head. It felt like the hand gesture was more for his own stability than as a romantic, sexual touch.

I quickly pulled my mouth away from his, trying again to catch my breath, hoping to find it easier to do without someone's tongue down my throat.

You're having a panic attack, The Voice said.

But I ignored my thoughts, searching for some sense of control.

68

My chest continued to grow heavy. I told myself to breathe. But I knew that was slowly becoming impossible.

I tried to take a deep breath once more.

I needed space and for people not to be so close to me.

The song changed over to another one with the same speed and tempo. I realized I had stopped moving. When had I stopped dancing?

I watched Ian turn to the girl next to him and proceed to grind his body with hers.

I got my body to work again as I tried to walk slowly to the door. But it was more like an ungraceful jog while trying to push through a sea of people.

I stepped outside the door, stumbling past a group of smokers who looked at me with entertained expressions.

They think you're pathetic, The Voice said.

Certainly, I looked as awful as I felt, both from the sweat that covered my body and the impending panic attack.

I leaned up against the outside of the bar and slid down to the ground. I rested my head on my knees and tried to take deep breaths to calm myself down. The cigarette smoke from the group near me lingered in the air. I began to cough as my lungs were ill-prepared for the sudden shift in pollutants that wafted into them.

My heartbeat grew louder in my ears. I glanced up briefly to see someone approaching, but before they could reach me, I buried my head back down as I tried again to breathe.

My thoughts shifted concentration as the feeling of deja vu hit full force, sending me back to a period in time I thought my brain had blocked out.

It was years ago; I had just left work for the day when Serena called and wanted to go out. She waited in her car for me as I ran inside to change.

I reached into the back of my closet, trying to grab a hooded sweatshirt. As I pulled one out, Caleb's scent filled the air.

I thought I had gotten rid of all of his shit. But I must have missed some.

I threw the hoodie into the corner and reached in for another one. I pulled it over my head and left my room without another look at the only piece of Caleb I had left.

"Took ya long enough," Serena said.

I mustered up a smile, then shrugged.

"That's what you changed into?"

"Yeah, why?"

"Well, when you said you needed to change, I thought you would pick something more—I don't know—provocative."

"I just want to be comfy."

"That's fine. It's just a little casual for a Friday night." She paused for a moment and looked at me sympathetically. "You're not ready to go out, are you?"

I wasn't, but not for the reason she was thinking.

"I'm fine. I really just wanted to be comfy."

"If you don't want to go out, I get it. I mean, things just ended with you guys. We could just hang out and watch TV."

Although it sounded like exactly what I needed, it was all I had done for weeks. And when I did have to leave to go to class or to work, I was awful to people. I was moody. I was frustrated. I was exhausted. I tried to reason with myself that my anger shouldn't be targeted at them. But it needed to be targeted at someone. And since I couldn't aim it at the person I wanted to, I was settling for the whole world.

"Harper?"

I had forgotten to answer.

"No, it's fine. I want to go out. I need a drink."

She continued to stare at me, contemplating her next move. "Okay, well, let's go out for a few drinks, and then we'll come back and just hang out."

I wasn't used to Serena not wanting to close down the bar. Patrick must have been having more of an effect on her than I thought. I couldn't help but feel a little jealous of their stability. Not so much in their relationship, but in their normality. Something I didn't know I would miss so much until I no longer had it.

She put the car into reverse and backed out of my driveway.

After a few minutes of listening to the engine hum and the bass rattle the old speakers, I tried to fill the silence. "So, things with Patrick are going good?"

Serena's smile reached her eyes. "Yeah, they are."

I gave a forced grin in return and glanced out the window, unsure of where I thought that would go.

"The guy for you is out there," she said.

But those words meant nothing to me. I wasn't searching for someone. That was why I had let things end the way they had with Caleb. I wasn't interested in having a boyfriend. I wasn't interested in being happy or in love. The dark cloud that had been following me for weeks had forced its way into every emotion, soiling anything good that had once been there.

I continued to stare out the window as I felt my chest get heavy and the rage inside of me reared its ugly head. I felt my fists grow tight and my jaw clenched.

"Are you okay?" she asked.

I wished she would stop asking me that. Because no, I wasn't okay. No, I wouldn't be okay.

"I'm fine."

"You know you can talk to me."

"There's nothing to talk about."

Her car pulled off to the side of the road; she put it in park and turned toward me. "Seriously, girl, what's going on with you!?"

"Jesus Christ, will you just quit asking me questions? Nothing's wrong. I broke up with Caleb. I don't give a shit about him or any of it. I just want to go out and drink. You know, you used to like to do that, too. Well, until Patrick anyway."

"What the fuck? Why are you bringing him into this?" she asked defensively. "I'm sorry I've been busy, but my life doesn't revolve around you. I don't know why you're being such a bitch, but I don't deserve it."

I opened the passenger door.

"What are you doing?" she asked.

"I figured you don't want a bitch riding in your car. I'll just walk from here."

She paused briefly. "Seriously?"

I slammed the door shut.

"Harper!" she yelled through the window.

I started walking in the direction of the bar.

Serena waited for a minute, then the noise of her tires burning into the pavement filled the air.

Fuck her. I wish she knew when to shut the fuck up. Why did she have to keep asking me shit? Why couldn't we just drink and not talk?

I folded my arms in front of me and took a ragged breath watching her taillights fade in the distance.

I looked up as the sun was setting on the horizon. A chill ran down my spine as I realized I was alone.

Within seconds I felt my heart start to race as a lump formed in my throat. I glanced around, trying to be mindful of my surroundings.

My breaths became shallow and hard to take. My hands shook, so again, I balled them into fists, trying to take control of my body.

"Breathe," I whispered to myself. But my heart continued to pound.

My vision blurred after briefly seeing a car heading my way. The streetlight in front of me flickered. My shallow breathing continued. A sob escaped as I put my hand on the light post to catch myself from falling.

The car pulled toward me. The lights from it filled my eyes. My body continued to shake, and my rapid heart rate forced me to my knees. Tears filled my eyes as I heard a voice.

I could tell someone was trying to talk to me, but the words weren't clear through the sound of thumping in my ears.

My heart sank as I felt hopeless. The darkness that had been invading my thoughts for the last month and a half were finally winning. My body was finally giving in.

Death had finally come for me.

I felt a hand rest on my shoulder.

A scream escaped my throat as my arms wrapped around the post and my knees dug into the damp grass.

"Harper!" I heard Serena's voice ring through my ears.

I lifted my head and was back outside the bar, knees to chest against the concrete wall. The smell of cigarettes still lingered in the air, tethering me to my reality.

I was able to make eye contact with her but was still unable to speak.

Her lips continued to move, but I couldn't concentrate on what she was saying.

"Breathe…" I finally managed to hear her say.

She knelt in front of me like she had years before. My body was just as tense as it was that night on the side of the road. She put her hands on my knees while I continued to concentrate on my breathing.

I hadn't known years ago what was happening. I had times when things had felt awful, but it was never out of nowhere and had never been a sudden onset of impending doom—the rush of death at my doorstep. I had felt many things over the years, most of them bad—some of them horrendous. But it had never taken hold of me in such an abrupt manner that I had been so sure that was the end.

Shortly after that night, Serena and I had learned I had had my first panic attack.

"Focus on me," I heard her say calmly as the smokers backed away to give me more space.

She titled my chin up and had me look at her.

"Harper—" I heard Caleb's voice say, but Serena put her hand up to stop him, keeping her focus on me.

I felt a tear stream down my cheek as my heart pumped slower and my trembling died down.

"Harper are you…" Caleb started to ask.

"She's fine."

"I'm just trying to help," he replied as she slowly got me to my feet.

"I think you've helped enough for one weekend."

I wanted to defend him. I wanted to tell her it wasn't his fault. But I felt too weak for words.

The group of smokers looked less amused and more sympathetic as we walked past them to Drew's truck that had just pulled up.

I glanced up at Caleb, whose intense look had given way to his concern for me.

I looked away as Cassy joined him at his side.

Thanks for coming to the shit show! The Voice said as if others could hear it.

But they couldn't. Only I knew the extent of the damage that lingered inside my head.

God, you're a fucking mess, it added.

And it was right. I was.

Chapter Seven

Monday took way too long to arrive. Most likely because I was waiting—almost wishing—for it, as work would be a good distraction from my chaotic weekend. But while Monday itself took forever to show up, the actual workday flew by, and suddenly I was rushing out of the office to get to my appointment on time.

I apologized to Sarah as I walked through her slightly ajar door. She was seated in her normal chair in front of the couch, reading.

Her expression stayed light as she greeted me, then motioned for me to take a seat. I complied and slid my journal across the coffee table to her.

It had taken most of Sunday evening to figure out where to begin. I had attempted to share a little about myself, hoping that what she said was true and it would be easier to do on paper than in person.

As it turned out, it *was* easier to write than to say out loud. However, being able to write it didn't make the thought of sharing that information any easier, which was why I ripped the page out of the journal and started over.

I chose instead to divert the intrusive glance into my life onto that of my father's. But the trip down memory lane brought about bigger emotions than I had intended on experiencing while jotting down a few key facts about him.

His sudden death, and subsequent absence from my life, did leave behind emotional scarring I had yet to dive into. I was certain, had I not been so dehydrated, tears would have smeared the ink, or at the very least, the remnants of Saturday's makeup.

***

(Journal entry)

My father was born Franklin Martin Jones on June 23rd, 1967. His parents died in a crash when he was 11 years old. An event I never heard much about and never found the courage to bring up. All I know is that sometime after their funerals, he was sent to live in Michigan with his Uncle Teddy and Aunt Ruth (I call them Grandpa and Grandma Jones).

It was a big change for my father, as he had lived in Southern California up until that point. He had told me once that his plan had always been to go back. That getting a job at the car place after high school had been to save money to get back there. But with college, meeting my mother, then having me, that never happened.

My father went to college to study business, and that was where he met my mother. While going to school, he was a car salesman, which he was very good at because he was very charismatic.

Since his parents had both passed, he received a grant to attend a state college for free. It was something he did not want to do, but his uncle made him. My father felt it was benefiting from their deaths; Grandpa Jones felt that not doing it was a slap in their faces for the life they would have wanted him to have.

His sophomore year, he met my mother, who was a freshman. I guess there was an instant connection between them. They met at her freshman orientation, spent the entire fall and winter inseparable, and eloped that spring.

Being married at that point wasn't out of the ordinary; neither was the short amount of time they had known each other. But them eloping devastated my mother's parents. She said they never forgave her for it.

My mother got pregnant with me her junior year— my father's senior year—of college. He stayed and finished, but with her horrible morning sickness that lasted most of the day and the entire pregnancy, she had to drop out of school. Something I felt she never forgave *me* for.

After my father died, the good memories stuck around, and the bad ones along with those feelings faded over time. I have heard that is what happens when people die, being able to forgive and forget more easily. I think of it more as me growing up and understanding the pressure my father must have felt, having to be responsible for a wife and daughter. A job I know I wouldn't have been ready for at that age.

Luckily for my parents, they had my uncle Sam. I think that was why I typically cut my father some slack, because Sam was always there for me. Sam wasn't really my uncle but was my father's best friend. Neither of my parents had siblings and, outside of my grandparents and me, he was the closest thing to a family they had.

Sam was the opposite of my father. He wasn't charismatic or charming in the way my father was, but he was lovable. He was liked by everyone and was handsome in his own way.

Sam was always around to help. He worked too, but he wasn't the boss, or as he always said, he wasn't anyone important. So, he got to put in his day of work and go home. He had explained that to me in my father's defense when I would ask why my father wasn't able to attend my school events like Sam could.

So, at least a few nights a week, Sam would come over and help my mother cook, or—as I learned over time—do the cooking, because Mom didn't like to do it. By bedtime, my mother would be exhausted from working, and from dealing with me, and my father would still be at work. So, Sam would put me to bed and read to me.

My father always seemed envious of Sam—even more so, when Sam could manage his time at work and be with the family. I think that's what eventually broke down the relationship. Although I was just a kid at that time, I could sense the tension towards the end.

Sam moved to Chicago when I was ten. He had knocked up a woman he had been seeing, and when she moved for a job, he followed to be in his son's life. That was hard for me. He had given my life stability; he was like a third parent to me, or sometimes what felt like my only parent.

About a year after Sam left, my father lost his job as a manager at a furniture store and was home more than ever. I feel like that is what stemmed my drama with him that led us to be at odds for the next few years.

Imagine going from having him home only late evenings and occasional weekends, to ALL THE TIME.

He found different jobs throughout the next few years, but nothing that he loved like he had loved being a sales manager. So, the jobs typically didn't last longer than a month, and then he spent the next few months angry and pacing around the house.

I was a pretty independent kid and, although my mother would already be home when I would get out of school, she never bothered me too much. When I turned eight, she started letting me do my own thing.

I did typical kid stuff—rode my bike to friends' houses, stayed out until dark, went to the local store to buy candy with change I found on my father's nightstand, things like that.

Since I had this independence from my mother, I wasn't used to getting asked questions. From the first day of my father being home, he would ask where I was going, who I would be with, etc. Stuff that I think now, of course you would ask your kid. But, at that time, I was just appalled that he thought I wasn't old enough to handle myself.

That was probably what led to a slight rebel streak that I had. Acting older than I was by trying cigarettes and booze, then having my first kiss, followed by other things. Looking back, I see how young and immature I really was, but I didn't feel that way at the time.

The last time I saw my father was at dinner on a Thursday evening. I was 16 years old, and he had finally found stable employment. I don't remember what we talked about, as I didn't know that would be the last time I saw him.

I'm grateful that it was a good dinner, and not one that resulted in one of the three of us leaving the table out of anger or annoyance.

I had left after dinner to go to my boyfriend's house as I did most nights at that age. Luckily, at that moment, I had the good sense to hug my father goodbye. That is a memory I'm eternally grateful for. I had gotten home after he and my mother had gone to bed, and he had left for work already the next morning when I got up for school.

I was in my last period of the day when I was called down to the office. I felt embarrassed by the attention I got when getting pulled out of class, but that soon turned into heartbreak, as Grandma Jones was waiting in the office to tell me what had happened. I hadn't wanted any of the details at the time, because honestly what did it matter? He would still be dead at the end of the day. But at the luncheon that followed the funeral, I overheard two people talking about the faulty machinery at his work that had killed him.

On the bright side, for my mother, his death at the factory left her with enough money that she didn't have to work again if she didn't want to. Though, over time, she found plenty of other ways to keep herself busy, mostly by joining a church and finding the Lord, and subsequently, Bernard.

At my father's funeral, I didn't cry. It felt weird to witness all these people who had come in and out of his life bawling for him, but not one single drop came from me. I thought I was broken. For a while, I had told myself I was just in shock. But months went by, and still nothing.

I felt sad. I felt the loss of him and his presence, but not enough to bring me to tears. It wasn't until the first anniversary of his death, when I heard his favorite song on the radio, that I finally lost it. At that point, it felt like a faucet had been turned on, and it stayed on for days. I didn't go to school. I didn't leave my house. Nothing.

Sam had come back for my father's funeral, consoling my mother, and trying to console me. I understood why he had left, but it didn't lighten the sting of abandonment. I think he would have stayed longer, but we no longer felt that same connection to him that we had six years prior. We had moved on to be a family without him, and he had started his own, too.

My mother and I started to be at each other's throats about two weeks after my father's passing. So, six months after he was laid to rest, and about a month after my seventeenth birthday, I moved out. Up until my father's death, my mother and I had been like two ships passing. We recognized each other's presence, and said I love you and such, but there wasn't a deep connection between us— at least not the kind I saw in movies or with my friends and their moms.

Our ambivalence toward each other had skyrocketed into sheer hatred. I don't know if my father had always just kept the peace in the house, or if his passing brought out the worst in us, but either way, six months of that was long enough for the both of us.

She didn't want me in the house as much as I didn't want to be there, so she bought me a small place in town. My boyfriend, Jacob, who had just graduated, moved in with me.

I kept it from her for a while, which was easy since she never visited my place, but after she signed the deed over to me on my 18th birthday, I stopped hiding it, knowing she couldn't do anything about it at that point.

She returned the punch by stopping all payments to my utilities. Something I didn't mind. I didn't want to rely on her for anything anymore.

It may have worked out for Jacob and me, had we not moved in that soon together. And after a few years, it became painfully obvious that neither of us were mature enough to handle that kind of commitment.

I often think about how different life would have turned out if my father hadn't died. What type of relationship I would have with him, if I would still be with Jacob, if everything would be less complicated.

***

Sarah liked my divulging about my father, his death, and a glimpse into my relationship with my mother. She started asking questions, but I couldn't find the right words to reply with. So again, I didn't say a word as I overthought every answer I wanted to give.

"You mention in here that you felt Sam abandoned you."

"That's what you got from all that?" I asked.

Her eyes narrowed as she looked to see if I was deflecting—news flash—I always was.

"Abandonment was probably a little harsh to use. I mean, he wasn't actually my parent."

"You felt like he was."

"Yeah, but he didn't owe me anything."

"No?"

"No."

"What about your dad?"

"What do you mean?"

"Do you feel he abandoned you too?"

I had always tried to keep the thought of my father's death locked away in the back of my mind. The only time I hadn't been successful was the first anniversary. At which point, I had gone through what I eventually learned was my first real bout of depression. Jacob had convinced me to talk to my doctor. But after a bad reaction to the medication they had put me on, I decided to handle things in my own way—with alcohol. Something that I wouldn't see the real consequences of until years later.

"I'm interested in learning more about your mother," Sarah said after I had let her question go unanswered. Maybe that was the point. Maybe she was planting a seed. I wished she would stop.

"Yeah, I can write about her next if you want."

"Only if you want to. No big deal if you want to wait on that."

My outburst the week before about my mommy issues made them very apparent. While the daddy ones lied beneath the surface, there was no covering up the mess the two of us had made for each other.

My mother seemed to hold a version of me in her head that I couldn't do a lot to refute. She saw me as a ticking time bomb—an imminent walking disaster.

A human that was both too dramatic, yet a tragedy of sorts all rolled into one. I liked to think her version was ill-fitted and more like a caricature. But in recent years, I had come face to face with the life I had created; only giving credence to the woman she claimed I was.

While some of my issues were of my own creation, others I could place at her feet. The main one being my internal voice that was unrelentingly critical of everything I thought, did, or said. It had started as more of a nagging reminder of my physical flaws, but over time it grew into pointing out all my mental and emotional ones, too. It was something I couldn't help but think she had a hand in creating—given that it often sounded just like her.

Being in therapy was something I had always tried to avoid, mainly because, while I knew there was something wrong with me, I would rather have kept myself in the dark about it. I didn't want it to be confirmed. Because then at least on my good days, I could deny it. I could deny my past, my traumas, and the real kicker—that sometimes I thought life would just be better without me in it.

"Do you feel like you had a good childhood?"

"I feel indifferent toward it. I have good memories and bad ones, but I don't have an overwhelming feeling either way."

My hands started to do their anxious movement on my lap. Talking about myself made my skin crawl. Everything I said needed to be calculated. I didn't want to end up walking out of there being labeled as crazy, psychotic, or, well, anything other than normal.

Chapter Eight

I stepped out of Sarah's office building and looked at the dull gray sky. Michigan could be so beautiful, but that day it looked how I felt— empty and somber. I got into my car and pulled out my phone.

The powerful tune of my post-grunge playlist filled my car, consuming the airwaves with the sound of pain and inner turmoil. My chest felt heavy as my fucked-up thoughts wallowed in self-hatred with the accompanied misery of the lead vocalist. I knew that immersing myself in the heart-wrenching tone of lyrical genius wasn't a healthy endeavor but listening to music was therapeutic to me. I needed a therapy session *for* my therapy session.

It was the kind that my mind didn't actively resist.

But in the times that even the music gods couldn't save my serotonin levels from plummeting into nonexistence, drinking was always a welcomed replacement. I found that it was more fun, and more socially acceptable, to go to the bar and drink, rather than medicate with the pills I needed to balance the chemicals in my brain. Again, not the healthiest choice, but my version of self-medication, nonetheless.

***

Arriving home, I kicked off my shoes and headed to the kitchen. I opened my fridge and grabbed the half-finished bottle of wine. While I cooked, I used both therapy tools at my disposal to go hard at my serotonin level by turning up the music and finishing my drink before pouring another one.

Cooking for one was depressing. But so was being alone—a disparaging thought that caused a light chuckle. I guess my therapeutic tool was broken.

Like you, The Voice added.

After plating my food, I carried my glass of wine to my couch.

The despondent feeling leftover from the weekend shifted about my body, leaving crumbs of despair behind to find its way back.

The feeling of loneliness, hopelessness, and despondency left me missing Caleb. A feeling that had become such a recurring sensation that it felt almost routine at that point. But routine as it may have been, it was always accompanied by guilt.

A feeling that *wasn't* habitual to me was the sense of missing Ben. A grotesque phenomenon that was egging on The Voice to attack.

Jesus, you're fucked up, it said.

Did I really think that being with Ben was better than being alone?

I took a ragged breath.

I didn't miss him. I missed the company. At least, that was how I rationalized it.

But there was no need for rationalizations because the reality was that when he was around, the sting of loneliness wasn't as apparent—not physically anyway.

But the reality of what I had felt, or was feeling, wasn't enough to justify giving that man any more real estate in my brain. Even if I thought *I* was trash, I was sticking to the immature childhood adage that it takes one to know one.

***

Just like with the bittersweet melodies of music, I indulged myself in movies that would produce the tears that I was holding captive. It was a weird psychological maneuver of telling myself that I was crying for the situation in the movie and not for any other reason—a way to feel and express the emotion without actually acknowledging it as my own.

While the credits ran down the screen, I continued to lay motionless—and surely quite pitiful looking—on the couch. The soft music from the television speakers was interrupted by the ping from my phone. I thought about ignoring it, seeing how it was my mother's name on the screen. But with a loud sigh, I decided to open the text.

Mother: Grandma Jones is in the hospital.

It had been a while since I had seen my grandma. Something I was confident my mother would remind me of the next time I saw her. But I didn't need my mother's help to feel the guilt. My own brain was great at making sure I was consistently racked with that.

I wanted to make myself feel better about not visiting, make excuses, as everyone does, about not having the time. Except not having the time had nothing to do with it as I typically had nothing *but* time.

The real reason for my limited visitations with her was her ability to see through everyone's bullshit, her proficiency in getting people to talk. I think her skill came from her lifetime career of being a nurse. She needed to be able to get the truth out of people so that she could help fix them. But whether she saw it or not, my defects weren't a treatable illness.

***

My decision to go to the hospital was made hastily and out of guilt. My feet seemed to drag a little, holding some resistance to moving towards the room that contained two women with polar opposite personalities.

I spotted my mother first. Her perfectly kept hair caught my attention as I neared the open door. The beautiful brunette dye helped hide her age and allowed us to be mistaken for sisters on a few occasions.

I had hoped that was just a compliment to her and not telling of how my life had aged me. She attributed her lack of wrinkles to her moisturizer routine. I attributed it to a lack of showing emotion.

Stepping into the room, I knocked on the door, gaining my mother's attention. She stood up, put on a forced smile, and hugged me like we were acquaintances.

But I guess acquaintances was a step up from strangers, which was the vibe I had gotten for the few years after my removal from the Christmas dinner party.

"Hi, G-ma," I said as I moved past my mother.

"Ruth, I'm going to go call Bernard and grab a bite to eat," my mother stated. "I'll be back in a little bit." She made no effort to look my way, and before my grandma could respond, she was out the door.

"I see things aren't any better with the two of you," my grandma commented as I sat down beside her bed.

"At least I got a hug," I replied with a small grin. But my lighthearted demeanor on the subject didn't seem pleasing to her. "Don't worry, we're fine."

She tried to match her grin to mine as she shifted in her bed. "You look tired, honey." She reached over and cupped my chin in her hand.

"Yeah, it's been a busy month."

It had actually been a *tough* month, but I wasn't going to get sucked in with her emotional vacuum.

"So, what are the doctors saying?"

"Nothing yet," she paused. "It's so noisy in here, and they are always coming and going."

"Yeah, hospitals suck," I responded, giving a little laugh.

"When you're the patient, they certainly do."

I moved uncomfortably in my seat as the room fell silent. It wasn't that long ago that I was in her spot. The memory sent a rush of nausea through my body.

"You okay, honey?" my grandma asked, her eyes full of distress.

I felt tightness both in my face and in the pit of my stomach from holding back the tears.

"Yeah, sorry, I just hate hospitals."

***

"Visiting hours are ending in 30 minutes," a nurse said as she wheeled in her cart to check Grandma's vitals.

The last hour with my grandma was the best and most genuine conversation I had had with anyone in a while. It was a conversation where I didn't have to worry about what emotion I was showing because, for once, she wasn't prying. She actually seemed to be doing everything she could to make me laugh.

My mother came back in shortly after the nurse left, causing the mood to shift in the room. Well, my mood did anyway.

"I'm going to get going, Grandma," I said. "I'll be back to visit this week, though, okay?"

"I would love that, honey."

I bent down to hug her, feeling the tightness in her squeeze. Her frail lips kissed my cheek. She squeezed my hand, her skin feeling oddly cold for her body being beneath layers of blankets.

My mother took the seat next to her where I had been sitting, and I moved toward the door.

I managed a half-smile and gave a slight wave to my mother. She returned the gesture with a simple head nod.

My grandma's smile wavered as she looked upon the two emotionally stunted humans in front of her. One, who seemed to have made peace with her past, and the other, who was actively trying to run from it.

Chapter Nine

On Tuesday morning, I walked into my office, setting my purse down on the desk and hanging up my coat on the door. As I took a seat, my skirt slid up, revealing my upper thighs.

"Shit," I said quietly to myself.

Wow, does someone feel they aren't getting enough attention? The Voice asked. *Why do you try so hard? No one's going to notice you anyway.*

I took a deep breath, trying to ignore my inner critic. But it had a way of deflating my self-esteem every time I was able to muster up even a small amount of it.

Was it so wrong to want to be noticed? Was trying to look nice and be liked not in the playbook of human nature?

I tugged anxiously at my skirt as the smell of coffee filled the air.

I walked to the break room, grabbed a bottle of water out of the fridge, and helped myself to one of the muffins on the table.

"Good morning, Harper," Noah said as he helped himself to the freshly brewed cup of caffeine.

"Morning," I replied.

Noah was the manager of the marketing department and was 13 years my senior. He had that George Clooney attractiveness about him, seeming to only get better looking with age.

He was tall, handsome, kind, a hard worker, and—unfortunately for all—married. I was sure his wife was very pleased with herself for landing someone like him. I would've been anyway.

"You look really nice today," he commented.

Yeah, because you look like shit the rest of the time, The Voice said.

I again tried to ignore my negative thoughts. "Thanks," I replied with a smile.

I didn't know if my low self-esteem was the catalyst behind my desire for all male attention. Some days my hormones were insane, and other days it felt like I did it just to feel wanted, or I guess even to just feel *something*. It was more likely the latter, but none of the options left me feeling particularly good about myself.

***

Before I knew it, three hours had gone by, and it was eleven. I loved getting pulled into whatever I was doing at work and losing track of time. The music blasting through my headphones did a lot to help that too.

"Knock, knock," my boss, Al, said as he stepped through my doorway.

I removed my headphones from each ear.

"Did you get those reports finished for Manny?" he asked, taking a seat in the chair opposite of me.

"Yeah, just finished and sent."

"Awesome. Some of us are going out to lunch. Wanna come?"

"Sure," I responded.

"Cool, we're leaving in a few."

His tone led me to believe the conversation had come to an end, but the fact he had yet to move from the chair told me he wasn't done.

"Did you need something else?" I asked.

Turning slightly in his seat, he pushed the door shut. His face changed to the concerned look that made my blood boil. But since he was my boss, there wasn't a lot I could say or do, so I sat back in my seat and waited for the question everyone loved to ask.

"I know I'm not supposed to, but I just wanted to check in on you. How's therapy going?"

I had been expecting the general question of how I was doing, not a specific one about therapy. I really hated that he knew about it, but when I needed to leave early on Mondays and Fridays, I didn't want to lie. Something I regretted not doing.

However, lying might not have been an option. I had missed an entire week of work when I had miscarried a little over a month before. So, when I returned, I had talked to Al about needing to leave early for therapy—leaving out the specifics.

But he could tell I wasn't okay—I think everyone could.

His face grew uneasy as I had yet to answer his question.

"It's going good," I finally responded, feeling embarrassed by the time-lapse. I tried to sound as convincing as possible. Because compared to a month before, I was okay.

"You never put in for any time off after that few weeks. You do have more time you could take—it's there for you to use."

I knew he was just looking out for my best interest, but work was a distraction for me, a place where I was around people. Why would I not want to be there?

"Al, I swear, I'm good. Please don't worry."

I think he had been growing more concerned for me throughout the year anyway. He had stopped in on different occasions to chat. He never had anything negative to say about my work, but you could tell he was just noticing things. Things that, at the time, I wasn't even noticing myself.

"Okay, well, I know you're not really a talker, but I'm here."

While I had been raised to not show real emotion to people, to stay composed at all times, I could feel my emotional suppression building up, waiting to be released.

Eventually, there would be a breaking point—an emotional collapse that would leave me burnt out and numb. All of which would befall me after an extreme release of whatever feeling had pushed me over the edge.

"So, where are we going for lunch?" I asked with a blatant shift in the subject matter.

He shrugged. "Noah extended the invite, so I guess wherever he picks."

As Al walked out of my office, the ping from my phone echoed off the walls. Ben's name, along with the deceptive words *I miss you*, lingered on the screen. I clicked the side to lock the screen without answering but knew I would have to at some point. If I didn't, he was sure to show up again.

I turned off my computer and looked at my jacket, trying to decide if Michigan's weather would keep to the same chill I had been greeted with that morning or if the sun had warmed things up since then.

Noah walked by my door, quickly stepping back into view. "You coming to lunch?" he asked, showing off his beautiful pearly whites.

"Yeah. Do you know if it's still chilly out?"

"You should be fine. If not, I'll keep you warm," he replied with a wink.

He was on his game today.

I tried to shake the thoughts away, telling myself to get a grip.

"I'll bring it just in case," I replied with a smile.

***

When we got to the restaurant, I slid into the booth-style seat. Al sat down next to me, and Noah picked the spot directly in front of me, catching my glance before I nervously looked away.

I liked flirting with Noah. It always seemed harmless. But after my lie of a relationship with Ben, I had no desire to end up in that situation again.

You mean like this weekend? The Voice asked.

I did my best to ignore the judgmental comments from my head and join the discussion happening at the table.

The conversation I jumped into was typical for that group. It would start with work topics and then lead into sports talk. It was all very surface level—and I loved that. It wasn't quite small talk, but nothing too deep either. It was a perfect balance.

Maybe that was why I loved work so much. I didn't have to worry about them seeing me for anything more than just one of them—well, I guess besides Al.

But for the rest, I didn't owe them explanations for the way I lived my life or apologies for my actions. I didn't have to worry about *how* my craziness affected them or *if* it affected them whatsoever. All I had to do was show up, fake confidence, and do my job. An uphill battle even on my best days.

Noah shifted in the chair, his leg grazing mine, pulling me out of my daydream.

I hated how often I disappeared into my own world. I hated even more how often people caught me doing it.

I looked at Noah, and he smiled.

"Welcome back," he said with a smirk.

I must have been zoned out long enough for everyone to notice. Everyone except Al smiled.

I felt my face get flushed. "Sorry."

I looked at Noah, who was still smiling. His leg shifted again, rubbing against mine. I could tell that our knees connecting a second time was intentional. I felt an ache in the pit of my stomach—the feeling of being wanted gave me an elated sensation. A high of sorts I seemed to be forever chasing—forever getting myself into trouble with.

I knew Noah was just playing around, but my mind took it to a whole different level. I pictured him coming to my office, pulling me in for a passionate kiss, unable to resist me any longer. Of course, in those fantasies, he was always single. Even in my daydreams, I had no desire to be party to wrecking a home—again.

With my sexual frustration building, that was typically where a call to Caleb would take place. He had kept the number of guys I had slept with lower than it would have been if we hadn't set up the arrangement between us years before. And any time he wasn't around to hold up his end of the bargain, I always had my self-help in the nightstand next to my bed.

The self-help was purchased for me by Serena at a Pure Romance party she had attended. She had no interest in keeping my number low, but she also had the frame of mind that you couldn't always rely on a man.

While I agreed and had upgraded to different vibrators since then, sometimes having the physical touch of another human being was the real desire I would be craving.

But in the times when another individual's touch wasn't possible, and the buildup got to be too much, my vibrator did the trick. Times like when Caleb had a girlfriend, when I didn't want to go to a bar on a weeknight, or when an attractive but very married man happened to be in the office.

The worst part of it was that, when I would finish, the emptiness of my bed would inevitably rush over me. The very apparent void that I had in my life would soon follow.

But with a man lying beside me, I typically had until the next morning for the lonely feeling to take hold—especially when I was with Caleb. We usually followed our nights together with breakfast or cooked some together. It was something that would keep the loneliness at bay for just a little while longer.

***

Once we had all finished our meals, we paid the waitress and got up to leave. Noah gestured for me to go first as he walked behind me.

While heading toward the door, I spotted a familiar face.

"Harper," Ian said, looking caught off guard.

He stood in front of me for a moment, then leaned in for an unexpected embrace.

It was awkward, to say the least.

"Hey, Ian."

From the expression he was sporting, I could tell he was uncomfortable, too, and had instantly regretted the hug. And, for a moment, my anxious thoughts fell silent as I thought about him having the same ones.

The sound of Noah clearing his throat reminded me he was still there. I glanced over and gestured for him to head outside.

"I'm really sorry about Saturday," he said.

What did he have to be sorry for?

"Yeah, me too," I responded. "I barely remember the whole last half of the night. I just know Drew dropped Serena and me off at my place."

Something in his expression told me Drew had already informed him of the panic attack. I felt the blood rush to my cheeks again.

"Yeah, I don't remember much either," he replied, rubbing his hand on the back of his neck. "But, I'm glad you're okay."

"Thanks."

"I'm sorry if I did anything to cause... you know..."

"You didn't," I interrupted. "I just had a lot to drink," I continued, wanting so badly to crawl into a hole and disappear.

The awkward silence started to build around us as our polite, but distressed smiles were wavering on our faces.

"Well, I need to get back to work. I'll see you around."

"Okay," he replied, moving past me toward an empty table.

There was nothing subtle about my exit, but neither of us seemed equipped for that conversation.

I walked outside, where Noah was waiting for me by his car.

"Jeremy took the rest of them back to the office," he said. "I told them I would wait for you."

"Cool. Uh, sorry about that."

It took me a second to catch my bearings, as I hated my two lives colliding.

"Is he anyone special?" he asked with a coy smile crossing his face.

"No—" I paused as I got in the car. "I met him at a bar this weekend. It was just awkward to run into him."

"Ah, to be single again," he said, running his hand through his hair.

I could tell Noah assumed Ian and I had hooked up. I didn't do anything to correct that assumption.

"So, do you go out often?" he asked.

I couldn't tell if that was the question he had really wanted to ask or if he actually wanted to know how often it was that I brought men home with me.

"I don't know, kind of. I had my ten-year reunion this weekend, so that stemmed some need to drink," I responded, trying to sound like I was joking.

"Oh yeah? God, I remember mine," he said as he trailed off.

"I'll give you time to think back that far."

"That hurts," he replied, playfully offended. He touched his hand to his chest.

"I'm sure everything does at your age."

An amused smile crossed his face as he placed his arm on the center console where mine was already resting. The warmth that radiated from his body made my mind go back to the fantasy of him and me in my office.

I removed my arm slowly and placed my hands in my lap. The thoughts in my head led me to tug nervously at the ends of my skirt.

He moved his hand down to his thigh and shifted his body like he was trying to get comfortable.

My pulse quickened at the thought of me making him flustered—the thought of him wanting his hands to be where mine was.

I took a deep but controlled breath, trying to hide my attempt at calming myself down. But my flustered thoughts only angered The Voice as it began to berate me for my choice in men.

You only want what you can't have, it stated.

I wanted to refute the claim, take offense, and prove it false. But my track record was hard evidence to the contrary. While I never actively pursued men that I knew were taken, I never shut down or discouraged their thoughts either.

Something I had convinced myself was okay since it had never gone any further than flirting. But my previous relationship with Ben left me questioning every decision I had ever made in my love life.

When I got home that evening, I decided to start with a shower as food was the farthest thing from my mind. The hot water cascading onto my skin did little to distract me from the ache that had seemed to take up temporary residence in my lower abdomen.

It was an ache that felt euphoric rather than painful, but the longer it went unsatisfied, the more I knew that feeling would shift.

After my shower, I slipped on my underwear and robe. The soft fabric against my skin did as much harm in my distraction as the shower had.

I walked barefoot to the kitchen to pour myself some wine but was met with only disappointment, stemming from the empty bottle on the counter. I took a picture of the tragic remnants and sent it to Serena with a frowny face. She replied with a laughing emoji, but then a crying one, as she felt my pain.

The sadness, or rather the annoyance, at my lack of wine, allowed me for a moment to repress the ache. There weren't many nights I wasn't able to tone down the unreasonable thoughts without at least a little help from my favorite form of fruit—crushed grapes. But since I was in no mood to go to the store, my night was going to end with me being tragically sober.

While I did my best to ignore any more wandering thoughts, for the time being, I heated up pizza rolls in the microwave, putting as little effort imaginable into making dinner.

I grabbed my mushy excuse for food and took a seat at my small kitchen table. The only thing missing was my staple glass—or bottle—of wine.

After I was finished, I cleared the table and let my hair down. I ran my fingers through the wet strands as I positioned myself comfortably on the couch.

With a favorite movie of mine playing in the background, I rested my hand in the opening of the robe. A few minutes passed as I lightly began rubbing the outside of my underwear, teasing myself.

But as the tension built, I moved the fabric to the side and slid two of my fingers in just enough so that my body was starting to beg for more. My eyelids closed while my mind drifted back to my fantasy of Noah in my office like I was watching a dramatization of how I felt it would have taken place. My thoughts shifted to Caleb and his jealous face from Saturday as I straddled Ian in the booth. Then quickly flashed to his face buried into my chest on Friday night.

I felt the ache shifting lower, taking over my legs as I pulled off my underwear and tossed them on the floor.

I moved my fingers deeper—my mind changing between scenes. But even with the scene change, and at times a partner change, my mind always returned to Caleb. Mostly on his ability to make my body feel whole every time his was on mine.

I closed my eyes and laid my head back on the armrest, letting out a soft moan.

The loud thud of a car door shutting pulled me from my euphoric state of mind. I wiped my fingers across the silk and jumped up, my body ill-prepared for the vertical shift—becoming as upset with the untimeliness of a visitor as my mind was.

I tried to compose myself while the sound of knuckles against the wooden door requested my response.

After pausing for a moment, I complied with the request as my body tried like hell to stable itself. My brain rushed through all the emotions it could experience in a small amount of time before I was finally able to speak.

"What are you doing here, Caleb?"

Chapter Ten

"Can't a friend just stop by?" he asked.

"Not a friend that I just fucked."

His twisted expression led me to take the bottle of wine from his hands. "At least you came prepared."

I walked into the kitchen as I heard him shut the front door.

"I just wanted to check on you," he said from the other room. "I was worried after Saturday night."

He came into the kitchen. He glanced at me, waiting for an answer. But instead, he got distracted. "Oh, was I interrupting?" He nodded toward my robe with a grin.

I glanced down at the spot that had started to dry, blushing instantly.

Caleb grinned mischievously while my hormones decided to play along.

"Maybe. Did you come to help?" I asked flirtatiously.

Are you seriously doing this again? The Voice said. *God, you're pathetic.*

I shut my eyes in disgust at myself before he could answer, then retrieved two glasses from the cupboard.

The Voice started to list all the compelling reasons not to tangle myself in the mess that was our relationship yet again. But my mind's inability to focus on the important details was having a field day with his close proximity to my body.

"You know I can't do that," he finally replied, with the reminder that I needed but didn't want. "But maybe we could just hang like we used to?"

Caleb reached for the bottle to open it, but my glance made him back down and then caused him to smirk.

"Unless you need to be alone," he continued in place of my silence.

His comment was meant as a joke, but just hearing the word sent a small amount of panic through my veins.

I poured the wine into my glass, then did the same for his.

"So, you're cool with me staying for a little bit?" he asked.

"Knock yourself out," I replied.

I curled up on the couch as Caleb sat down in the chair. He seemed preoccupied as he stared at the floor. I followed his eye line and saw my underwear lying shamelessly balled up on the ground. I tossed the blanket on top of them while he glanced over at me, amused.

"You know it's not a good idea for you to be here," I said.

"Can't control yourself, huh?" he asked, raising his eyebrows.

"Caleb, I'm serious."

He exhaled frustratedly. "Hey, there's nothing wrong with me checking on a friend."

"Yes, but you haven't had sleepovers with your other friends."

"Don't pretend to know what Milo and I do in our friendship."

I laughed.

He did too.

It was nice not being alone. But my mind didn't want to let it go that easily. The Voice kept telling me I was making a name for myself.

"Seriously though, does Cassy know you're here?"

"No. I mean, at least I didn't tell her. It's not like it was intentional."

Did he mean it wasn't intentional to sleep with me or to cheat on her?

"Can I sit by you so we can watch TV?" he asked, looking over at me.

I shook my head.

He sighed again. "Seriously, I won't try anything."

He seemed much more confident in his self-restraint.

After a moment of hesitation, I brought my legs closer to my body as I shifted to the end of the couch, leaving him room to sit.

***

I finished my second glass of wine while we sat in silence watching TV. I imagined that to be what life would have been like if things hadn't gone so wrong when we had dated years before.

For a split second, my ache of desire turned to sadness as I thought back to the time before everything had changed for us. A time when there was only excitement, mystery, and lust. Instead of fighting, lies, and traumatic pasts.

Our relationship, or whatever it could be labeled, had changed so much, mainly because *we* had changed so much, or at the very least, *I* had changed.

He was with Cassy now.

He'd be stupid to fuck things up with her for you, The Voice said.

I felt guilty for flirting with him when he was with someone else. I would have liked to say it was harmless flirting, like with Noah, but could I really call it that if I knew what his kiss tasted like? If I knew what it felt like to have him inside of me? If I still wanted those things to happen?

"Hey, are you good?" he asked, looking at me distressed.

I sighed as my emotions did a 180.

"Yeah, I'm fine. Why?"

"You just seem different," he answered, angling his body to face me. "I thought maybe it was just everything this weekend, but something still seems off."

What was I supposed to say to that?

"Nope, same old me," I replied, pouring the rest of the wine from the bottle into my glass.

I was confident that my drinking did little to reassure people I was fine. But I had always been able to put back the wine—or any booze really—with the best of them. So, my alcohol consumption shouldn't have been considered a factor in my healthy mental state or lack thereof.

"What happened between you and Ben?" he asked, finishing up his second glass.

"We broke up," I replied, purposely being evasive.

He thankfully took the hint, and we both fell silent.

"My grandma's in the hospital," I blurted out as the silence got uncomfortable.

"Oh, I'm sorry. Is she going to be okay?"

"Yeah, I think so. I don't really know what's up yet. Not a whole lot of updates coming from my mother."

"Well, that should be expected," he said with an eye roll.

While Caleb had heard a lot about my mother over the years, he had been fortunate enough to never have to meet her.

"Yeah," I responded, turning off the TV.

"Calling it an early night?" he asked.

"Well, the wine is gone," I replied, shaking the bottle in his direction with a chuckle.

We looked at each other but remained silent.

The wine was just antagonizing me to take care of the ache that was making my body feel like it was going to explode. Caleb *not* trying to have sex with me was just as much of a turn-on as when he did try because I knew he was holding himself back, too.

He needed to leave.

"Seriously, though, I have stuff to do," I said, slowly standing up, unsure if I could trust my legs at that point.

"Are you finishing what you started earlier?" he asked with a goofy smile and glossed-over eyes.

I could tell the wine was starting to get to him. Caleb wasn't a big drinker, and although he had a good hundred pounds on me, I could drink him under the table on any given night.

"You should sober up before you take off. I'll make you some coffee," I commented as he followed me into the kitchen. "I only have the instant kind," I commented.

"That's fine."

I placed it in the microwave to heat it up. I tried to act distracted by my phone so that he wouldn't feel the need to fill the silence, but he did anyway.

"Don't let me stop you from *finishing* your night," he said as he leaned back against the counter next to me.

"You're such a lightweight," I joked again, briefly giving in to his demeanor.

I reminded myself not to let the wine get the best of me. But who was I kidding? The wine was just an excuse.

Caleb looked at me longingly. "I mean, *I* can't do anything, but that doesn't mean you can't *think* of me doing something," he said with a devilish grin.

I pulled the coffee mug out of the microwave and set it down by him, trying to figure out what was the right thing to say.

Really? The Voice questioned. *Are you that far from the line that you can't see it, or did you just erase it entirely the last time you crossed it?*

I ignored the morality police inside my head—taking a minute to consider Caleb's thoughts. I had already planned on handling things myself—so what did it matter if he knew I was thinking of him? I usually did regardless.

If you need loopholes to justify it, then it's wrong, the righteous voice reasoned.

I knew I needed to be careful, or I was going to make a name for myself. But I couldn't help but think, whoever took the time to consider me?

"Good night, Caleb. Lock up on your way out," I finally replied as I looked intensely into his eyes.

I grabbed my headphones out of my purse, slipped off my robe, and hung it on the back of the chair in the kitchen. I turned my head enough to catch his stare as I smiled sinfully before retreating to my bedroom.

Well, line officially crossed, The Voice scolded.

I started to close the bedroom door but instead decided to leave it open.

I placed my headphones into my ears as I lay back on my bed. I turned my music up to drown out the silence of being the only one in the room.

Thinking of Caleb listening made the ache throb inside of me. I grabbed my vibrator and slowly pushed it into place, moaning loud enough that I heard it over my music.

Caleb's shadow moved in the light outside of my door.

I knew he wanted badly to come into my room and take care of it himself. I knew it was wrong, but it didn't *feel* wrong. The guilt for that would kick in later.

At that moment, the only feelings I was letting in were the good ones—the feeling of desire, him wanting to be in there, him listening to me moan, jealous that only the Caleb in my mind was making it happen. All of it was what the ache in my body was craving. It was exactly what I needed to allow my body to release the buildup of sexual energy I had been hoarding all night.

I saw his shadow move in the hallway as my breathing started to return to normal. I was unsure if he would leave right then or if he would stick around for even a few minutes. But moments later, his shadow disappeared, and when I pulled out my headphones, I heard the front door shut behind him.

The pain of loneliness traveled through my stomach and took over my chest. I felt a tear stream down my cheek.

This is all you're good for, The Voice said. *You're not the woman they come home to. I'm surprised anyone even wants you. You're pathetic.*

The way I had ended my night was not on my list of proudest moments—scratch that—I didn't even *have* a list of proudest moments.

It did, however, make the list of the most inappropriate things I had done.

The Voice echoed Ben's harsh words into my head, reminding me that I was the crazy mistress. I was just good for a lay and nothing more.

My chest grew tight as The Voice continued with degrading remarks. But soon, my regular thoughts took hold, making me almost prefer the slanderous statements to the hurtful questions.

Was I even capable of having a relationship that was more than just sex? Was I capable of loving someone in a normal functioning way? Could anyone ever really love me once they knew the real me?

Chapter Eleven

After work on Wednesday, I stopped at the hospital for a visit, hoping to rid myself of a little guilt from everything that was plaguing my mind. When I arrived, my mother was there with Bernard. They moved over so I could sit by my grandma, who began talking to me about the visitors she had been having over the past few days.

Sometime during our conversation, Bernard and my mother left to get a bite to eat. Once they had adequately vacated the proximity of the room, I felt my grandma's tone shift, her mind undeniably preoccupied with something else.

"Grandma, are you okay?" I asked as she struggled to make any sense while starting and stopping each sentence she began. "Should I call a nurse?"

She shook her head. "No, it's nothing like that, honey." She paused, then continued nervously. "I don't know how much your mom has told you about why I'm in here."

"Nothing really. You know my mother—not very forthcoming with information."

She sighed, visibly upset.

"I'm going to call a nurse," I stated, starting to move toward the button.

"Harper Eleanor!" she responded. "I don't need a nurse. Just listen."

She looked at me sternly, so I sat back down as she took my hand in hers. "I'm not leaving the hospital."

I sighed, giving a light smile. "Grandma, you're going to be fine. You look better already."

"No, Harper, I've been sick for a while. I'm afraid this is it."

I sat back in my chair. "What do you mean you've been sick?"

"Harper, that's not important. What's important is that I need you to know the truth about something."

I was annoyed, but not surprised, that my mother would withhold information like that from me.

"Harper," my grandma said, pulling me back from my thoughts. "I'm sorry I didn't tell you this a long time ago. I'm sorry I let myself be convinced that it was the right thing to do because now, being at the end, I see that it wasn't."

I was intrigued at what she needed to get off her chest. But as she struggled to get the words out, my mouth went dry, and my hands began to fidget, suddenly wondering if I wanted to hear it. Wondering if I could handle whatever it was that was causing my grandma such distress just from having to say it out loud.

After another minute of collecting herself and me squeezing my nails into the palm of my hands, she was finally able to form the words she had been searching for.

"Harper—your dad's death wasn't an accident," she continued as she avoided my eyes and looked down at her blanket. "He killed himself."

The words coming from her frail voice didn't soften the blow.

"What?" I finally managed to say.

"He suffered for a really long time... It just got to be too much for him."

"*What* got to be too much?" I asked as I felt myself pulling away.

"He battled depression for years. We really thought he had it under control, but, about a week after he died, your mom found a note he had left for her."

A rush of nausea ran through my body as my head began to throb.

It didn't make sense. She was lying.

"But we got all that money for his death...he was killed by the faulty machine," I replied hesitantly as I no longer knew what was real.

She nodded. "He somehow made it look like an accident so that you guys wouldn't be left with nothing." She took a deep breath and continued. "He had called me that morning. I didn't realize he was saying goodbye, you know, for good. But once your mom told me about the note, I knew that's what it was for."

I put my head in my hands. The pounding in my ears was making it hard to hear my grandma's words. My face flushed, and the nausea intensified. I was worried I was going to have another panic attack, so I did my best to calm myself down.

"I'm so sorry I kept this from you. You deserved to know a long time ago," she continued. "I couldn't leave without you knowing the truth."

I could see she was in pain. I knew I couldn't offer up any amount of reassurance that what she kept from me was okay. But I also knew that it all boiled down to my mother and her need to control every situation—her need to keep all secrets buried.

She took my head in her hands and kissed my forehead. "You're such a wonderful girl. Your dad would be proud of the woman you have become."

No he wouldn't, The Voice said.

I heard my mother step into the room behind me. "What's going on?" she asked as she set her purse on the chair next to the bed.

I turned and looked at her. She knew.

Her face went pale, and there was no need to ask if it were true—her expression said it all.

"Seriously, Ruth?" Her voice shook with anger. "You just couldn't help yourself, could you?"

"You should have told her when it happened," my grandma snapped back, her voice unsteady. "She could have handled it."

"That wasn't your call to make," my mother replied. "Did you know that she's in *therapy*? Did she tell you *that*? Did you think to check and see if she was suffering from the same thing that killed Frank before unloading your guilty conscience!?"

My mother must have been shouting because a nurse came into the room looking very concerned, but I didn't hear anything after her comparing my therapy to my father offing himself. My brain hadn't processed that part of it yet. It hadn't pieced together that I could have gotten my fucked-up way of thinking from him.

I calmly wiped my face, realizing at some point that tears had escaped the corners of my eyes. I kissed my grandma on the cheek, grabbed my purse, and walked past my mother—side-eying her like I was a teenager again.

I heard her call my name as I walked toward Bernard, who stood up from his chair in the hallway. I could tell he was unsure if he should try and stop me. The look I gave him told him not to; luckily for him, he complied.

***

I felt my mother's presence as I got outside; I knew she wasn't far behind. I unlocked my car and sat down before she reached me.

Her hand gripped my door, holding it open. "We need to talk about this, Harper."

"No. *You* had your chance to talk. Twelve years, in fact," I said, glaring up at her.

"It isn't that simple," she replied, looking around before she continued, lowering her voice. "He was very sick."

"Clearly. And, apparently, so is Grandma, and you didn't mention that either."

She pulled her hand back as she saw I was going to close my door, with or without it there.

"Harper!" she said through the glass.

Fucking bitch.

I put up my middle finger and peeled out of the parking space. Getting a little bit of delight as I had always wanted to do that to her. But in my wildest dreams, I would have never imagined that being the reason I would finally do it.

Chapter Twelve

After the week I had had, I was happy that it was finally Friday. As per usual, work was a welcomed distraction, as was the wine and bingeing of shows that had filled my past few evenings. All I had left to get through was my session with Sarah, and I could do my best not to think about my father—or my mother. I wasn't sure how I was going to accomplish that, but it was my weekend goal, nonetheless.

Luckily for Sarah, I had already written in my journal about the wretched woman who birthed me before everything went south at the hospital. I contemplated ripping it out but didn't want to write a new entry about her or anyone else. Though there was certainly more that could be added to her section—like how she was a lying bitch.

When I walked into Sarah's office, I set my journal down on the coffee table as I had Monday and took a seat opposite her. She glanced at me like she was trying to gauge my reaction to something. But without saying anything more, she picked up my journal and began to read.

***

(Journal entry)

My mother, Lorelai Edith Vanderwit, was born September 15th, 1968, and was raised in a small northern town in Michigan. She was at the top of her class the entire time she was in school and, from a young age, was dead set on being valedictorian.

While happy that my mother wanted to do well, my grandma Van Warren (or Grandma V. as I call her) felt that this would make my mother less appealing to men. Saying they wouldn't like a woman who was smarter than them. This old way of thinking just pushed my mother further into her studies, and less onto the opposite sex.

My mother did graduate top of her class and was awarded the honor of being valedictorian. The night of graduation she got drunk at a party and lost her virginity to a boy she barely knew. That was the extent of us ever discussing sex. I don't know if she considered that the sex talk. A warning of some sorts. But I was 15, and I didn't care for any cautionary tales, especially from my mother.

The only reason she shared her story about her graduation night was because I had approached her about getting on birth control. I had waited until after she had finished a bottle of wine, so that led to her oversharing.

I ended up just forging my mother's signature to get what I needed, since she either didn't remember the conversation, or purposely didn't want it brought up again.

After moving out of my house at 17, I had stopped by to see Grandma and Grandpa V. when they had returned from their winter in Florida.

I talked with my grandma about what had led to me moving out, which led into a discussion about my mother in general. I knew my mother's pregnancy with me was hard on her physically, and I knew that I was the reason she was never able to finish her degree, which is a big reason she was upset that I didn't finish mine.

My grandma told me that she had actually lived with us for the first month of my life, to help with my mother's introduction to parenting. Something she didn't take to very easily. And as soon as my mother was physically able she went back to work.

My grandma said that she felt that my mother suffered from postpartum depression. But it wasn't something widely recognized at the time, and my mother wasn't willing to bring it up to the doctors, as she was afraid to be labeled "crazy."

All this information helped our relationship make more sense to me. But it also left me with so many questions that I haven't felt comfortable enough to ask my mother yet. My grandma said the more she tried to help with me, the worse their relationship got.

My mother blamed my grandma, and the help she had given in my first year for why she had a lack of connection with me. She said my grandma did it on purpose to make her feel like she wasn't good enough—even though motherhood was something she had never been interested in.

My grandma felt she was just projecting and never took what my mother said to heart. However, while I don't think it was her intention, hearing that your mother didn't feel like she had a connection to you was really fucked up and painful.

After I moved out, I didn't see my mother much. She met and married Bernard Vanderwit two years after my father's death. Which caused her to pull even further away from me. It felt like she was trying to forget the life she had with us.

Bernard had two kids from a previous marriage that left him widowed as well—a twelve-year-old boy and a fourteen-year-old girl. My mother's wedding to Bernard was small and intimate. So intimate in fact, that I wasn't even invited.

I know this entire thing makes my mother sound terrible, but she wasn't all bad. We had good times, too. I remember my mother in those good moments. I remember her teaching me how to ride my bike and playing Barbies with me. The good times just got to be less and less frequent over the years.

I did see signs of that kind mother from those moments again when she started dating Bernard. Her smiles seemed genuine, and her laugh was full. I guess that had just been something my dad and I couldn't give her at some point anymore.

***

Sarah could tell that I was riled up. I was sure she felt that was a good thing, as it meant I would share more. But thankfully, she didn't rush me into it.

"So, I just want to be completely honest here because that's what I want between the two of us," she said, setting the journal back down.

I wasn't sure where she was headed, but I nodded anyway.

"Your mother called me Thursday morning. She was concerned about you."

Funny. I hadn't heard from her since I had found out she had been lying to me since I was 16.

I folded my arms and exhaled. "Sounds about right."

"She didn't go into any details. And she didn't want me to mention it to you. But I don't keep secrets; that's not what this space is for. I told her that as well."

I appreciated her candor.

"My father's adoptive mother is in the hospital. I went to visit her Wednesday night." I paused, trying to decide if I wanted to get into everything about my father. I sighed before I continued. "I learned that he didn't die from a malfunctioning machine. My grandma told me he killed himself." I hadn't said the words out loud yet. They hadn't sounded as powerful while leaving my lips as they had in my head.

We sat in silence as I decided how I should continue.

"My mother and grandma knew the entire time and never said anything. But now my grandma is dying, and I guess she didn't want to take it to her grave."

Sarah stayed silent as I took a deep breath.

"My family has just been so secretive my whole life," I continued. "I keep finding shit out. I just don't understand why they felt they couldn't tell me anything. My mother is so worried about what people may think. I just, I can't deal with her anymore. I mean, we basically never talk anyway, and I'm not really welcomed at holidays, so what's just one last push to have her completely out of my life?"

"Is that what you want?" she asked.

I sat still, thinking for a minute. "Yes," I said firmly. I immediately felt hesitant about my answer. "Well, I don't know. I mean, I do, but I want answers first. I want to know why she gave up on my father long before he gave up on us. I want to know why she didn't fight for me when I left. Why she just let me go. She *literally* bought me a house, for Christ's sake. That's how bad she wanted me gone. Why have I never been important enough to her?!"

I pressed my arms tightly against my stomach.

"Have you ever asked her any of this?" Sarah questioned, pushing the tissues closer to me. But I didn't need them.

"You don't understand her. She doesn't talk about her emotions. That isn't the way we handle things. You can't let people see you at your weakest point. You *can't* be weak."

Saying that out loud brought me back to a time in middle school when I had my first crush on a boy. That boy, however, turned into an ass when his friends called me a slut. At that time, I had never even kissed a boy, but they didn't care. I had developed early, which made me an easy target—kids can be as cruel as adults.

I went home that night and cried to my mother about it. She was annoyed that I was interested in boys already, saying that she sent me to school to learn, not to date.

Right after that, she was remorseful and had given me what she thought was sound advice. She had said that I couldn't show weakness with boys, that they could sense it and would use it against me. I needed to keep my mind sharp and on the prize of graduating.

I never did take her advice on staying clear of boys. But I had doubled down on the part of not showing weakness, doing so not just with boys, but with everyone.

Sarah continued to ask questions, trying to dig deeper into my father's death and how it affected me. Although I still didn't have answers to her questions, it did give me some good things to reflect on. The biggest thing I was worried about, at that point, was that if my father's depression was how he met his ultimate demise, would that happen to me, too?

While I had never brought up my depression again with my doctors, I was sure it was still noted in my charts from my test run with the medication years before. I had always been able to pull myself out of my low points without the help of a medical professional. But, from what my grandma said, my father had always been able to do that, too. Until one day, he couldn't.

While I would have days that I wouldn't get out of bed, I had never really thought it was all that bad. It felt like I was just taking a mental break. But maybe that wasn't as normal or common as I had thought. Everyone had their bad days, but I was becoming increasingly worried about the severity of mine.

"What if I kill myself like my father did?" I blurted out.

"Are you thinking of harming yourself?"

"Not currently. But what if I do? What if something changes, and it happens?"

"Well, that's why you come here, Harper. You're working on things. You're opening up."

"What if that's not enough? What if it's something that just catches up to you?"

Sarah got up and grabbed a card out of her desk; scribbling something onto the back. "I wrote down the number to the suicide resource here in town. If any feelings like that come up at all, I want you to call them. Plus, you know you can call me anytime."

That was it? That's what I should do if I get into a bad place?

I could tell she sensed my skepticism.

"Harper, you're making progress. This is hard news to take, but as you can see, you are here—you are talking. We will keep working through this. You *will* get through this."

Chapter Thirteen

I was not wanting to spend a third evening in a row drowning in the nothingness of my home life and disparaging thoughts. I decided to go to the movies.

When I arrived at the theater, I purchased some candy and pop and found my seat. I snuggled into the couch-like seating and propped my feet up in front of me—preparing to do what I could to extract myself from the real world.

As the lights dimmed for the previews to begin, a few people trailed in, attempting to find their seats.

I ignored the silhouettes of the cute couple who entered in behind the others as I put the box of raisinets to my mouth and tipped it back.

While the screen lit up the theater, the outlines of the adorable duo became detailed, allowing me to recognize Ben's face.

I sank further into my seat and put my hand to my temple, hoping they would find their seats quickly.

Finally, they moved to their spots a few rows in front of me. He draped his arm around her as she intimately nestled against his chest.

She's much better looking than you, The Voice said.

I ignored the remark, more upset that I had been planning on immersing myself in the movie. But instead, I knew full well that I would be spending the next hour and a half staring daggers into the back of his head.

As the film progressed, Ben moved his hand to her leg, getting bolder with every sensual touch.

Though annoyed, little shade could be thrown from my seat, as I had let him do the same thing when we had come to the movies together only a few months before. A memory I felt stupid about for a few different reasons.

***

By the time the movie wrapped up, everyone in the theater could tell Ben would be getting lucky later that night. Realistically though, I was probably the only one who noticed—or cared for that matter.

He stood up as the lights came on and turned enough so that his glance caught my stare. There was no possible way at that moment I could have avoided being seen.

You should have left during the movie, The Voice said.

But the words of advice were a little too late, leaving me exposed to his smug smile that hung disgustingly perfect on his face.

I placed my feet on the floor and focused my attention on slowly cleaning up the few things I had—hoping to avoid a run-in with him outside the door.

While they disappeared into the sea of people piling out, my thoughts changed from being bothered overseeing him to angry that he had been trying to get back together while still seeing other women.

But I guess it was true—once a cheater, always a cheater. I was just glad he was no longer my problem. I had hoped that, given enough time, he would just move on, and it seemed he had.

As I stepped into the hall amongst the last group of people, I felt a hand rest on my back. I turned around, coming face to face with the good-looking man I was hoping to have left in my past.

"Are you stalking me?" he asked, with too much enjoyment in his tone.

I held back an eye roll, taking a step backward so that his hand fell. "Nope, just here for the movie."

He kept his smile and glanced around.

"What, did your date ditch you?" I asked.

His grin wavered a little as his eyes narrowed, but his look quickly shifted to delight. "Is someone jealous?" He chuckled. "You have nothing to worry about; it's a harmless date."

I was annoyed at his delusion and his incessant need to get what he couldn't have. The more I tried to repel him, the more he tried to break me. He knew it was possible. And as much as I hated to admit it, I knew it was too.

He was handsome. He was charming—until he wasn't anyway.

I was hoping I was smart enough not to fall for his manipulations again. But I had little faith in my intelligence when it came to many things—most of all when it came to men. It didn't matter the amount that I despised his personality, how much I loathed his treatment of me or the extent that I hated how he made me feel.

I had a bad habit of using sex to block everything out so that my fractured self-esteem could try and repair itself. Something that had yet to ever work.

He noticed his date come out of the bathroom and look around for him. "I still want to get together and talk," he added before heading off to her.

***

After downing two glasses of wine from the bottle I had picked up on the way home, I called it an early night. I was hoping to get enough alcohol in my system to make my sleep more restful and thoughts of Ben less maddening.

Unfortunately for me, despite the alcohol consumption, my mind had other plans. Plans that I wasn't privy to until I was drifting in and out while my head rested comfortably on my pillow. Moments with Ben played like a movie projector on the back of my eyelids. My fight to change the content of the film was futile against my tired mind.

I felt like my mind had strapped me to a chair and forced me to watch my bad decision-making. Though, at the time, it hadn't appeared all that bad. I was blinded by his gorgeous smile, his nicely pressed suit, and his suave demeanor.

It wasn't until a couple of months later that I was able to start noticing his manipulative behavior. All of which could be traced back to the night of our first date—our first kiss as adults.

It was one that so gentle and easy. One that made me, for a split second, think that maybe my heart could love someone who wasn't Caleb. But I had been wrong. I had been stupid. I had been trusting and vulnerable with a horrible man.

I had let him take my control.

While my mind resisted the images of Ben, my father came into view instead. He stood smiling at me in the kitchen of our first house, where we had lived until I was seven. His jet-black hair and green eyes were vibrant.

He looked as I had remembered him, although I could see the happiness from his smile wasn't forced like it had been for as long as I could remember. It was a contrived look that, when I gave it, I was told I resembled him.

But I had known it was the smile that made us look alike. What I didn't know was that his head was full of disparaging thoughts. I hadn't known that what was wrong with him would someday consume me in a similar way.

The sound of a bell rang loudly throughout my old kitchen. I felt panic for a moment, but his relaxed—almost serene—demeanor allowed my worry to drift away. I don't know if my mind knew I was dreaming, and therefore allowed me to control the circumstances, but I willed myself to feel his warm embrace.

Without any real lapse in time, I felt his arms tightly around me. His newfound tranquility transferred through his hug, as it felt more meaningful—more intentional—than it had when he was alive.

Our relationship had been so different from what others experienced. I felt most women I knew had either an amazing relationship with their fathers or a completely disastrous one. And though my sex life seemed riddled with daddy issues, our relationship had been so straightforward.

I knew he was the father who did his best to provide and give us a good life, and he knew I was the daughter who tried my best to stay within the lines and do as I was told. It was a weird ground of mutual respect that really only shook a little when Ben was in my life. A warning sign I should have seen all on my own.

As he loosened his hold on me, I found myself missing him more than I ever had. But his smile and his embrace weren't from the man I remembered, and it left me wondering—was I really missing him, or missing some contrived *idea* of him?

I felt myself shift in my bed as the bell continued to pierce my ears. My father, who had been standing before me, suddenly disappeared, and then there was nothing but emptiness. Everything had gone dark, yet I still felt awake in another world.

Then, just as quickly as it had gone, the world I had created was back. That time, in unfamiliar surroundings. As the bell continued to sound, I spotted Ben across the room. He smiled lovingly as he approached me, passing by beautiful women on his way.

His eyes were glued to mine like I was the only thing that mattered. My body tingled as his mouth grazed my neck and his hands moved to my hips.

The hatred I had felt earlier in the day seemed to dissipate. The man looked like Ben, but his touch and the happiness I felt from his presence made me think it was a lie. A lie like the counterfeit man that had appeared to me as my father.

When he lifted his head from my neck, Ben was no longer the man who stood in front of me. Caleb smiled as he moved the bangs out of my eyes. Before I could react, the image of him standing there, and the touch of his skin on mine, faded away, and so did the world around me.

The noise that had been in the background of my mind continued to grow louder. I felt myself getting pulled out of my dream, reaching for my phone to shut off my alarm. As I continued to wake up, there was a pungent odor I couldn't quite identify.

I opened my eyes, again trying to turn off the alarm on my phone. While my eyes focused on the screen, I realized it was too early in the morning for an alarm and that it was a Saturday. The noise continued to shriek while I stumbled out of bed to my door.

I reached for the doorknob—immediately pulling back—as blinding pain shot through my palm. Within seconds I was woefully awake—grasping the full reality of my situation.

Panic started to set in as I saw an orange glow from under the door and heard sirens in the distance. I felt like I couldn't move, couldn't breathe. Not from the smoke, but from the panic—maybe a little from both.

I tried to remind myself to calm down, to not panic—to breathe.

I looked around the room as my eyes set on the navy-blue curtains.

I jumped on my bed and pushed the window open as the fire trucks pulled up in front of my house. I took out the screen and clung tightly to my phone as I attempted to pull myself through.

Two people dressed heavily in fire gear helped me the rest of the way as the others got things ready on their truck.

"Is there anyone else in the house?" one of them asked.

"No… no, just me," I replied, my head still spinning.

They brought me to the ambulance as it pulled up next to their truck. "They will take care of you, okay?"

The firemen went to work containing the flames that consumed my house. I watched in horror as there wasn't a room untouched from the raging inferno.

It took me a few minutes before I realized the paramedics were talking to me. "Can you tell us your name?"

I don't know what questions they had been asking before that, or if they had repeated the same one, waiting for an answer.

I tried and failed to talk. I swallowed and then tried again, moving the oxygen mask off my mouth.

"Harper," I responded, looking at my hand that was gripping my phone.

Why did it hurt to hold my phone?

I moved it to my other hand, exposing the varying degrees of burn marks on my palm.

"Um—" was all I could manage as I lifted my hand, showing it to one of the paramedics.

She told the other one what to grab and then looked at me. "Is there someone you can call?" she asked.

I unlocked my phone and scanned through my contact list—continuing to scroll until I came to the end.

No. There wasn't anyone I could call. Serena was hours away. Caleb had Cassy. Ben had whoever he had. And calling my mother would be something that would happen over my dead body.

Honestly, would anyone even give a damn that my house was disappearing before me in the form of billowing black smoke?

I shook my head at the paramedic, who eyed me wistfully, putting the oxygen max back over my face.

"Okay, well, we're going to take you to the hospital to be evaluated," she said, motioning to her partner.

While I was certain the hospital would once again be able to treat my external wounds, I was equally as confident that whatever internal ones were received that night wouldn't be as easy to recover from.

Chapter Fourteen

When I got to the ER, it was busier than I had expected for 5:00 am on a Saturday.

When they put me into an empty room, they let me know someone would be in shortly and then closed the privacy curtain. Still feeling the effects of the wine, or possibly even the adrenaline, I tried to contain the nausea that was building in the back of my throat. The pain from my hand allowed for a brief distraction from the changing of my reality—a transformation in my existence that left me with more questions than answers.

However, my mind's inability to focus sent my thoughts wandering quickly in another direction. Where would I go when they released me? Where does one even start? What do people do when their entire lives literally go up in smoke?

As I was mid-thought, a woman in a white coat pushed the sheet aside and walked in. "Hello, Harper," she said, flipping through my chart.

"Hi," I replied with the forced smile my father had apparently bestowed upon me.

"I'm Dr. Thomas. I'm sorry about the wait. It's been pretty busy here this morning."

I nodded.

"We just want to get your lungs checked out for smoke inhalation and get the burn on your hand looked at before we release you," she continued with a comforting smile. "Do you have any questions? Anyone, we can call?"

I shook my head.

She put my chart back in the holder. "Tricia will be in as soon as she can to get everything checked out and get you discharged, okay?"

I nodded as she smiled once more and then disappeared behind the curtain.

My bed began to vibrate as my phone's screen lit up. "Hey," I said casually as the phone reached my ear.

"Hey? Seriously, girl? Are you okay? What the hell is going on?" she asked each question one right after another. Before I could respond, she continued. "I got a call from the hospital saying they brought you in because of a house fire!"

She didn't know I had changed my emergency contact from my mother to her about a month before. Honestly, I had been so high on pain medication that I had forgotten I had done it as well.

"I'm fine," I managed to say as if I had been asked the typical, *how are you doing*, that I was so used to getting.

Serena exhaled loudly. "Good, but I'm on my way, and I don't want to hear anything about it," she said, clearly expecting a fight from my end. "I called Caleb; he'll obviously be there before I am, though."

That was where she should have braced for the fight.

"You called *Caleb*?"

"Yes! Harper, you need someone there with you. Would you rather I called your mom?"

I sighed.

I didn't know why I had let my brain convince me that they wouldn't come. But maybe it had little to do with whether they would come or not, and more so of them taking care of the situation—taking care of *me*. Maybe it was them getting a glimpse of the weak side of the self-professed girl who was perpetually *fine*. It was a lie that wasn't demonstrated well when she was sitting homeless on a gurney with a flesh wound on her palm.

"Okay," I said reluctantly. "I'll text you if I'm discharged before you get here."

"Alright, I'll see you in a little bit," she responded.

I hung up the phone and looked down at the shirt and leggings I had on. They smelled like smoke, but I preferred them to the gown they had offered when I first arrived.

I looked at the dirt on my feet that had clung tight in my walk to the ambulance. I needed a shower.

I undid my ponytail and let my hair fall to my shoulders. I sniffed it before turning to look at my reflection in the small mirror on the wall—barely recognizing myself.

Caleb's troubled voice trailed in from the other side of the curtain. "Hi… I'm looking for Harper," he said, followed by a slight pause. "Sorry, uh, Harper Jones."

After a few seconds, the sheet moved, and he came into view. His face looked anxious as he gazed upon the mess of a girl lying on the bed in front of him.

"I'm fine," I said, almost laughing at the preposterous nature of my habitual lie.

He got closer, and without hesitation or permission, he hugged me. His embrace felt warm and safe. I reluctantly wrapped my arms around him but then gave in and held him tight, savoring the moment.

"Why didn't you call me?" he asked, moving to sit in the chair next to the bed.

"I didn't want to worry anyone."

I wasn't badly injured—homeless, yes, but there wasn't anything they could do about that. There wasn't any real reason for them to come.

I unlocked my phone screen, trying to use the tips of my fingers to scroll.

"What did you do to your hand?" Caleb asked.

I looked at it, then at him. "I tried to leave my room, and the doorknob burnt me." I chuckled, but his look of concern didn't change.

I opened to my Facebook page and began moving through the posts as a means of distraction—a diversion that was short-lived. "Sweet, my house is all over the news," I said, swallowing a lump in my throat as the pictures of my incinerated home flooded my news feed.

"You really should have someone closer listed as your emergency contact," he commented, breaking the silence again.

"That's a pretty big ask from someone. I figured putting Serena down was safe because I didn't think she would make the drive."

"What kind of friend would she be if she didn't?" he retorted.

"The kind that would understand that I can take care of myself."

He sighed.

He had always told me that I was too stubborn. I definitely didn't disagree. But I also couldn't help but feel like a burden most of the time with people. I was worried that the more overwhelming I proved to be, the less they would want to be around. So, to keep them in my life, I had to distance my real self from them. Unfortunately, somewhere along the line, I forgot who that real self was.

In my eight years of knowing Caleb, that was my third stint in the hospital, but it was the first time that he had seen me in one. A visual I was sure would have him trying to take care of me for months, that was unless I somehow stopped it.

I glanced over at him as he sat in the chair beside me. His expression harbored the same anxious look he had sported seven years before when I had seen him after being discharged from the hospital the first time. The day after I was attacked.

I had known I wasn't going to be able to hide how I looked. So, I had told him a version of the story I thought he could handle—a version *I* could handle.

Not wanting to spend any amount of time in my head thinking of the past, my thoughts quickly switched back to my current state of affairs.

But once they were there, it was hard to get them out. I wanted to be comforted by him. But I knew that was wrong. Allowing him to comfort me was even worse than allowing him to hear me moan. To let him know I was thinking of him. Because letting him see me at my weakest would drive him away. It would make him see the damage and lead him to do what I knew was inevitable—him leaving for good.

I took a deep breath as I felt the tears well up. I resisted the urge to let them out. My throat tightened, and my chest ached.

That seemed to be a shitty pattern of mine, pushing away someone who clearly gave a damn. Maybe I wouldn't be where I was at if things hadn't gotten so fucked up for me when we had been dating. Maybe things wouldn't be where they were if I wasn't so crazy.

Typically, over time, wounds healed. But I had made it worse from my lack of dealing with any of the big traumas in my life head-on. It seemed that any time I felt like I was starting to repair, the wounds would rip open again.

Soon the blinding pain would set in, eventually consuming me. This caused me to reach for a numbing device, usually in the form of alcohol, a continuous cycle I had been swirling in for the better part of a decade.

My ability to hold back the tears failed as greatly as I seemed to in life, falling silently onto the pillow.

Caleb motioned for me to move over and shifted in the bed beside me. Our bodies pressed tightly together on a one-person gurney.

"Caleb, I think we need to take another break. A little longer this time," I said, as I started to fidget with the gauze on my hand.

I felt his head turn to look down toward me, but I didn't move. I didn't want to look him in the eyes.

"I don't think it's fair to Cassy," I continued. "You guys need more time without me in the picture."

I took a breath and swallowed the lump that had formed in my throat. "I can see a difference in you... since we stopped talking. She's *good* for you."

He sat in silence, but I felt his chest tighten.

I knew our breaks were as tough on him as they were on me. But the months away from me the last time allowed him to become more serious with Cassy. They allowed him to be less intense, to be more of the man he had always talked about being. They allowed him to be Caleb the boyfriend, eventually it would be Caleb the fiancé, and ultimately Caleb the husband.

***

I had unintentionally fallen asleep and was startled by the sound of a cart rolling in. Caleb moved back to the chair so the nurse could do my evaluation.

"Sorry about the wait," she said, grabbing things out of a nearby drawer. "I'm Tricia. Let's get you checked out, so we can get you discharged. I bet you're eager to get home."

She cringed as soon as the words left her mouth.

I hid my smile as I repressed a laugh. Despite my less-than-favorable circumstances, I was that same type of person—the one who stuck her foot in her mouth or who made jokes at inappropriate times. Though, I could tell that it wasn't her intent to joke at that moment.

"I'm sorry," she said, avoiding eye contact.

"It's fine."

I put my injured hand into hers as she gestured for it.

She pulled off the gauze, wincing simultaneously with Caleb.

"How bad does it hurt?" she asked.

It had been hurting quite a bit, but when the realization crossed my mind that Caleb and I needed to stop talking to each other yet again, the pain in my hand dwindled. Instead, it was my heart that was left with an agonizing burning sensation.

"It's not that bad," I finally answered.

"Well, you must have a high pain tolerance because it looks painful."

She grabbed a tube of something from the drawer and smeared it on the burn. "I'm going to send a prescription home with you for pain. Your body may still just be in shock."

She conducted a routine checkup for people who endure smoke inhalation. I figured the fact that I didn't burn up with my house was enough to discharge me. But I guess around 3,000 people die every year just from the inhalation of the smoke itself. Something I would have felt better not knowing.

***

I signed the discharge paperwork and stepped out into the hallway where Caleb was waiting for me. His phone began to ring while I approached him. He talked briefly before hanging up.

"Serena's going to meet us at my place," he said. "She's stopping to get you something to wear and some shoes."

"Caleb, I—"

"What? Where else are you going to go?" He gave me no time to respond before continuing. "We can talk about all that shit later. Please just let me help you for once."

While he didn't try and hide his annoyance, I could tell, behind his irritation, that I was hurting him all over again.

I nodded, giving in to his stubborn but thoughtful demands.

As we walked towards the exit, my mother appeared in the main doorway. She looked distressed and less put together than normal. I didn't know why I would think it was out of the question for my mother to express anything other than disdain for me. But her unusual tactic of showing hesitation to approach me caused me to go to her instead.

"I had to hear about your house on the news!" Her worried expression was fading fast.

"It just happened. I'm sorry."

"Well, *he* had time to get here," she replied, gesturing toward Caleb, who was right to keep his distance.

"Serena called him. It's not a big deal."

"Not a big deal? Your house burnt down! It's a total loss!" She took a deep breath. "Harper, you look—" She stopped, possibly realizing that her criticism wasn't needed nor wanted. "Have you been looked at?" she asked, switching gears.

"Yeah, I just got discharged."

"Why didn't they call me? I'm your emergency contact."

She glanced around like she was trying to find the person responsible.

"I don't know, Mom. I just want to go shower."

"Okay, I'll take you back to my place," she began. "You can shower there, and then I'll take you to get some new clothes."

For a second, it felt like she cared and that her worry was genuine. It even caused me to briefly consider her offer—until she continued.

"I called Sarah on the way here. She can see you at noon for a session," she said, pulling out her phone as if she was checking for confirmation.

I felt my expression shift as aggravation took hold. "Mom, I don't need to see Sarah. I'm fine," I replied, lowering my voice so that Caleb wouldn't overhear. "I have an appointment with her Monday. I can talk about this then."

"Harper, this is a big deal. It's a lot to take on. I will not have you spiraling out of control."

"Jesus Christ, I'm not spiraling. My house burnt down. And yeah, it sucks. But I'm *alive,* and shit can be replaced."

God, I was starting to sound like her. But I wasn't wrong. It could be replaced. I wasn't emotionally attached to my stuff, and really, what kind of memories did the place hold for me?

"It can, and it will. But Harper, I can't help but feel this was a cry for help."

My cavalier attitude was quickly dissolving as I laughed under my breath. "Are you *seriously* implying that I set my own house on fire?" I asked as my voice shook.

Caleb approached us. He must have sensed it was time to get me out of there. "Harper's coming to my place," he said, staring directly at my mother.

I should have warned him against that.

She returned his look with a rigid expression that showed both confidence and contempt. "Yeah?" she began. "And where were *you* to take care of her a month ago? Where was *Serena*? I didn't see anyone come to the hospital while she was there then!"

Her unexpected words left my mind playing catch up. Before I could speak, she turned to me. "Was it *his* fault? Was he the one…"

I cut her off as my mind panicked at the words that had been ready to deploy next. "Could you, for one second, resist the urge to make things worse for me and just leave me the fuck alone?"

Chapter Fifteen

We pulled into Caleb's driveway, where Serena's car was already parked. She was leaning against it and biting her nails.

I opened the door and stepped down, immediately being pulled into her embrace.

"You scared the hell out of me, girl!" she said, sounding a little choked up.

I winced as her grip remained strong. Caleb looked amused at the scene and certainly at my expression. I knew I looked uncomfortable.

But it wasn't from the act of her embrace or even from the pain that had set in as the adrenaline had dissipated. No, my comfortability was taken with someone showing such deep emotion for me.

It was something I had a hard time coping with. It gave me the same amount of distress as someone watching me open a gift. That cringe-worthy feeling of possibly letting someone down if not reacting the exact way they had been waiting for weeks to experience.

"Sorry," she said as she stepped back, giving a deflated smile. "I got you some stuff from the store. Nothing special. We can go shopping tomorrow—or sometime soon—for better stuff, whatever you're up for."

"It's okay. I'm sure it will do just fine. Better than what I'm wearing," I replied, looking down at my clothes and the grippy socks the hospital had given me. "I really just need to shower."

I glanced over at Caleb, who grabbed the bags from the pavement and led us into the house.

Serena closed the door behind her as I peered around the room. His house was small but had a comforting, homey feel to it. But maybe that was just to me, and the comfort I felt from all the memories there.

He opened the closet door adjacent to his bedroom to grab a towel. I glanced in his room at the evidence of the painfully real relationship he had with Cassy. It was vomited about the surfaces in the form of cliché decor. There were things like flowery scented candles, wall signs that said *Live Laugh Love* and *kiss me goodnight*, and my least favorite, the useless decorative pillows on the bed.

I wanted to be annoyed, but really it just furthered the thought that Cassy was good for him. I knew it was all hers, and he loved her enough to let her put up stuff he thought was cheesy.

I tried to ignore the pain that had formed in my chest when I told him we needed to pump the brakes once again on our very unusual and unhealthy friendship. But the pain continued to grow as I saw a picture of the two of them on his nightstand. A spot he had once tried to put a picture of us, and I had asked, or more so demanded, that it be removed.

I followed him into the bathroom as he hung the towel on the bar.

"Your house looks… clean," I said, trying to act as if my stomach hadn't just been sucker-punched on the way in.

He gave me an apathetic smile. "Yeah, Cassy spends a lot of time here," he replied, with what felt like an unintentional blow.

154

"Looks nice."

I set the bag of stuff down on the bathroom floor.

"Well, you know where everything is," he said. "Enjoy your shower," he added, closing the door as he exited.

I turned on the water, realizing the bandage on my right hand would make things rather difficult.

"Caleb, do you have any Saran wrap?" I shouted from the bathroom door.

"Are you cooking in there?" he asked as a small trail of laughter echoed down the hall.

I watched as Serena swatted his chest and then smirked. "She needs it for her hand."

"No, sorry, I don't," he finally replied.

"I'll help you," Serena said as she walked towards me.

"Well, this is a tease."

Serena rolled her eyes. I just laughed and shook my head.

***

Although I felt like I really had no one to call that morning, I was glad I had listed Serena as my emergency contact. It took a good friend to drive from a few hours away, spend her own money on clothes for me, and help wash my hair. It was something up until then I didn't think we would have done for each other. We must have been closer than I had given our friendship credit for.

The tranquility of the water on my skin made my mind grow tired, and soon after, my body did as well. I turned off the water and climbed out of the shower. While the rush of exhaustion continued to trample over me, I decided to leave my mess of a head to post-nap Harper.

I opened the door in time to hear Serena and Caleb's voices trail in from the kitchen. It hadn't been my intention to eavesdrop, but when I heard my name, I switched gears to listen.

"Why didn't you tell me that Harper was in the hospital last month?" Caleb asked as if they were close friends who told each other everything.

I had been expecting him to ask *me* that question on the ride from the hospital. While I was happy that he hadn't, asking Serena was not a welcomed alternative.

"I didn't know she was," she said, sounding surprised. "I wonder if that's why she's in therapy."

I rolled my eyes. Thanks, Serena.

"Therapy?" Caleb asked, his tone switching from annoyance to concern.

"Yeah, I don't know why she's in it specifically; her mom's paying for it though. She goes twice a week, I think."

Even though my mind was shouting for her to shut the fuck up, nothing of that nature left my lips.

"Her mom asked if it was because of *me,*" Caleb continued. "Do you know if I did something? Has she said anything?"

I needed to stop the conversation from going any further.

"No, it wasn't because of *you*," I replied, throwing my dirty clothes by the washer and walking toward the two of them. "And I would appreciate it in the future, if you want to know something, you ask *me*."

"If I would've asked you, you wouldn't have told me."

"And what does that tell you, Caleb?"

"I'm just worried about you," he responded with a sigh, leaning up against the kitchen wall.

"Yeah, I know—apparently, everyone suddenly is. There is nothing to worry about. I'm *fine*. Everything is *fine*. My mother overreacted to some shit and put me in therapy."

"Harper, you're a grown-ass adult," Serena chimed in. "If you don't want to be in therapy, then don't go."

I acted as if what she said didn't faze me. "It's free therapy, Serena. Who doesn't have shit they want to talk to an unbiased person about? I don't have to be *crazy* to be in therapy. It's actually a very healthy thing to do."

I was certain I was saying that more for my benefit than for hers, as she had been the one who had given me that advice when I had first told her about it. But clearly, my brain needed a little more convincing.

I grabbed a bottle of water out of the fridge.

She was right. I could stop. There was nothing forcing me to be there.

But while I wasn't thoroughly enjoying it, I had become worried about what would happen if I didn't go anymore, even more so with the revelation of my father's mental state.

Serena and Caleb exchanged glances but ultimately let the conversation fall flat.

I felt the pain and exhaustion in my body take over once again. So, I grabbed the bag from the pharmacy off the counter, attempting to open the bottle myself. But any way that I had tried to hold it, it put pressure on my injured hand.

Seeing me struggle, Caleb walked over and opened it for me. "These are very addicting… please be careful," he said, looking into my eyes.

"I will," I answered, taking two pills and washing them down with my water.

His concern was understandable. However, I didn't share it. I wasn't worried about becoming addicted. I had a few vices— prescription medication wasn't one of them.

***

After a while, I started to feel very calm. I hadn't noticed that my pain had been temporarily eliminated, but I did detect a strong sense of peace.

I had been on pain medication a few times before, but I had been under such distress I guess I hadn't noticed the full effect of them.

As the medication took hold, everything became funny. Serena had wanted to record me, but Caleb reminded her that sober Harper would hate that. But sober Harper wasn't around, and I didn't care. I thought I was funny, too.

"You should try and sleep while I get us some food," Serena said.

I giggled at her and hugged her arm. She laughed at me and pulled away, getting up to leave.

I snuggled closer to Caleb; whose body felt warm against my cold skin.

"You feel nice," I said with a goofy grin.

He looked at me with a shy but enamoring smirk as his eyes locked into mine.

"And you have a beautiful smile," I added, gazing back at him.

I rested back on the couch, looking up at the ceiling and stretching my legs out onto Caleb's lap.

He placed his hand on my shin. "Are you okay?"

"You need to quit asking me that," I replied, giggling unintentionally.

I thought back to earlier in the day—Caleb holding me in the hospital bed, comforting me, stroking my hair, making me feel safe. He was always trying to take care of me.

"Why did you come to the hospital this morning?" I asked with a sweet and gentle tone.

"Why wouldn't I?" he questioned, looking almost offended.

"Because you're with Cassy…" It was getting progressively more difficult to concentrate on what I was trying to say. "—and you *love* her."

"What does that have to do with *us*?" he asked.

"Everything," I replied, my tone sounding almost blissful. However, the words we were exchanging were anything but.

I went silent again as my mind drifted.

He sighed. "I came to the hospital this morning because I was scared. I wanted to make sure you were okay." His tone was soft, but his face still expressed his annoyance.

He was never going to move on if I was always around for him to take care of.

My relationship with Caleb seemed to resemble the first real relationship I had had—my relationship with Jacob. Caleb had been there for me in a time that I needed someone, just like Jacob. Caleb had taken care of me in a way I couldn't take care of myself, just like Jacob. And just like my relationship with Jacob, Caleb and I would inevitably part ways, leaving me to be fucked up by myself in a world I already hated.

Luckily, Caleb didn't seem as easy to scare away as Jacob had been. Something I was sure had a lot to do with his past.

Seeing the parallels in two of my biggest relationships worried me. The fact that I saw it while high on pain medication scared me, too. Would I remember that breakthrough when the medication wore off? Would it change anything? *Could* it change anything?

I inhaled sharply as my body sprung forward on the couch. I was drenched in sweat, my mind still reeling from my nightmare. I put my hand on my forehead and took a few deep breaths as the remnants of the dream were already starting to fade. I glanced around, taking a moment to realize where I was and why I wasn't at my house—why I wasn't in my bed.

I looked at the clock on the wall. It was 5:00 in the evening but, aside from the sweat that lingered, I felt refreshed and ready to start my day.

As I walked toward the bedroom, I heard voices coming from outside. The front door was opened, allowing the screen door to filter in the cool Michigan breeze. I was close enough to hear Caleb and Cassy's conversation as their backs were to me on the porch swing. She was snuggled up against him in the same position I had been earlier at the hospital. It made me feel angry. Angry at myself for seeking comfort in him. Admittedly, I was a little jealous, too.

"—I understand you want to be a good friend, but she has other friends," Cassy said.

"But she really doesn't. Serena lives two hours away. Plus, Harper's super closed off…"

"I know, babe, but you have to understand. I mean, how would *you* feel if my ex was staying with me?"

She had a point.

"We ended things seven years ago, Cassy. She needs a place to stay. Just for a little bit." I was thankful he hadn't shared our years of sexual liaisons with her. I was sure, if he had, they wouldn't even be having that conversation.

"Okay, well, how about you come and stay with me then? I mean, she's used to living alone. She can still take care of herself."

"I don't know. She's been through a lot. Serena told me that she's in therapy…"

I felt my face get flushed.

He thinks you're bat shit crazy, The Voice said. *He wants her to feel bad for the lunatic inside his house. Maybe this will be a fun side conversation for them to have later. What will Harper do next?*

My nails dug into my palms as my body grew tense. I wanted to interject. I wanted to make both of them, and The Voice shut up. But before I could, she began again.

"Babe, I know you want to be a good friend, and I love you for that, but this isn't your problem. If she's in therapy, then she is getting the help she needs. Let her lean on Serena or her family or whoever. You take on way too much," she responded, resting her head on his chest.

I sighed.

She wasn't wrong.

He did take on so many of my problems. I tried so hard not to burden him with them, but it always seemed to happen anyway. I was sure that was why he looked so together when I saw him the week before. And all it had taken was a little over eight months of me bearing the brunt of my own created chaos and him spending that time living the script of a Hallmark movie with Cassy.

"What are you doing?" Serena asked, making me jump out of my skin.

"I was just—" I began as I walked over to her.

"Eavesdropping," she said, cutting me off with a smirk.

I exhaled. "I was just looking for you guys and heard them talking."

"Well, I can tell by the look on your face that you didn't hear anything good."

I shrugged. It didn't matter. Everything she had said was right.

Serena scrunched up her face. "Why are you so sweaty?"

We both turned our heads as we heard the screen door open and shut.

"Harper?" Caleb asked, seeing that I had disappeared from the couch.

"In here."

Serena and I stepped into the living room.

"How are you feeling?" he asked.

At least he was polite enough not to inquire about my perspiration.

Cassy stepped inside and walked over to Caleb. She weaved her fingers with his, most assuredly looking to assert her position as his girlfriend in front of us.

"Uh…fine. I think I slept off the pain meds," I answered, distracted by their hand-holding. I finally broke my gaze away. "They probably should have given me a smaller dose," I said with a laugh.

Cassy and Caleb just silently stared at me, but at least Serena shared in my humor.

"I told you to be careful with those," he responded.

I looked at Serena who rolled her eyes.

An awkward silence filled the room. I watched Cassy squeeze Caleb's hand, undoubtedly motioning him to tell me what they had decided outside.

"I'm going to go stay at Cassy's place," he said, not making eye contact with either of us. "You can stay as long as you need to, though."

I looked at Cassy. Her expression seemed smug, but maybe that was just how I perceived it.

"I shouldn't be too long," I replied. "I'm sure there's stuff set up for situations like this."

What could I say? I didn't really have anywhere else to go at that moment.

Again, the silence crept in.

"I'm going to pack some stuff up," Caleb said, pulling his hand from Cassy's and walking toward his room.

Serena jumped off the counter and opened the fridge. "Caleb, you got any whiskey? Vodka?"

"No, he doesn't really drink much," Cassy replied sharply.

Serena peered over the fridge door, looking bothered both at the answer and the person who gave it.

***

After a few minutes, Serena had gone back to sitting on the kitchen counter, I was leaning up against the wall, and Cassy had moved to the arm of the couch. Everyone was looking at their phones, trying to avoid any conversation.

Caleb walked in with his bag. The tension in the room seemed to hit him like a ton of bricks.

"So…uh, here's my spare key," he commented. "I'll swing by tomorrow to check on you."

He looked to be actively avoiding Cassy's glance.

"Sounds good," I responded.

I took the key from him as our eyes met for a split second before we both looked away.

That key had been in my possession for years prior. We had exchanged them with each other for easier access to our places—to each other.

But it was returned to the rightful owner when I had thrown it at him after our fight—after the confession of his feelings. Honestly, I had assumed he had given it to Cassy at some point since then.

I dropped the key into my purse and moved over by Serena.

"Sorry about your house, Harper," Cassy said, giving a small apologetic wave.

"Thanks."

Caleb nodded in our direction and shut the door behind them.

"*Sorry about your house, Harper,*" Serena repeated. She rolled her eyes and jumped down from the counter. "What a bitch."

I took a seat on the couch before responding. "She was trying to be nice," I replied, but not really believing it myself.

"You know she's the reason he isn't staying here," she said as she sat down next to me. "She doesn't trust him or you."

I laughed. "Would *you*?"

Although I was smiling, I felt guilty thinking back to Caleb's and my hangout. If I told Serena about the other night and the fact that I had let him listen to me finish, she would probably cut Cassy a little slack, too.

She shook her head and put her arm around me. "I know you're sick of people asking. But *are* you okay?"

I nodded, not wanting to say anything.

She put her head on my shoulder. "You know I love you, right?"

"I know. I love you, too," I replied, tipping my head to rest on hers while I waded through the uncomfortable feeling that came with saying so out loud.

Our relationship had always been a weird one. I would've said a month earlier that we had started to drift apart. With both of us working and her living two hours away, it had started to take a toll on our friendship.

But I was glad she had come. I was glad for once that I had someone who could hold me without bringing about shame and guilt. Someone who would hug me, even though my body became stiff like a board at the slightest sign of emotions being tied in with physical touch.

Chapter Sixteen

On Sunday morning, I had woken up the same way I had from my nap the day before—covered in sweat, reeling from my nightmare, having been stuck in a fiery inferno. Faces continued to flash through my mind from the dream, with the vision of everyone sitting calmly and quietly, living their best lives as I remained trapped—waiting to be burned alive.

Through the course of my morning, the visions had finally started to fade, with my mind returning to its normal anxious hell. That was until we pulled up to my house, or the ground at which my house had stood. Fragments of my home laid about the lawn, having been torn through trying to contain the fire. The roof was almost non-existent, and the walls that were still standing were covered in black soot.

My throat grew tight as my memory from Friday night played in my head like a picture film. The feelings of panic, confusion, and horror settled into my chest and stomach, as I opened the car door and stepped out onto my brown, patchy lawn.

An article I had read the night before said I was lucky to be alive, that my bedroom was the last room to be taken down. Beneath that article in the comment section—that I knew not to read but did anyway—people shamed me for my response time, saying I must not have had proper smoke alarms installed.

I stupidly continued to read their ignorant and crude comments. The hard hitters were sharing in my mother's thought process—that I had done it myself. Others said things like, thankfully she was alone—although I was sure the intent wasn't the same from those ones. Lastly, and probably the most aggravating, were the ones implying that I deserved it.

Realistically I knew they were just internet trolls, and people were attacking them back on my behalf. But I was having a hard-enough time trying to get my mind to stop telling me I deserved it, so I didn't need the confirmation bias from the comment section of the local media's page to make me feel any worse.

"Should we go?" Serena asked, as I realized I hadn't moved or spoken in minutes.

I shook my head but continued in my silence as I walked to my car. I looked it over, taking note of some smoke damage to the front half. But outside of that, it looked salvageable. It was a bright side that I would have to take as there wouldn't be much more of that found during my walkthrough.

Against Serena's wishes, I moved the caution tape out of the way to get inside. The chopped hole in the side of my bedroom wall made for a gut-wrenching door. I slowly and steadily moved about the room to the closet. The once plush carpet installed by Caleb and me years before was scorched right down to the floorboards.

I reached under a pile of charred and tattered clothing and pulled out my safe. I tried to wipe away the ash that had floated on to me, but all that succeeded in doing was making a bigger mess on my skin.

When I stepped back onto my lawn, a man stood beside Serena; he said he was there to investigate the fire. The expression his face held was the same as hers. I knew it didn't look good that I was back at the scene of the crime, but at that point, I was past caring what people thought—even him. I knew I hadn't burned my place down, so no evidence would say that I had. Though I may have read a lot more into his look than necessary, he might have been just annoyed that I had gone in myself.

After a short but stern scolding about safety, he told me a little about the process and what to expect. I hoped Serena had been paying attention because my mind wasn't retaining anything he said. She was taking mental notes, though, not just of his words, but my lack of them. Her concerned expression from the conversation stayed planted on her face the entire way back to Caleb's. At which point, she had dropped me off at his house and reluctantly left for hers.

I took to curling up on the couch that I had made into a bed as Caleb's scent filled the air from the blanket I wrapped around me. The smell was comforting—almost like he was there with me—like I hadn't gotten what I wanted and been left all alone.

I finally returned Al's call Sunday night. He was understanding of the delayed response and made me agree to take off as much time as I needed. I tried to reassure him that it wouldn't take longer than the week, hoping just as much to myself that that was true. We ended up settling on me calling to update him the following weekend on where I was at with everything.

I spent my Monday morning getting in touch with the car dealership. After I told them what had happened, they made me a new key and hooked me up with a detailer. Which only took a few hours, allowing me to make it to Sarah's office with 10 minutes to spare.

Sarah called me in as her previous client moved past me. Once in the room, I handed her my journal and took a seat as if it had been our routine for longer than it actually had been.

I had jotted my entry into the book Sunday night after Caleb and Cassy had stopped by to check on me. They hadn't stayed long; it felt like Cassy was babysitting us. She was clearly not wanting him there—or to be there herself.

I needed to find a new place to stay. Seeing them together regularly was not something I was emotionally equipped to handle. The previous time it had sent me into the arms of a manipulative adulterous asshole. Though, my emotional unavailability may have forced my hand on that one. A topic I was sure Sarah would be all too eager to dive into once I showed my cards.

The contents of my weekend had left me reminiscing about my previous life. A time where I was a completely different person. Part of that had to do with my naive grasp on the world, but most of it had to do with Jacob. The boy who showed me what love was supposed to look like. The boy who got me through my first real-life problems—the boy that, realistically, I should've married.

***

(Journal entry)

I met Jacob when I was 15. That was when we officially met anyway; I had known who he was since he was a sophomore on the varsity baseball team. I never would have thought to even try to talk to him. But later, when I told him that, he thought it was funny. I had come to learn that he may have been popular, good-looking, and outgoing, but he was incredibly nice and down to earth as well.

The day we officially met, his car had broken down on my street. He had been on his way home from baseball practice when it stalled out. He wasn't among the few kids in our school that had cell phones at that time. So, he needed to use someone's phone to call his dad.

I was lying on my roof outside my window which faced the street. It was where I did my homework, listened to music, and read books. It was something I had loved to do since I was little. But my favorite thing to do there was to clear my head and just be. Taking the time to let everything drift away and just relax.

I had been mid-daydream, when I heard someone yell, "Hey!" I remember being startled and him laughing at my reaction.

He told me what happened with his car, and I climbed back through my window and let him in downstairs so he could call for a ride. My father wasn't home yet from one of his temp jobs, and my mother was visiting a friend. So, we sat outside and talked until his ride showed up.

I expected him not to acknowledge me the next day at school, especially with me being a freshman and him a sophomore. But he did. He even brought me a sunflower and left it for me in my locker. I found out later he came in early and got the janitor to open it for him. I remember feeling embarrassed for it being so messy.

Jacob and I grew very close, very fast. We were together all the time. No one at my home seemed to mind, and his dad loved having me over. He had lost his mom when he was eight, which explained a lot about him. But he had a very close relationship with his dad and older brother. Something I was very envious of.

He was so helpful when my father passed. He knew exactly what to say, and what not to. He knew what to do, and when to let me be alone. It really helped. When shit got bad between my mother and me in the six months following the loss of my father, Jacob would sneak me into his bedroom, and I would stay there.

While other memories have faded over time, those nights haven't. Every detail was seared into my mind. Not just because Jacob was my first, but because of how he made me feel. He took care of me when I needed it, back before anyone doing so made me cringe.

After my seventeenth birthday, when my mother bought me my house, Jacob graduated and moved in, too. His dad tried to talk him out of it, telling us both it was too fast. But as young people often don't realize, love isn't all you need, and relationships can get messy.

Jacob always stayed amazing though, and he did everything he could to make it work between us. At some point, he got it in his mind that marriage would solve our problems. So, on our four-year anniversary, he blanketed our house in sunflowers, got down on one knee, and asked me to be his wife.

This led to one of the first big regrets of my adult life—telling him no.

When I came home from work the next day, he was gone, along with all of his stuff. At first, I was more relieved than sad. I had started to get antsy, thinking that was it, that I was with the man I was going to marry. That, at 19, I was facing the life my mother had seemed to work so hard to get away from.

I knew our relationship had to mature too quickly. But looking back, I wonder how much of that was just my mother's thoughts and fears that she had embedded in me. Because I did love him and wanted to spend my life with him. A realization that left me broken-hearted and emotionally numb for a while after.

Jacob had seen me through a hard time in my life that I probably couldn't have handled without him. I felt completely responsible and guilty for the damage I was sure saying no to him had left him with.

But years later, he popped up on my Facebook as a friend request, which I accepted. I wasn't sure if he wanted to rub his new life in my face or just to let me know he was happy. I was hoping he wanted me to know that it was okay to let go of that guilty feeling I'd held onto all those years for what I had done to him. But whatever his intention had been, I was grateful for the closure.

***

"So, it's been a very tough week for you," Sarah said, shutting my journal. "Is there a reason you decided to write about Jacob?"

"I don't know. I've thought about our relationship over the years, and even more so recently," I replied, taking a brief pause. "He took care of me. He got me through some rough patches. I often wonder how different life would be if I had just said yes to his proposal. Like maybe my life wouldn't be so... what it is, and I wouldn't feel so, I don't know, *alone*."

Thinking about our relationship gave me a weird sense of deja vu. I had a slight recollection of going down a rabbit hole of sorts the previous Saturday. But my mind was too foggy to recall any specific thought.

"Why do you feel alone?" she asked.

"Because I *am* alone," I answered as if it were the most obvious thing in the world. "If anyone had been there with me the night of the fire, it would have just been some guy from a bar."

I instantly regretted adding in that last part—too much sharing for my taste—though I was sure she had deduced I was the type to indulge in the occasional hookup with strangers.

Sarah shifted in her seat. "What's so wrong with being single?" she asked.

"There's nothing *wrong* with it; I just feel better when people are around."

"How do you expect people to stick around if you can't be honest with them?"

"Excuse me?"

"It isn't hard to see that you have a hard time opening up to people."

"Okay? That doesn't mean I'm lying."

She gave a light smile. "I didn't say you were. But that doesn't mean you're being honest with them either."

"They know what I need them to know."

"But don't you think them knowing more would help them understand you? Wouldn't you feel closer to them if they knew the things you have been through?"

I shrugged, although I knew that it would, in fact, help them understand me. But understanding my past didn't equate to accepting it. It didn't mean they would be able to get past it—especially since I had yet to overcome that hurdle myself.

After a minute of silence, she shifted in her seat and began again.

"Listen, I know you have a lot going on right now. And, when we left our last session, you had me a little worried. I really want you to understand that I'm here to listen. I want to help in any way I can.

It's okay if it takes time. I want you to understand *why* you do the things you do. And to do that, we need to identify *what* it is that you do."

I wanted to trust her. I too, wanted to figure out what I did, and even more so the why behind it. But I was also worried about learning the answers. To take a glimpse into my past and see how everything I had ever done led me to be the fucked-up person I was. Someone who needed a therapist to spell out everything I had done wrong in order to figure me out.

"I know it's only been a few days, but how are you doing since the fire?"

I was okay with the change in subject matter but didn't have a thoroughly thought-out answer on my feelings towards what happened. My emotions hadn't settled enough for me to properly convey them, even *if* I had wanted to do so.

"Fine. It was just stuff; it can be replaced."

Cold and *emotionless,* The Voice said. *Soon you won't even need a relationship with your mother. You will* be *her.*

"Harper, it's okay to be upset about it. The loss of your stuff, and the loss of the security you had in sleeping—"

"I know, and I am, but it will be fine. I've dealt with worse before."

Sarah's expression shifted briefly to an annoyed look but quickly returned to normal.

"What?" I asked but probably shouldn't have.

She sighed. "I want you to open up on your own time, but I want you to understand that not everything just works itself out. You need to start owning some of these feelings."

"What feelings?"

"Any of them," she replied. "The scared feelings, angry feelings, sad feelings—all the bad ones I know you are hell-bent on burying."

Damn, you did it now, The Voice commented.

"I *am* owning them. I know they are there, and they are being dealt with."

"Okay," she answered. "So, *how* are you dealing with them?"

I sat silently as I didn't have an answer—well, I didn't have a *good* answer. While, yes, I hadn't had a drop of my typical coping mechanism, I couldn't very well claim sobriety—though the pills were taken for the pain in my hand.

You had no other motive behind taking them? The Voice questioned.

"I'm here, aren't I?" I finally responded, but my tone had lost some steam.

"Harper, that only does so much if you don't open up."

"I thought you wanted me to open up when I was ready?" I asked, with my tone emulating a teenager's.

She sighed again. "I do want that, but you seem bound and determined to ignore any trauma and hope it will eventually just go away."

I felt anger build in my chest. While her tone was calm and collected, her words were sharp and seemed to rip a hole in my mind's diabolical plan. "Well, maybe I don't want to think about those things," I bellowed as I stood up. "That's why they're called traumas, right? They're not easy to talk about, and I think it's really shitty of you to push me."

I walked toward the door and put my hand on the knob as she calmly said my name.

"Please sit back down," she continued.

I took a deep breath, and, after a minute, I complied.

"I didn't mean to upset you," she began after a moment of silence.

But my anger had been misdirected at her. I knew it had really been meant for me.

I closed my eyes and inhaled slowly. "I've been having nightmares the last few nights," I began, opening my eyes again. "I keep waking up in a panic, dripping with sweat, feeling so anxious. And the feeling takes a long time to go away, so I end up with this uneasy feeling in the pit of my stomach all day until I have to do it all over again."

I felt stupid for bringing up something that wasn't even real; I was hoping she wasn't annoyed by it.

"Have you suffered from dreams like this before?"

"Once, yes."

"How did you get rid of them then?"

I did what was socially acceptable. I drank copious amounts of alcohol, passing out, and repeating the process every day for months.

"They just stopped over time," I answered.

She seemed skeptical, but she moved on anyway. "Stress exacerbates post-traumatic stress disorder."

"You think I have PTSD?"

"I think it's a distinct possibility. And if it is, in fact, what you have, you need to do your best to minimize your stress levels."

"That's easier said than done."

She smiled.

Cutting myself off from Caleb could either help or hurt my stress levels. Thinking back, he may have been the reason the dreams stopped the first time. But I needed to tackle my problems without him. I needed to learn to handle things on my own.

Sarah asked me a few more questions, nothing too personal. I think she was still trying to keep from setting me off again—which I appreciated. She also gave me some advice on what to do and what to look out for moving forward to help manage my stress and hopefully help with the nightmares.

The session bell dinged, and I picked up my journal from the coffee table.

"So, how did your journal survive the fire?"

I looked down at it—one of the only things of mine I had left. "It was in my car. Luckily, I had this, a sweatshirt, and a few other things in there."

She smiled as she opened the door for me. I stepped out of her office and saw my mother sitting in the waiting room reading a magazine. Sarah gestured for her next client, and my mother looked up at me.

"Glad you still made it to your appointment." She stood up, putting her purse over her shoulder. "Can I give you a ride?" she asked, looking like she was mustering up all the kindness she could for that one sentence.

"It's fine. The dealership was able to give me a key this morning for my car," I responded.

She nodded. "Very good. How about dinner then?"

I didn't really have an excuse prepared since she bombarded me. "I guess that would be fine," I replied.

"Wonderful!" she exclaimed. "Meet me at that little Bistro place on 44th.

Chapter Seventeen

When I walked into the restaurant, my mother was already seated at a booth. I had been in my seat maybe two minutes before she began the discussion on my *situation*.

"So, what have you done so far?" she asked.

"What do you mean?"

"Have you found a new place to stay? Have you talked to your insurance company? Do you know what next steps you need to take?"

I must have looked overwhelmed, because she continued without an answer from me.

"Well, my friend Miranda lost her house and, tragically, her dog as well, two years ago to a fire. Good thing you didn't have any pets." She paused to take a sip of her drink.

"Anyway, she told me everything you need to do to get things done. The insurance money takes a little while to come in—depending on the investigation—but she gave me some numbers for people that can help with other things like temporary housing and all of that."

"I'm staying at Caleb's," I responded. Although, I wasn't sure why I had said it, since I had no desire to stay there.

How could we stop seeing each other if I was sleeping on his couch and he was stopping in to check on me daily?

"Harper, you don't need to be shacking up with some guy. You need to get back to your own place," she responded, flipping through her menu.

I really wanted to set the record straight on Caleb and me, but the less she knew about my life, the better.

"Can you send me the numbers?" I asked politely, picking up my menu and glancing over it.

She probably expected me to put up more of a fight. To be honest, I expected that from myself as well. But I didn't have a whole lot of fight left in me. If I was going to move past everything that had happened, I needed to let someone help me. And who better than my own mother? A thought that I was hoping didn't come back to bite me in the ass.

"Well, I already called a few of them for you," she said, making no attempt to look up at me.

Of course she had.

While my mother wasn't very involved in my life, I had learned over the years that she loved to handle everything. Whether it was because she didn't want her family looking bad or because she genuinely wanted to help—something I didn't think I would ever truly know. Even after my father's death and her second marriage, she had continued to look after Grandma Jones, which was one of the better things she had done. But that also may have been to spite her own mother, which was an explanation that seemed more up her alley.

"If you have time after this, we can stop by a house a few blocks over from here," she began again. "The lady said she would be there until 6:00 tonight if we wanted to see it."

"Yeah, that would be fine," I responded.

I was sure I was throwing my mother off with how agreeable I was being. But she was throwing *me* off by her helpfulness without all the side comments.

It did confuse me that she hadn't mentioned anything further about her thoughts on me being an arsonist. So, either that would come up later, or she had gotten the good sense to shut her mouth on the subject.

***

We both pulled into the driveway of the house around 6:00. The place was a little smaller than mine had been but appeared to be newer. We both got out of our cars, and at the same time, the lady walked out of the front door.

"Hi! You must be Lori," she said with a large grin. "And Harper," she continued as her tone went lower and her brows furrowed.

I responded to her sympathetic expression with a forced, uncomfortable smile.

"I'm so sorry to hear about your house. Your mom told me all about it."

While my mother didn't like airing dirty laundry, she loved to soak in the tragedy of sudden events that were out of our control. I felt like anything that tragically happened to me, she used as a way to justify my behavior in life, and therefore made her feel better about calling me her daughter publicly. But I guess I couldn't blame her. I used the same excuse to justify my life too.

"Harper's interested in taking a look around," my mother said with a smile. "As I suspected, her current living situation isn't working out. So, she would love to have a place to stay while she gets everything figured out.".

The lady smiled and gestured toward the house. "My name's Rachel, by the way."

"Nice to meet you, Rachel," I responded.

We looked around the house. It had two bedrooms, a bathroom, and a one-car garage, which in the wintertime would come in handy—if I had to stay that long. But the garage also made me nervous; not having one was the only reason my car had survived the fire.

"There's no time requirement for the lease. This house is for people who have been in situations like yours," Rachel said as I walked back into the living room. "There is a security deposit, which I already discussed with your mom."

My mother nodded at Rachel in a way that told me she was taking care of that. She made it hard to hate her when she was being so helpful.

They talked for a few minutes while I finished looking around. My mother seemed pretty set on me living there. But it was probably, so I didn't stay another minute shacked up with *the boy*. Something I agreed with but wasn't going to share with her.

"I can give you the keys tomorrow night if you are able to meet to sign some papers," Rachel said, looking at me as I looked at the furniture.

"Uh, yeah, that's fine. Does the furniture stay, too?" I asked, confused.

"Yes, dear. It comes fully furnished. Wouldn't be much of a place to stay if you didn't have something to sit and sleep on," Rachel replied with a laugh.

I forced another grin. "True."

"Can you make it tomorrow at four, or are you heading back to work?" my mother asked me.

"No, I called Al. I'm taking a little time off," I responded.

"Good," she said. Then she shook hands with Rachel. "We will see you tomorrow."

***

When I got back to Caleb's place, his truck was in the driveway. I expected Cassy to be with him like she had been the day before. But when I went inside, only his shoes were by the door.

I could hear the water from the shower running, so I made myself comfortable on the couch while I scrolled through Instagram. After a few minutes, he came out in a t-shirt and basketball shorts with a towel around his neck.

I loved those shorts on him. I quickly looked away, annoyed at where my thoughts were heading.

"Hey," he said as he walked over to the couch and sat next to me. "I thought I heard you come in."

He rubbed the towel on his head and then rested it on the back of his neck.

"Yeah, just got back from dinner with my mother."

He looked surprised. "Everything okay?"

"Yeah, it's fine," I answered, picking up the remote and turning on the TV.

"You've been saying that a lot lately," he replied.

"You've been *asking* a lot lately."

He nodded in defeat and rested his back on the couch.

"So, where's the girlfriend?"

"At her place. I went to the gym and then came here to shower."

"Why didn't you just shower at the gym?"

He didn't respond.

Because he wants to shower with you, The Voice said. *He wants a taste of the crazy life once more.*

I was worried The Voice was right. And that was exactly why I couldn't stay.

But while my head was being rational, my body was begging for his. Wanting to say *fuck it* to my overthinking mind, his responsibility to another woman, to anything that stood in the way of me being with him in that moment.

But my head would win. My bad decisions only seemed to really pan out if mind-numbing substances were involved. I was too painfully sober for me to throw my guilty conscience out the window. But, even with my brain winning the war in my head, it didn't change the way I was feeling. It didn't take away my ache for him.

And with my self-help burning up in the fire, how would I be able to help myself now?

"You didn't need to check on me," I said, as I covered up with the blanket.

"Why are you sleeping on the couch? There's a perfectly good bed in there," he responded, moving past my comment and eyeing the pillow next to me.

Did he really expect me to sleep where him and Cassy have sex?

"That's okay," I replied, with more disgust than I had intended.

"My bed isn't good enough for you?" he asked, raising an eyebrow.

"I don't think Cassy would like your *ex* sleeping in your bed."

The room fell silent.

We didn't typically refer to each other like that, so I was sure he understood that I had overheard his conversation a few nights before.

"I'm going to change," I said, breaking the silence and heading to his bathroom.

Part of me hoped he would leave while I was changing; the other part of me was begging for him to stay.

Chapter Eighteen

I had fallen asleep the past two nights in the clothes Serena had picked up for me, so that was the first time I saw the pajamas she had also gotten. Judging by the lack of coverage, she was aiming to make things tough on Caleb, obviously thinking the plan was for him to be staying at his house with me, too.

I put on the tank top and matching pajama shorts, then looked at myself in the mirror.

She could have at least bought a bigger size, The Voice said. *Look at your ass! Not to mention your arms. You shouldn't wear tank tops. Maybe don't turn to the side, and he won't notice how fat they look.*

As I continued to get berated by my own internal voice, I thought about having a drink to shut it up. With Caleb's dry house, it had been days since I had had a drop of alcohol, and that trend was looking to continue since I had forgotten to purchase anything while I was out.

You can't even go a few days without craving your fix, The Voice continued.

I wanted to refute that claim. To reason with myself that it had just been a tough few days. But when didn't I have tough days? When wasn't I able to find a reason to dissolve my lucid state?

I closed my eyes. I needed to get out of my head; I needed to focus on something else.

I took a deep breath as my mind showed images of Caleb kissing my lips, then my neck.

I put my hands to my head. "Stop," I demanded of my own thoughts.

Yeah, nothing's going to happen between you two, The Voice said. *He isn't going to fuck things up with Cassy. If he wanted to end it, he would have told her, you guys had sex last weekend. And he didn't. So, case closed. Move on!*

My inner critic was brutal but had a point. Had he wanted to leave Cassy, he had an opportunity. A misunderstanding that still could have led to their breakup, but he didn't take it. It was clear he didn't want to ruin things with her.

I looked at myself in the mirror again. I wished I didn't hate my reflection. I wished I was able to see the girl I once was.

I exhaled. I wished I wasn't sober.

I grabbed the pill bottle out of the bag and set it on the counter—staring at it while I searched for reasons to end my sober thoughts.

I just wanted to quiet them down.

You might as well just blame it on your hand, The Voice said.

While my hand pain would be the reason I would tell myself that I took them, the real reason would be because I had planned on that being my last night with Caleb before another break.

Before another amount of time, he would need to move forward with Cassy. Before he would officially move on, marry her, and give me what I had been fighting for. To keep our friendship intact, to keep him in my life—to forever have him at arm's length.

I popped one of the pills in my mouth and sipped from the faucet to wash it down. I tucked the pill bottle back in my bag as I heard Caleb yell through the door.

"Harper, you want some popcorn?"

I opened it. "Aren't you leaving?"

He looked me up and down. "I thought I would hang for a few," he replied, giving a flirtatious grin. "So, do you want some?"

I felt my face get flushed, and butterflies flew through my stomach. I wasn't sure if it was a rush of nerves stemming from the possibility of him finding out that I took something I realistically didn't need, or if it was from the way he was looking at me—the way he always looked at me.

"Some what?" I asked absentmindedly. "Oh, popcorn, no, uh, I'm not really hungry."

He stood silently for a moment at the door, I wasn't sure what was going through his head, but I was also trying hard not to care.

"You done in there?" he asked.

I nodded, and we walked back to the couch, him trailing closely behind me.

"So, Serena picked those out for you?" he asked as I sat down.

"Yeah, I think she got them a little small, though," I replied. "They're kind of tight."

I glanced at him to see his reaction as I hadn't intended to sound flirty. I didn't want to cross any lines like we had the week before. But I knew us. I knew we possessed the ability to make those lines invisible every time we were near each other.

He adjusted his position on the couch.

I wrapped the blanket around my back and brought my knees to my chest.

"Did you want to watch anything?" he asked, clearing his throat.

"Whatever's fine. I'll probably go to sleep soon," I answered, hoping he would take the hint and leave.

But he didn't budge. He didn't even make his popcorn. Instead, he continued to make himself comfortable on the couch and put his feet up on the coffee table. As he flipped through the queue, I glanced over at him.

The medication was starting to take hold of my mind and body. The tension I had held in every muscle turned to jello as the worries trapped inside my head floated away.

At that moment, I waited for The Voice to chime in with some ruthless words to cut me down for my possible future addiction. But nothing came; the silence was enchanting.

"What?" Caleb asked with a grin.

I hadn't realized I was still staring at him.

"Nothing," I replied with a smile.

An empty feeling quickly grew in the pit of my stomach.

What if Caleb found out that I took the pills for reasons other than my hand? What if I did become addicted to the feeling of being free? The feeling he had warned me about so many times.

As easily as the anxious thoughts had flooded in, they settled down and disappeared within a matter of minutes. Then my body returned to its tension-free state.

I ran my fingers through my hair and continued to breathe steadily as Caleb again shifted in his seat.

"You're restless tonight," I commented flirtatiously, pulling my hair up into a ponytail and grazing my fingers gently along my neckline.

His breathing was balanced, but I could tell I was getting a reaction from him—something which only fueled me in my medicated state.

I wasn't sure if an ingredient in the medication delivered the feeling of euphoria or if it was the resistance to sleep propelling it forward. But either way, every movement felt magnificent.

Without any contemplation or hesitancy on my part, my subconscious took hold and, before I knew it, I stood up, grabbed my pillow, and went and settled in on the love seat.

For a moment, Caleb looked confused at the move. But then I started softly stroking my fingertips on the top of my thigh. I wasn't sure what my mind's intention was, if it was to get him riled up or if I was just enjoying my own touch. But both were happening regardless of any intent.

The lack of attention he was giving to the TV was becoming increasingly noticeable. For a moment, I hoped he didn't detect my calm, elated demeanor from the pills, but that quickly dissipated with any other worry that tried its best to creep in.

I put my hand at the top part of my shorts and touched myself with my fingertips. There were moments I forgot he was still in the room, and other moments him being there pushed me more. It was not my intent to give him a complete show, but I wasn't leaving much to the imagination. Fighting the need to sleep was pulling me in and out of a state of mind not able to make any level-headed decisions.

I made eye contact with Caleb. He still appeared restless. I was sure he was dying to touch me—I wanted to do the same to him.

After what seemed like an eternity for me, and probably for him too, I saw him slip his hand into his shorts. A sight that sent the butterflies fluttering through my midsection.

I moved my hand back down to my underwear, letting them disappear beneath the fabric. While the medication was heightening the feeling of my hands on my body, it seemed to block the release I had built myself up to. It was like I was right on the edge but couldn't jump.

As I moved my fingers deeper, a moan escaped my mouth. After a few minutes passed of just the sounds of our heavy breathing over the television, I heard him finish.

That left me to quickly come to terms with the fact that my constant harmonious state was going to prevent a push off the ledge. So, I gave into the exhaustion I had been fighting as I rolled over and shut my eyes.

I heard Caleb grab his keys off the counter, then felt a blanket cover my body. His lips touched my forehead—lingering for a moment, allowing me to feel the warmth of his skin one more time.

I wanted badly to kiss him on the lips. Kiss him passionately like we had many times before. But, even in that state, I knew not to trust myself to stop. The image of me sleeping on the couch after yet another weak moment of blurred lines was going to have to be the last one he had of me until we were able to learn some self-control.

***

For the third morning in a row, I woke up drenched in sweat, having the same dreadful nightmare. The lack of restful sleep was starting to catch up. A part of me had taken that pill the night before in hopes it would block out everything in my imagination.

But all it did was serve as a knife so that I was able to slice through the boundaries of someone else's relationship. A relationship I had admittedly been pushing to keep intact. I could blame the pills like I blamed the alcohol, but in the end, it was still me who did it.

I wrote Caleb a note and tore the page out of my journal. I was sure Sarah would say the journal exercise was not meant to take the place of an actual conversation with someone. But it did seem like a good way for me to do it—not having to break down in front of anyone, and not having to hear I love you before I would leave again.

But the hard part wasn't leaving; I had done that before. That had become a thing for us. The problem was we were always looking at it like, after the break, things would resume like normal.

But how could he ever move forward with someone like Cassy if he was always holding out for me? Eventually, there wouldn't be a next time, and when I would come back into his life, he wouldn't want me anymore, not even as a friend. And I couldn't have that. I needed to learn some self-control.

I know a permanent way for you to stay gone and not ruin things for him, The Voice said in a way that made a pain form in my chest.

The words were dark, even for me.

I really did hope Caleb and Cassy would work out. I didn't know her very well, but I could see why he was with her. She was stable and seemingly undamaged—not that he ever said she *wasn't* or that I *was*, but I could tell. Besides, I could see she loved him.

It was kind of like how Jacob had loved me. They had been able to see past all the reasons to not be with us and all the damage that we came with. I just hoped that she and Caleb ended up better than Jacob and I had. And with me out of the picture, they had a chance.

One of my biggest regrets was saying no to Jacob. My life had really changed after he left. Things happened—things that changed me to my core. Although, without Jacob leaving, I would have never met Caleb.

But it was something I wouldn't have needed had Jacob stayed. I would have been happy, or at least what I thought happiness could have been. The happiness that comes with being married at twenty to the first boyfriend you ever really had.

Caleb had only gotten the slightly blemished Harper for a little while before I would become the completely damaged goods he would come to know for the next seven years.

I missed the girl I had been when we had met. I may not have liked her at the time. I may have had too much of my mother's emotional wreckage instilled in me even then, but at least I was hopeful. At least I saw the world as a place I could see myself enjoying. At least then, I wasn't plagued with the constant need to overthink everything in life to a detrimental point.

I left Caleb's key under the mat after locking up. I needed to distance myself from him, his place, and everything we were when we were together. I drove around for a little while until I ended up in Grand Haven on the main strip that followed along the coast of Lake Michigan.

I parked my car and stared at the almost empty beach. In a beautiful state surrounded by water, I spent my free time gazing upon my TV, men at bars, and the inside of my eyelids. I couldn't remember the last time I had been to the lake on a weekday. The last time I had been to one, in general, was on a Saturday years before with Caleb.

I grabbed a blanket out of my trunk and laid it out on the sand. A cool spring breeze blew in from the lake as the waves rushed in.

The sun was hidden by the clouds, but the warmth of summer was beginning to arrive.

I rested my head on my sweatshirt and put in my headphones, trying to enjoy being the most relaxed I had been while sober in years.

Chapter Nineteen

My phone pinged, and I realized I had dozed off. It was a little after 3:00, and my mother was reminding me to be at the house. I had never been more grateful for her lack of faith in my responsibility, but like everything else, that was something she didn't need to know.

I walked to my car and then headed to the place that would soon be known as my home—at least for the foreseeable future.

***

When I pulled up a few minutes before four, my mother and Rachel were already there. We went inside so I could sign some papers and my mother could write a check.

Around 5:00, Rachel left, but my mother stuck around. I brought in the few bags that I had and put the clothes into the drawers. I heard my phone ping, then watched as Caleb's name appeared on the screen—something I had been anxiously awaiting all day.

However, he hadn't even been home yet to find the note. He was texting me to see if I was at his place because he was on his way over. So, my anxious feeling continued as I closed out of the message and placed the phone back in my pocket.

"We need to get you some groceries," my mother said, opening the kitchen cupboards. "Would you like to stop and see Grandma and then go to the store? I'll drive."

I wasn't used to her being that nice, especially without any strings attached. It was hard to stomach. Maybe she was trying to make it up to me after lying for 12 years, or maybe she was genuinely scared when my house burnt down. Or it could have been what my cynical mind kept saying—that she was just there to control my mess. There to make sure I didn't, in fact, *spiral*, as she had so lovingly accused me of.

But, from an unfamiliar part of my brain, I was also being told to soak it up and enjoy the time we were being civil to one another. Besides, I needed a distraction. And as uncomfortable as time with my mother would be, I knew it would keep me from caving with him.

***

On the way to the hospital, my phone let me know that Caleb messaged again. By the question he had asked, I knew he still hadn't found the note, and my anxiety over the situation was starting to feel like it was manifesting into an ulcer.

But, as we pulled into the hospital, my phone started ringing. My mother seemed annoyed at the constant noise that had been coming from my purse, so I turned it on silent. Both to appease her and to ignore him.

While we approached the door to my grandma's room, three nurses walked out, with a doctor trailing behind them. The exiting staff looked somber, and the doctor stopped as she reached my mother.

"Lori, I'm so sorry," she began. "We were about to call you." She paused, glancing briefly at me, then back at my mother. "Ruth just passed."

My mother didn't seem shocked—or it was possible she had just gotten good at holding in any reaction.

My grandma had told me she had been sick for some time, so I guess it shouldn't have shocked me either. But I selfishly hadn't asked how long she still had. I had thought—or hoped, rather—that it would've been a little longer.

A sob got stuck in my throat as I sat down in the chair just outside the room. I repressed the tears that tried to escape the corner of my eyes.

But although it was a devastating loss, she had told me she had lived a good life and was ready to go when the good Lord needed her. So, I guess that was comforting, knowing she was okay with it.

My mother went with the nurse to sign some papers, and I stayed outside Grandma's room. She was covered with a sheet, which I was thankful for. I wasn't ready to see her gone or the lifeless body she had left behind.

I never saw my father's corpse either. My mother said she had him cremated right after they released him following the accident. I was fine with that—not knowing what he would have looked like after what had happened to him.

I glanced at my phone. I had six missed calls from Caleb, along with a few texts. His words were apologetic. But as I read them, my screen changed, and Serena's name came across it.

"Harper, what's going on?" Serena asked.

I was confused by her tone and by her question. How would she have known?

"My grandma died," I responded.

The other end of the phone went silent for a moment.

"Shit, I'm sorry. She was a really nice woman," she finally responded. "Are you okay?"

"Yeah, I knew she was sick…"

And yet you didn't stop back to visit her, The Voice chimed in.

"Still, I'm sorry. I'll call my boss and let him know I'm taking a personal day tomorrow."

"No, don't do that," I told her. "I'll be fine."

Serena sighed. "Will you?"

"What do you mean?"

"Caleb called me."

I rolled my eyes. "Why are you guys suddenly talking to each other?"

"We aren't. I mean, I wouldn't have picked up if I knew you weren't talking to him again."

Fair enough.

"Sorry, I didn't think about him having your number," I replied.

"So, what happened? Where are you staying?"

"Nothing happened. We just needed a break from each other."

"You guys just *had* a break."

"Clearly not for long enough," I replied. "And my mother helped find me a place. I moved in a few hours ago."

"Well, next time, give me a heads-up, okay?"

My mother walked to where I was standing and looked down at me—clearly wanting to leave.

I glanced once more into my grandma's room, feeling the hard-hit of guilt sucker-punch my stomach.

"Yeah, sorry. I will. I have to go. Call you later?"

"Yeah. I'm coming into town this weekend, whether you like it or not," she replied, causing a small smile to form on my face.

***

After we left the hospital, my mother still insisted on taking me to the grocery store. But the car ride was filled with more silence and awkwardness than before. She tried to casually bring up that she would ask for some donations from her church to get me on my feet again. But I insisted that she had done enough already—that I could manage the rest on my own.

The church she was referring to was one that she and Bernard had started attending when they first got together. I thought it was funny since neither of my parents were particularly religious growing up.

The little I did know about God was from the occasional Sunday school class my grandparents would stick me in when I stayed with them on a Saturday night. My parents' lack of religious conviction was something none of the grandparents were exceedingly happy about.

***

My mother pulled up to my house around 9:00 that night. I paused before getting out, wondering if a hug was in order. I mean, I knew one was, for all she had done, and due to my grandma's passing, but they were always so awkward with her—so forced.

She must have sensed the awkwardness, too, because she said "bye" and picked up her phone to call Bernard. So, I seized the opportunity and exited the vehicle.

Once inside, I put away the groceries and started to get ready for bed. As I pulled the toiletries out of the bag, my bottle of pills fell to the floor. I stared at them for a minute as I thought back to the previous night and what they, along with my poor decision-making, led me to do.

I picked them up and opened them—peering inside the bottle.

While they helped fuel my bad decisions, they also helped fuel my escape from reality. I wanted to stop making crummy choices, but I also wanted to experience that sensation again. To get back to that carefree feeling—even if it was for just a small moment in time.

But for the first time in a long time, I fought against the pull of self-destructive behavior and poured the pills into the toilet— having a sense of relief rush over me as they disappeared into the drain.

Once in my new room, I curled up in the strange bed that smelled like mothballs instead of Caleb. A few tears broke free and rolled down my cheeks. They soaked into the fabric beneath my head as my emotions from the day took hold, leaving me with a pillow that held more water than cloth and a heart that held more emptiness than anything else.

Chapter Twenty

As I opened my eyes, I picked up my phone to look at the time—10:00am. Again, I was waking up drenched in sweat, wishing the nightmare would end already. Either having them conclude with my rescue or in my death. I was sick of spending the entirety of my slumber trapped inside my old house, feeling the heat from the flames and the sting from my hand—watching as everyone carried on their lives without me.

I sat up in bed. Not having to get up for work on a weekday was so strange. The two previous mornings, I had things to do or places to run from. But that wasn't the case anymore.

The guilt started to creep in from not visiting my grandma more. I braced myself for the tears to form, but either my tear ducts were out of commission at the moment, or I really was becoming as emotionless on the inside as I tried to show everyone I was on the outside.

I took a deep breath and tried to block out any thoughts of her—I wasn't ready to process that grief. However, that just meant she would be placed alongside everything else that had taken up permanent residence in the *things I wasn't ready to deal with yet* part of my brain.

I picked up my phone, wanting to distract myself.

I was thankful it had made it out with me the night of the fire. I was also glad Serena had bought me a phone case for my birthday that held my ID and credit cards.

I wasn't sure about it when I first put it on, but not having to always carry a purse with me did have its benefits. And since said purse was a casualty of the flames, I supported the invention even more.

I sighed, knowing I wasn't mentally prepared to deal with— well, anything. But I unlocked my phone anyway, seeing the missed text messages from the previous night.

Both messages were from Caleb. When he had texted me earlier in the night, he had sounded sad and confused. But the ones later were angry, something I felt was good. If he was mad, then he would hopefully stop trying to talk to me.

He had done it before. He had allowed us a break from each other. He had continued to grow with Cassy. I was confident he could do it again. I was more confident in him than I was in myself.

I wouldn't have gotten through the months without him before had I not had Ben to keep me strong. Or rather, cause me to be weak. I had gotten so lost in the situation I had put myself in, that running to Caleb during the midst of it all hadn't seemed like an option. I had lost myself in the misery I had created, so I felt deserving of my time spent in the purgatory of disillusions.

Was life supposed to be that complicated? Was it really that complicated? Or did I just make it that way?

You make it that way, The Voice chimed in. *You bring so much drama, and no one likes to be around you.*

I put my phone down and slid to the edge, letting my toes rub against the carpet. I pulled tighter at the comforter to hide my entire body as I nestled like a caterpillar inside.

With Caleb being the last man I had climbed into bed with, I was determined to cleanse my palate to help with the process of moving forward. Typically, the idea of going out to meet someone was met with at least *some* excitement, a little bit less of a forced, have-to mentality.

But the forced feeling wasn't new. I had felt the same energy into moving on from him when we had originally broken up. Although, I hoped to have a better success rate than I had had that time around. Success both in resisting the urge to need him and being able to get in bed with someone else.

While it was a Wednesday, and most people my age weren't looking to rage on a weekday, I was hoping to find at least one halfway decent male to bring home. An uncomplicated rebound that didn't lead to anything more than thanks for the sex—have a nice life.

The universe must have wanted the same thing as my phone pinged and Anna's name crossed the screen.

Anna: I heard about your house! I'm so sorry :(I'm going out with some friends for a drink tonight if you wanna come :)

Although I hated going out with people I didn't know, I accepted her invitation to join them. Because, when it came down to it, needing to get laid trumped my loathing of small talk.

Anna and I had worked together at the store a few years back. She was a couple of years younger than me but lived a similar single lifestyle. I would question why our friendship never blossomed into much more than the occasional text and hangout, but Sarah had rightfully pointed out that I don't let people in. So, we stayed casual acquaintances as I had with anyone who came into my life post early twenties Harper.

***

By 7:00 that evening, I had showered, shaved, and gone to the store to get something cute to wear. I picked out new eyeliner and mascara and some protection for my assumed planned activities that night.

While Serena had bought clothes for me, they weren't the girls-night-out or pick-up-men-in-a-bar type outfits I had found myself in need of.

I rebandaged my hand to make it less noticeable, hoping to avoid any conversation about my burnt-down house. I wanted casual sex, which came from easygoing conversations, not from my steady stream of drama.

I called an Uber and met the girls at Joe's Sports bar downtown, a bar I hadn't been to in years.

"Harper!" Anna exclaimed as I walked in the door.

"Hey," I replied, smiling politely at everyone.

"Harper, this is Maggie, Tara, Miah, and Sammy."

I saw that they already had drinks in front of them, so I didn't want to wait to order one for myself. "I'm going to go order at the bar," I commented as Anna pulled out a chair for me.

She nodded, then turned and started talking with Miah again.

I walked up to the bar and waited for the bartender to free up. As the other customer walked away with her drink, the bartender turned toward me and smiled.

"What can I get ya?" he asked.

"A cranberry vodka, please," I replied, but I knew I would need more than that to kick the night off. "And a shot of vodka."

"Bad day?" he asked, pouring the shot and setting it down in front of me.

"Bad week."

He filled up my shot glass again. "This one's on the house," he responded with a grin.

I tossed it back while my mind reminded me to pace myself. But I didn't know if that was even going to be an option.

I gave him my card to hold open my tab for the night and brought my drink to the table.

The waitress came around after a few minutes and took orders for food. I knew I needed to eat. If pacing myself was out, then I at least needed something to soak it up with.

I glanced around the bar. It was slim pickings on men. It seemed any guys there were either already with a girl or looked as if they were barely legal to drink. I was probably being pickier than I should have been, but I knew that would change as the alcohol started taking over the decision-making.

***

Around 9:00, karaoke started, something the girls tried to coax me into doing, but that was a whole other level of drunk I needed to be. But they, on the other hand, had no shame—picking the cheesiest songs and having a blast together on the small stage.

I craved to be that carefree, not restrained by my insecurities, not needing copious amounts of liquid courage to jump any tiny hurdle placed at my feet.

"What? Too good to sing with your friends?"

I turned my head, and the bartender stood next to me with his arms crossed.

"Something like that," I responded with a smile.

He paused for a second. "Jenna went out for a break; can I get you anything?"

"Uh, yeah. I'll take another cranberry and vodka," I answered, quickly finishing the rest of mine.

When he brought me a new one, he took a seat in the chair next to me.

"Don't you have customers?" I asked with a smirk, though I didn't mind the company.

"Nah, it's a slow night," he responded, returning the smile.

"Just looking to enjoy the music then?"

I looked toward the girls on stage who were now making gestures at us.

"No, just enjoying the view," he replied, as his eyes stayed on me.

"*Wow,* that was cheesy," I said, lifting my eyebrows and laughing.

He chuckled. "Yeah, I regretted it as soon as it came out."

For a moment, a genuine smile crossed my face.

He wasn't my usual type, which typically consisted of clean-cut, preppy-looking men like Caleb, Jacob, and Ben. He had more of a broody, bad boy look. Like someone who I imagined owned a motorcycle and had a different girl in his bed every night.

He did, however, have soft eyes and a smile that could have been used for dental ads. So, who cared if he ended up being a self-professed fuck boy? The *men* I had been with were, too; they just didn't seem to be able to admit it to themselves.

"I'm Harper."

"Jesse."

I turned back toward the girls as they finished their second song and exited the stage towards us. Jesse got up from the chair to let Anna sit back down.

"Hey, cute bartender, can we have a round of tequila shots?" Maggie asked.

He nodded and then winked at me as he walked away.

"Harper Jones, are you flirting with the *bartender*?" Anna asked.

"Definitely."

Jesse came back with the round of tequila and dropped it off on the table. He stood next to me as Maggie made conversation with him.

I started to get a little nervous as Maggie was very pretty, with her long red hair and beautiful green eyes. I felt like nothing in comparison.

"Maggie's married. She's a harmless flirt," Anna whispered to me.

Oh, good, he could just think about her while he's in bed with you, The Voice said.

Anna also added that Maggie had been married since she was 19 and was fully committed to her husband. Kind of what I assumed life would've been like for me if I had said yes to Jacob.

For a moment, it made me feel less guilty for flirting with married men as the married women did it, too. But The Voice seized the opportunity to remind me that flirting stopped a lot shorter than where I seemed to let it get to.

The shame and regret forced my hand to the shot glass. The bitterness I felt from all of it mandated it down my throat.

Jesse went back to the bar to help another customer. As the burn from the shot weakened and the liquid courage took hold, I found myself in a rare moment of confidence as I approached the bar.

"What time are you off tonight?" I asked him.

"We close at midnight—shouldn't be too long after that."

"Wanna come over?" I asked, trying to sound casual in my bold approach.

"Yeah, I can do that," he answered as he opened a beer for another customer.

I walked back to the table and waited impatiently for the next three hours to pass by.

***

In the course of that time, Maggie had gotten so drunk she was puking in the bathroom. *Oh, tequila.* Sammy was texting her ex and lying to Anna about it. Anna wasn't dating Sammy, but it seemed like she wanted to be. It was possible they had dated before, but I didn't know Anna that well to know her exes.

Miah had called an Uber shortly after the tequila shot. She seemed to have the good sense to wrap it up before she couldn't handle herself.

All said and done, they were pretty fun to hang out with. It never got to the small talk or anything since they were already slightly buzzed when I showed up. It may have helped too that Jesse and I had spent a good portion of the night making eyes at each other.

We also had a few short conversations, but they always got interrupted by someone needing a drink.

***

By 12:20, everyone had cleared out, and I sat at the bar waiting for him to wrap things up. Since I had Ubered, he was going to drive us to my place.

After he locked up the front, he took my hand and led me through the back of the bar. As soon as we stepped out the back, he gently whisked me around and pinned me up against the building. He put his hand behind my head and brought his lips to mine. His kiss was soft and left me breathless.

"I've wanted to do that all night," he said, pulling his lips away from mine but keeping his body close.

I smiled and pulled him back in for another one as the ache moved about my body. He moved his hands to my hips and brought his lips down to my neck. His five o'clock shadow brushed against my skin as he kissed me hard.

A quiet moan escaped my mouth.

I buried my hands into his hair, giving it a slight tug when he hit all the right places. He brought his face back up to mine, kissing my mouth once more.

"Let's get out of here," he said, taking my hand again and leading me to his car.

I laughed silently at my wrong assumption about the motorcycle as I climbed into his Corolla.

The car ride to my house was full of sexual tension. If we had had a condom with us, I was certain we would've pulled over to finish what we had started behind the bar. I hadn't had sex in a vehicle since my first time with Caleb. An enjoyable memory that I quickly shook away.

Jesse put his hand underneath my dress, caressing my thigh, inching closer to being completely between my legs. He slipped his fingers beneath my underwear and let out a soft moan as he felt my excitement for his touch.

We pulled into the driveway and he turned off his car, leaning over to kiss me.

Once we made it to the door, I grabbed out my keys and unlocked it. He moved my hair away from my shoulders and started kissing my neck—making it hard to concentrate.

When we finally made it inside, I unzipped the back of my dress and let it fall to the floor. He pulled me close, wrapping his arms around my body.

God, he was a good kisser.

He pressed me against the wall, pulled off his shirt, and tossed it in the same area as my dress. I took his hand and led him through the dark hallway to the bedroom.

Once in the room, I felt his arms around me as he lifted me up and placed me gently on the bed, never allowing his lips to leave my body. He undid his pants as I handed him a condom which he slipped on before joining me once more. He promptly pulled me on top of him, like he knew exactly how I liked it.

His body shifted upwards. He put his hand on my ass, and the other tugged at my hair.

My mind, for once, was at ease. Free from the guilt of what I was doing and who I was doing it with. His kiss, his touch, his movement—everything we were doing was completely in sync. It was something I had never experienced with someone I had no history with—something I had desperately needed.

***

When I got out of the bathroom, Jesse was in the living room putting his shirt back on.

I turned on the hallway light to give some glow to the living room. "You can stay if you want," I said, leaning on the wall while I tied my new robe shut.

"I have to get home," he replied, buttoning his jeans, then looking up to give me a smile.

"You're not like, married, or something, are you?"

"Shouldn't you have asked that before?" he questioned with a chuckle. "No, I'm not married," he added with a smile. "But I do have a dog that needs to be fed and let out."

I smirked.

He walked over and put his hand behind my head and brought my lips in for a kiss. "I had a really good time tonight," he said, gazing into my eyes.

I looked down at the floor anxiously. "I did, too."

"Can I get your number?" he asked, pulling out his phone.

I wanted to be more hesitant since I hadn't intended on seeing the person I brought home for a second time. But I entered it in any way and handed it back to him.

He grabbed the ties on my robe and pulled them loose so that my naked body was exposed once again. He then pinned me back up against the wall for another kiss, pressing up against me tightly with his whole body. After a minute, he stopped and grinned.

"Go feed your dog," I said, giving him a playful push toward the door.

He smiled and winked at me as he walked out.

That had gone better than I expected it too. Most hook-ups ended with an awkward morning or weird conversation, knowing neither person would call.

I just hoped he wasn't lying about the dog. I couldn't take getting involved with yet another committed man.

Why? Then he really would be your type, The Voice said.

Chapter Twenty-one

The next morning the sound of a received text message ripped me out of my nightmare. But I was grateful since it was starting to feel like I was trapped in one of Dante's circles of hell.

I grabbed my phone off the nightstand.

Unknown: I hope you slept well :)

For a moment, I was irritated, thinking it was Ben. But I saw the unknown number was different than the one he had texted from before.

My mind flashed to Jesse.

Harper: I did. ;)

I showered, cooked breakfast, and got ready to start my day, though I wasn't sure what it would consist of. Thankfully, Serena would be in town Friday night, and at the very least, would provide me a partner to drink with.

I decided to spend my day shopping for some household basics and a few more outfits. I stopped by the insurance place while I was out as well. I was trying to do anything to keep me busy and out of my home—anything to keep me from falling asleep and slipping back into the wretched inferno.

I had received a call while I was out in regards to my house, or my former house anyway. They said they were still waiting on the lab for confirmation, but that it appears it started through old wiring in the kitchen. That didn't surprise me. It was an old house.

I got back to my place around 4:00. When I pulled in, my phone pinged from the passenger's seat.

Jesse: Dinner tonight

Harper: Is that a question?

Jesse: ;)

Harper: Okay

Jesse: I'll be over around 6

***

I had spent the better part of an hour leading up to Jesse's arrival, trying to cover up the bags that had taken up residence under my eyes. When I heard his car door shut, I met him at the front door and locked it behind me.

"No work tonight?" I asked as he opened the passenger door for me.

"Nope, I usually have three nights off a week; this is one of them."

Already trying to learn his schedule? The Voice asked. *Desperate much?*

He smiled and put the car into reverse. "Did you work today?" he asked. "What do you even do? Sorry that I never asked."

He didn't ask because he doesn't really give a shit, The Voice commented.

I must have been more nervous than I had thought I would be. The Voice seemed oddly queued up and ready to go. I hoped that whenever Jesse was taking me, they had mind-numbing refreshments. Something to take the edge of the questions and the comments that not only The Voice would be making, but Jesse as well.

My face flushed as I knew I was off to a bad start, realizing I had yet to answer. "I'm an office manager. I usually work all week, but I have the week off..." I replied and left it at that.

***

After a few minutes, we pulled up to a restaurant I had been to once before—with Ben. I pushed the unwanted memories away and walked in with Jesse.

We passed the time, asking each other questions. The questions were informational without being too invasive. I was glad he took charge because I tended to get anxious with silence and would end up word-vomiting all kinds of inappropriate things. I preferred to get to know other people and have them not really get to know me.

Jesse was originally from Michigan, growing up only a town over from mine. He left when he was in his early 20s to take care of his Grandma Mary in South Carolina. Both she and her husband, David, had moved there when they couldn't stand the snow anymore.

His grandpa had passed away when Jesse was 19, and his grandma had gotten sick when he was 20. His parents were going to move her back to Michigan so they could take care of her, but she didn't want to leave her house. So, Jesse dropped out of school and moved down south to take care of her full-time. She died a few days after his 23rd birthday.

She had left her house—and all her earthly possessions—to him. So, he stayed there for a while. He got a job as a bartender since he was used to staying up late with his grandma, which was when she was at her sickest. Plus, he enjoyed meeting and talking to new people.

After a while, it got lonely there, being away from the rest of his family, so he moved back to Michigan when he was 27. Three years had passed since then.

I was glad he had a lot to say because I didn't really want to share anything about myself. I didn't want to come off as the damage-filled human piñata I knew I was. Although, at that point, the stuff I would share was only a little dive into the wreckage. He didn't need to know that either. But as soon as he gave me time to talk, the word vomit spewed out.

I told him I was also from around there, that my father had died when I was 16, and that I had moved out shortly after that when things fell apart with my mother. I talked a little about the company I worked for and what my job entailed.

Then I got bold—or anxious, rather—and told him about my grandma's passing. I quickly rounded off the unusual conversation by talking about my house fire the previous weekend. I hoped things were going well enough that sharing such heavy content on both our ends wouldn't divert the night.

"Holy shit!" he said. "You weren't kidding that it's been a week. I'm sorry about your grandma—and your house." He shook his head and took a bite of his dinner.

"Yeah, but it's fine. Everyone's been super helpful."

He nodded and then grinned.

"So, whose place did we go to last night?"

"Oh, it's just temporary housing until I find something."

"That makes sense."

My brows furrowed. "What do you mean."

"It just looked like no one lived there. Really impersonal."

I looked down at my plate. "Yeah, I haven't had time to decorate yet."

I was glad he saw that at the temporary house. My former house had looked the same. No pictures. No knickknacks. No sign of real human existence. Post fire Harper couldn't be judged on her clinical-like housing decor because it wasn't her house. Post-fire, Harper had lost all her sentimental things in the fire.

After he paid, he took me to a mini-golf course nearby. I hadn't been to one since I was little. My uncle Sam used to take me to the one by my parent's house when they would be fighting or when I felt they didn't want me around. After he moved away, whenever my parents would fight, I would walk there and play the course by myself. That was until I had met Ben and started hanging out with him instead.

While mini-golf wasn't hard, Jesse seemed to really struggle—or maybe I was just really good. Halfway through, he confessed he had never been before but that he thought it would be fun and easy to do. Fun, sure. Easy? Apparently not.

"You want to try the batting cages next?" he asked, seeming more confident in his abilities with a bat than with a golf club.

I grinned and nodded.

"Let's make it interesting. If I can get more hits than you, we go back to my place tonight," he said, putting on a helmet.

"What if *I* win?" I asked, as if I hadn't planned on the night ending at my place or his regardless.

"*If* you win, you can pick what we do," he replied with confidence ringing from his voice.

Little did he know, I had spent many weekends at the batting cages with Jacob. He had taught me how to properly stand, how to watch the ball, how to hit, everything I would need to win the bet. Well, if I still remembered how to do it all.

Jesse came out proud of himself, hitting twelve out of fifteen pitches. I took the helmet from him and placed it on my head.

I walked into the cage and stood at the plate. I settled into the stance Jacob had taught me years earlier and looked back at Jesse with a smile.

"*When* I win, I would like ice cream," I said.

I turned to face the machine. And, with that, after all those years, I still had it—fifteen for fifteen. My teacher had taught me well. I think he would've been proud.

I walked out, pulling off my helmet and letting my hair cascade down my back.

"How did you get so good?" he asked.

"My high school boyfriend was on the varsity baseball team," I replied with a laugh.

"Cheater."

"Hey, dude, you never asked."

"Alright. Well, ice cream it is," he responded with a smile, taking the bat and helmet from me.

We stopped at a little ice cream stand on the way back to his house.

"The second-place prize seems to be better than first place," he commented with a grin.

"Clearly, you've never had Moose Traxx."

We pulled up to his place a few minutes later. He had told me at dinner that he was able to buy his house in Michigan from selling the one his grandma had left to him. He had been sad to give it up, but it was more room and work than he needed and could handle. He liked the new one because it was small and simple. And being just outside the city, he had a good piece of property that made it feel like an escape from life—the one I had anyway.

We were greeted at the door by his dog, Mike. Jesse didn't have an explanation behind Mike's name other than he always liked dogs with human names. He had gotten Mike shortly after his grandma had passed, as he had gotten lonely in her big house by himself.

"Have you ever had any pets?" he asked me.

"No, they're a lot of responsibility."

He laughed. "Tell me about it!"

We finished our ice cream as we talked on the couch. It was nice having the first time out of the way. No, "will we, won't we " type of date. We both already knew it would end that way, and we both already knew how it would be.

Jesse's carefree attitude was a welcomed change from people walking on eggshells around me and always asking if I was okay. I finally felt relaxed. Funny how easy it could be if I just took things that made me feel bad or guilty out of the equation.

Mike scratched on the back door, and Jesse let him out. He had built a fence the summer before, so he didn't have to worry about Mike wandering off. I hadn't taken Jesse for the handyman type like Caleb. But I had been wrong about many things in my short time of knowing him.

If he's as stable as he seems, then he isn't your type, The Voice commented. *It's only a matter of time before you fuck it up.*

Jesse sat back down beside me. He placed his hand gently on my cheek then put his arm around my neck—pulling me in for a long, erotic kiss. I didn't waste any time climbing onto his lap and continuing the connection of our tongues from on top. His hands pressed firmly on my lower back, pulling me closer to his body.

He moved his hand into my hair, pushing my lips into his. Then his kiss drifted down to my collarbone, starting from the right side and moving to the middle.

Mike jumped up on the door, startling us.

Jesse smiled at me. "Life with a dog," he said with a shrug.

I climbed off so he could let him in.

"Did you want to stay tonight?" he asked, walking back over to me and leaning over the back of the couch for a kiss.

"Sure," I answered, not wanting to sound too eager.

But God was he fun to kiss.

He put his lips back against mine. After a minute, he pulled back, took my hand, and led me to his room.

Mike tried to come in, too, but Jesse stopped him. "It's just for a little while, buddy," I heard him whisper as he shut the door.

The only light coming in was from the small space beneath the door, but Mike's nose was blocking part of it.

My lips curved into a smile as Jesse walked toward me. He pulled off his shirt and then helped slip off my dress—our motions in sync once again. He was touching me in a way as if he knew me well, caressing my body in a familiar, almost caring, way. That time more in line with Jacob than how it had been with Caleb.

Caleb's movements were intense, raw, passionate to the nth degree. But Jesse's soul didn't seem to harbor that same drive. Something I was confident made being in his bed an even better, more guilt-free decision.

I felt Jesse's lips move to my neck, sending a rush of pleasure through my veins.

My mind wandered briefly, wondering how Caleb was doing—wondering if I had set Cassy and him back onto a better path. Hoping I hadn't caused any detrimental issues for them in my brief return.

He's fine. He's not even thinking of you, The Voice said.

Although I wasn't sure if that was true, I couldn't help but get sucked into my roaming thoughts of him. I shut my eyes as my heartbeat quickened, and I saw his face.

Stop! The Voice yelled, scolding me like you would a child. *You told him no. You left him. Move on!*

I willed my thoughts of Caleb to stop. I hoped that Jesse hadn't noticed that my mind had strayed. Even when I was enjoying myself, my thoughts tended to overwhelm my ability to focus—*Caleb* overwhelmed my ability to focus.

I was worried that the thoughts of Caleb were what stemmed my orgasm. I couldn't be sure as I had been thoroughly enjoying my time with Jesse. But with visions of Caleb and thoughts of our passionate sex, it was hard to know for sure. Either way, Jesse seemed satisfied with the conclusion of our time together as I slid off him and rested beside him on the bed.

***

Jesse put on a pair of sweatpants and let Mike in the room. He went to turn off the lights in the rest of the house as I reached for the t-shirt he had left on the floor.

I watched while Mike jumped up and sniffed the bed. I pulled the t-shirt over my head and went across the hall to the bathroom to pee and wash my face.

I rested my hands on the edge of the sink as I looked at myself in the mirror. My favorite thing about putting such little effort into doing my makeup was the lack of catfishing I could be accused of when I stayed the night anywhere. But with having just washed off the little I did have on; I was left feeling more self-conscious than usual.

The bags under my eyes looked grueling. I was thankful for the dim lighting in the room. Before I could give The Voice anytime to weigh in, I went back into the bedroom.

"That t-shirt looks good on you," Jesse said, pulling me in for a kiss.

"Thanks. I thought so, too."

He grinned.

As I curled up to him in bed, the usual sting of guilt set in— that time for thinking of Caleb during sex. I tried to rationalize to myself that when you've been with a guy as much as I had been with Caleb, it wasn't easy to just block him out. That was something that would take time. Or at least that was the positive outlook I was telling myself to have.

Chapter Twenty-two

I hadn't considered my nightmares when agreeing to stay. I hadn't slept next to anyone since they had first begun. I didn't know to what extent they affected me physically while they were happening. But it didn't take long for me to find out.

"Harper—"

I heard my name as I felt a hand resting on my upper arm.

"Harper—" I heard again.

I opened my eyes.

"I think you're having a nightmare."

"Y—Yeah," I mumbled as I came to. "Uh, sorry, I should have warned you," I replied, sitting up in bed as sweat ran down my neck.

"This happens a lot?" he asked.

"Just since the fire," I responded with a shrug, glancing at my phone that said 3:00 a.m.

His expression was sympathetic. "Do you want to talk about it?"

"Uh, no, it's okay. I'm going to go splash some cold water on my face. I'll be fine," I replied in the same regurgitated manner I had been using for years.

"Okay."

"Actually, do you mind if I take a shower?" I asked as I stood up, knowing sleep wasn't going to be an easy feat to get back to.

"Not at all," he replied. "Towels are in the bottom cabinet."

***

As I stepped into the shower, the hot water scalded my skin. Typically, I enjoyed my water so hot that it felt like it was burning my soul, but the feeling of it at that moment pulled me right back into my nightmare like I had never woken up. I turned the knob to cold and stood under the stream of water until it shifted temperatures.

Although the cold water itself wasn't enjoyable, it at least washed away my sweat. I was hoping the chill would be enough of a distraction that I wouldn't slip into my usual whirlwind of overthinking, but it wasn't.

When would it end? I needed sleep. Restful sleep.

I knew I needed to start talking to Sarah. I knew I needed to start taking her advice. But knowing I needed to, and actually doing so were two very different steps in the right direction.

I closed my eyes as my skin became numb to the frigid water. A familiar feeling from years before. Not from taking a cold shower to wash away the fragments of a nightmare, but from the short time I had spent as a normal couple with Caleb.

The better part of a year that I had tried for so long to repress; memories of what could have been, too painful to think about. But the harder I tried to forget them, the clearer they appeared, like I was still in the moment—almost like we had never left.

A shiver had run up my spine as I clutched my sweatshirt closed in the front. Caleb laughed as I yelped out at the icy waves of Lake Michigan crashing into my feet. While the sun made the temperature outside appear warm and inviting, it was deceitful.

232

Caleb took my hand and brought it to his lips. He kissed it softly, giving me an adoring smile. We continued to walk on the shoreline as the sun set—life was just slightly shy of perfection.

I was experiencing feelings of pure joy and happiness— feelings I hadn't experienced since my time with Jacob. They were feelings I was so sure I was never going to get again when I had said no to his proposal.

Another wave rolled in, splashing higher that time. The bottom of my jean shorts were soaked with cold water, and goosebumps littered my skin.

Caleb laughed as my teeth chattered. He pulled me close to his body to keep me warm. I was struck with an overwhelming feeling of his arms being the safest place in the world.

The feeling of my teeth vibrating stole me away from the moment I had gone to. One moment of many that I always fought to keep away, but when they would reveal themselves, I found myself fighting to stay in them.

I looked down at my goosebump-covered body as my hands tightly clutched my arms; holding myself to try and stay warm.

I turned off the shower and stepped out. I put Jesse's t-shirt back on and a clean pair of underwear I had stashed in my purse. I didn't have the good sense to avoid the mirror, looking again at the reflection of the unrecognizable woman.

Outside of the unsightly bags that I was sporting, my physical appearance really wasn't playing a part in the unfamiliarity of myself. Caleb was right when he could see something was different—I could see it too.

***

I opened the bathroom door and saw the light on in the living room. Jesse sat on the couch with Mike asleep on the chair.

"You didn't have to get up."

"It's okay. I just wanted to make sure you were alright."

I sighed. There it was again. I was forever running into the trap of being checked on.

"I'm fine, really."

For as much as I repeated those words, I really needed to work on a more convincing tone.

Jesse extended his arm to me and I sat next to him. I rested my head on his shoulder and curled my bare legs up underneath me.

"Jesus, you're cold," he commented as he did a slight twitch in his seat.

"Yeah, sorry."

I didn't want to go into me showering in cold water to avoid the memories of my hellscape, so I was hoping he would move past it, and he did.

"Do you wanna go back to bed or watch some TV?" he asked.

"I'm going to stay up, but you should get some sleep. I feel so bad that I woke you."

"It's really not a big deal. Why don't we just turn on something to watch and we can just fall back asleep on the couch."

I looked up at him and smiled. "Sounds good."

We moved to lie horizontally, and he let me pick what to watch.

"Oh, I love this show," Jesse said as I clicked on *The Office.*

At least he didn't have the same taste in shows as Caleb.

Stop thinking about Caleb, The Voice said.

I made it through almost two episodes before I fell asleep again, but I had tried hard to fight it, worried I would go back.

***

When I woke up again, I felt Jesse's body behind me. It was the first time I wasn't startled awake because of my nightmare, and the first time I wasn't drenched in a pool of my own perspiration.

I went into the bathroom to change, unfortunately only having my dress from the night before.

When I came back out, Jesse was up letting Mike out.

"You hungry?" he asked.

"Yeah, I could eat," I replied with a smile.

"Well, I don't have any food in the house besides Mike's, so unless you like your meal from a can and all blended together, we should probably go somewhere."

"Well, the first option *is* tempting, but going out is fine, too."

When we got to the café, I was overdressed. It was like doing the walk of shame down a very public street. I requested a booth in the corner, wanting to hide.

Jesse thought it was funny, and soon I felt like I was being a little overdramatic about it. Realistically, no one cared. My self-conscious tendencies always made me think people hung on to moments or things like I did. A trait of mine I had been trying to correct for years.

"So, how is it that you are so healthy?" I blurted out. "Like mentally. You're, so, put together—"

"You're very straightforward," he replied. "It's refreshing."

I was glad he found my word vomit refreshing.

He smiled and took a sip of his coffee. "I don't know. I guess living with my grandma and being responsible for her made me have to grow up. My parents and siblings weren't willing to move, so I just kind of took on that responsibility."

I nodded. That made sense. Being forced to mature did help. I had been on that same type of path with moving out at an early age.

It made me have to take responsibility for getting myself out of bed, getting myself to school and work, paying my bills, everything being an adult entailed, while barely being one.

"You seem to be pretty put together too—" he said, with a sincere smile.

"If only things were as they seemed."

I wasn't trying to scare him away—or at least I don't think I was. My subconscious had pushed away potentially good relationships before. It was like my brain was looking out for me—or fucking things up just as they were getting good. I could never tell what devious plan my mind had in store.

***

We finished eating and he took me back to my place. He stood at my door kissing me good-bye. I pulled him inside, shutting it behind us. I pushed him up against the door, feeling his lips with mine.

"You're making it very hard for me to leave to work," he said.

I smiled as the feeling of butterflies again erupted in my stomach. But even in the trance of newness and possibilities, I felt the dark shadow of doubt looming overhead.

He's just fooling around with you, The Voice graciously reminded me. *You are just good for sex. You're not wife material. You're barely girlfriend material. Someone like him will never stay with someone like you.*

I pulled away from him, allowing him to reluctantly exit our embrace. And while I watched him walk out the door, my mind started to question its own motives.

Was my devious brain really trying to save me? Or was it trying to save him *from* me?

Chapter Twenty-three

After Jesse left, I wrote in my journal for my session that afternoon. I decided I needed to talk to Sarah about Ben. I felt it was time I started working toward moving past him. Working through all the damage our relationship had brought me, or more accurately, brought *out* in me, in the short time we were together.

My sessions had been getting better since I started answering her questions. I still hadn't allowed us to dive into talking about my father's true cause of death. But that would come in time. The whole subject of his death, no matter how it happened, was something I had buried deep inside of myself a year after it happened.

I hoped I could slowly work out my emotional shortcomings. That I could push through each part of them one by one. Maybe then I would feel like I was good enough for someone. Maybe my brain didn't have to work against me. Maybe I would no longer have to be the damaged girl I had grown into.

***

(Journal entry)

I met Ben when he transferred to my school in fifth grade, but I didn't really get to know him until the summer after our sixth-grade year. He was the one who I shared my first taste of booze with, my first hit off a joint, and my first kiss.

He gave me butterflies every time he looked at me, and to me, that was what my parents had talked about from when they had met. So, he became my everything. Although I couldn't tell how he felt in return.

However, looking back, it may have just been the hormones, since they run rampant at that time in life. But back then, it felt like so much more.

We hung out almost every day—usually along with his friends. Although we had kissed and fooled around a few times, we were never anything official. Our first kiss was the summer we met, at the broken-down train car in our hometown.

Kids went there often to drink, smoke, etc. We had gone there that night with a group of friends, but they all had to get home. Ben didn't seem to care if he was late, and if he didn't care, neither did I. It would be worth a scolding from my parents to spend just a little more time with him.

We sat on the end of the train car. The older kids were making out and drinking in different areas around us. Although it was summer, the night was crisp, and I wasn't really dressed for it. Ben took off the zip-up sweatshirt he was wearing and put it around me. He wasn't really one for words, especially when his friends were around, but it felt different when it was just the two of us.

I had never kissed anyone and was very nervous and didn't know what to do next. As I thought about letting him know I wanted him to kiss me, he did. It was quick, but nice. I remember feeling knots in my stomach, but in a good way, something I hadn't felt up until that point.

After that night, I thought it would turn into something more official between us, but it didn't. He actually kept more of a distance whenever the guys were around than he had before. But, when it was just the two of us, he wanted to kiss and fool around. I was confused by it all, but didn't want him to stop, so I never asked why.

I really thought that, after a while, it would change, and we would start dating, but then he started dating Mia. It felt very sudden, but it may have been going on and I just didn't notice. By the time I did, she was around all the time.

Up until that point, I had been the only girl hanging around them. It wasn't hard for me to be the only girl, because I preferred to be one of the guys. I always had a hard time with girls. I don't know if that stemmed from the lack of connection I felt with my mother or the very real connection I had growing up with Sam.

Either way, having their relationship thrown in my face every day wasn't a form of torture I was willing to subject myself to. Looking back, I think his sudden drop of me, and love for her, is what stemmed a lot of my insecurities. Along with the feeling of not being good enough, or at least the beginning of it. I was replaced without a second thought. I felt abandoned for the second time in my life.

I've spent a majority of my time on earth nitpicking myself, so it's hard to pinpoint an exact moment it all started. I wish I would have realized at the time that Ben's feelings and actions said more about him than me. But I think that was way too complex for a fourteen-year-old to diagnose.

I blamed Mia for a long time, too, thinking she stole him somehow, not understanding that he was never mine, and that he probably never even told anyone about anything we ever did.

I felt lonelier than I had ever had up until that point in life, and being a teen, it really felt like I was going to die from heartbreak. I couldn't talk to my mother about it, as she still didn't support my interest in boys, even at that age.

After a very lonely summer, and first half of freshman year, I started dating Jacob. Doing what I could to forget Ben.

Ben had grown up on the wealthier side of town but did his best to not associate himself with it, and rarely let me interact with his parents. Although, the times I did meet them, they seemed like fine people, but he hated them.

Sometime during my senior year, rumors had gone around that his dad was abusive to him and his little brother. The summer after we graduated, I ran into him at a party. He was really drunk and got into a fight with another kid.

Amid the fighting and trash talking, his abuse got brought up. After the fight was broken up, I helped get him home since Mia hadn't come to the party, and none of his "friends" wanted to leave. On the way to his house, still drunk, he admitted that everything people had said about his dad was true.

I didn't really see him after that, so I never got the chance to talk to him about it again. Not until we were together anyway, and by then, I didn't know how to bring it up. So, I never did.

Ben was with Mia the entirety of high school, and I found out shortly after the party that night, that she had announced they were pregnant. Not long after that, they had a small wedding at a local church she attended. I still hadn't gotten over my feelings for him. Or I guess more so the closure of those feelings.

I think that was part of the reason I said no to Jacob. He had asked me to marry him shortly after their wedding. I know now what I felt for Ben all that time wasn't love. Something I would learn the hard way by dating him.

A little before my 25th birthday, Ben friend requested me on Facebook around 1:00 a.m. I was always up late those days since I worked second shift. Over the next few years, he would make the occasional comment on a picture, or like a status, but no real conversation would ensue. His wife tagged him in a lot of photos, but he rarely posted anything himself.

A little over eight months prior, he wrote to me on Facebook Messenger, keeping the app for that, but deactivated his actual Facebook. Shortly after his first message, we exchanged numbers and started talking via text.

About two weeks in, it started becoming an everyday thing, with an occasional Facetime. I started to feel bad and told him that we shouldn't talk, that it wasn't fair to Mia. He told me not to feel bad, that he and Mia were getting a divorce.

After a month of texting, we started meeting up at bars on the weekends, which quickly turned into actual dates that, not too long after, led to my bedroom. I had waited a long time to know what sex was like with Ben. I had fantasized about it many nights that I had spent alone. But the reality didn't live up to the fantasy I had created.

Not to say he wasn't good; I think I had just built it up a lot more in my head. Plus, like every other man that came after Caleb, I felt myself comparing them to him in most things. I didn't care that the sex wasn't some stupid fantasy that I had created in my mind. I wasn't alone anymore; that was all that mattered at that point.

Caleb had been with Cassy for almost five months right after I started talking to Ben. That is when Caleb and I had gotten into it. That was what really pushed me to start seeing Ben, even though part of me knew he hadn't left Mia. I had let myself believe he had, so I didn't have to be alone after everything with Caleb imploded.

One of the things I liked about Ben was that he didn't talk about subjects I didn't want to. He didn't worry about me, or constantly ask if I was okay. He didn't lovingly hold me after sex or stare adoringly into my eyes. All things that Caleb did. Things that made my anxiety grow and my body feel suffocated.

And while I found myself craving those things from Caleb once they had stopped. I knew it was better to give him up as that was the way it would inevitably end up regardless.

"Okay, so there are a few different things I would like to unwrap in there," she started with a smile almost appearing on her face.

I nodded hesitantly, worried at what specifically her takeaways were.

"So you said, 'I knew it was better to give him up as that was the way it would inevitably end up regardless'," she said, reading directly from the journal. "Why did you think you and Caleb would end?"

"Because that's the way all my relationships end up."

"What way?"

"With them leaving."

We both went silent.

"Is that why you are scared to open up to anyone? Because you think they will just leave?"

I exhaled a small laugh, "I don't just *think* they'll leave; I *know* they will. And I don't know if that's why I do it—that's why I'm here. To figure it out."

She gave a light smile. "What makes you so sure they will leave?"

"I mean, look at my past. Sam, Ben, my father, my mother, Jacob, Caleb—"

"Caleb is still around," she replied almost in his defense.

"Yeah, but he left the first time when he broke up with me."

"Why did he break up with you?"

244

"I don't know."

"You've never asked him?"

I went silent for a moment. I knew why he had left, and it had much more to do with me than him.

"Why do you think you liked that Ben didn't do the same things that Caleb did, or look at you in the same way?"

"I don't know, some sort of daddy-issue I'm sure," I replied, trying to make light of the conversation.

She didn't laugh, so I chose a different answer.

"I don't know; it just felt easier."

"Easier how?"

"There just wasn't all this baggage in the relationship. It was just us hanging out and having sex. I didn't love him, and he didn't love me."

"If you liked that, then why leave him? Was it because you found out he was married?"

I looked up at her and then back at my hands. "Partially."

I knew that made me sound like a bad person. Not running when I found out he hadn't actually left his wife.

I continued to fidget with my fingers, remaining silent for a moment while my anxiety began to build. I knew there was more she wanted to get out of me. There was more I wanted to get out in that session, too.

Despite not wanting to divulge more on the topic, my inability to hold in my word vomit, coupled with my crippling anxiety, was proving to be too much for my brain to continue in the silence.

"I found out I was pregnant around the same time that everything came out about his wife."

My throat became dry and my heartbeat quickened. But I pushed through to carry on the conversation like it wasn't an emotional black hole for me.

"How did you feel about that?" she asked. "About being pregnant, I mean."

"I didn't really know what to think or feel. I mean, financially we were fine. We were old enough. It was the direction everyone had always told me that life would go in."

She looked at me like she was trying to *will* the information out of me. "That doesn't really answer my question."

I sat completely still as I contemplated my next words carefully. "I was nervous."

She nodded like she was proud I identified a feeling. But saying it out loud just made me feel miserable.

"It's okay to be scared about something like that," she replied after a minute of silence. "A lot of people are nervous, even if they were *trying* to conceive."

"It wasn't the same. I wasn't nervous-*excited*. I was nervous-*dreadful*."

"That's still okay. What was it specifically that you were nervous about?"

"Everything," I responded with a loud exhale. "I wasn't ready to be a mother—to take care of another human being."

"People rarely are."

"Exactly, and my mother certainly wasn't, and look how that turned out. I didn't want to raise a kid and have them end up like me," I continued as I shook my head. "And I definitely don't want to end up like her."

I was worried she would take a dive down that rabbit hole, so I began again. "Besides look at Ben's parents, the pain they put him and his brother through. These are the models Ben and I have for parenting."

"Okay, well, what did Ben have to say about the pregnancy?"

"Nothing good. He was upset too. Blamed the whole thing on me. Saying I was trying to trap him like Mia did." I collected my hands in my lap and started fidgeting with my fingers. "As if he was some fucking prize everyone was just trying to hold on to."

After a brief pause, I began again. "I had a few weeks to think about it before I told him. I had considered having an abortion. Then I considered that, if I had a baby, I would have someone all to myself. Someone I could hold and teach and love freely without worrying about getting hurt or it leaving me. Because I would try to be the best parent I could. And it kind of just made all the other worries fade."

I paused for a moment. "I decided to tell him and went in with the expectation he would be angry and leave, though he was angrier than I had anticipated," I said, but then carried on. "When he left, I was upset, but I got over it. I was going to do it on my own. I didn't need anyone's help."

She smiled at my confidence—my determination—something I was sure I had yet to show in our sessions. But her smile faded, knowing the story didn't end there.

When I remained silent, she cleared her throat. I knew she was wanting me to say it out loud. She was wanting me to let the pain in.

However, instead of the pain, I felt the anger.

"But I didn't get the chance to do that," I began again. "Because It left me. It left me just like everyone else does."

Chapter Twenty-four

"Did you tell Ben you lost the baby?"

I shook my head. "But I'm sure he can guess. I saw him a few weekends ago and I wasn't exactly sober."

"Maybe he's waiting for you to say something to him. Maybe he needs that closure too. It's possible he came around and wanted to raise it with you."

Even if he had, I would have a hard time believing that he wouldn't use the circumstances to further his manipulation of me. What if he used the fetus as a pawn to try and reel me back in? What if he tried to use it as bait to try and get me to open up? To let him in? All while just wanting to hook, line, and sinker the remnants of any self-worth I had until I gave up completely.

"I know it's outside your comfort zone, but I think you both need closure. I think you should talk to him."

While I disagreed about needing the closure for myself, maybe if it really was what he needed, then telling him would end the obligation he might have thought he had to me.

I thought for a moment how it might be easier to talk about the whole experience in my journal. Or maybe writing a letter of closure to him instead of talking about it in person.

But would writing it down have been easier? Would it have been less difficult to write about the sudden pain I had been in one Thursday afternoon than to say it out loud? Or the sudden panic I felt when no one was around. What about finally calling 911 when the pain got so severe that I thought I would pass out?

Would writing down the words about being rushed to the hospital have made it less painful to relive? How about jotting down that I had learned that it was an ectopic pregnancy? Or the feeling of being relieved that I wasn't having a baby with Ben.

All of which was ultimately followed by the undeniable fact that, no matter who it was or how strong the bond could be, everyone always left. A crippling realization that trapped me in my house following my discharge from the hospital.

***

I felt bad when Serena showed up that evening, and I wasn't in the partying mood. Although, I was in the state of mind for drinking; the two were not mutually exclusive.

But I did my best to play my part of being okay and decided to lighten up my night a little more by choosing Jesse's bar as our girls' night-out spot. Hoping that having two different people for distraction would help my mind from slipping to somewhere grim.

As we walked into Joe's Sports Bar, it was completely packed, apparently far more popular on the weekends. I saw a small table near the wall open, so I grabbed Serena and went for it.

Jesse stood behind the bar, swamped with customers. There would be no time for flirting, which was a letdown. But it was nice to watch him work. He looked good back there, making drinks, smiling at women—something he did for better tips—at least that's what I told myself anyway.

Jealous already? The Voice questioned.

I ignored it, trying my best to enjoy my night out.

Fifteen minutes went by, and we hadn't even seen a waitress, so I offered to go get the drinks while Serena saved our table. I squeezed in at the bar and leaned in, hoping to get Jesse's attention.

He made his way over but was completely oblivious to my presence.

"Hey, can I get some service over here!" I yelled over the music.

He smiled as he noticed me. "Hey, good lookin'."

I smirked. "Can I get service sometime tonight?"

"I can arrange that," he said with a grin, moving up against the counter.

"I meant booze, buddy. Serena and I are thirsty."

He smiled. "What will it be?"

***

Lucky for me, sleeping with the bartender equaled free drinks. He leaned over the counter and gave me a peck kiss and a wink before going back to more orders.

"Did you just kiss the bartender?" Serena asked when I sat back down.

I smiled and took a sip of my drink. "Yeah."

"When did *that* happen?"

"The other day, Anna and I went out. I met him here and we ended up back at my place."

She clinked my glass with hers.

"So, you didn't really tell me what happened with Caleb."

I sighed. "Nothing happened. My mother found a place for me, and I moved out."

"That doesn't explain him calling me."

My eyes narrowed as I stared her down.

She knew.

"So, I'm guessing he told you about the note," I said, drinking my liquor a little faster.

"Yeah, he did. Question is, why didn't *you*?"

I shrugged and then downed the rest of my drink.

"Harper, you have been keeping a lot of shit from me lately, and I don't understand why."

I was supposed to be having fun, not diving headfirst into another therapy session.

"It's just not a big deal. Caleb's with Cassy, and we weren't being good, so I cut him out."

"What do you mean? Like you guys were still sleeping together?"

"No. Not since the reunion. But, I mean, we definitely crossed some lines. I just can't control myself with him; it's unhealthy."

"It's because you love him."

I looked at her unamused. "Of course I love him. But it's too complicated. We are better off as friends. Which we have yet to figure out how to really do."

I needed a shot.

She continued to stare at me, clearly wanting more out of the answer.

"We're supposed to be having fun tonight. I need fun!" I said, giving her a pitiful look.

"Does that really work on people?" she asked, making us laugh.

"Sometimes."

She rolled her eyes.

"But usually because there is sex involved," I added with a grin.

She laughed and then finished her drink.

"I need a shot," I finally said out loud.

She nodded and went to the bar, coming back with four shots and a drink for each of us.

"Bartender guy seems to be smitten with you," she commented, as she set the tray of drinks down on the table.

I looked over his way, catching his gaze, and we exchanged smiles.

Jesse was what I needed. He was fun and kind. It was like how it had been with me meeting Caleb after Jacob had left. Currently, I wasn't looking for love. But I was also trying to steer clear of a path that led to someone like Ben.

Trying to find someone just too dull the loneliness was a problematic road to travel. And I was confident that the roadmap of my life would show grooves in the pavement.

My time with Jesse had me driving off-road, tracking through unfamiliar territory. He made for a fun time, and maybe, someday, the potential for more.

Not very likely, The Voice stated. *Men don't marry girls like you.*

They only fucked girls like me.

I downed a shot as if the sting of alcohol would set fire to the nagging voice and incinerate the derogatory thoughts.

I quickly followed it up by downing the second one. Serena was too preoccupied with my Caleb mess to give me her raised eyebrow glance and the "are you good" line of questioning.

It left me wondering how long he had talked to her on the phone. I hoped they weren't becoming friends. It was supposed to be a break from seeing each other. I didn't need us to be forced to be around each other by sudden mutual friends. I really didn't need the two of them talking in general. I was worried they were forming a pact to show a united front on how to handle Harper.

After another two hours of hard-drinking, Serena and I called it a night. She called for an Uber back to my place, while I went to say bye to Jesse in private.

He got Jenna to take over at the bar, and we went out back, right outside the door where we had been just a few nights before.

"I'm having a really hard time not ripping that off of you right now," he said kissing me on the lips.

"Don't fight it."

He moved his lips down to my neck. "You're making this night seem like it's taking forever."

"Tell me about it. Now I have to go home and lay naked in bed with no one there."

He sighed and kissed my lips again. "Alright, I'll go quit and we'll leave together," he responded, acting as if he was going to march back inside.

"Don't do that," I replied with a laugh, pulling him back to me. "I will sleep fully clothed until you can join me."

"That doesn't really help," he said, looking me up and down.

"There's no winning with you," I replied, biting my bottom lip.

We stayed pressed up against the building with lips locked for a few more minutes before he had to go back in.

"I'll text you tomorrow," he said, as I headed away from him.

I nodded and gave a small wave as I concentrated on doing a sober walk.

But the heels mixed with the four shots and four drinks were proving to have more control over me than whatever my mind's intentions were.

As I turned the corner, I spotted Serena past the sea of people in line. She was looking at her phone, standing next to what I assumed was our Uber. I looked at my phone as I walked toward her. She had already texted me three times.

"Harper?" a familiar voice said, stopping me in my tracks.

Ben looked at me perplexed, but then his expression shifted. The ends of his lips curled into a smile.

I, on the other hand, felt the hard-hit of his presence and the sudden exit of all breath in my body.

"Harper, dude, let's go!" Serena shouted as she spotted me.

"Uh, hi. I, uh, have to go," I said, trying to walk past him.

He stepped out of line to block me. "I've been calling you. You said you would answer."

I tried not to look annoyed, but I wasn't sure how well I was doing with that. "I've been dealing with a lot—"

"Yeah, I saw your house burned down last week," he interrupted. "I was trying to see if you were okay."

He put his hand on my upper arm.

A rush of nausea ran through my stomach. I didn't want him or his hand anywhere near me.

"Yeah, I'm fine. Just a little burn."

I moved slightly so he could tell his touch was unwelcomed while showing him my injured hand.

"We really need to talk," he said. "Could we please have dinner tomorrow?"

I glanced over at Serena who literally looked like she was going to murder me.

"Uh, yeah, I guess," I replied, trying not to sound like I was dreading it too much.

"Great," he said with a smile I hadn't seen since we had first started dating.

"I'll call you tomorrow for your address," he continued as he caught my glance at Serena, so he turned and waved.

Her death glare didn't waver at either of us, so I broke eye contact.

"Uh, no, I'll just meet you."

"Okay, well, let's meet at Johnny's on Northland Drive. Does six sound good?"

I chose to nod as I was confident if I opened my mouth right then that there would be more than word vomit spewing out.

I walked past him and met Serena at the Uber. She shook her head—I knew it had nothing to do with me being late.

"What the hell was that?" she yelled as she shut the door behind her.

"I'm sorry," I responded and gave the Uber driver an apologetic look.

He didn't seem to notice.

"I didn't know he was here," I continued. "I was saying bye to Jesse."

She looked at me with disbelief.

"Seriously. I just ran into him while he was standing in line."

"What did he have to say?" she asked, calming down some and looking out the window.

"He asked me to dinner tomorrow," I replied, although I should have kept that to myself.

She turned to look at me. "And you said *hell no*, right?"

I remained silent, keeping the answer I gave him to myself. But she didn't need me to speak; the lack of reply was enough for her to know.

She shook her head. "Jesus, girl, you really know how to fuck things up."

I wished I could give her an explanation. But it was a little too late as there was far too much baggage to unpack in the situation I had found myself in.

***

Although I had made plans with *Ben* and had spent some time kissing *Jesse*, I couldn't help but think about *Caleb* as I fell asleep. He was so easy to talk to, whether it was as a friend or more than that.

Jesse seemed to be the same way, but it was so early, and I barely knew him. I was so nervous at the possibility of getting myself wrapped up in another Ben-type situation.

Though Jesse didn't seem at all like him, I had thought Ben was different in the beginning too. He was so charming and charismatic and, as if I had never seen a soap opera or a drama-filled movie in my life, I ignored the signs that I was being manipulated and controlled. So, before I knew it, he had hung up all the red flags for me to see. And instead of running for the hills, I looked at the beautiful shade of red and thought, *I can work with that.*

With Caleb, though, his flags were yellow. They served as a caution for me, but only after I had fallen for him, and vice versa. But his flags were different. They didn't have to do with shitty personality traits or ways he could tear me down. They were a warning of what we could do to each other because of how we felt. I knew that sounded stupid to people; I was reminded of that often by Serena. But our past, my lies, our conflicting views on almost everything, all stemmed into one intense relationship.

It was an intensity that brought down all the barriers around us, one that could be felt so deep that, when we were together, we threw all caution to the wind. I was confident he would eventually see me for the horribly damaged person I was and finally leave for good.

While I had purposely ignored any conversation he had attempted to have over the years on how he felt about me, I knew he held similar insecurities that had set the stage for both of us to be ticking time bombs for one another's happiness.

But although the yellow flags had flown for many years, staying away was hard. Because, in the good moments, the rationalizations I made for us being together, even as fuck buddies, made sense. And whether I said it to him or not, I did love him.

It was something I hadn't allowed myself to admit until he told me he loved me eight months before. I didn't say it back to him, but I had felt it in my entire body that night as I had cried myself to sleep.

Chapter Twenty-five

The following evening, I pulled into the restaurant's rear parking lot at ten to six and saw that Ben's car was already parked. I knew I had to go in and face him—have the conversation with yet another person about something I would have rather never brought up again. But if that was the only way to keep me from having to see him again in any formal capacity, I would do it.

As I stepped out of the car, my phone pinged, allowing me to delay my arrival for a few seconds more.

Jesse: Are you coming to Joe's at all tonight?

Harper: No, I'm having dinner with a friend. Text me tomorrow?

I would have felt worse about seeing Ben if I thought anything could potentially happen between us. Serena didn't seem as confident in my inability to backslide. I understood given my track record, but a little assurance that I *could* resist his charm would have been nice.

Instead, before she left, she gave me a lecture about how I shouldn't be getting mixed up with Ben again. Reminding me about Jesse, and that I had a tendency of messing things up. But at least her voice sounded more reasonable than hurtful—unlike the one in my own head.

***

When I got inside, he was already seated at a small booth in the back of the restaurant. The softer lighting made his suit and posture look less severe. But the severity of his appearance told me nothing; it was his eyes that were the direct giveaway to his mood.

"Hey, beautiful," he said, as I walked to the table and took a seat.

"Hey," I responded, avoiding eye contact, then looking down at the menu.

He sighed and reached across the table for my hand. "I know we left things in a really bad place before—"

I glanced at his hand that rested on mine, scowling at him as our eyes met.

He smiled, seeming almost intrigued by my demeanor and pulled back his hand. He shifted comfortably in his seat and opened the menu. "I wanted to let you know—the divorce is final."

I had absolutely no idea what he expected me to say to that, so I didn't look up right away. But when I finally did, he looked annoyed at my lack of reaction.

As he was known to do, he quickly moved on. "I was so worried when I saw your house on the news," he began again, nodding at the waiter who was dropping off some water.

"What can I get you to drink?" the waiter asked.

"I'll have a neat scotch, two fingers please," Ben replied, "and she'll have vodka cranberry."

"Oh, no thanks; just the water is fine," I responded as I smiled politely at the waiter who nodded and walked away.

"Still hungover from last night, huh?" he asked with a chuckle but still seeming annoyed at the same time. "You looked pretty wasted, not to mention when I saw you at your house."

I didn't know what to say, but from his ability to do all the talking, I was sure that wasn't a problem.

"Seems to me you've been hitting it pretty hard lately," he continued again with feigned amusement.

He sighed as my perplexed expression had yet to fall from my face.

He set down his menu on the table and looked almost sympathetic. "Listen, I just want you to know that I appreciate you... you know, taking care of the— *problem*," he said, quickly glancing down at my stomach, then back up to my eyes.

It took a second before I finally understood that he thought I had an abortion.

"How do—"

"I thought maybe I was wrong," he interrupted. "When I showed up to your house the night of the reunion, I thought you were drunk. But I knew you wouldn't drink if you were still pregnant. So, I thought maybe I was just mistaken. But then last night... I knew for sure. And I—I just really appreciate you understanding the situation."

I wasn't angry that he thought I was capable of having an abortion because it had been an option I was seriously considering. The anger I felt was stemming from his narcissism on the subject, from the clearly illogical thought that I would do it for *him*.

His eyes glistened off the chandelier that hung above the table. His modest grin grew twofold, showing the elation he was experiencing over me "understanding the situation." I couldn't quite tell if he had it in his mind that his leaving his wife and me no longer being with child indicated that we could start over. But I hoped that, by the end of the night, he would understand that while I *was* trying to do just that, it certainly would not be with *him*.

He went on to talk the night away about his pending divorce and how glad he was that he was finally going through with it—stating how rough it was feeling *stuck* for years.

The whole conversation made me nauseous. My brain hurt, wondering how I had put up with how self-involved he was. How little he actually cared for the people around him.

Did he even notice I was having a shitty time? How could he not tell I didn't even want to be there?

After finishing our meal, he insisted on walking me to my car. Something I only complied with to avoid making a scene in the restaurant. I was hoping the walk to the car was the last time I would ever have to see him.

After exiting the building, we walked around the corner to head to my car. I watched as his shoe caught on the pavement causing him to lose his balance for a moment.

"Maybe you should call an Uber," I stated.

While I was more worried about the safety of others rather than him, I still knew as soon as I said it that I shouldn't have.

His expression shifted. "Jesus Christ, Harper. I had a few drinks, not an entire bottle like some of us are known to do."

I took a deep breath, wanting to get the night over with and be done with him for good. Although he didn't know the truth of the situation that had severed the one thing that had tied us together, he was at least aware that it had, in fact, been severed.

"I'm sorry. That was uncalled for," he said in a surprising change of pace. "I've always found your intoxication charming."

I leaned my hip up against my car. "Thanks," I replied. "Well, good..."

"I'm sorry," he interrupted.

I looked at him perplexed, wondering if he was drunker than I originally thought.

"Yeah, you already said that—"

A genuine smile crept to his face. One that showed me a small glimpse at the boy I had met so many years before at the concession stand at a football game.

"I mean, I'm sorry about what you had to do. I know it must have been hard for you," he said, taking my hand in his, and annoyingly enough, I didn't resist.

It was hard to tell if he was experiencing genuine emotion or if he was just trying to reel me in with his manipulations once again.

But whether it was just another manipulation or not, I couldn't help feeling bad knowing that I wasn't any better than him and that I messed with people's heads and hearts in my own way too.

"Thank you, but…"

As I geared up to tell him what really happened, he continued instead.

"I really think you did the right thing, Harper. I mean, not just for me. You would've hated the whole mom thing. It was hard for Mia, and she was actually good with kids."

The moment of sympathy I had for him vanished from my body, leaving only bitter, resentful thoughts in its place. My mind shouted angrily at him while he continued to list all the reasons that I couldn't have handled it.

"—That's what I love about you," he said, pulling me away from my thoughts.

He had never said he loved me before.

"What?" I asked without the slightest hint of fury, as I was so confused at where the conversation had ended up in my daydreamed absence.

"You're crazy," he said sweetly as if the tone of voice made the connotation behind the word any better. "And sexy, and well, a little spacey, but I can get past that."

I was having a hard time understanding what exactly was happening.

"And now we can start over. We can be more careful this time," he continued.

He put his hand on my cheek, gently stroking it with his thumb.

And with having felt almost every emotion that night, my brain had a litter of reactions to choose from. And while fucking things up and sleeping with him was my default, my mind did something completely unexpected.

I laughed.

It was a laugh of disbelief, so more like a deep exhale with furrowed eyebrows, but a laugh, nonetheless.

The world moved slowly as I realized what I had done. My audible rejection of his feelings sent the calm and loving man into hiding.

His expression changed, along with his tone.

"Oh, I'm sorry, do you have someone better in mind?"

He let his hand fall to his side.

I tried to fight the urge to be combative and just talk to him straight.

"This has nothing to do with me and you. Single or not, I don't want to be with you," I replied blankly.

Leaving noncombative Harper to play catch up, I continued. "Ben, you lied to me for months. You *used* me for months. And then, when I tell you about the baby, you say I'm trying to trap you." I shook my head and turned to open my door.

"None of that matters anymore," he responded as if he was confused by my outrage.

I turned back to him, losing the fight against the urge to compress my combative nature. "Why? Because *you* say it doesn't?" I questioned.

I hated that he didn't understand why I wouldn't want to try again. Not just because of that night or his wife, but because he was controlling, selfish, and, well, a prick.

"I'm sorry for everything I said. But we had good times, too," he replied, putting his hand on my hip.

And as if my words weren't combative enough, my eyes did a twirl, glancing briefly at the night sky.

Fuck.

I had been so good at keeping that in check all night. I had a moment of hope that he would let it go, but his expression changed, and his hand fell once again back to his side.

"Seriously?" he said.

I swallowed hard as my heart started to beat faster. But my nerves changed as my jaw clenched and my body grew tense.

"God, Ben, were you even *there* the whole time we were dating?" I took a ragged breath. "You really don't see how much of a controlling asshole you are, do you?" I shook my head and started to open my car door once more to make a swift exit. I was hoping to not let my anger get the best of me as it had before.

But while my rational side had prevented an outburst of anger from me, Ben's didn't seem to be doing its job. He slammed the door back shut. "Did you ever think that maybe I'm a controlling asshole because of *you*? That maybe *someone* needs to be in control since you don't seem to have any over *yourself*?"

Before I could come to my own defense, as if I had a defense, he continued.

"You are nothing but a broken, pathetic *bitch* and have been since the day I met you."

His eyes were narrow, and his grin was wicked. The words came out smoothly like he had wanted to say that for some time.

Rational Harper jumped ship as my brain capsized in a sea of insecurities. My impulse control floated away and left my temper to go down with the ship. A temper that manifested itself into another round of physical assault as my palm connected with his face.

I felt a rush of pain as I held back tears of anger and then, in the same moment, felt the sting of his hand across my cheek. Then once more, from my head hitting the car.

"Are you serious?" he said as he ran his hand along his jawline. "Is that all you got?"

I should have punched him. I should still be punching him.

You won't do anything, The Voice said. *You're too fucking scared.*

"Fuck you!" I shouted.

I felt as if I was reliving our last night together all over. And again, I had come ill-prepared with comebacks and forethought as to how I was going to handle the situation.

"Didn't think this one through, huh? No bedroom to hide in this time."

His eyes got darker than I had ever seen them before. He pinned me up against the car with his hand pressed firmly against my throat.

My chest tightened as I gasped for the oxygen that was freely floating around us but was unattainable to me at that moment.

"Bitch, I've been fighting grown-ass men since I was eight," he said in a sinister tone with his grip growing tighter. "Do you really think anything you could do would hurt me?" he whispered into my ear.

I should've seen that his temper could lead to that. I should've known he was capable of hurting me. As my resistance grew weak and my arms grew heavy, he released his grip and shoved me to the ground like a discarded rag doll.

To be fair, you did hit him first, The Voice said as I laid amongst the dirt and gravel, trying to refill my lungs.

The Voice had been right on cue. Of course it was my fault.

My body tensed up seeing him bring his leg back, looking to do what karma had been doing to me for years—kicking me while I was down.

"I called the cops!" I heard an older man shout as I stared at the front of Ben's over-priced shoe.

He stepped back, as I lay frozen between the two cars. He paused only briefly before storming away, climbing into his car, and driving off.

I was pissed that, after all my time spent in the ring boxing with Caleb, I didn't use a single thing I had learned. I wanted to blame it on being caught off guard, but we had trained for that, too.

The man who had shouted at Ben approached me as I moved to rest my back on my car. "I haven't called the cops yet. I just wanted to get him to stop. My phone's inside. We can call from in there."

I shook my head. "No— no, I'm fine."

He knelt by me. "You don't look fine. Your face is bleeding."

I touched my hand to my right temple and felt warm liquid on the tips of my fingers. I could taste it coming from my lip as well.

"It's okay. I can drive. I'll just head to the hospital," I replied, using the car to help me stand.

"Please, just come inside," he pleaded.

I was sure he gathered that I had no intention of actually going to get checked out.

"It's fine, really. I'll head straight to the hospital and get looked at," I responded, trying my best to be convincing.

I gently took my purse from his outstretched hand and got into my car. I wiped the blood from my fingers onto my jeans as I turned the keys in the ignition. While pulling away, I caught his stare in my rearview mirror. His dejected, sorrowful look seized my chest, setting free a singular tear that was only the prelude for the others that would follow.

Chapter Twenty-six

My vehicle slowed as I approached a red light. I gripped the steering wheel tightly as my mind relived the entire night. It replayed everything I had said, everything I had done, causing me to wonder what specifically it was that got me on the universe's bad side.

I looked to my right, catching a glimpse of an old sign I had seen many times before. Although the sign rang familiar to my memory, the building itself had changed. The facelift took away the chipped paint, replaced the missing shingles, and filled the potholes in the cement.

Everything looks better without you around, The Voice said.

I felt tears well up in my eyes as I thought back to why I had started going to the gym in the first place. And the vow I had made to myself that I would never again be the victim.

My chest felt heavy.

How did I let it happen again? How was I not prepared? I knew better. Everything Caleb had taught me. Everything I had learned—wasted.

The sound of impatience erupted from the car behind me, causing my eyes to notice the glow of the green light. I quickly signaled a turn and pulled into the almost empty lot.

How did I keep finding trouble? What was wrong with me?

I put my head on the steering wheel as my heart started to pound in my ears.

Are you really asking that? The Voice questioned. *You can't possibly be this stupid. Look at yourself. You're a fucking mess!*

"Shut up!" I said to myself, gritting through my teeth.

I swallowed a lump that had formed in my throat.

Was that really how my life was going to go? One bad decision after the next?

I felt my chest tighten again as it grew hard to breathe.

Oh great, another panic attack, The Voice said. *Caleb wouldn't have done this to you,* it added as the heartbeat grew louder. *You brought this on yourself.*

It was right; I had.

You chose to say no to Jacob. You chose to go to that party alone. You chose to leave Caleb. You chose to be with Ben. You chose to see him tonight instead of seeing Jesse. You did this—all of this. You have no one to blame but yourself.

I gripped the steering wheel tighter, shutting my eyes, doing my best to concentrate on my breathing and drown out my thoughts.

"Harper?" a barely audible voice questioned.

I chose not to respond as I continued to concentrate on controlling my breathing, doing my best to pull myself out of the sea of hopelessness I was starting to drown in. I continued to firmly clutch the wheel. I still felt the tears rolling down my face, but they seemed to be falling at a faster pace than what everything else was moving at.

I heard the door open. "Harper."

I felt a hand touch my shoulder, making me flinch. My eyes shot open, but the blurriness of the tears prevented me from seeing clearly.

I blinked to remove them as I turned my head, noticing Caleb beside me.

"Jesus, Harper!" He knelt by my car and took my face in his hands. "What the fuck happened?"

Our eyes met briefly.

I had happened—my bad decision happened.

I let my hands fall from the steering wheel, not realizing how tight I had been gripping it. They proceeded to tremble as I balled them into fists on my lap.

While my focus shifted once more, I turned my body toward Caleb.

I tried again to speak but couldn't. I took another deep breath. I could tell my silence was making him think the worst.

I was so glad to see him. I was relieved he was there. I didn't want to be alone.

Of course you don't, The Voice rang in again. *That's literally the feeling that fuels all your dumb decisions.*

I closed my eyes and put my hands over my ears as if the thoughts were coming in externally.

How about you quit dragging people into your chaos? The Voice continued once more.

"Stop," I responded in a barely audible tone.

But telling it to do so didn't make a difference as it continued to berate me. *I mean, why are you even here? Why did you pull in? Why didn't you just go home? Because you're needy! You're pathetic! You're crazy! You're everything Ben described. If Caleb didn't see it before, he sees it now!*

"Stop!" I shouted, that time hearing myself very clearly through my plugged ears.

"Harper!" Caleb repeated. "Harper, talk to me," he attempted to say sternly, but his voice trembled.

I remained silent for another moment, hoping The Voice was letting up.

"Harper. What happened?"

I took a ragged breath.

"Nothing," I finally managed to say, successfully quieting the noisiness in my mind.

How was it that even when my brain couldn't control anything else, it still held the reflex to lie and say that nothing had happened? Why was my autopilot reaction to try and control the narrative that I was fine? That I was *always* fine.

His worried expression lingered on his face, but it didn't hide his frustration. Which I understood, as I was, too. I was frustrated that I let it happen again. Frustrated that I ran to Caleb. Frustrated that I was repeating all my same bad habits.

I took a deep breath as I looked at him again. "It's nothing, really." I tucked my hair behind my ear and tried to give a reassuring smile. "You should see the other guy," I joked, swallowing back a sob.

"Who was it?"

His concerned look turned to rage in one fell swoop.

"Don't worry about it, please," I replied but knew he wouldn't let it go at that. "I shouldn't be here. I need to go," I continued as I reached for the door.

His expression softened a little. "Don't," he responded, putting his hand on mine. "Please let me help."

I wanted to leave. I wanted to listen to my brain that was shouting to continue with the break I had made us take. To stop bringing other people into my mess, to stop showing him all the crazy that would eventually push him away.

I wanted to listen, yet, I couldn't bring myself to shut the door.

Just once I wished I could do the right thing.

Caleb helped me out of the car and walked me inside the gym. There were only two other people there, but they seemed focused enough on what they were doing to not notice the frail woman in their midst.

Caleb took me to the locker room and grabbed the first aid kit out of a side locker.

We sat in silence as he wiped down the cut on my temple, and I held a cold washcloth to my cheek. I felt bruises forming on my ass, elbow, and hip. Ben's words to me bounced around in my head, syncing with my own internal voice.

You're a broken, pathetic, crazy bitch, it said on repeat.

It was right; *he* was right. I had always known how shitty of a person I was, but I let that be my excuse to do shitty things. Caleb was the person who usually ended up with the shit end of the stick in my self-centered mess of a life.

I was pathetic. I was broken. I was crazy.

I was a bitch.

I didn't need The Voice to tell me that.

"What happened to everything you learned?" Caleb finally asked, breaking the silence with his disappointment.

"I... I don't know. It all happened so fast. I wasn't expecting it. He's never done that before."

He stopped moving his hand. "You *know* him?"

Oops.

"Yeah, but it's okay; it's done with. I won't be seeing him again."

His face was frozen with anger. "This isn't okay, Harper. You need to stop getting yourself into these situations."

While he was right, I couldn't help but be defensive. "Are you implying this is *my* fault?"

He sighed. I knew that wasn't what he meant. Even worse, I *did* think it was my fault.

"No, I'm just saying, if you're not going to let me look out for you, you need to look out for yourself."

A tear ran down my cheek as my adrenaline had run its course. I started to feel helpless and tired. "I don't know what I keep doing wrong."

He sighed again and then put his arms around me and pulled me into his chest.

"You're not doing anything wrong. I'm sorry I said that."

We stayed like that, in silence, for a few minutes as he stroked my hair.

I lifted my head from his chest to look up at him. "Why are you here? I thought you only came during the week."

"I have nothing better to do with my time. And you just kind of took off," he replied with no real inflection.

"How about doing what I said and spend time with your girlfriend?"

"We broke up," he responded way more casually than I felt he should have.

"You *what*?" I shifted back from him.

"It just wasn't working."

He stood up from the bench and put the first aid kit back into the locker.

"Why? Because of *me*?" I asked.

"No, because we just weren't connecting."

I stood up frustrated with both him and I. "Maybe because you were spending too much time *connecting* with *me*."

"Hey, I wasn't the only one there," he said, like that somehow made it any better.

The room fell silent again, causing my anxiety to start spinning its wheels.

He was right. Both of us were complicit in any wrongdoing. But that was exactly why the break was needed.

"You should call her, see if she'll take you back. I'm giving you some space—"

"But I don't *want* any space from you," he replied, taking a step toward me.

"Caleb, I really can't do this. We've had this talk already. I can't keep having it."

I was dumb for being there. For doing that to him again. For letting him be my knight in shining armor. I had gotten exactly what I was looking for. And he was getting the emotionally repressed woman who did nothing but make bad choices.

"I shouldn't be here," I continued exasperatedly.

"But you are. You're here for a reason. Listen, I promise no more shit between us if that means you'll stick around."

"It's not that easy, Caleb, and you know it. I want that, too, but I think we just need more time apart. Maybe a little longer this time."

"What is a little longer going to do? Doesn't it tell you something that we can't just be friends?" he asked, looking defeated. "We had something good before. Why can't we get back to that?"

I sighed.

I wished he understood that we weren't those same people. Or at least, that I wasn't that same girl.

He walked the rest of the way towards me and took my hands in his. I looked up at him, and he brought his lips down to meet mine. I let them linger for a minute before I pulled away.

He looked down at me, and I rested my head on his chest. The close proximity to the man I loved sent my thoughts into a tailspin.

When would he see that we wouldn't work? That we shouldn't be together? That I made his life harder. That I was no longer the woman that he once loved. That I was saving us both from heartache—from the potential of losing each other for good when he finally saw that.

We both ignored the sunshine-colored flags that were warning us that we weren't going to work. One of us had to stop disregarding them and take action. One of us had to pull away before hate became the only feeling we had left for each other.

Because I didn't want to hate someone who had done all that he had for me, and I didn't want to live in a world where he despised me. And at some point, I knew I would do something that would make that happen.

My eyes met his as I felt hopeless against the decision I had made for us years before.

I didn't know why I wasn't saying any of it out loud. Maybe I wasn't ready to admit to him that I wouldn't change my mind. I had told him he shouldn't love me, but I had never said that I didn't love him back. I had never told him anything that would take away any hope of him getting what he wanted. But I was worried that taking away that hope might take him away for good. A fear that would continue to drive my every move.

I pulled away and wiped a remaining tear from the corner of my eye. "Thank you for helping me," I said.

I looked down, grabbed my keys off the bench, and walked away.

***

I almost made it to the front door when the sound of fists landing on the punching bag tugged on a long-forgotten memory. The smell of sweat, cologne, and musty carpet made it break free, bringing it to the forefront of my mind.

I shut my eyes as a flash of Caleb holding the bag steady in front of me appeared. A recollection that seemed suddenly so clear as if it was yesterday and not almost seven years before.

I became flushed thinking of the sweat that ran down my back, soaking into the tank top that clung to my skin. My gloves pounding against the smooth leather that remained strong at my feeble attempts to injure it.

I continued to swing, landing every punch I threw. My form wasn't where it needed to be at that point. I could feel that with every swift motion. But the pain just fueled me.

I could hear Caleb's voice instructing me—coaching me along, but I didn't care about that either. I didn't care if my form was right or that my body ached. I wanted to not only break the heavy bag but break down its will to live.

You're projecting, The Voice said.

I was projecting. The bag was nothing more than me taking the anger out on myself. With every punch, every ragged breath, every shot of pain, it brought me just a little closer to ending the life I once had. Letting go of the woman I had been and would never again be.

As I landed my final swing, Caleb called it quits and stepped aside.

"It got pretty intense there for a minute," he commented as we walked to the locker rooms.

"Yup," I managed to say, still trying to catch my breath.

I dabbed the sweat off my forehead with a towel and took a swig out of my water bottle.

"Anything you wanna talk about?"

"No," I replied, trying to act unfazed as if I hadn't just pictured myself as that bag. As if I hadn't metaphorically left my former self lying beaten to death on the gym floor.

"Wanna grab a bite to eat?"

"I wanna shower," I responded, trying my best to still seem casual about my latest workout.

He shook his head. "I meant after a shower."

"I'm not really hungry. But you're welcome to stop by my place."

His brows furrowed.

"If you want," I added as I disappeared into the locker room.

***

Caleb's truck pulled into my driveway shortly after I myself had arrived home.

He was barely inside the door before I pushed him up against the wall, my lips meeting his for the first time in what seemed like centuries. But I sensed some hesitation on his end. I was sure he was confused. I certainly couldn't blame him if he was.

He pulled his jacket off the rest of the way and then wrapped his arms around me.

"You look really beautiful," he commented like I was the one who needed the warm-up.

"Shut up," I responded with an eye roll.

As we got to my bedroom, he pulled off his shirt, and I pulled off mine. I pushed him onto the bed and climbed on top of him. Moving my lips to his neck, I felt his body shift as he gently pulled away.

"Harper, what does this mean?"

Was he seriously asking that now?

I moved my lips back to his mouth, trying to subtly shut him up.

Once again, he removed mine from his, that time making eye contact with me. "What are we doing?"

"What do you mean?" I asked, being purposefully obtuse.

He put his hand on my hip and motioned for me to move.

I sighed, climbed off of him, and sat on my bed.

He stood up and ran his hand through his hair, pausing briefly before turning to me. "I don't understand what's going on. Four months ago, you broke up with me..."

"Actually, you left me..." I started to say, but the look he shot at me shut that right down. While, yes, he had been the one who left, we both knew I was the motivating factor behind that happening.

"— then you show up to the gym, ask to train with me, and now what?"

"Sex," I replied, raising an eyebrow.

"Yes, sex. Now sex?"

"I don't understand the problem?" I asked, throwing my head back onto my pillow.

"Are you wanting to get back together?"

I let out a small laugh.

His expression told me he wasn't as amused as I was.

"Sorry. Uh, no. I'm not looking to get back together."

"Then, what is this? Why did you start coming to the gym? To my gym?"

"Because I wanted you to teach me how to box."

"Okay, and I've been doing that. So why am I here in your house?"

"You're here because I invited you, and then you accepted."

Again, he didn't look amused.

I took a deep breath. "I'm not looking for anything serious. I just want to have some fun. I thought you would be into that."

"I am."

"Okay, then why are my pants still on?" I asked with a smirk.

His lips curled into a grin, but I knew that wasn't going to be the end of the conversation.

He climbed back into the bed, gently putting his body on mine.

I knew that he still felt something for me. If I hadn't gathered it from the brief conversation we had just had, his kiss would have given it away.

Guilt started to reveal itself, but I didn't have time for guilty thoughts or the feelings he had that wouldn't be reciprocated.

But while I pushed away the guilt and the feelings I was in denial over, anxiety was able to take over.

His body suddenly felt heavy on mine. At the same time, my lungs seemed to stop working, and then my mouth went dry.

Even with Caleb, it was happening. It didn't matter who I was with. I was broken.

I pushed hard at Caleb's body. For a moment, I knew I had him worried. But I played it off as part of the role. We were fuck friends now. I didn't want to make love. I didn't want to be held and cared for. I just wanted to be in control.

I climbed on top of him, taking charge of my room, my bed, and my body. He did what I wanted and touched me where I wanted.

And with that, he made me release months upon months of built-up rage and sadness, along with emotions I never even knew I was capable of.

Caleb didn't know how big of a moment that was for me. He didn't know what the months before that had been like. But I had done my best to make it seem as casual as I had previously presented it as.

***

After we had finished, I stood up and pulled my underwear back on. I glanced at him as he appeared to be making himself comfortable. He placed his hands behind his head while my eyes drifted down until they met the beginning of the sheet. I swallowed hard as I told myself to stay strong.

I tossed his jeans to him and reached for mine.

"What? I can't stay over?" he asked with a grin while he rolled on to his side.

"No."

"Do you have plans?"

"No."

"Is this all I'm good for?" he asked with a quiet laugh.

"This and boxing lessons."

The room fell silent. I looked over as his expression softened.

"I'm kidding," I began, taking a seat on the bed next to him. "But I wasn't kidding when I said I don't want anything serious. I don't want you staying over. I don't want to go to dinner. I don't want presents or long talks—"

I continued my list until I felt his hand on mine. "I don't want to hold hands..." I added, causing him to slowly pull his hand away.

"I get it," he replied.

But I knew he didn't. He was just saying that so that I would stop talking. But I needed him to if he wanted to continue doing what we had just done.

"Do you?" I asked, making eye contact to get a feel for his true reaction.

"Yeah," he answered after a brief pause. "So, does this mean this is going to happen again?"

"Only if you want it to," I replied with a grin.

The sound of a door shutting loudly echoed through the gym. The men that had been practicing were nowhere to be found, leaving me embarrassed at my ability to drift away to another time.

I walked to my car as the feelings from that first day of Caleb's and my arrangement clung tightly to my chest.

The memory came with such torment to me. While it was a big step for me personally, it was just the beginning of our teetering relationship.

My brain continued to play memories of the two of us on loop in my head as I drove home and climbed into bed. The images of our time together finally succumbed to my exhaustion, and I soon felt relief as they faded out to black.

Chapter Twenty-seven

I woke up the next morning the same as I had been, only that time, I was able to add a stiff, achy body to the list.

My phone lit up, and I slowly reached for it, trying carefully not to make any sudden moves. Jesse's name on my screen only made the feelings of stupidity from my previous night reveal themselves and take up shop.

I read his text. His nice, normal invite to lunch didn't help the feeling subside. And as much as normal sounded perfect right then, I was in no condition to go out. In reality, I was in no condition to be seen.

Harper: I'm just not feeling well today. Raincheck?

Jesse: I'm sorry, I could come over and take care of you;)

Harper: it's okay, I'm sure I'll feel better tomorrow.

Jesse: How about I at least bring you some soup?

I didn't want him to get the impression that I was blowing him off, so I allowed impulsive Harper to take the driver's seat. She was usually right there anyway.

Impulsive Harper? The Voice questioned. *Don't you mean* deceitful *Harper?*

It wasn't deceitful to tell him I wasn't feeling well. But it was both impulsive and deceitful to say it was because I had taken a fall down the stairs when attempting to do laundry.

But deceptive behavior allowed me to have my cake and eat it too. Jesse would be able to see me, and it prevented all follow-up questions of my past.

When he didn't respond, I took that to mean he was coming over.

That, or he knows you lied, The Voice said.

But, for once, that wasn't a worry of mine. Jesse didn't know me and my past well enough to even think I would lie about that. Although, the excuse itself had me a little worried. But I let impulsive Harper do the talking, so I had to trust she could see it through.

***

When Jesse arrived, the door was barely opened before his expression shifted to the worried look I had come to loathe.

"Holy shit, Harper," he said, taking my face into his hands just like Caleb had done the night before.

I winced, gave a soft smile, then gently pulled away.

We walked to the couch as my body tingled with embarrassment.

His worried expression didn't leave his face. "Did you go to the hospital?" he asked, taking my hand in his.

"No, I'm okay, just a little banged up. Besides, I'm way too embarrassed."

290

"What if you have a concussion?" he asked as his brows furrowed.

"I woke up this morning, so I must be good." I chuckled.

"Still," he began, smiling back. "I think you should get checked out."

I shook my head. "I'm fine, really, just having some bad luck lately."

"Is there anything I can get you?" he asked.

I thought about the pills I had flushed a few days before. I regretted my sudden strike in morality.

"I'll take some Tylenol. But I don't think I have any here."

He kissed me before exiting out the front door.

I ran my fingers across my lips as a wave of guilt rushed over me. I thought back to my moment with Caleb the night before.

***

Jesse stayed with me all day, watching movies as we laid curled up on the couch. With his arm around me and his fingers intertwined with mine, I felt uncomfortable with the resistance my heart held to my head. But as distressed as my insides were at the affection he showed, I stayed planted in place. Hoping the affection would eventually smother the resistance out completely.

When dinner time came, he insisted on cooking for me. I didn't put up much of a fight against that one since I had forgotten to eat breakfast or lunch.

While he attempted to charm me with his chef skills, I decided to shower, hoping to relax my body. Between the terrible excuse of a fight the night before, and my body's knee-jerk reaction to tense up at someone showing a fondness for me, I needed a moment to unwind.

I tried and failed to lift my shirt over my head as I avoided myself in the mirror. I instead attempted to take off my pants, but the muscles in my legs worked against me, causing me to let out a small but audible sob.

I gave up.

I wished at that moment that Serena was there again to help me. But I knew her being there would bring on the judgmental tone of seeing Ben, and then, shortly after, the concerned look of not being able to take care of myself.

I opened the bathroom door and looked at Jesse in the kitchen. Voices emerged from the speaker on his phone, playing one of the few podcasts he listened to. I smiled sweetly as he concentrated on measuring something out.

He glanced up and caught my stare. "Done already?"

I smirked, trying to hide my second round of embarrassment for the day. "No, uh, I—"

I paused, standing silently for a second, unsure of what to do next. Seeing someone's body naked outside of being in the throes of passion could be awkward. Of course, my silence was making it even more so.

"I—I need your help getting undressed," I continued.

He smiled as he turned the knob off on the stove and followed me into the bathroom.

After shutting the door, the steam materialized from behind the shower curtain.

Jesse, seeming a little nervous himself, pulled off my shirt, revealing the bruise on my arm from where I had connected with the car. I was trying hard not to think about the night before, but every time I moved any muscle, the pain sent me back.

As he slowly tugged on my pants while moving towards my feet, I caught my reflection in the mirror. The condensation had almost relieved me from the misfortune of having to see myself, but to my dismay, a small clearing allowed me to catch a glimpse of my scar. One that I was certain Jesse had now seen too.

I had forgotten there was more to my being naked in front of him than I had considered.

It was another thought I didn't want to be having.

After he finished taking my pants off, a very large bruise was revealed. As he slipped off my underwear, he kissed the bruise on my thigh and then looked up at me and grinned. It was helping me forget the bad thoughts. But my body was in pain, and I had yet to wash away the memories of another reminder of how ill-prepared for life I really was.

"Sorry, I couldn't help it," he said, standing back up.

I attempted to take my bra off myself but inhaled sharply as I failed. He reached his arms around me to unhook it, kissing my neck and shoulder as he slipped it off.

I gave a light laugh. "This is really not fair," I said.

The fact that he didn't know the truth brought me some comfort. Mostly in the fact that he wasn't concerned about my safety and stupid decision-making but thought I was just embarrassingly clumsy. A version of myself I could be comfortable with—even if that version wasn't real.

"Sorry, I really can't help it. You're just so beautiful."

My body resisted the urge to believe the compliment, causing my eyes to dart downward. My mind did its best to remind me that what he was saying wasn't true.

"Thanks," I replied.

I gave him a kiss on the lips and climbed into the shower. I heard the door close behind him as the water cascaded down my body. While it did help relax my muscles, it didn't do anything to relieve my mind from everything that had been building.

My body grew tense again as I thought about the possibility of running into Ben.

How would I handle it? How should I handle it? Should I ignore him? Should I sucker punch him?

I took a deep breath, trying hard not to rile myself up.

My mind tried to shift subjects, landing on Jesse. The only person in my life that didn't look at me like a defective toy.

While I liked the idea of people looking out for me, I felt their need to protect me wasn't as much from others as it was from myself. A constant reminder I got from any of them the second they gave me their looks of concern.

Don't do things for them to be concerned about, and they wouldn't look at you that way, The Voice said.

But I didn't do it on purpose.

Whatever. You love the drama, The Voice said. *You live for the attention. That's what everyone thinks. Why do you think Caleb is always trying to fix you? At what point do you think they will give up on you? They won't be around forever, you know. They will do what you did to Caleb and leave. The difference is, they will have the self-control to actually stay away.*

As The Voice continued to lay into me, my brain felt as if it was emulating the punching bag that was also known as my body. My rational thoughts tried to chime in saying that I wasn't really that bad and that people did love me. It even tried to reason with my biggest fear, that I was going to someday be abandoned by everyone. But I wasn't in the right state of mind for the sensible thoughts to triumph.

I couldn't help but feel defeated as everything hurt inside and out. I was certain the physical pain only felt worse because of the agony that was spreading on the inside.

The misery that lingered internally could only be shown in the confines of the safe space known as my shower. In there, no one was around to be concerned about me; no one was there to ask if I was okay.

Because alone in my shower was the only place I could let down my guard and admit what everyone else already knew—that I wasn't.

***

After I finished my shower, I toweled off as best I could and looked at the hot mess of a girl staring back at me in the mirror. My temple was bruised, and there was a small cut on my lip. The handprint on my neck was starting to become more apparent.

I wasn't sure how to explain how the fall had caused that. Maybe I could make a fashion change to some scarves or turtlenecks for a few weeks. That would be enough to hide it from others. But it wasn't everyone else that I was concerned about. It was my time spent alone with Jesse. The time that would be spent without the need for scarves or turtlenecks.

On top of that, I couldn't go in to work the next day looking like I did. Al would just send me home anyway, and there would be so many questions, so many looks. I was confident that, with my history, the falling down the stairs alibi wouldn't cover it there, especially since it was starting to unravel already.

Besides, Al had wanted me to take more time off after the fire. I guess he would be getting his wish. Maybe I could spin it into a healthy move. Me finally listening to my boss and taking some time off to just chill out. Taking a mental break for a good reason, or so I hoped that was how he would see it.

I hated that I felt I had to spin it into something. Why couldn't I just take some time to chill out, to relax?

Because you don't know how to relax, The Voice said.

I slipped on my robe that hung on the back of the door. A smile crept to my face thinking of my first night with Jesse. Him opening it up, pressing his body up against mine, kissing me like he was going to miss me—despite us having just met.

I took a deep breath and stepped out of the bathroom.

I was greeted by a pleasant aroma as he set down two bowls on the small dining room table.

I don't know what I had been expecting, but as we both took our seats, I looked down to see a bowl full of macaroni and cheese.

"Sorry, uh, I don't really know how to cook," he said looking a little nervous.

A smile instantaneously leapt onto my face and touched my eyes. "Are you kidding me? Mac and cheese is my favorite."

His nerves seemed to dissipate as he grinned.

I stuck the fork in, suddenly overwhelmed with hunger.

"Thanks for coming over," I commented.

"Of course," he replied, giving me a wink.

***

I got up from the table and rinsed out my bowl. Thinking to myself that maybe it was possible for me to just relax. But as I tried for once to be positive, The Voice did what it was best at and shut down the good feel.

It won't always be like this, it said. *Jesse will have work, have Mike, have other responsibilities. At some point, you will be alone again.*

And once alone, I could never seem to just relax.

My chest started to feel heavy as nerves sank in, knowing my alone time was just a little ways off.

Again, I regretted dumping those pills.

"How are you feeling?" Jesse asked, snapping me out of my thoughts.

He set his bowl in the sink next to mine and carefully wrapped his arms around me.

My eyes met his, and I smiled. "I'm fine."

It's already beginning, The Voice said.

But I couldn't help but defend his reasoning for asking. I did look awful. He was just worried about me.

So is everyone else, The Voice stated. *Why is it different with him?*

It was right. Everyone else was just worried too. But he was worried about clumsy Harper. Not possibly-suicidal-with-an-abusive-ex Harper.

298

My sobriety was catching up with me. It was mentally exhausting to be me in the first place, but without anything around to alter my state of mind, my thoughts were more crippling than usual.

Although my eyes burned from fatigue, I did my best to avoid shutting them. I knew that, once I did, Jesse would have to leave, and I would have to be alone. Alone to sleep. Alone to dream. Another place that no longer led to a short escape from my reality.

I felt a tinge of resentment toward Mike. And an even bigger resentment towards the universe.

"You should get some sleep," he said, leaning up against the counter as my body pressed onto his.

"No, I don't want you to go."

"I can lay with you until you fall asleep."

Even though I knew that wouldn't be enough, it was going to have to be. I was going to have to take what was offered, which was better than nothing at all.

He walked with me to my bedroom. And, although my body was still hurting something fierce, I slipped off my robe, hoping it would entice him to stay.

"Now who's not being fair?" he asked while he got under the covers with me.

I grinned.

But my grin quickly faded as I started to feel stupid. Using sex to avoid being alone had become my default for most of my adult life. A band-aid I had created to cover up the broken girl underneath it all.

I exhaled. "I'm sorry I'm so broken," I said unintentionally, immediately feeling the blood rush to my face.

He put his arm around me and kissed my cheek. "I'm sorry you're broken, too."

I smiled, letting the misunderstanding slide.

While we rested close to one another on my bed, Jesse stroked my hair. He was very sweet and had a gentle and calming way about him. It was the opposite of Caleb.

Caleb could be gentle and sweet, but his type of calm was chaotic like mine.

But maybe it wasn't. I had seen a glimpse of a changed man. Maybe my chaos just spreads. Maybe I would take away Jesse's calm too. Maybe he too would become intense and chaotic like Caleb, once he was given enough time with me.

I grew frustrated with my thoughts. Frustrated at their inability to shut the fuck up and let me enjoy the moment I was in. Sobriety didn't suit me. But sobriety was my only choice at that current moment in time. So, my brain shifted to its default setting and used the only band-aid left at its disposal.

"If we were to have sex, could you be gentle?" I asked, but not really caring if gentle was an option. Maybe the pain would help kill the thoughts that were ravaging my brain.

He smirked and brought his lips to mine. "Just tell me if it's too much," he whispered as his lips moved to my neck.

The cold sheets and his soft lips against my skin felt serene. His hands moved around my body in a gentler manner than other times before. But that didn't extract any of the excitement that I felt from him.

I watched as his lips moved lower on my body with each kiss. It didn't take long before he had disappeared under the blankets, causing me to stifle my moans in a nearby pillow.

The motion of his body and tongue caused my back to arch as my moans grew louder. Pain shot through me, but it was in the same intensity as the pleasure, so I let it continue.

A few minutes later, he shifted to again be face to face with me. I pulled him close as my lips explored his neck. His body moved in unison with mine, while my brain released all thoughts of chaos and crazy that I brought to the table. Presenting me with a small window of enjoyment before the pandemonium in my mind would consume it once again.

Chapter Twenty-eight

My room was silent. The stillness of the world was unnerving, but I didn't yet know why. I had been in the same realm of discomfort before. The same unstable universe that shook me to my core years before. But back then it wasn't a fiery pit of hell I dwelled in, but a small wooded patch of land that trapped the girl I once was.

So, if I was trapped there, how was it I was trapped again? Had I finally escaped that hell and traded it for a new one? Was the new hell more bearable than the last?

I climbed out of bed as my room filled with smoke. Breathing got harder, but I wasn't scared of dying from asphyxiation; it was something else altogether that terrified me.

As I reached my door, I calmly took the knob in my hand. I didn't pull away in pain as I had before. Instead, I continued to hold it while the metal seared into my palm. I felt tears form but heard my mom's voice whispering to not show weakness, so I continued to clutch the knob, finally getting up enough nerve to pull it open.

My hand fell to my side as I stared out into my world. People I knew and loved, even some that had passed, all sat around in my mother's living room. They were laughing, smiling, discussing things I couldn't hear. I tried to listen—to speak—and like every other time, I tried to enter the room, but my body was frozen in place.

The intensity of the heat grew around me as the flames began to take over my room. I wanted so badly to join the others. To laugh and joke with them, to look as calm as they all did, but I started to feel weak as I began to swelter.

I tried my best to push through the fragility, to see it through to the end, to finally finish it. But, as my weakness grew, I felt my body shift and my eyes open.

***

I lay motionless in the pool of my sweat for a few minutes as I let my mind focus on what I could remember. I was bound and determined to overcome the nightmares as I had once before. I couldn't remember the exact day they had stopped and therefore didn't know what I had done to make it happen. So, I wasn't confident I was capable of doing it a second time.

I stretched my arm out to the side, feeling pain first from the movement, then from the realization that Jesse had left. I didn't remember drifting off. I wondered how long he had stayed after I did. At least my band-aid helped me sleep, but it didn't help the hurt when it was ripped off the next morning.

I let out an exhale as I moved to sit up. The stiffness wasn't as intense as the morning before, but the pain was greater in certain areas. That was most likely due to the previous night's physical exertion. Something I was willing to endure the pain for.

I reached for my phone and called Al on his cell, knowing he was on his way to work. I did my best to avoid any questions that would involve me outright lying to him. So, I kept it as short and sweet as I could.

***

I had waited all day to hear from Jesse. A guilt-free sense of excitement that I hadn't felt in a while. But every time my phone rang, I had only been met with disappointment.

Though the disappointment didn't last long with the first call, as Sarah needed to cancel our session due to the flu. I was grateful for the excuse on her end, as I was sure she wasn't going to buy mine.

The second call had come from my mother. A conversation that left me feeling hopeful that maybe we had made some advances in our relationship the week before. But, like anytime I felt hope, I also reminded myself to be realistic, to not get too excited, to remember what happened when life seemed to be getting better. It suddenly wouldn't.

But somewhere amongst the hopeful feeling, I had offered to help clean and pack up my grandma's house on Saturday. A gesture she accepted but gave zero indication of how she actually felt about it.

For dinner that evening, I had contemplated making another sandwich since that was all I had in the house. But I was getting restless inside and figured a quick trip to the store would be good for me. Both for forcing me out of the house, and for acquiring the alcohol needed to kill my sober thoughts.

As I walked into the store, my phone went off. I again felt my hopes rise as I reached for it in my purse but was met with Caleb's name flashing across the screen. I stopped the ringing and put it in my pocket. After a minute, I heard a ping from a text, and then a few minutes later, I heard it again.

> Caleb: Just checking in on you. Making sure you are okay.
>
> Caleb: Come on. I just want to make sure you're alive.
>
> Harper: I'm alive.
>
> Caleb: That's what a killer would say if they were answering for you. How do I know it's really you? ;)

A goofy smile came to my face, but an annoying feeling crept into my brain. My pit stop at the gym Saturday night blew our break right out of the water. It had been a few days since I had heard from him, so I thought he had finally agreed that we needed some time apart, just for a little while.

But my pull to appease him led me to send a picture of myself, although the lighting did little to help the dark circles that ungracefully took over my eyes. My quick trip to the store for some food and wine hadn't required full makeup, so I had applied just enough that I didn't alarm the cashier when I went to pay.

Caleb: Perfect :) Beautiful as always

While he may not have felt guilty saying that since he was no longer with Cassy, I was starting to feel guilty because of my time spent with Jesse.

While it had started as a casual hookup, I had hoped that we could pave a path to something more. It was a path I enjoyed being on and wanted to continue traveling. But I was muddying the trail with texts, visits, and thoughts of Caleb.

As I mindlessly put groceries in my cart, my thoughts drifted to the previous week. I started to get nervous that I was getting my hopes up. That I was setting myself up for another person to leave.

He'll find out about the real you, The Voice said. *And then he'll leave like everyone else.*

I hadn't even recovered from my breakup with Ben. A breakup that seemed to just be getting messier. Then add Caleb on top of it. A break I had attempted to make that, again, just seemed to be getting more chaotic.

Jesse was seeing a version of me that didn't exist. A clumsy adorable girl who lived a quiet simple life. But that girl hadn't existed for a long time. No matter how much I pretended that she was still around, in reality, pretending couldn't raise the dead.

I needed to tell him about the real me. Tell him everything that was going on in my life so that he knew exactly what he was in for.

I knew I was being impulsive, but if I told him and he called it quits, we wouldn't be in too deep. I felt I could handle the small amount of rejection now, over the larger-scale version of it later.

At which time we would have entangled each other in one another's lives and had started to build a future together. While I wasn't sure what exactly from my past would come back to haunt me and lead to the demise of my life with him; I knew that there were many things to choose from, and any one of them could be lying dormant waiting to fuck things up.

***

After paying for my groceries, I drove to Jesse's work and parked in the back. I texted him that I was there, hoping they weren't too busy so he could step out for a minute.

He replied that he would be out in five.

But five minutes was too long as insecurities filled my head.

Was that really the right time to be doing that?

I shifted uncomfortably in my seat. I had carelessly convinced myself that he needed to know the real me. But wasn't doing so just me pushing him away on purpose? Wasn't I stopping something good yet again because I was scared I would fuck it up? Wasn't that, in turn, me doing just that?

Maybe I *did* want to be the version he saw me as. Maybe I could play that part for him and be the girl I was before. I sucked at lying, but maybe if I believed in the lie enough, we could both stay blissfully naive to the eventual demise of the girl he thought I was.

Jesse's smart, The Voice began. *He'll see it's just an act sooner or later.*

I saw the back door to the bar open. I hesitated, still trying to decide what to do.

"Hey, good lookin'," he said when I opened my door and walked towards him.

His lips touched mine the moment I was close enough.

"Hey," I responded with no inflection as my mind was still preoccupied.

"What are you doing here?" he asked, putting his arms around my waist.

The time had come to decide. And for once, I put impulsive Harper in the passenger seat.

I smiled. "I was just thinking about you," I replied, pulling him in for another kiss.

My insecurities, or possibly my better judgment, got the best of me and I let go of the real reason I had come.

"Sorry I didn't text you earlier," he said. "I had to do inventory today before my shift."

I smiled, thinking it was sweet he felt the need to explain.

"It's okay. I just hung around the house. It was nice to relax."

The ease at which the lie left my mouth was frightening.

"Do you want to come in for a drink?" he asked.

I scrunch my nose up. "Looking like *this*?"

"You look great," he responded, moving the bangs out of my eyes. "If anyone asks, just tell them you showed those stairs who's boss."

I laughed. "Okay, I can do one drink, but I can't stay too long. I have groceries in the car."

He smiled, taking my hand and pulling me along as we walked inside. He went back behind the bar, and I took a seat in front of it. He gave a flirtatious grin and poured me a vodka cranberry. I took a sip and looked around as he helped another customer.

Looking at the almost-empty bar made me feel bad for him. Weekdays there seemed so boring. The weekends brought wall-to-wall people and tips that made me question my career choice. But on nights like those, where people drank from the comfort of their own houses, I would have been bored to tears.

I did a double take as my eyes caught a glimpse of what looked like Caleb at the back-corner table. I was angry at myself for having a moment of excitement at the possibility of seeing him. I missed him more than I was letting myself believe.

Thankfully I was aware my mind was playing tricks on me. Excitement was not a feeling I would be having if Caleb were in the same place as Jesse. If my life with Jesse were to collide with my life with Caleb.

I took a large sip of my drink as the table of people cleared out from the back of the bar. Their untimely exit from the establishment freed up plenty of space for me to see just how much the man at the back table resembled Caleb. So much so that I could tell it *was* Caleb.

Chapter Twenty-nine

Why was Jesse's bar suddenly a hotspot for my exes?

I left my drink on the bar as my curiosity got the best of me. Caleb didn't spot me until I was almost to his table, at which time his eyes met mine.

His glazed look was hard to miss as his lips twisted into a goofy grin.

"Caleb?"

"Harper," he replied casually.

It wasn't that it was weird to see him at a bar, only that he was by himself. Well, and the fact that he was drunk. I had only ever seen him drunk two times before, and those were not good times for him. He was never against a buzz, but he never liked to get to the point where he wasn't in control. Something he had been preaching that I needed to learn for years. I knew that was mainly due to his past.

You did this to him, The Voice commented.

"Are you okay?" I asked, seeing the irony in the question.

He put his arm around my hip and brought me closer to him. "I'm great!" he responded, taking another sip of his drink.

You broke him, The Voice said. *And now you want to do this to yet another guy? How about stopping the already-derailing train and cleaning up the messes you've already made?*

"I was hoping you would stop by," he said with a smirk, not removing his hand from my hip.

"How did you even know I come here?"

I looked toward Jesse who was watching us from the bar.

"You've been tagged here twice in the last week on Facebook. I thought I would take a lucky shot," he replied.

"Caleb, you don't even have a Facebook."

"No, but Milo does," he replied with a mischievous grin.

I sighed. "Great. You're keeping tabs on me through Milo now?"

The goofiness that had lingered on his expression faded and his stern look arrived on cue. "I wouldn't have to keep tabs on you if you would stay out of trouble."

I was annoyed by his tone, and apparently so was Jesse, because I watched as he headed over.

"Everything good here?" Jesse asked.

He eyed Caleb's hand around my waist.

"Yup!" Caleb replied with a smile.

"I was asking *her*," Jesse responded sharply, but I could tell he was trying to appear casual at the same time.

"Yes, everything's fine," I replied reassuringly. "He's a friend."

"Yup, just a *friend*," Caleb said.

I wanted to tell him to shut up, but instead, I let my eyes do the yelling, hoping that Jesse didn't notice the inflection in his voice. But the look I gave Caleb didn't have the intended effect, as he seemed amused.

I slowly pushed Caleb's arm from around my waist as I stepped closer to Jesse. "He doesn't usually drink like this," I tried to whisper. "I think he just needs to go home."

Jesse glanced at Caleb and then back at me. "I wish people could hold their alcohol better," he responded in an intentionally louder tone.

Impulsive Harper had made her way back into the driver's seat and pressed on the gas before my brain could stop my bad habit of defending the wrong person. "Yeah, well, who's been pouring the drinks?"

My retort came with instant regret.

It wasn't his fault. It wasn't my fault. Only Caleb could control what Caleb was doing.

But, while my head did its best to try and convince me of that, I could feel the guilt shifting about in my stomach. Knowing I had to take responsibility for at least a little of what was fueling Caleb's need to drink.

I lowered my voice and stepped closer to Jesse. "Listen, he's going through a breakup. He just isn't handling it well."

Jesse sighed, looking more empathetic. "I understand. I'm sorry. I'll call him an Uber," he said as he started to pull out his phone.

"It's okay. I have to get going anyway. I'll just drop him off on my way home," I replied.

With his brief pause, I thought I was going to be able to get out of there without any real problems resulting from the collision of the two of them. But as I started to turn around, he began to speak.

"I'll swing by after work, okay, babe?"

Under normal circumstances, I would have liked being called that. But I didn't like it being used to mark some kind of claim on me. Ben manipulated his words to control me, too. It made me feel small and insignificant like I was nothing and could do nothing without that man beside me.

Jesse's word choice had gained Caleb's attention as I knew it would.

But before I could show my annoyance at Jesse that time, Caleb showed his.

"Babe?" he said the word as if he had never heard it before. His expression shifted. "Is he the one who did this to you?" He stood up from his seat.

I turned and glared at Caleb. "Of course not," I replied.

"How do I know it wasn't him?" Caleb snapped back at me, his eyes searing into mine.

I glanced at Jesse who looked perplexed. "Jesus, Caleb, just stop. We need to go."

"You don't know what you're talking about," Jesse said, finally speaking up. "She fell down the stairs."

I felt even worse at that moment that I had gone with that excuse. Caleb knew it was a person, and I was sure Jesse was moments away from knowing that too.

I diverted my eyes from Caleb as I glanced at Jesse. Seeing the exact moment he not only knew I had lied about that, but I also suspected the entire version of me he had created had imploded.

I could have come clean when he texted me the morning before, or when he came over, or at dinner, or minutes ago in the parking lot. I had multiple chances to explain about my ex. I had time to let him process the information. But I had been so hell-bent on keeping his false idea of me intact that I had chosen the easy way out. I had chosen to lie.

I watched as Caleb's eyes grew dark. I could tell he thought that someone explaining away my bruises from a fall down the stairs clearly was responsible for making them happen. I saw the gears turning as his hands curled into fists.

I stepped towards Caleb and gripped his arms. "Caleb, look at me," I began. "I'm serious. It wasn't him."

I needed him to listen since my body was the only thing that stood in the way of him lunging at Jesse. An object that could be easily moved *if* and *when* he decided to do so.

He still didn't look convinced or to be backing down.

Maybe it was the alcohol. Maybe I wasn't going to be able to get through to him. And although Jesse looked like he could hold his own, I had seen Caleb in the ring. I knew what he was capable of.

I felt Caleb start to shift forward. Without knowing what else to do, I put my hands on his chest.

"It was Ben!" I shouted as my voice cracked.

His eyes reverted from Jesse's back to mine. "*What?*"

Then I heard Jesse ask, "Who the hell is Ben?"

I turned to Jesse, feeling like I owed him an explanation first, trying to figure out how to control any damage my lie had caused.

"Ben is my ex. I went to dinner with him Saturday night. *Nothing* was going to happen, I swear. We were just talking and shit just got out of hand."

I felt the eyes from the other patrons on us.

See, you're a mess, The Voice chimed in.

Jesse exhaled and shook his head but stayed silent.

"Harper," Caleb said, his voice full of disappointment.

I felt a sob get stuck in my throat, but I pushed through it. "Shut up, Caleb," I replied, turning toward him and then back to Jesse, giving him an apologetic look.

I waited for him to say something.

"I have to get back to work. Get him out of here," Jesse said, turning around and heading back to the bar.

I wanted to talk to him, to chase after him. But I didn't know what to say. I felt like I was getting the answer to the question I had yet to ask—that he could in fact *not* handle my chaos.

The slow melody of a country song played over the radio as I rolled down the window. I had worked up a sweat in my panicked state of unraveling lies.

Usually, I enjoyed the silence when placed in a situation like I was currently in. One that led me to be inches away from someone who had questions they wanted me to answer. Answers I wasn't ready to give.

But the silence came with thoughts of how I had fucked things up yet again. How my lies and deceitful actions ruined another good thing. How my bad decisions fueled by my lack of impulse control would forever be the reason for my inability to keep anyone close.

"Ben?" Caleb questioned, breaking the silence. "Really, Harper?"

His tone was full of disgust. I suddenly missed the silence.

"Don't act like you know anything about him."

"Serena told me all I need to know," he replied.

I rolled my eyes. Of course she had.

"Since when do you and Serena talk?" I asked.

"Since you seem to be falling apart," he responded with his hand pressed to his forehead and his eyes shut.

"Me? I'm not the one wasted in a bar on a Monday," I said as if I sat on some pedestal of righteousness.

"No, you're just beaten and bruised by a married ex."

The low blow caused a resentful pit to form in my stomach. I swallowed hard, as my eyes narrowed.

When I didn't respond, he continued. "Plus, you're in therapy and haven't even told us why. So, who knows what the fuck else is happening with you?"

"It's none of your fucking business. Not everything I do concerns the two of you!"

He shook his head. "You mean like you dating the bartender?"

I exhaled. "Yes, that falls under the category of *not your fucking business*."

"So you are dating him then?"

I stayed silent as I felt his eyes on me.

Finally, I gave in to the bitterness that was radiating from him. I rolled my eyes as I shot him a side glance. "I don't know."

He scoffed, "How do you not know?"

"Because we met like a week ago. I don't know what it is yet."

My headlights lit up his house as I pulled into the driveway. I immediately opened my door, wanting to end the conversation right there. But I knew it would be carried inside. He never knew when to quit. It was a fault we both shared.

He fumbled with his keys as he attempted to get them out of his pocket. They hit the ground as his patience seemed to be wearing thin.

But mine was too, so I picked them up and opened the door.

I retrieved him a glass of water from the kitchen, hoping he would sober up a little before I left. Or, at the very least, I hoped to curb the hell of a hangover I knew he would have the next day for work.

"How could you start seeing someone?" he asked. "I broke up with Cassy—"

I walked back into the room and looked at him as he sat on the couch.

"Don't put that shit on me, Caleb. I told you to stay with her. I told you we couldn't be together."

I took the seat next to him on the couch, although I knew it was already past time for me to go.

I handed him the glass, and he held it in his hands as his expression changed once again. "Which I don't get..." he sighed. "Am I really that clueless? Do you really not love me?" he asked, glancing at me, then back at the floor.

"Jesus, Caleb," I replied, rolling my eyes and standing up. "You know that I do. Just... I don't know. You know how shit went down before."

"No. I don't. One day I'm dating a fun-loving girl who enjoyed waking up next to me every morning, and the next you could barely be in the same room with me. I don't understand what I did."

"*You* didn't do anything," I responded, hoping my calm tone would calm his.

"Then *what?*" He stood up, clearly not taking the hint. "You got what I thought you wanted. I broke up with you because *you* wanted space. Then, out of nowhere, *you* come to *my* gym and want to be *fuck buddies?*" He shook his head. "I didn't understand it then, and I don't understand it now. What do you *want* from me?" he asked with pain in his eyes.

"Caleb…" I began, then thought better of it as my insecure feelings rushed in. "I'm sorry. I'm not doing this. I'm not going to have this fight when you're drunk."

"You won't when I'm sober either. You keep this shit bottled up. You don't talk to anyone. No one has any idea what's going on in that fucking head of yours!"

"This is my fault. I shouldn't have gone to the gym back then or now. I should have just let you live your life."

I knew I had fucked up. I had known it for years. And yet I continued to repeat the same behavior over and over again.

Before he could speak, I began again. "I don't get how you don't see how much better off you are without me. Six months without me in your life… almost an entire year with Cassy, and you were like a whole new person. I took that from you."

Amongst the yelling and the blaming of myself, I had made it back to the door, ready to flee again.

"I may have *looked* better, but I wasn't," he said stopping me in my tracks. "When you're not around, I feel nothing. Nothing good anyway. Cassy was a nice girl, and life *was* easy with her. But I'm not interested in *easy*," he said, as I heard him approach me.

320

I turned to face him. "Caleb, it would be too complicated between us. Why do you have to keep making this so hard?" I asked as I lowered my voice.

"Me? Harper, I have been in love with you the entire time I've known you. You're the one making things difficult."

"If it has been so hard on you, why did you agree to this? To *us*?"

I thought he would need time to answer, but he didn't.

"Because having you even a little bit was better than not at all."

I went silent. My chest hurt, like a boulder was suddenly placed on top of it. He was doing the same thing I had been doing—anything necessary to hold on to us.

I pushed through the feeling of understanding, knowing there was more to my side of things than to his. Mine was realistic; his was just some fantasy life, where just being in love automatically meant things would work out.

"I can't be the girl you want me to be," I said.

I hadn't realized how true those words were until I started opening up in therapy. Thinking about my past self. The girl he was really in love with. I started to hear all of Ben's words flow through my head poking at each one of my insecurities as The Voice echoed the sentiment at the same time.

Caleb walked over to me and took my hands to calm the fidgeting that had mindlessly begun.

I swallowed a lump that had gotten stuck in my throat.

"Harper, I don't want you to be anyone but yourself. I love everything about you."

How could he say that if he didn't know everything?

I looked down in defeat. I had been keeping things from him for years. How could he be in love with someone he knew so little about? He was so blinded by our past that he couldn't see what I saw. The only way I could think to show him he couldn't handle my past and the trauma that stemmed from it, was to be honest.

I exhaled. "Okay."

"Okay, what?"

My honesty was going to come with a price. A price that usually only *I* paid. I knew telling him the real reason that led to our breakup would cause him pain that I couldn't easily prepare him for. There was no softening the blow to secondary trauma.

"I've kept things from you," I replied, finding my way back to the couch. "And while I stick by my sentiment that you don't need to know everything, I understand that it may be hard to see the problem if you don't know all the facts."

His confused expression continued.

I patted the seat cushion next to me and he complied. I put my hands in my lap and again began to fidget as I tried to think of the words I wanted to continue with. I stood up and took a deep breath.

"What's happening? What facts are you talking about?"

I was too engrossed in my thoughts to reply. I started to pace back and forth in front of his TV as my brain screamed at me to rip off the band-aid.

"Okay," I said again. This time it was in response to my brain, but he didn't need to know that.

"You said that already," he replied.

I took a deep breath, trying to stall for just one more moment. "If I'm going to get through this, you can't talk. You can't ask questions. Just let me get it out, okay?"

He nodded.

"I lied to you about the night I was attacked." I shook my head realizing I had to be more specific. "When I was attacked seven years ago."

Chapter Thirty

I watched as Caleb's body grew tense. I tried to ignore it and work on getting out my words so that I didn't have to say them again.

"I don't know how much you remember from what I told you before," I began as the fidgeting started right on cue. I stared down at my hands to keep from making eye contact with him. "I went to Ryan's party that Friday. You had to help with some project up north for work, and Serena canceled on me *again* to be with Patrick. I knew I was going to drink, so I had walked there since it was only a few streets from my house." I paused, thinking back to that night.

Although it had occurred almost seven years before, I could feel every moment of it like it had just happened. I remember it was unseasonably cold out for a summer night in Michigan. I had consumed a large portion of the alcohol I had brought to the party but still felt good enough to walk myself home. It was something I had done many times before.

I realized I had gone silent, so I began again. "As the party started to die down, I decided to head home. On my way, I saw a girl being bothered by some guy. I didn't know exactly what was happening, just that she looked way drunker than I was, and clearly couldn't handle herself against whatever he was trying to do."

I paused again. "She wasn't yelling, but I could hear her saying no, and she was trying to pull herself away. I walked a little bit closer and asked loudly if she was okay... it was like her eyes were screaming at me." I felt a tear run down my cheek. I took a deep breath, wiped it away, and fought the urge to let any more come out.

"He pushed her to the ground and took off. It all happened so fast I didn't really know what to do if I should yell or call for help. We were still close to the party, so she asked me to take her back; she had friends there."

My mind ran the play-by-play as I sorted out the relevant information for Caleb, but really, I was just prolonging the inevitable, wanting to avoid talking about what had happened just a little longer.

I thought back to her friends who had been looking for her; they were so happy I had found her. I tried to talk to them about what had happened, but they were drunk too, and it was hard to hold their focus. I had somewhat sobered up at that point, very scared of what I had witnessed or what I had possibly prevented from happening.

Ryan, the kid who was throwing the party, overheard what I had said and was angry that I had suggested calling the cops. He kicked everyone out and, although I had known people when the party had started, I looked around and didn't know a single person who was left. Any of the guys could have been the one who had tried to hurt her. He could have followed us back to the party.

I remember starting to panic, not knowing who to trust. I reached for my cell to call someone for a ride. But it was dead.

After a minute, I realized I had gone in my head once again. My stomach was in knots making me feel nauseous. Every feeling I had that night was fresh in my mind.

I exhaled, preparing myself to start again. "Before I knew it, everyone was kicked out of the house and had gone their separate ways. And there I was, left outside in the dark by myself."

As I got closer to the truth, I felt my brain wanting to back down, run for the door, abort mission.

"I... uh... I tried to be vigilant in watching my surroundings. I even tucked my key between my knuckles like my dad had shown me," I said, glancing at Caleb, who hadn't moved a muscle since I had started talking.

My legs grew weak as my stomach started doing somersaults. I took a seat on the other end of the couch. Leaving enough space between us that I didn't have to worry about him trying to take my hand.

"He came out of nowhere. I didn't hear anything," I said tucking a strand of hair behind my ear before gathering my hands back together on my lap.

I felt the tug on my hair and the arms around my chest, finding it hard to breathe like it was happening to me again.

My hands curled into fists. "He pulled me into the bushes... I was only a street away from my house... there's a little patch of trees... I used to go running there in the morning sometimes—" I took a breath, again taking a moment to delay. "He hit me a few times while having me pinned down." He told me that I was stupid. That I shouldn't have helped her. That it was my fault.

I felt my heart start to race as it grew louder in my ears. "My body felt cold against the ground. And it hurt. Not just because of the hitting, but I think I was lying on sticks or something; they were digging into my back." I felt my face get hot. I knew it was only a matter of time before the tears fell or I sent myself into a panic attack. "I... I had told you that he beat me."

I glanced at Caleb and he nodded.

"He did... I had tried to scream. But he had shoved something in my mouth." A rush of nausea swept over me. I swallowed hard to try and keep it down. "I don't know at what point I realized that it was my underwear." I stopped again and saw Caleb's body tense up from across the couch, but I didn't make eye contact with him.

"I don't remember a lot of what happened once I felt his body on top of mine; it was like I was suffocating." I swallowed the lump in my throat, feeling suffocated again. "I think I kind of left my body. It feels more like I watched it happen rather than having it happen... *to* me."

His body had been heavy. His fists against my head had made me disoriented. I wanted to continue fighting, but I didn't know what to do.

When he forced himself inside of me, I felt the vibrations of my scream. But the sound was muffled by the fabric. I kept trying to yell louder, to make enough noise that someone would hear— someone would help. But I never could, and no one ever did.

My chest grew tight again, and nausea settled in for the long haul. Although I had finally talked about it out loud, it didn't relieve the pain like I had hoped.

"I pushed you away because I didn't feel like myself anymore," I said. "I felt like you looked at me differently."

The palm of my hands started to sting. I realized I had dug my nails deep into them, so I loosened my grip. "I understand you didn't know… that you couldn't have possibly known because I didn't tell you. I see now that it was because I looked at *myself* differently. That it had nothing to do with you."

For months I couldn't even look in a mirror. When I finally could, I didn't recognize the girl looking back at me. Both physically and mentally. The reflection was a stranger. The helplessness that had befallen me after everything happened had consumed me entirely. That was until the anger had set in.

As the feelings from that time returned in full force, the anger resurfaced all at once. I felt it spread out over my body reaching all my extremities. I closed my eyes as my heart raced once again and my hands balled back into fists.

Caleb started to speak. "I'm so sorry, Harper. I'm sorry I wasn't there for you. I'm sorry I let you push me away—"

I could tell he was going to beat himself up over my confession, but I could do little to comfort him as I felt myself losing control. My heart was beating like a drum in my ears.

I hadn't been ready to say that yet. I pushed myself too hard—again.

I stood back up and he did the same. I looked at him, which was a mistake. The look in his eyes was more than just sympathy, more than pain from anger, or any sort of rage at the vile piece of garbage that did that to me. It was like the revelation of my true past had mutilated his version of me. Maybe it made everything make sense, maybe it had made all the pieces fall into place like I had hoped, and he now understood why I felt it couldn't work.

But a small part of me, or a big part that was stored deep, had hoped nothing would change. That he would still love me—still look at me—the same as he always had. But as he stepped towards me, undoubtedly, to hug me, hold me, comfort me from the pain I was feeling, I put out my hand to stop him. Reacting the same way I always had to any loving, vulnerable touch.

"I'm sorry, Caleb. I can't—"

And, without another word, I shut the door behind me and ran for my car.

***

After pulling away from Caleb's house, I parked on the side of the road to calm myself down. I was able to return my heart rate to normal, but not without a pounding headache in return. I put my head on my steering wheel, exhausted in a way that I hadn't been in a long time.

I grabbed my phone off the passenger's seat and saw that I had a missed call. I turned it on speaker to listen as I pulled back onto the road to start driving again.

"Hey. I'm really sorry for earlier tonight. I had no right to get pissed about any of that. I know we just met; it just feels like we've known each other a lot longer. And I just… I really like you. I don't know if you feel the same way, or if this was just a one-night stand that got out of hand. But I just wanted you to know that I'm not upset and that, if you wanted to, I would love to see you again. I understand you have a past… I mean, who doesn't? Just let me know… you know… if you still want to try this out."

The phone went silent.

I was unsure of myself and my life choices as it was all starting to build up. I needed an escape from it. I needed time to think. To be away. To be anywhere but there.

On the two-hour drive to Serena's, my mind drifted back to the aftermath seven years before. Back to the birth of the girl I had become. I felt my hands grip the steering wheel tighter as I visualized myself slowly getting up from the dirt patch next to the wooded area.

I had taken my underwear out of my mouth and found my jeans tossed aside. I didn't even remember feeling cold at that point, just numb. I had found my keys in the spot where he had grabbed me. Unfortunately, there was no time to put them to use. I picked them up and finished what seemed like a walk that took hours but, in reality, was probably five minutes.

I had gotten into my car and driven myself to the hospital. Luckily there hadn't been a lot of people there. When I walked in, the lady at the counter didn't look up. She asked for my name and reason for being there.

I tried to answer but, when I opened my mouth, I couldn't speak.

She had let out a sigh and then glanced up. Her face changed from annoyance to grave concern. I didn't know what people she was used to getting at that time in the morning, but I'm guessing it wasn't whatever I looked like.

She picked up her phone and called the doctor, or maybe a nurse.

After she hung up, she came around the corner to walk me toward the back.

She pulled up a wheelchair and helped me sit down, I managed to get some words out, but I don't remember what they were. I remember the pain as my adrenaline seemed to have run its course. The doctor or nurse or whoever she was came shortly after and got me. I don't know what they typically do with patients to check them in, but that seemed different.

I was moved to a different area, and it was only that lady and two other women. They were talking to me, but I either couldn't hear them or couldn't concentrate on what they were saying. I could only see their lips moving. Finally, things started to calm in my head, and I could hear their words.

They asked me a lot of questions and ran through what I assume was protocol for victims of rape. Once they did everything they needed to, I showered, changed, and got in the hospital bed. I thought about calling someone. Maybe they had even asked if there was someone I wanted them to call. I don't remember. But I didn't want anyone coming to the hospital. But given the circumstances, I was able to refuse them calling my emergency contact.

In the late morning, I asked to be released. They insisted I wait until all my tests came back, but I didn't want to be there. But once home, I realized I didn't want to be there either.

Before Caleb got to my place, I had decided I would tell him only about the first part of the attack. While I knew that would be hard for him, that was a part I couldn't really hide.

I had thought I could handle it all myself, but after things started to heal on the outside, he wanted to be *us* again. Which meant sex, something even from the beginning we had been very good at together and had lots of.

But I couldn't. I told him things still hurt or would use other excuses. After a little while, I felt like he was angry with me.

Which he was, but I shouldn't have been angry back. I was the one who lied. I had stopped returning his phone calls and texts to hang out. When I *would* see him, all we would do was fight. He even accused me of seeing someone else, since I didn't want to sleep with him. I couldn't even share a bed with him. I would end up sleeping on the couch any time he stayed over. I could see how it all looked, but I was just so angry all the time, I didn't care what he thought or what happened.

Before I was discharged from the hospital, the nurses had gotten me to file a police report, to go with all the evidence they gathered from my body. But during my statement, the officer asked me questions, all alluding to it being my fault. Or at least that was how it felt. Because I didn't understand why it mattered if I had been drinking, what I was wearing, or why I was out so late. Or maybe it did. I don't know.

I had a really hard time letting go of the anger at everything and everyone surrounding my attack. Even Caleb. *Especially* Caleb. Even more so when he broke up with me.

I was angry at him for doing it, angry at myself for pushing him to do it, and angry at the world for being so fucked up in the first place.

I stopped going to classes. The only reason I still even went to work was because Al kept checking in on me when I wouldn't. He knew something was up but didn't know what. People could just tell that my entire personality had shifted.

I wasn't as friendly to my customers at work. I was super jumpy and moody all the time. I had stopped sleeping—well when I could help it anyway. The nightmares had consumed me, causing me to go into a zombie-like state. So, I started getting shit-faced almost every night so I could blackout and get some rest.

One day, after I had moved from hopelessness to the anger-filled woman people had come to expect, I showed up at the gym where Caleb had learned to box, asking him to teach me. My original motivator was to find the guy and beat the shit out of him. But, after a while, it was just a good way to get my anger out. And after that, it just became something Caleb and I did together.

Everything that happened made me a very cynical person, as I kept hearing my mother's words of "no good deed goes unpunished" from when I told her the same story I had originally told Caleb. She also added, "nothing good happens after nine." Such helpful advice.

I had tried to sleep with a few guys between the time Caleb had left me and me showing up at the gym, but the few attempts ended with panic attacks or angry outbursts.

Being at the gym with Caleb, and releasing a lot of my aggression, brought us closer, but nothing compared to what it had been like in the beginning with us. Caleb was the only man I was able to have sex with for a little while, and even then, the start of that required a lot of pep talk.

During that time together—even more so after things ended between him and Alyssa—unhealthy parts of our relationship grew like weeds in a garden. Arguing was one of our main pastimes, which always led to sex. And since I wouldn't date him, jealousy from both of us steamrolled into making those arguments happen.

The easygoing relationship we had once had was buried beneath the overgrown weeds, and neither of us was willing to dig it out. We were both angry, passionate, and trying like hell to not get hurt again.

Chapter Thirty-one

The spring night in Michigan was colder than I had anticipated. Enough so that the idea of putting my seat back and waiting until morning to wake Serena didn't seem like a viable option. I was able to knock out a journal entry for Friday's session while procrastinating having to announce my arrival. But that proved to take no time at all.

My knuckles tapped on her front door. I took a deep breath, knowing I hadn't done it loud enough to wake her. So once more, I bawled my fist up, hitting it louder.

I pulled out my phone as the crisp night air allowed goosebumps to appear on my skin. I typed out a text to Jesse and slipped it back into my pocket.

> Harper: I got your voicemail. I'm glad you're not upset. I just need some time.

However, while my text bought me a little time, I didn't have an infinite amount of it. And with everything beginning to unravel—myself included—I needed to figure things out before I let Jesse throw away the normal and quiet life he had become accustomed to.

Moments later, the light above me came on and the door cracked open.

"Harper?" She opened the door the rest of the way and stepped aside so I could enter. "What the hell are you doing here? What time is it?"

"A little after midnight," I responded, as she shut the door behind me. "I had to get away. I'm sorry."

She flipped on the light to the living room and gasped as she stepped toward me. "Holy shit! What happened?"

In my hasty exit from my problems, I had forgotten not only about the ice cream in my backseat, but also the remnants of the dinner she had told me not to attend.

She put her hand on my chin to examine me in the light, moving my hair out of the way with her other hand to look at the bruising around my temple. "Who did this to you? Was it Caleb?"

I shifted my face away from her hand and let out a quiet laugh.

"How the fuck is this funny?" she asked, taking a small step back from me.

"Sorry, it's not."

How would she have known Caleb wouldn't do that? I had never been very forthcoming about the details of our relationship.

Her brows furrowed.

She knew.

"Goddamnit, Harper. Ben?"

My eyes fell to the floor, which was all she needed for confirmation.

"I told you not to go to dinner with him," she said, shaking her head at me in disbelief. "Why don't you ever listen?"

I felt my chest get heavy, again annoyed with myself and my stupid decisions.

She sighed. "I'm sorry. This isn't your fault," she continued as she hugged me. As she pulled away, her expression filled with rage. "I'm going to ruin that bastard's life."

"Don't worry about it. He's not worth it—"

I could tell she wasn't fond of my casual response. But I really just wanted him to be a part of the past.

She moved past my comment and continued. "Did you go to the cops?"

I shook my head.

"Harper," she said. "Wait, is this why you came here? Are you scared of him coming to your house?"

"No," I replied. "He doesn't know where I'm staying. I met him at the restaurant."

She sat down on her couch and I followed suit.

"So, why are you here? Not that I'm not happy to see you but coming for a visit at midnight on a Tuesday isn't something you typically do."

I buried my face in my hands and took a deep breath before looking at her. "I talked to Caleb last night. I told him why we broke up."

She exhaled as her expression softened.

While Serena didn't know what had happened either, she knew whatever it was, was something I had a hard time talking about. Things had become rocky between us during that time, too. I had blamed it on her relationship with Patrick, but I suspected that she was very aware that had nothing to do with it.

"Are you okay?"

I nodded. "It was just really overwhelming. I thought I was going to have another panic attack."

"How often are they happening? I was really nervous after that night at the bar."

I stayed silent, not knowing how much I wanted to divulge.

"Harper."

I sighed. "I've just been dealing with a lot. With Ben, the fire, my grandma, Caleb, Jesse, the nightmares…"

"Nightmares?"

"Just since the fire," I replied, trying to sound casual.

But Serena knew I had had nightmares before. She knew I dreamt about being attacked. Although she didn't know the extent of what was happening in them.

"Harper, why didn't you call me?"

"I thought I could handle it."

She sighed. She knew how stubborn I was.

"What about therapy?" she asked. "Are you talking in there?"

I shrugged. "Yeah… about some things."

She sat silently for a moment. "Okay, well you're here now. Let's talk."

The insecurities I had had about driving two hours in the middle of the night to talk to her became very apparent.

"Uh, no. God, I'm so sorry," I stammered as I stood up. "It's the middle of the night. You have work tomorrow. We can talk another time."

You're trying to avoid shit again, The Voice said.

I felt guilty for waking her. For taking up her time. For thinking that my chaos deserved more than an evening phone call.

Just continue to avoid the issues until they eat you alive, The Voice said. *One day they will kill you just like they killed your father.*

The Voice's words stopped me in my tracks.

"Harper?"

I turned back toward Serena whose expression hadn't shifted. Her eyes still held concern, her

"I've been keeping things from you," I said.

She nodded.

I knew that was obvious. But she didn't know the extent of the secrets, or just how much they impacted my entire life.

I paused for a moment as I swallowed a lump that had formed in my throat. I knew, once I told her, I wasn't going to be able to take it back. That she was going to worry about me more. That she would possibly even tell Caleb.

But before I could talk myself out of it, I began. "Last week before my grandma died, she… uh, told me that my father killed himself."

"What?"

"Yeah. Apparently, he made it look like an accident so that my mother could get the insurance money."

"And your grandma kept that from you this whole time? God… does your mom know?"

I side-eyed her, and she gave a small, annoyed, laugh.

"Of course she knew," she replied, shaking her head in frustration.

I swallowed hard and gathered my hands in my lap. "She thinks I'm going to do the same thing," I said as I shifted about on the couch.

Her eyes slowly moved to mine. "What do you think?"

"I'm scared she's right. What if one day it all gets to be too much?" I began. "I mean, I do take after him." I added with a small, ill-timed grin.

"Harper, you're not your father."

"I know."

"And you're getting help. Everyone gets overwhelmed."

"I know, but it's not just that."

"What do you mean?"

"It's everything. It's my life, the decisions I make, the nightmares, the men… How do I know what my breaking point is? None of us noticed when my father reached his. He thought it through carefully, waited for the right time, and then just did it."

"Harper, I couldn't possibly know what you're going through and what this is doing to you…" She paused. "Why don't you stay for a few days? I'll call my work in the morning and tell them I'm working from home the rest of the week."

"I don't want to put you out."

"Girl, shut up. It'll be nice having someone around."

"Are you sure?"

"Yes. Clearly, we have stuff to catch up on."

***

Over the course of the next few days, I lounged around Serena's house, still getting restless sleep as the nightmares continued. After her eyes would close, I would sneak out of bed and watch TV on her couch until I couldn't keep my eyes open any longer.

Since I had arrived at the dramatic hour of midnight a few nights before, I knew I had made her worried about me. She hid her concern about me as well as I hid my need for concern. Any time that wasn't spent working on her laptop was spent with me having to divulge more information about what was going on.

As usual, I did my best to avoid any major traumas that I didn't want to resurface, but the wine she provided helped the conversation on other topics flow just a little easier.

The discussion on Ben was open and shut. I wasn't to see him again. Instructions I would gladly follow. She promised to no longer tag me in at any place on social media, hoping the chances of us running into each other would decrease. If Caleb had done that to find me, Ben might have done the same.

When the topic switched to Jesse, I was eager to share. He was fun, handsome, and sweet. Although only a short time had passed, I had plenty of things to tell Serena about him. But while we talked, I felt a sadness set in my chest. I wasn't sure if it was from missing him, or if it was more than that.

Once Caleb got brought up, I started in on her talking to him. She claimed it wasn't as much as he led me to believe. That they were just comments made in passing or a quick phone call. Either way, she agreed to not say anything else about me to him.

***

While nothing was resolved while I was there, it was the time away that I needed. I had taken a few days to stay clear of my phone—no texts, calls, or social media of any kind. I just spent my days vegged out on Serena's couch while she worked, and my evenings drinking wine, talking, and laughing.

Since I was sharing things and genuinely enjoying myself, each night I had gone to bed with the hope that the nightmares wouldn't come. But every night, like clockwork, they still arrived.

On Friday, Serena returned my phone to me after I had given it to her for safekeeping. Both so that I didn't get wine drunk and text anyone, and just in case something important did come up she could let me know.

When I got my phone back, I was disappointed that I hadn't missed any calls or texts. There had been nothing new from Caleb or Jesse. But it had been what I wanted—more so what I needed.

I took a deep breath and allowed my apathetic demeanor to take control once more. I knew I had taken a pause from my life long enough. I had to head back to the chaos I had left behind.

After a shower, I got ready, dressing in the clothes she had loaned me. I pulled the shirt over my head and looked in the mirror for the first time in days. "Shit," I said.

"What?" Serena asked from the other room.

"Sorry, nothing."

Nothing except I was supposed to see Sarah that afternoon and my mother the following day. How was I going to explain the bruises?

The stairs excuse would *not* work on them.

I took a deep breath.

Although it was starting to heal, the healing just meant it was turning purple and yellow, instead of black and blue—not that it was disappearing.

Chapter Thirty-two

I parked my car in front of Sarah's office and grabbed the small bag from the passenger's seat. I pulled out the concealer and dabbed it over the bruises. The makeup appeared heavier than usual, but there was no avoiding that. I was just happy the swelling had gone down because I had no excuse for an inflated face.

I smeared some of the concealer under my eyes, as the dark circles almost matched my bruising. But as I gazed in the mirror, trying to make sure everything looked to be sufficiently covered, I caught my own stare.

I slammed the compact back into its folded position and grabbed my purse from beside me.

Before I could even take a seat in the waiting area, Sarah's door opened, and she ushered me in.

***

(Journal entry)

I met Serena in high school and hung around with her and some of her other friends. I wasn't very outgoing even then, so I would kind of be on the outside of the group. Serena dated one of Jacob's best friends for a little bit our sophomore year, which is how I came to be friends with her in the first place.

We went to parties, football games, and all the typical high school stuff as a group. While my presence at any event wasn't usually remembered by much of anyone, Serena's was. She was fun. Loud, but fun.

She has three older sisters and two younger brothers, so she has that typical need for attention outside of the home. I'm not downing that at all. That's what makes her, well, her. She's one of the only people I know that doesn't come from a dysfunctional home.

While her parents did get divorced her junior year, they did the co-parenting thing right. They didn't fight over the kids or in front of the kids. They didn't try to turn the kids against the other parent. They even shared a house for a little while after the divorce because finances were tight.

Don't get me wrong—the split still affected Serena, but I don't know if, at that age, there was any way around that. I think that fueled her more outgoing streak toward the end of high school.

After we graduated high school, Serena went away to the same college her oldest sister had attended. That college was two hours away. It was good for her. She did a lot of growing up during that time. After college, she got offered a permanent position at a company she had been interning for, so she bought a house and stayed there.

She had a serious boyfriend for the last two years of college. His name was Patrick. Although you will never hear her talk about him. When they graduated, he asked her to move back to Georgia with him. But she couldn't imagine being that far from her family. Two hours was already hard enough.

She asked him to stay, but his degree was very particular and there wasn't much call for it here in Michigan. I went and stayed with her for a week or so after they broke up, as she had done when Jacob had left me. We determined at a very early age that we weren't fit to be in long-term relationships. We were both too stubborn. I had already dated Caleb at that point and was still working through my own shit.

Since then, she has started with a new company and is doing really well. Despite being only 28, she has a lot of say in how the company runs and seems vital to their operation. I admire her leadership ability. She is a force to be reckoned with for sure.

Serena and I didn't really become super close until the summer of my 18th birthday. I had been having some issues with Jacob and he went and stayed with his dad for a couple weeks. Serena didn't want to follow the curfew still set for her at home, so she moved into my place for the summer, before leaving for college. We really got to know each during that time, way more than the surface level shit it had been up until then.

After she left, I visited her most weekends, or she would visit me. And boy did we party. Jacob got annoyed at how often Serena and I went out after graduating high school. I think that was one of Jacob's and my main problems. He wanted me to settle down and be his version of a responsible adult. And I wanted to be an adult that had fun.

I still went to my college classes and work when I was scheduled. But that wasn't good enough for him; that didn't prove I was responsible. He even told me one time that responsible people don't get drunk as often as I did, which I wholeheartedly disagree with, but even more so at that age.

He blamed Serena for my drinking, since the partying had become more frequent when she moved in, but I think he was just making excuses for me. She didn't care though. She knew I was my own person, who made up my own mind. I loved her for that.

For a few years of our friendship, I had told her everything. But that all changed when *I* changed. When my life had been turned upside down right before my 21st birthday. After everything happened, I went back into my shell and stopped sharing stuff. My anxiety had really taken off at that time, and I had a billion thoughts on everything at every moment.

I don't think she ever understood that. Serena never experienced anxiety. She just did stuff and was positive that the outcome would be good. At least that's how it's always seemed to me.

After a while, we talked less and less, because I had a hard time fighting my anxiety and didn't visit as much. Luckily, that didn't ruin our friendship completely; she still came when she could. She forced me out of my comfort zone, or sometimes out of my bed.

I don't know if she ever really understood the depth of my anxiety or, on occasion, my depression. I mean, why would she if I never told her? When I told her I had started therapy, I think she was more shocked that I was telling her something personal since it had been a long time since I had shared something like that with her.

I guess I wanted it out of my head and to hear from someone else that it was a good thing and not having all the stigma hanging around it. She did reassure me it was good and healthy and even told me she had gone before. That did make me feel better, but I didn't share it with anyone else besides my boss.

While I do feel safe with Caleb and even Jesse at this point, Serena is my getaway. When everything at home gets to be too much, I always have a place with her.

***

"Serena sounds like a good friend," Sarah commented.

"She is."

"So, why do you feel like you can't tell her things?"

"I don't know. I mean, I've spent the last few days with her, and we talked a lot actually. It was really nice."

"Great. So, do you think you can keep doing that?"

"I don't know. I guess it depends what it is."

"Why is that? Shouldn't your best friend be the person you tell even the worst things about yourself to?"

I shrugged. "I mean, I guess it should be. But what if I don't want anyone to know those things?"

"Well, that depends on you. It's okay to keep some things a secret, as long as those secrets aren't hurting you."

And she knew they were.

"Do you feel like she will judge you?"

"I guess—maybe." I paused. "Maybe because I feel like everyone is always judging me."

That was probably one of the most honest things I had shared with Sarah.

"Why do you think that?"

"Because I'm always judging others," I responded without hesitation.

"If the things you have been through had happened to Serena, would you judge her if she felt the way you do?"

"No."

"Would you still love her the same?"

"Of course."

"Then why do you give your friend such little credit to be able to do the same?"

I paused, "I don't... I just don't want to talk about things. I don't want people to pity me or see me as weak."

"Do you consider sharing things to be a sign of weakness?"

I shrugged. "Not necessarily. I just... I've been to support groups, and when I heard their stories, I felt sorry for them. I felt like their damage was very apparent."

She took a deep breath, pausing for a moment. "Did you share with them? The support groups?"

"No, I stopped going before I ever actually spoke."

"So, why don't you give them another try? If you can talk about it with them, maybe you can share it with the people you know."

"I shared some of my past with Caleb earlier this week. Stuff I had been keeping from him for years."

"That's great."

"I guess."

"Did it not go well?"

"What constitutes *well*? I mean, I got the information out to him that was needed."

"Did he react badly?"

"He reacted exactly like I knew he would."

"Meaning?"

"He looked at me like he could *feel* my damage for once instead of just seeing it."

"It's called being empathic. Why would that be bad?"

"Caleb's been through a lot in his life, and he's already helped me more than he could possibly ever know. I don't want to be the source of more pain for him."

"But he's in pain because he cares about you."

"Pain is still pain."

"True, but I'm sure he stays around because the joy you create for him outweighs any pain you bring him."

"Maybe it's that way now—but if I start sharing everything..." I paused. "What if I share things and he decides then that it's too much?"

"And what? Leaves?"

"Yeah."

"You shut him out before he even gets a chance to make that choice."

"Because I know that's what he'll do; it's what everyone does," I replied, starting to feel overwhelmed by the topic—by the thought of him leaving for good.

"Harper, you've shared with me the past you have had with many different people. And from what you have told me about the things you do—the way you are with people—I think you may suffer from fear of abandonment."

I looked at her incredulously. "I think that's a bit extreme. I just don't want to lose Caleb from my life. He's helped me through so much."

"Why would that be extreme?"

"I just think labeling it like that makes it a bigger deal than what it is."

"So, you think the way you push Caleb away is *healthy*?"

"I'm not pushing him away; we just need some space sometimes."

"—to love each other less," she added matter-of-factly.

"No... yes... I mean, just so things don't get more complicated."

"Yeah, so you don't get hurt this time around."

"That's not what I meant."

"No? You have said before how everyone leaves—Sam, Ben, your father, your mother, Jacob, Caleb... Even Serena left you, moved two hours away. You don't think that your inability to open up to them has anything to do with that?"

***

I wasn't sure if Sarah's question or my lack of sleep had pulled the strings on my sudden exit from her office. But, as I found myself once again in my car trying to calm myself down, I realized it had been occurring more frequently lately. My heart would race. My chest would tighten. My hands would curl into fists. And suddenly, I would be saying or doing something I knew I shouldn't.

But, per usual, once I was alone, I knew I was only upset with myself. With the way I had left things, I knew I would need to reach out and apologize for storming out.

But for now, I needed a moment to sit with what she had said. I needed some time to come to terms with the new issue she had labeled me with.

Chapter Thirty-three

When I arrived at my grandma's that Saturday morning, Bernard and his kids were there. The awkward tension mounted on the front porch as my mother unlocked the door. It had been a while since we had all been in the same place. Four Christmases before, to be exact.

Caleb had been dating Alyssa at the time and spent the holiday with her and her family. I spent mine with my mother, her friends, and her perfect nuclear family.

Her new home was decorated with lights, garland, and pictures of the type of family she had always wanted. She had spent most of the time talking about Bernard's daughter—and, subsequently, *her* daughter—Hannah, who was attending college to be a nurse. She had never struck me as the proud mother type. But I guess that was just because she had never had anyone to be proud of.

At some point that night, between Bernard cutting the ham and the white elephant present exchange, I had opened the wine that was gifted to my mother by a guest. It was almost an accomplished feat that I was able to go through the entire bottle myself before anyone even noticed it was missing.

My grandma Jones was the only one who didn't make me feel like a pariah, but even so, my drunken words and actions aimed at my mother were uncalled for—at least in front of her guests anyway.

And although I blamed myself for my behavior, I didn't talk to my mother for almost a year and a half after that. Understandably so, I had yet to be invited back.

I felt horrible for being jealous of Hannah. She had never done anything to me. But the angry green monster always revealed itself the moment her name rang from my mother's lips. I had been replaced as a daughter, and I couldn't even blame her for it; she was seemingly perfect.

"Are you coming, Harper?" my mother asked as I stood alone on the porch.

I felt my face get flushed as I stepped inside. My mother divided out the assignments, separating us from them. Surely a calculated move on her part.

***

Laughter echoed up to us through the hallway, Bernard and his children reminding me that not every family was as dysfunctional as mine. Sarah would come at me with the fact that, technically, I was their family, too. But a technicality didn't erase the reality that I felt nothing for the people bound to me through my mother's remarriage.

The no-talking order my mother and I seemed to be under made the laughter even harder to listen to. It made me wonder if we could have ever had a family like that. Or had the three of us been so fucked up that it wouldn't have worked?

I had a few memories of us laughing together, but not a whole lot stuck out in my mind. Honestly, I had more memories of laughing with my uncle Sam than with my parents. And although over time, we had grown apart, it made me miss him.

"Have you heard from Sam?" I blurted out without thinking, something I had a tendency of doing in her presence. I seemed to always be trying to fill the harsh silence that clouded around us like a dust bowl.

She took her time to respond while continuing to pack stuff into boxes. "I heard he got divorced earlier this year."

"Oh. I tried to find him on Facebook a while back but couldn't."

She continued to keep her eyes and focus on the task at hand. "Yeah, I think he and uh… Marissa had theirs together."

"I see," I replied, surprised she had any idea about social media at all.

The room fell silent from our words, leaving only the noise of old books and trinkets being packed away to fill the air.

"Why do you want to get in touch with him?"

"I don't know. I've mentioned him a few times in therapy and just kind of wondered how he was doing."

Her nervous glance toward the door the moment I said *therapy* caused my eyes to twirl. One could assume she hadn't mentioned that part of my life to her husband and didn't intend to.

My annoyance didn't stem from her withholding that truth from her other half. It came from the fact that not telling him didn't come from a sense of privacy for me, but rather how it made her look as a mother.

"Is there a reason he would come up in *there*?" she asked.

No wonder I had a hard time opening up. The woman couldn't even say the word therapy.

"He was a big part of my past. I was just talking about growing up."

"Oh," she responded. It didn't seem like she wanted to continue the conversation, but then she began again. "Do you think it's helping?"

I was surprised she was asking, at least in that tone. Was it possible she was showing sincere concern for my well-being?

"Yeah, I've been talking more about stuff, which was really hard at first," I replied, conveniently glossing over my teenage-like storm-out the day before.

I waited for her to ask a follow-up question, but she didn't, and like most of our conversations, it fell back into the harsh cloud of an awkward silence from which they all came.

***

I walked around the upstairs and checked in each room and closet to see if there was anything left to pack. I reached the last door on the right side and opened it. The walls were navy blue with white trim. There was no furniture, only boxes, and dust bunnies.

How had I never seen that room before?

I stepped in to open one, seeing that there was an inch of dust on the boxes.

"This was your father's room," my mother said as she stood in the doorway.

"Who packed the stuff up?"

"Your father did before he left for college."

"He never took any of it?"

"He was going to, but we just never got around to moving it over to our place."

"What's in them?"

"Mostly clothes, probably some books."

"Shouldn't we go through it?"

"Harper, we have too much to do. This can all just be donated. There's nothing of value in here."

Her poor choice of words caused my face to flush. How could she say there was nothing of value? It was my father's stuff.

"Lori, the donation truck is here!" Thomas yelled up the stairs.

"Okay, we'll start bringing stuff down!" she yelled, sticking her head out of the door frame.

She pulled her head back in and looked at me. "Just bring them down, Harper," she said before exiting the room.

I ignored her orders and opened the box, sending the dust floating into the air around me. I quickly rifled through it, finding that it was as she had said—full of clothes. I pulled a few more over to me and checked those as well. Again, finding only the evidence that my father had once been a teenage boy who wore jeans and eighties hairband t-shirts.

I wasn't sure what I had expected. I had already discovered his biggest secret—his purposefully untimely death, so what more could I find? And if there were still things to discover, did I really want to have them revealed?

My mother walked back up the stairs as I grabbed the box of jeans to bring down. I was annoyed by her ability to leave my father packed away. To donate his past to charity without a second glance at the life of the man she had once fallen madly in love with.

But I couldn't say I was surprised. She had not only done the same with all of his things following his death, but she had also done the same with all of mine the weekend I moved out. She had left no trace of her former family, allowing a perfect new start for Bernard and his kids upon their arrival only a short time after.

I continued to empty out my father's room, snatching a sweatshirt from the top of the box before walking the box down to the truck. When I picked up the last one in the room, it was heavier than the others. Upon opening it, I saw that it was filled to the brim with pictures, books, and papers.

I picked up a glossy photo from the top of the pile. It was of my father and Grandma Jones. He looked to be around 13. He was lanky and awkward looking, having yet to come into his good looks and, I'm sure charming personality.

Although later he would become very photogenic, he was never a big fan of pictures. Even if he had been, it wasn't like he was around a whole lot to be in them, and he hardly ever smiled for them.

But the one I held in my hand captured the smile I had seen him have at times, perfectly. My lips followed suit, curving into a similar shape as I stared at his bright green eyes. Ones that looked haunted, even then.

I had gotten lost in the box, looking through a few more photographs that gave me a little glimpse into the boy my father had been.

"Harper, the truck's almost full. We're going to try and fit the last of it in!" my mother yelled down the hallway.

"Okay."

I grabbed the sweatshirt off the ground and put it in the box, having to push it down to get it to close. I walked the box down the stairs, and once everyone was out of sight, I took it to my car and put it in my trunk.

After the truck had been packed and driven away, the five of us stood outside the house to enjoy the small breeze that gave relief to our sweat-soaked bodies. Bernard handed us all bottles of water as he and my mother discussed the option of renting the property instead of selling it.

I hadn't realized my grandma had left her house to my mother, but I guess it made sense given how close they had become over the years.

A bead of sweat ran down my forehead to my neck. My body was becoming accustomed to being a sweaty mess. At least my current state didn't derive from a hellscape created by my own fucked-up mind.

I ran the bottle of cold water around my face, letting the condensation restore my body to a normal temperature. I untied the sweatshirt from around my waist and used it to wipe off the clammy mixture of elements on my face.

"Harper, what the hell did you do?" my mother exclaimed, taking me off guard.

Her expression of both horror and concern caused the other three to glance over, too.

My brows furrowed, and I wondered what I had done to strike such a powerful response. For once, I had been standing still, not drinking, not talking, not doing a damn thing to warrant an accusatory tone.

But as the makeup smeared on my sweatshirt caught my eye, my mind said what my mouth wanted to.

Fuck.

"I—uh—just fell. No big deal. It was like a week ago."

I was happy I had yet to wipe off my neck.

Bernard and his kids took a moment before going back to the conversation of renting as my mother continued to look at me. Her concern turned to anger. She somehow always knew when I was lying, not that that particular lie required a real detective to figure it out.

My mother looked at Bernard and then walked over to me and lifted my hair to see the rest. She appeared perplexed as to what to do, being in front of her flawless family and all.

"Well, you should be more careful," she commented, trying to sound casual, but the look on her face was anything but.

Although her need to look perfect in front of them always made me mad, I was grateful in that moment for it. Her need for the appearance of an unblemished first daughter outranked whatever situation she was sure I had found myself in. But it prevented me from having to divulge any information, subsequently also stopping the need to spew further lies.

***

While my mother and Bernard left to grab us all a late lunch, Hannah and I sat in the living room, taking over where my mother and I had left our awkward silence.

Thomas could be heard talking to his girlfriend over the phone on the front porch, another daughter my mother would be gaining soon if that relationship stayed on its current trajectory.

I scrolled mindlessly through my Instagram, trying to look like the silence wasn't slowly consuming my brain.

"Did your boyfriend do that to you?" Hannah asked.

"I don't have a boyfriend," I replied, with my tone unintentionally harsh as I kept my eyes glued to my screen.

"I had a boyfriend who did that to me."

I glanced up at her.

She gave me a soft smile and continued. "I started dating Adam in college. He didn't do it at first, but I still should have seen the signs. He was controlling, lied all the time, and blamed me for everything. When I told him I needed some space, he threw me down the stairs."

She paused. "He said it was an accident—that he would never intentionally hurt me. And I believed him."

She paused again, longer that time. "It took three hospital stays before I realized he wasn't going to change." She took a moment, looking around the room and then back at me. "My dad tried to pull me out of college when he found out."

I couldn't help but think that seemed a bit harsh.

At least he cared, The Voice piped in.

My expression must have given away my thoughts on the subject.

"I know that sounds extreme," she replied. "But my dad was just really worried, and Adam still had another year before he would graduate. My dad was convinced I would go back to him, and I couldn't really blame him for that. But I agreed to check in with him weekly and to join a support group off campus."

That answered my question as to why she seemed so mentally stable, but maybe things weren't as they seemed. I certainly would have had no idea she had been through that. Maybe she was just better about hiding her sordid past.

"So, if it's happening to you, it won't stop, I promise," she said, looking back down at her phone.

I took a deep breath feeling compelled to share since she had. "It was an ex," I began. "It happened after we broke up. I was just trying to get closure. I don't intend to see him again."

"Well, you dodged a bullet. He sounds like a real prick."

I smirked. "He really is."

She gave a small genuine smile before she redirected her eyes back to her phone.

It was weird how just a short conversation with someone who was essentially a stranger made me feel a little better about my own damage. Maybe I *was* ready for group therapy. If I was able to share something with Hannah, maybe I could talk to people I didn't know. Could it really be that easy? Could my damage just go away as hers had seemed to?

"How are you not angry?" I asked, finally getting up enough nerve to continue the conversation.

She set her phone down in her lap. "I was. Mostly at myself for letting it happen, but then, the more I talked about it with others, I saw that the problem was with him, not me. I just knew I would never let it happen again. I just needed to learn from it."

We sat in silence for a few minutes as I thought about what she had said. "I'm in therapy," I said before I lost my nerve. But the word vomit came with a nervous glance towards the window in case she had a reaction to it that I didn't want to see.

"That's good. It's a start in the right direction. I still go from time to time when I feel overwhelmed."

My body let out the breath I had been holding in.

Bernard's truck pulled into the driveway, and Hannah picked up her phone once again, moving on as if the conversation had never occurred.

***

The linoleum floors shined as my mother finished the last corner of the kitchen. I avoided the wet spots as much as I could while carrying the vacuum to the front door. I watched as she pulled off the rubber gloves and tossed them into the trash.

"Done," she said proudly; I think more to herself than to me.

Bernard and Hannah had left to get dinner started a short time before. Thomas left right after that to go see his girlfriend. I had taken my mother by surprise once again by offering to stay and finish up.

I even offered to drive her home. While I knew she hadn't expected that from me, I hadn't anticipated a yes to either—let alone both—offers.

***

When I pulled into my mother's driveway, Bernard and Hannah could be seen through the kitchen window. Hannah sat at the island, looking deep in conversation with her dad while he cooked. The genuine smiles that graced their faces made my internal green monster claw at my insides. But I tried to remain casual as always, acting as if the pain I felt was only a figment of my imagination.

"I'm sorry you never got that," my mother said, looking very passive, but her tone suggesting her actual condolences.

Not knowing how to reply, I didn't.

She didn't seem to mind my lack of response. More than likely, she preferred it.

"Did you want to come in for dinner?" she asked, extending what felt like an olive branch.

My phone pinged, and I looked at Serena's name.

Serena: Caleb's in jail. He Needs $500 for bail.

"Sorry, uh… thanks for the invite." I clicked the side of my phone and looked over at her. "Another time?"

Her lips stayed together as they curved into a small, almost disappointed smile. "Sure," she replied.

She didn't get out right away like I had expected. Nervously I wondered if she wanted a hug. Which left me questioning, when would it just come naturally for us to do that? When would it not be forced?

Before either of us could commit to taking an actual step forward with a goodbye hug, she opened the door.

"See you Monday," she said, shutting the door behind her.

Once she was out, my mind was given proper space to allow it to travel down an adjacent rabbit hole of worries and nerves.

Why was Caleb in jail?

Chapter Thirty-four

I sat in an uncomfortable chair for what seemed like longer than the two hours it actually was. I was tired from a day of manual labor and needed a shower desperately. Had I known it would take as long as it had, I would have gone home for the wait.

But my sweaty, smelly body fit in well amongst the others that hung around, waiting for their fellow jailbirds to be released. The room itself reeked of old gym shoes, and the bulb inside the vending machine blinked like a strobe light.

The only thing that looked to not belong was the tall blonde who sat the furthest away from everyone. She clutched her purse tightly as she avoided looking up at all. I wasn't sure what she was so scared of. The supposed bad people were locked up; the ones in the waiting room were the ones bailing them out.

The door buzzed as the middle-aged woman shifted behind her desk. The alluring blonde in the corner glanced up for the first time since she had arrived, only to be disappointed as the noise hadn't been for her person—but for mine.

Caleb stepped through the door. The right side of his face was swollen as a dark shade of black set in. He didn't look to be hurt badly. I wasn't sure if that meant the fight was broken up quickly or if he had used the blocking techniques I had forgotten—allowing him to be virtually untouched.

Serena had given almost no details over the phone. Whether that was because she really didn't know anything or because she was keeping it from me, I didn't know. I had thought the air had been cleared during my week spent with her, but maybe my information dump just left things messier than they had been before.

I certainly wouldn't have expected her to notify me that Caleb had been arrested. Maybe she had been testing me to see if I would bail him out or if I would let him rot.

If that had been what she had intended to do, I had failed. Or I had possibly succeeded, depending on what exactly she had been trying to prove.

Caleb didn't seem to notice me as he walked up to the lady at the front counter. He looked dejected and sullen. I wanted to hold him—comfort him—but I also wanted to be angry at his inability to take his own advice and stay out of trouble.

I moved to lean up against the wall while he signed some papers. He picked up his bag of stuff off the counter as the lady pointed to me. His briefly furrowed brows indicated that I wasn't who he had expected.

His expression tightened. "What are you doing here?" he asked as he walked over to me.

"Bailing you out."

"Why?"

"I think the words you're looking for are *thank you*."

He exhaled. "I didn't need you to come."

"I mean, you obviously did," I said as I gestured around. "No one else came."

"That's because I didn't call anyone."

"Why?"

"Because I was fine sitting in there."

I rolled my eyes. And he always said I was stubborn.

"How did you find out I was here anyway? Did your boyfriend call you?"

I wasn't sure what he meant by that, but before I could ask, the buzzer for the door went off again.

I watched the now perky blonde jump to her feet. I watched as the well-dressed, but beaten man was immediately embraced by the woman. The anger that Caleb had just put into place with his comment grew as my mind caught up to what exactly Caleb had done and why exactly Serena had led me there.

"Are you fucking kidding me?" I said although I hadn't meant for the words to leave my head.

Caleb glanced back at Ben, looking almost prideful in his handiwork.

I couldn't help but enjoy the sight of Ben's blood-soaked collar and tattered blazer. His slight limp and clutching of his ribs was a beautiful moment in time I hoped to never forget.

But the annoyance of Caleb interfering in something that had nothing to do with him stole the moment from me, causing my hands to ball into fists and my face to feel flush.

I should have been the one to do that to him. He should be limping and bleeding because of my fists.

I glanced at Caleb, who was staring daggers at Ben.

"Let's go," I said, putting my hand on his arm.

I caught Ben's glance in our direction as Caleb recoiled from my touch and moved past me to the door.

***

As I left the parking lot, the moon reflected off his eyes. I could tell by the shine that he had been drinking.

While I was certain he had sat in the cell long enough to sober up, at least enough to drive, I didn't want to risk him going back in. That was part of the reason anyway. The other half of me wanted to get to the bottom of what I had done to piss him off.

Wasn't I the one who should be angry?

"You can just crash at my place tonight," I said.

He stayed silent, continuing to look out the window. It hadn't been a question, but I expected at least an acknowledgment of some sort.

"Caleb?"

"I just don't get it," he began but didn't offer up anything else for me to go on.

"What do you mean? What don't you get?"

He didn't respond to my question, so I started in with different ones. "I'm sorry. Did I miss something? Are you mad at me for some reason?"

His expression softened a little, but not enough to convince me he wasn't upset with me.

"Never mind… I just didn't need you to come."

But never mind wasn't okay with me.

"No, what are you talking about? What don't you get? What did *I* do?"

***

We finished the ride to my temporary house in silence. He followed behind me as I opened the door and set my purse on the side table.

I found a spare blanket and pillow in the closet and threw them on the couch. If he had been expecting to crash in the bed with me, he didn't show it. He continued to play the quiet game as he slipped off his shoes. I stood with my arms crossed, leaning up against the wall while he pulled off his shirt. It caused me to be annoyed, and in the same intensity, to be flustered.

He glanced up at me as he unbuttoned his jeans. I was certain my breathing pattern had changed, leaving me to concentrate on controlling that in front of him. My eyes darted from his as I exhaled louder than I had intended and walked to my room.

I climbed under the cold, comfortable sheets. The workout from my day of moving and cleaning made falling asleep a seamless transition. The drift into my unconscious state felt almost immediate as my nightmare began to consume my mind.

As every time before, my room filled with smoke, and my hand seared with pain. I watched as the people from my life enjoyed themselves while I was trapped in my own personal hell. Again, my room became ravaged by flames. I expected to be pulled out at that moment as I usually was, but while the flames crept closer, I got nervous that they would actually reach me that time.

I watched in horror as they got within a foot of me. I could feel the heat pushing up against my skin. I turned to the room full of people and screamed. No one flinched; no one looked. They couldn't hear me—couldn't see me. I really was trapped and, as the flames reached my feet, I screamed once more.

"Harper!"

I inhaled as my eyes shot open. Caleb sat beside me on my bed, looking horrified.

I propped myself up on my elbows.

"Are you okay?" he asked.

"Yeah. I'm sorry for waking you."

He shrugged.

"What time is it?" I asked, reaching for my phone.

"A little after four."

"You should go back to bed," I replied, laying my head back down.

"What was your nightmare about?"

"The fire," I responded.

He put his hand on mine. "Do you want to talk about it?"

"No, it's okay. I know it's just a dream."

He gave me a half-hearted smile and got up. I wanted to ask him to stay there with me. But I didn't want to be sending mixed signals and, since I didn't know what I wanted, I let him go.

***

When I came out of my room after four hours of tossing and turning, Caleb was sound asleep on the couch. I grabbed a Pop-Tart from the cupboard and sat at the kitchen table.

After a half-hour of picking at my breakfast and scrolling through Facebook and then Instagram on my phone, Caleb joined me in the kitchen. He searched through the cupboards, finally finding the cups. He pulled one out and ran it under the tap.

"Are we going to talk about last night?" I asked.

"About your nightmare?"

"No, about the fight."

I watched as he shook his head. "There's nothing to talk about."

"Caleb, I had to bail you out of ja—"

"I didn't ask you to for this exact reason. I don't want to be having this conversation."

He finished the water, set the glass in the sink, and walked back into the living room.

I followed behind him. "Okay, well, then why don't you tell me what it is that has you so pissed off at me."

He rolled his eyes and took a seat on the couch. I waited a moment for him to respond, but instead, he pulled out his phone, ignoring me completely.

Not wanting to let my anger get the best of me, I left the room to get dressed.

***

When I came back to the living room, he was still on his phone.

"We need to get going," I said.

He nodded and put on his shoes without saying a word. We walked to my car and climbed in.

"Where's your truck parked?" I asked.

"Joe's Bar," he answered.

My head swung in his direction. "Seriously?"

He stayed silent, avoiding my eye line.

I let out a deep sigh and backed out of my driveway.

So that was what he had meant the night before when he asked about my boyfriend. I knew full well Jesse would have been working last night. What I didn't know was why didn't he call me?

Probably because you told him you needed time, The Voice said. *All this did was prove how much drama you bring. I wouldn't be surprised if he never talks to you again.*

I exhaled.

I would be more worried about you proving how much drama you bring to Caleb, The Voice continued. *In one night, you probably lost them both.*

The harsh realization of The Voice's words made my chest tighten, and my mind begin to unravel.

Chapter Thirty-five

Though I had made some progress in my nightmare the night before, Monday morning played out as it had every other night, with me waking up early, then lying in bed until my alarm went off.

As it rang, I slowly sat up, feeling the exhaustion try to pull me back down. I forced myself out of bed and into the bathroom to get ready for my grandma's funeral. Yet another day—another experience—I wasn't mentally prepared for.

***

When I arrived at the church, there was already a large group of extended family there, none of whom I knew. I hadn't known much about my grandma's side and, selfishly, I had never thought to ask.

I really didn't think there were many of them, if any, since she had always spent her holidays with us after Grandpa passed. But the turnout at the funeral showed just how wrong I was.

I took my seat next to my mother, at the front of the church, with the rest of the immediate family. I asked her if she knew who everyone was, and she did her best to recall them all.

She told me about my grandma's four sisters, two of whom were still alive. My mother was sure that each sister had at least two kids themselves, but she wasn't confident about which kids belonged to which sister. She talked about how three of her sisters had moved out of state, but one had stayed in Michigan, though she had passed some time ago. Of the remaining, my mother didn't seem to be a fan of theirs, and I sensed the feeling was mutual.

Soon the sanctuary filled with friends and old colleagues of hers. The awkward silence from those in the front few pews caused me to play I Spy with myself, trying to avoid having to stare at my grandma's casket or my own fidgeting hands.

My last moments spent in a church were at my father's funeral. It looked about the same with the crowd of people, a propped-up photo, and flowers lining the steps leading up to the podium. The entire dreadful view was one I was looking forward to not seeing again for a long while.

Serena appeared in front of me, blocking my line of sight from the minister that had taken a seat upfront. I stood up and gave her a quick hug. A hug that came more naturally to me with her than with anyone else. A thought that made me feel a little out of sorts when I thought of my mother beside me.

My mother showed unexpected kindness as she told her she could sit by me. I was incredibly thankful that she was able to put aside her feelings about Serena to see that she was my family.

I turned towards the door as one of my grandma's favorite hymns erupted over the speakers—the last of the guests filed in, including the man who was giving me the silent treatment.

Outside of his shiner, which was only accentuated by his black suit, Caleb looked good. I would have said the bruise itself was a welcomed addition to his intensity, but I still had mixed emotions behind why he had gotten it in the first place.

I kept my eyes on him as he took a seat in the very last pew.

I turned back towards Serena, who had noticed him too.

"He asked. I'm sorry," she answered before I was even able to speak.

I rolled my eyes. "You could've lied," I replied, turning my head slightly in his direction.

"He just wants to be here for you."

I couldn't help but be comforted by the thought that whatever he was mad about didn't keep him away.

But I thought you wanted the space, The Voice said. *Oh, that's right, you're selfish and indecisive. You don't know* what *you want.*

As a new song began and the minister prepared his books on the podium, the large door in the back creaked open. The noise caused me, along with a few others, to divert our attention in that direction.

I watched as Jesse looked hesitant, glancing around for a spot. My eyes immediately darted to Serena's, but she appeared to be just as surprised as I was.

The song faded out, and the minister began to speak. I peered over my shoulder, catching a glimpse of Jesse as he sat across the aisle from Caleb. He shifted awkwardly in his seat, looking as uncomfortable on the outside as I was sure he felt on the inside. When he glanced up, I saw what looked like a cut on his lip, though I couldn't be completely sure from where I sat.

Jesse's eyes veered over to Caleb's. They appeared oddly okay with one another's presence. Caleb gave a slight head nod to Jesse, and Jesse returned it before bringing his attention to the main stage.

My eyes narrowed as questions started filling my head. The first one being, what the fuck was that? Then the rest followed. Had Jesse interjected last night? If he did, why didn't Caleb tell me? Were they friends now? Was any of that why Caleb was mad at me? And lastly, was Jesse mad at me now too?

My mother caught on to my distraction, pinching my leg like she had used to when I was a little girl. Even then, I was always off in my own head—always in a daydream.

I gave her an apologetic look and faced forward.

I listened as different people went up and talked about my grandma—the love they had for her and the life she had lived. It was beautiful. There were so many things I didn't know about her. The realization just allowed for the pile of guilt that had already formed to grow bigger.

I learned that her family was originally from the Netherlands. Her parents came to the United States right after they had gotten married. Soon after settling in Michigan, they had her—the oldest of the five girls.

My grandma was a nurse in World War II and remained one her entire working career. I had known about her time working at the hospital downtown, but not about her part helping in the war. I felt my face get warm as the tears rolled down my cheeks.

Surely, she had lots of knowledge to share. I should have asked more.

Always so selfish, The Voice stated. *No wonder your family is always leaving you.*

I ignored the thoughts and the guilty feelings that were dogpiling onto my stomach.

The biggest revelation to me was her and my grandpa's struggle to have kids. They had tried for a long time to start their family, having numerous miscarriages. I choked back a sob as the one last round of guilt charged for the pile and landed on top, making my insides feel like they had exploded.

Wow, you are such a piece of shit, The Voice continued. *Even your mom visited her. The woman you claim is the reason you don't show your feelings at least had enough feelings to care for a woman she had no actual blood relation to.*

I tried to convince myself that she was just secretive like my mother and I, but in reality, I was the reason we hadn't been closer.

Her sister continued talking about their life and how, after years of struggling, they got an answer to their prayers. The answer was an eleven-year-old boy—my father. Though he came to them out of the tragic loss of Grandpa's brother and sister-in-law, they saw the blessing amidst the tragedy.

I envied people's ability to have belief in something they couldn't see, touch, or prove—just blind faith. It must have been comforting to find peace in their losses; instead of anger like I always seemed to feel with mine.

The minister invited us all to stand up to sing a hymn my grandma had chosen. After we finished, we continued to stand for prayer.

I shut my eyes as everyone grew silent. I heard sniffling from the crowd and even the whimper of a small child. My mother's perfume wafted past me but soon faded into the background of the stagnant church air.

The smell and the sounds brought me back to a day I had tried like hell to repress. A day, not unlike that day, that had left me racked with guilt.

Pain crept into my head as I pictured my father's urn right where my grandma's casket was.

I felt my heart rate quicken as my father's closest friend, Steve, gave a speech, choking up after almost every laugh in his stories. My mother's gorgeous features were reduced to a stone-cold appearance, her bloodshot eyes the only indication that she was grieving at all.

I wished I would have known he was struggling. I hated that I had missed how much pain he was in.

But would it have mattered if I had known? Could I have changed things? Could I have made him talk to me—made him get help?

Maybe if I had, he could have been around to help me deal with the same thing he was going through. Then maybe I wouldn't be worrying about the possibility of the next funeral, my mother attending being mine.

I wouldn't have to worry about her having to stone face her way through another round of grieving. Another person in her life who couldn't keep their mental illnesses in check and their secrets from getting out.

I felt my heart start to pound in my chest as the minister said amen, and the sound of everyone taking their seats ran through my ears. A rush of nausea raced through my stomach as I opened my eyes to follow suit with everyone else. But in that same moment, the room suddenly went void to any sound, and as my body grew heavy, the world around me went black.

***

As my eyes fluttered open, I was staring into the eyes of a stranger. He was talking to me, but it took a few moments for my hearing to return. I didn't know how long I had been out, but it was obviously long enough for paramedics to arrive. When I tried to get up, they told me to stay lying down just until they could ask me some questions.

The only people left in the entire sanctuary were Serena, my mother, Caleb, and Jesse. The embarrassment I felt was only masked by the lack of focus I seemed to be having.

Everyone except my mother appeared concerned. Even the paramedic looked more sympathetic than the expression she held. But I was sure my mother knew I had forgotten to eat since I had done the same thing leading up to my father's funeral. But when I had passed out that time, it was in my room at home—not a big dramatic show, as I was sure she would call it.

After the paramedics finished their checkup and gave me the all-clear, Jesse and Caleb jumped to help me up, but Serena gave them a look to back off and helped me herself.

I wanted to explain how my subconscious always got so nervous about funerals and turned the part of my brain off that regulated things like remembering to eat when you're hungry. Well, that, and I'm sure the lack of quality sleep I had been getting as of late was a factor. But I didn't think any of that would help reassure them that I was fine and there was no cause for concern.

Seeing that I was indeed okay, my mother went to help with the guests who had moved to the after-funeral luncheon. I was certain I would hear about how my dramatic faint cut the funeral short later—another thing I would have to feel guilty about.

Serena took a seat beside me on the pew as the three of them did little to hide the look of concern they left plastered across their faces.

"You can all stop staring," I commented. "I'm fine."

Serena's face shifted into a smile, but the boys' didn't.

"I'm sorry if I freaked you out," I continued, glancing at Jesse.

Being up close, I could tell his lip was injured, and I was scared to ask for a reason.

When no one said another word, I stood up, instantly regretting how fast I had done it, almost sending myself back to the ground.

"I'm going to go eat," I said, looking at Serena as I held the edge of the pew.

Walking into the gymnasium was like having one of those dreams where you go to school naked, and everyone stares. But in this nightmare, instead of laughter and finger-pointing, there were concerned, pitiful looks waiting for me.

As I successfully dodged all conversations in the line, I found an empty table and started to pick at the food on my plate. My stomach was in no condition for consuming anything, let alone with a room full of watchful eyes. I knew, if I wanted to leave, I needed to give my body some fuel to do so.

After filling their plates, Serena, Caleb, and Jesse joined me, taking seats around the table like a group of old friends.

It was fucking awkward.

"So... thanks for coming. You guys didn't have to," I said, breaking the silence before I lost the nerve to.

Serena grinned, and the boys nodded.

I watched Serena shift her eyes between Caleb and Jesse. I knew what she was wondering. I was wondering about it too. But, unlike her, I wasn't sure I wanted to know.

"Well, since Harper isn't going to ask, I will. What the hell happened Saturday night?"

Caleb looked annoyed, and Jesse looked like he just didn't want to speak first.

He glanced over at Caleb, who then rolled his eyes before starting to explain. "I went to Jesse's bar because you told me that's where Harper ran into Ben."

I glared at Serena.

"You could have left that part out," she snapped back at him.

Caleb shrugged then continued. "Ben *did* show up. Then, after a few drinks, I started asking him some questions he didn't like, so I gave him the opportunity to hit me, and he took it. Since *you* called her, and *you* picked me up, I'm guessing you two can piece together the rest."

His expression was smug. I was annoyed that he was purposefully glossing over the details we specifically wanted to know.

"That doesn't explain Jesse," Serena said, looking his way.

Caleb looked at Jesse too.

"I went and tried to break it up until Caleb told me who he was fighting," Jesse responded.

"So, you got hit trying to stop it?" I asked as guilt somersaulted about in my stomach.

Caleb smirked. "No, he got hit by one of Ben's friends when he jumped in and helped me beat the shit out of him," he replied like it was a fond memory.

Jesse looked down as he smiled, too.

"So, why wasn't Jesse in jail?" Serena asked, and the boys looked at each other.

"Caleb told the cops I was just trying to break it up," Jesse answered with a slight nod to Caleb.

What the fuck was happening.

The fact that they were even in the same room, sitting calmly next to each other, was weird enough. But them working together and helping each other was a different level of crazy. I was sure I still looked annoyed because Jesse started to defend himself.

"He was saying a whole bunch of shit about you. What else were we supposed to do?"

I was still too nervous to ask for specifics of what was said, so I took the conversation down another path. "You didn't know what else to do except beat someone up?" I asked, trying not to sound too harsh since my anger wasn't meant for him.

Caleb's ability to hit first, ask questions later was a big problem for me. He did everything so intensely when I was involved—*especially* when I was involved. His behavior had a way of amping me up so that I was on his level, which was wonderful when it came to things like sex, and terrible when it came to any kind of fighting.

"I really can't deal with you guys going around handling my shit," I began. "I had put that to bed, and now Caleb is going to have shit on his record because of me. I don't want that."

"So, he was just supposed to get away with hurting you?" Caleb asked as his eyes narrowed, staring directly into mine.

His annoyance intensified when I didn't answer.

"So I was just supposed to let *you* handle it? You don't even know how to do that. You just ignore shit, hoping it will go away."

My face felt flushed with anger as I got up and headed to the bathroom. But what was I supposed to do? Fight with him there—in the gym of a church? Give an encore performance to Harper's dramatic life in front of my grandma's friends and my long-lost extended family? Give my mother yet another reason to be embarrassed of the daughter that kept her from having the perfect family?

I walked into the bathroom and stood in front of the mirror, questioning myself. Questioning why the hell I was even still there.

After calming the pit of anger that pulsated inside of me, I found my mother and told her I was leaving. I was sure the stares from people weighed in my favor of her not caring. I had become a pariah, and she didn't like the attention.

***

Serena took me home, not wanting me to drive, while my mother said they would drop my car off once they packed up. I had Serena tell the guys I was leaving, as I didn't want another minute around whatever bizarre friendship they had created while "defending my honor."

Serena left shortly after dropping me off since she had work in the morning.

I turned my phone back on, listening to a message from Sarah. I had canceled our session for that day due to the funeral. Something I had planned on doing Friday, but with my swift, angry exit, I wasn't able to reschedule.

In her returned message she said she was rescheduling me for Tuesday morning so that I didn't miss any more sessions.

After my emotionally draining day, I waited for my mother to drop off my car, then decided to call it a night. I turned off the light in the kitchen and headed to my living room to lock up. As I approached the door, there was a knock.

I peered through the window, seeing it was Jesse.

I opened the door and stepped back so he could come in. He looked uneasy. His lip appeared a little less swollen than it had that morning, but the bruise by it looked darker.

"Shouldn't you be at work?" I asked.

"I switched shifts with Jerry for his Tuesday night," he explained.

I shut the door behind him and gestured toward the couch.

"I just wanted to apologize for Saturday," he began. "I shouldn't have gotten involved."

I nodded but stayed silent, taking a seat next to him.

"I didn't really consider your thoughts on it."

I understood heat-of-the-moment bad decisions better than anyone.

"Thank you. But it isn't your fault. Caleb was intentionally looking for a fight with him," I replied, leaning my head up against the back of the couch.

"Can you blame him?"

"Yeah, I mean, if he happens to run into him, then I guess not. But he was looking to start trouble."

"I think he was just trying to protect you."

Why was he trying so hard to defend Caleb?

"I don't need protecting," I responded.

Keep saying that until you believe it, The Voice said.

He paused for a moment. "So, what's the story with you guys?" he asked.

"Me and Ben?"

He shook his head with a reluctant smile. "No, Caleb."

I didn't know how much detail I wanted to go into with him. "We used to date," I decided to say, choosing my words carefully. "It didn't work out. But we've been friends since."

I had hoped he would leave it alone. Neither of us wanted to be having that conversation.

"Just friends?" he asked.

After a moment passed, I answered. "No."

Was that what he wanted to hear?

"Is he why you kind of went MIA?"

I nodded, resting my chin on my knees and curling my arms around my legs.

"So, where does that leave *us*?"

He had so many questions. But could I really blame him for that either?

I took a deep breath. "I don't know. This is just really hard. And I'm still dealing with other shit. It's all just really overwhelming," I replied, feeling pain creep to my forehead.

"I don't want to put any pressure on you. I just like spending time with you."

That *was* pressure. Just being in the same room with either of them was hard.

"I know. I just feel bad I got you involved in my shit show of life," I responded, making him smile.

The cut on his lip did nothing to dampen the beauty of his smile. It did give him a little more of the edgy look he had lost when I found out that he wasn't the bad boy I had pinned him as.

"I got myself involved," he replied, moving a little closer. But he did so, slowly, I assumed, in case I stopped him.

"I really don't know what is going to happen, and I just don't want to hurt anyone," I said as he moved the rest of the way to be right next to me.

"Don't worry about it. We're all adults. We can handle it."

I rested my head on his shoulder.

As great as that sounded, I knew that wasn't true for at least two of us. "I just... I really didn't want to have to think about all of this right now," I said.

"So, don't," he replied, rubbing my arm with the hand he had put around me.

We sat in silence for a few minutes, that was until the close proximity to him got too overwhelming for me. I put my hand to his cheek and shifted his face towards mine. I ran my thumb gently across his injured lips.

I felt bad for having him involved, well, for having *anyone* involved—no one needed to be brought down by my bullshit. I swallowed back a lump that had formed in my throat as I looked into his eyes.

Every time I was with him, everything seemed so easy. So that made him the obvious choice, right? Like the same choice, I should have made years ago with Jacob. But, without leaving Jacob, I would have never met Caleb. And I didn't know what I would do without him.

Jesse put his hand into my hair and pulled me in for a kiss. I wanted to resist, to not be *that girl,* to not play mind games. But I couldn't. I wanted it just like he did.

I moved my hand from his face to behind his head and pulled him in harder. It didn't take long, and he was lying on top of me, pressing his body up against mine.

I pulled off his shirt and kissed his chest, then pushed myself up onto my elbows so he could unhook my bra. I took it off the rest of the way and threw it on the ground, moving his lips back to my neck.

"Uh, I don't have a condom," he said with a nervous laugh.

"You didn't think this through."

I grabbed his hand and led him toward the bedroom. But once in the hallway, he spun me around and pinned me up against the wall, kissing me once again in a way that made me never want him to stop. When we finally made it to my room, he laid on top of me—taking his time with each kiss and every touch, just like I was.

***

After we finished, I rested my head on his shoulder while he rubbed his hand slowly up and down my back. I think both of us were savoring the moment, not knowing if it would ever happen again.

As usual, he couldn't stay. Mike needed to be fed and let out. He had tried to draw out his leaving—so had I—but, ultimately, the time came for him to go.

After he left, I tried to sleep, but my thoughts were very active, and I could tell my brain was fighting to have to go back to the hellscape I had created. So, I got up and grabbed my journal.

I was seeing Sarah in the morning and had put off my hardest entry for too long. So, I curled up on my bed and put my exhausted brain to work, trying to escape my own pain by writing about someone else's.

Chapter Thirty-six

(Journal entry)

The things Caleb went through as a child are hard to stomach. Though he rarely talks about it, I learned about his past the morning after we met. Well, some of it. The rest came about a year later.

Caleb was born in a city right outside of Detroit. His mother, Alice, was seventeen years old when she got pregnant with him and was also addicted to heroin. Her parents had forced her into rehab when they found out. But in her ninth month of pregnancy, she ran away from the facility and started using again. Caleb was born two weeks later addicted to heroin. Luckily, with no permanent damage.

His mom was found passed out on the street while in labor and taken to a hospital. Due to the positive results on the drug test that the doctors had run, Caleb was taken from Alice and placed with his grandparents.

He doesn't know what happened to him up until the age of four or five, but he does know he didn't like his grandparents and was very happy whenever Alice was able to get him back. He does remember living in a foster home for about a year around that time, but he doesn't know if that was his first one or not.

Over the years, Alice had gotten clean at different times and always got custody back of Caleb and her two younger sons, Caleb's half-brothers. But that never lasted very long.

Caleb and his brothers would be with her for several months until CPS would get the inevitable call from the school and they would be taken away.

Caleb never knew his father. That part was even blank on his birth certificate. Alice did tell him once as a kid that his father was her dealer, but later she had also said he was the quarterback on their school's football team, so he didn't even know if she knew.

The father of Caleb's two half-brothers got clean and stayed clean. When Caleb was seven, and they were five and three, the brothers went to live with their dad who had moved to Texas. This left Caleb alone to bounce back and forth between foster care and whatever motel Alice was living out of.

Caleb tried hard to be a good kid and to stay out of people's way, but as he got older, he struggled with the bullying from the foster homes and from school. I don't know the extent of his juvenile record, but he said it was very long. Mostly small stuff, some of it even unreported, because some of the cops knew who his mom was and felt bad for him.

When Caleb was fourteen, Alice got clean again. He told me once that it felt different than other times. That he really believed her—that he believed *IN* her. For once, she was sober for more than just a few months. And for the first time in his life, she was even sober for his birthday. It was the only time in his childhood he remembers experiencing actual happiness.

Even though Caleb's home life had drastically improved, his school life hadn't. A few months after his fifteenth birthday, he fought back against his bullies. The problem was, he had a lot more built-up anger than he had realized, and he put one of them in the hospital.

He was expelled from school and sent to a juvenile detention center for six months. During which time his mother died of a heart attack.

He has only talked to me about it once. A conversation I was barely sober enough to remember. But I remember the pain in his voice, the sadness in his eyes, and the blame he carried on his shoulders.

While the years of drug use had weakened her heart, he was convinced that his trouble was what caused her death. They were finally happy, and he had screwed it up. He had ruined everything.

After his mother's death and his eventual release from juvie, he was placed back into foster care. The home he ended up in was nicer than the ones before, but he was too far gone at that point to care if the universe was finally trying to be on his side.

His best friend Milo had moved away after Caleb had been arrested and Alice's dead. So, with no one left, he ran away from the home. He lived on the streets for a few days before running into Ian, a kid he had met in juvie. Ian had let him crash on the couch at the place he had been staying with some guys he knew, but the crash pad came at a price. One that had gone against everything Caleb believed.

But Caleb didn't feel like he had any options, so he complied, becoming a dealer of the very thing that had ruined his life.

After a while, the pain, the anger, and the restlessness had become too much. He stayed away from heroin and all the drugs he had seen used around him while growing up. And instead, he went for the opioids, having the thought that those weren't as bad since doctors prescribed them to people.

He said, after taking his first one, he completely understood why his mom had used all those years, why the drugs felt more powerful than time with him. In his short life, he had seen and dealt with more than most do in a lifetime, and it seemed to all melt away when he was using. That feeling led to him losing all track of the next two years.

And as he approached eighteen, he had found himself being exactly what he had always hated in life. When he was young, he swore he was going to do better, but after a while, it turned into you do what you need to do to survive.

Right before Caleb's eighteenth birthday, Ian overdosed. Caleb was the one who found him. He said he still relives that moment over and over in his head. But he also said that it was the push he needed to change how he had been living.

It took a while to distance himself from his group. They weren't the type of people to let go easily. So, Caleb made himself less and less reliable. He made it seem like the drugs were really wearing down his ability to do anything. A role he had seen Alice play for years.

After a while, they stopped relying on him, and then stopped talking to him altogether.

That was when he got in touch with Milo. They had been best friends growing up, but when Caleb was sent to juvie, Milo's parents (who had been like family to Caleb) moved just outside of Grand Rapids, worried that Milo was heading down that same path. They agreed to let Caleb live in their basement, which he did for a year until he and Milo got an apartment together.

But it's not like things just magically get better when you decide to get clean. Milo tried his best to help, but when he knew his support wasn't enough, he convinced him to do something else. Which is when Caleb tried N.A., however that didn't last very long as he didn't feel it was for him.

Another man from the group, who had been Caleb's sponsor for those few months, tried to convince him not to quit. But when he knew Caleb wasn't coming back, he called and gave him some advice. He said to get a hobby, something to fill his time, so that he could do it whenever he got antsy, whenever he felt like he needed to use.

So, he walked into Ray's Gym and learned how to channel that feeling into boxing. Over the years, I could tell when he was stressed, because he spent more time there. I knew that was his sanctuary, his place to go when everything else was falling apart. It was the place that kept him clean.

For a short time, it had become my safe spot as well, which I think is another thing that bonded us. I had asked for him to work with me on boxing after everything had happened, hoping I would find the same thing he had in it.

And while it did work for a little while, over time I had found other methods of coping with my demons. Methods that to this day we still disagree on.

Caleb and I first met at a party Serena had dragged me to one of the weekends she was home. By then he was 24 and well into his recovery, enough so that he felt fine being around drinking and drugs and trusted himself not to do them. Although I'm sure it was tough.

Jacob and I had broken up about a year before that party, and while I had slept with someone else in that time, I hadn't really put myself out there.

Instead of my typical night spent liquored up, I joined in on smoking pot with a few people I had met at the party, something I had only done a handful of times in my life.

After a while, I found myself alone on the front porch. Caleb came out and saw me lying down, staring up at the sky. He was concerned for a second because of my stillness, but it was just because I was so calm and very high. I remember telling him he was cute, and that he should look at the stars with me, and so he did.

I do remember some of our conversation despite my state of mind. And at the end of it, I remember a very good, very gentle kiss. It didn't feel like he was expecting anything more from me. I got the sense he just really enjoyed my company, and I enjoyed his.

Serena walked out shortly after, and we left. Luckily for me, at some point in our conversation, he had written his number on my hand. I called him the next day and we got breakfast. That was the morning he told me the shortened version of his past.

The rest of the story came around a year or so later when I got in my dark place and he tried like hell to pull me out. Something that didn't work, but I was grateful later that he had told me.

While Caleb avoids drugs of any kind, he does have a drink on occasion. I should have seen the excessive drinking coming when he had started going to the gym so much, but I was too wrapped up in my own shit to notice.

Cassy was the first serious girlfriend he had in years. While I do admit in the beginning, I wanted it to fail, I realized how selfish that was, and stepped away. I wanted him to get the girl I felt like I had been when we had first met.

She is that girl, and I am someone different entirely. Part of me feels like I am just someone for him to watch over and take care of. A girl who can't seem to stay out of trouble or handle her own shit.

The other part of me has a whole different worry completely. That the feeling he has for me isn't just love, but a replacement for the addiction he once had. I sensed it from the intensity I always felt when he looked at me, the way life just heightened when we were around each other.

Each other's presence and touch is a type of high we can't seem to get anywhere else. His drug of choice was once opioids, but since he had gotten clean, I was worried I had now become his vice.

I was nervous about going to my appointment that morning. I wasn't sure how Sarah was going to react to my walkout the Friday before. Although, she had seemed fine on the voicemail she had left me.

But what did I really have to be worried about? I was an adult. A little reprimand from my therapist would be nothing worse than a typical conversation with my mother.

When Sarah called me into her room, I waited for her to shut the door, and then I began.

"I'm so sorry about Friday," I said. "I don't know why I reacted like that. It was rude and uncalled for."

"Harper, there's no need to apologize."

"There isn't?"

"No," she responded, taking a seat and motioning for me to do the same. "You are going to have sessions like that. Sometimes things get to be a bit much. I hope that, in the future, you let me know if it's getting to that point so that we can stop, but I understand it's not always something we see coming. Sometimes it's out of our control."

I had been expecting more of a pushback. Something more on par with what my mother would have said. More irritation at my lack of control over my emotions rather than the understanding of them.

"Have others done that to you?" I asked.

"A few times," she answered with a light smile.

"I don't know why I did it," I replied, looking down at my hands. "I've been so angry lately, mainly because I'm just… really tired."

"Are you still having trouble sleeping?"

"Yeah, I keep having the same nightmare from the fire," I responded and then paused for a moment. "I feel like, if I just finish the dream, it will stop."

"How do you know there is an end?"

"I don't know. It just seems like there's information I'm missing."

"What happens in your dream?" she asked, looking intrigued.

I felt stupid for bringing it up as I was sure it didn't mean anything and hated wasting her time on something my subconscious was making up. But it was better than diving headfirst into our previous discussion.

"It starts out like the night of the fire. I'm in my room, but there's a lot more smoke than there was before. I reach for the doorknob, and the same pain I felt in my hand happens again. But even though it's painful and I'm scared there's fire on the other side, I open it anyway." I glanced up at Sarah. "But when I open the door, it's to my mother's living room, and everyone is sitting around talking, laughing… just enjoying themselves."

"Who's everyone?"

"My family, friends, co-workers, even people who have already died, like my father and grandma."

She nodded, and I continued.

"I try to go to them, but I can't. They can't hear me either. Then the fire starts taking over my room and, as it reaches me, I wake up."

"How do you know that's not the end?"

"I don't know," I answered. "I just have this *feeling*. Like there is something more that's happening. Something I'm not understanding."

"Maybe it's not meant to be understood. Maybe it's just a dream… or nightmare, I mean."

"Maybe," I replied with a shrug.

"I, in no way, mean to imply that it isn't scary or something worth discussing. We talked a little before about PTSD. Nightmares can be a symptom of that, and it's possible you are having a hard time processing what happened."

I nodded again, but I had hoped for more of an answer.

"It's important that you do your best to keep your stress to a minimum."

My audible exhale at the hilarity of that repeated advice gave her pause, but then she continued. "That also means not turning to alcohol or any other unhealthy coping mechanism."

I was able to control my laughter on that advice. However, I wasn't sure I would be able to comply with it.

Wanting to change the subject before she dove into my unhealthy ways of coping, I quickly reached for my journal. "So, I wrote about Caleb this time," I said. "But I don't know if I should share it. I know you're a therapist and all, but after I wrote it, I kind of felt like I invaded his privacy. Only a few people know about his past, and I feel bad being the one to share his secrets."

"I understand. You don't have to share the journal entry with me."

I nodded, feeling relieved.

"How are things going with you and Caleb?"

"It's complicated."

"Do you want to talk about it?"

I shrugged. "I don't really know what to say. I had tried to make a clean break from him, but after the whole thing with Ben—"

"What whole thing?"

I felt my face grow warm as I started to backpedal. "Just with telling him about the baby."

"Oh, so you told him? How did that go?"

"It could've gone better."

"Was he disappointed?"

"No, he thought I had had an abortion."

"Oh, and what did you tell him?"

"Nothing. He was happy that I had done that for him, so I figured it was best to let him think what he wants."

She nodded. "And what about Caleb? Did you tell him?"

"Not about the baby."

"No?"

"I only told Ben so that there was nothing left to be said between us. I didn't really want to discuss it with anyone else."

"That's understandable. You have every right to keep it to yourself."

After I went another moment without talking, she began again. "Listen, Harper; you have made tremendous improvement over the last few weeks."

"I have?"

She nodded and smiled. "Yes, a few weeks ago, I could barely get you to say two words—"

"And Friday, I stormed out like a child," I said, interrupting.

"You are learning how to handle your emotions, how to talk about things… the questions I ask can be tough, and you're not always going to have an answer. Sometimes you'll need to take some time and think to really reflect on some of the things I ask. I want you to really think about what your goals are here. What you want to get out of seeing me. I know Friday was hard… I know having things pointed out about yourself can be scary. But until you start identifying the problems you may have; you can't very well expect to work through them."

"I know," I responded before drifting off into my own thoughts.

The more I talked to Sarah about my past, the more I realized that I was even more fucked up than I had thought. I saw that some of my problems might have started long before I had been shoved to the ground, beaten, and raped.

The trauma of emotional and physical abandonment I had experienced as an adolescent had laid dormant. The perfect storm of past and present trauma had been set into motion in the moments following sticks poking into my back and underwear being shoved into my mouth.

Chapter Thirty-seven

After my session, I drove to a small café downtown for lunch. While I picked at my sandwich, my thoughts wandered to Sarah's questions. What did I want out of therapy?

The answer seemed pretty easy. I wanted to get better. I wanted to not be so fucked up. I wanted to be normal.

Normal?! You will never be normal, The Voice said. *It's literally in your DNA to think the way you do.*

But I told myself, just because my father died from it didn't mean I would end up the same way. But The Voice didn't agree.

No? Do you think you're stronger than someone like him? It asked. *You think there is anything in your future that leads you down a different path? No one truly knows you because you don't let them, and if they did truly know you, they would most definitely leave you.*

A single tear rolled down my cheek and fell onto my plate. I quickly wiped my face and picked up my phone, determined not to let my thoughts bring me down to my dark place.

I opened my Facebook and aimlessly scrolled through as I finished the rest of my lunch. A shared picture of my grandma's house appeared on my timeline. Bernard and my mother must have decided to go with renting the property rather than selling it. I scrolled past it as my heart sank further, thinking of my grandma.

The waitress brought me the check, and I laid my card on top of it.

Sarah's voice rang through my head. Asking, where do you see yourself in the future?

I scrolled back up and clicked on the pictures of my grandma's place. I had been a homeowner since my mother had changed the house into my name when I turned 18. I had never rented. I had always had permanent roots down—planting me in place.

The idea of renting made me feel a tinge of excitement; It gave way to some possibility that I didn't have to stay in one place for very long. The possibilities were there to do something else, to be somewhere else, to *be* someone else.

Although I was sure being somewhere else and someone else wasn't what Sarah had in mind, I couldn't help but ride that high of the excitement of eventually getting away from the place and the people—my current self-included—that had failed me so many times in my life.

With the rush of adrenaline coursing through my veins, I picked up my phone and clicked on my mother's name.

***

When I arrived at my mother's, only her car was there. I sat for a moment. It had been a while since I had gone into her house. The memories of the last Christmas we had spent together made me shudder. I had sensed some hesitancy on her end when she had invited me to dinner to discuss the possibility of me renting my grandma's place. I wasn't sure if the hesitancy was from renting to me, or from me coming over for dinner.

I stopped stalling and walked up to the door.

I sat down at the kitchen island while she finished cooking. "Where's Bernard?" I asked.

"He is out with his friends. He won't be back until late tonight."

That information made the invitation to dinner make more sense.

She stayed silent as she continued to prepare dinner for the two of us. The whole setting really took me back. While our old home didn't have an island, I would sit at our very well-loved table as my mother cooked. My father had saved that table from going to the dump when it was being discarded by a friend of his. He reasoned that it still had some life left in it.

My mother had always hated that table. It was the first thing she changed in our house after he had passed. I was very angry about it when she did, but as I got older, I understood that it was just a table and didn't need to stay.

It was funny that I was mad, because I always hated it, too. One of the legs was shorter than the rest, and there were a lot of scratches on it—it was ugly. I was angry because it felt like that was the first of many things she upgraded after my father's death.

I glanced over at her new kitchen table. It was different from the one she had bought back then. She had made a very hasty decision on the one she got after he died. She had complained about it almost immediately after getting it home.

I had been annoyed and told her that nothing ever made her happy. In those days, I wasn't cutting her any slack.

Lately, it seemed like she was getting more bearable to be around and, well, *nice*. But I was starting to think it wasn't her and that it was me that had actually changed. I was getting older and was starting to see and understand why she was the way she was.

It didn't change the fact that she wasn't the most open mother, and it wouldn't make our relationship become something it had never been. But maybe at some point, we could have holidays together again. Maybe at some point, we would be more than just two people existing in the same world together.

"I'm really sorry we don't have a good relationship," I blurted out, taking us both by surprise.

"What do you mean? We're fine," she replied, but with little confidence in her tone.

"It must have been hard to watch Dad struggle with his depression," I continued.

If she didn't regret the invite before, I was definitely changing that.

She stopped what she was doing but didn't look up. "It was."

"Why did you stay with him?"

"That's a dumb question, Harper," she started to say as she continued to stir. I assumed I wouldn't get an answer, but then after a moment, she continued. "I loved him."

I was surprised she answered at all. I knew it wasn't a subject she liked talking about. I chuckled to myself, feeling a bit like Sarah. "I don't see how love can be enough."

She stayed silent.

"When did you find out about his depression?" I finally asked, breaking the silence I had created.

"Pretty early on. He wasn't very good at hiding it."

I could relate to that.

"Why didn't you make him get help?" I asked, sounding more accusatory than I meant to.

"I tried." She stopped what she was doing and looked up, then continued, "He was a very stubborn man, and he thought he could handle it on his own."

I could relate to that, too.

"I see that same stubbornness in you," she said without skipping a beat.

I took a deep breath as my stomach knotted up. I could sense the concern in her voice.

"Yeah, me too," I replied after a long pause. I had never realized how much I had in common with my father. "Is that why you put me in therapy?" I asked.

"I knew you wouldn't talk to me, and I figured you weren't into sharing things with the people around you without a push. So, yes."

I wanted to question back where she thought I had learned such behavior, but instead, I chose to ask something else. "Did Sam know?"

She sighed and came back to stir. "Sam knew what I told him." She paused for a while, like she was contemplating continuing or not. She turned off the burner and removed the noodles from the heat. "Harper, what are you looking for?" she asked, leaning her back up against the counter, appearing defeated.

"I… I guess I just want to understand everything better. You guys never seemed close. I don't think I would have even known there was love between you two without knowing how you had met."

She smiled and looked down, probably reflecting on that day. She always remembered it fondly. But her expression quickly changed from pleasant nostalgia to hurt.

I immediately wanted to kick myself. I probably should have thought that over before saying it out loud.

"I'm sorry to hear you feel that way. But I did love your father very much," she said, moving the food to the table and motioning me to sit down.

I took the seat across from her. "I understand that not all love looks the same. But with him gone all the time, I don't know… you didn't seem to care," I responded as she took a bite.

I really needed to stop. That wasn't going to help my relationship with her at all. If that was, in fact, what I wanted. But we hadn't been that honest with each other in a long time—if ever.

"You seemed to get along with Sam way better," I added after another moment of silence.

Her hurt expression changed to defeated once more.

I think I finally did it. I think I had made us take three steps back.

"Why do you keep bringing him up lately?" she asked, taking a sip of her wine that she had yet to offer me.

I really didn't have a good answer, so I started eating, ignoring her question, as she had been trying to do to mine. We sat in silence for most of the meal. As I finished what was on my plate, chalking the night up to another failure of ours, she began to talk again.

"I loved Sam, too," she said, staring down at her plate.

I had started to agree, but she held her hand up to stop me. "I didn't just *love* Sam. I was *in* love with Sam."

Over the years, when I would talk about Sam to others, my friends would joke about the fact my mother was seeing him—that they were having an affair. While I didn't put it past my mother, I never thought Sam was capable of it because of his relationship with my father.

"I met him about a year after I met your father. He had gone to high school with him and had left for college out of state. But he moved back when he struggled with his classes."

She stopped to take a sip of her wine, still not making eye contact. "He had a way of making me feel like a whole different person. Like more than a housewife, a mother, a college dropout—" She trailed off, seeming to remember the feeling, and I could see her smile touch her eyes as she tried hard not to cry at the same time. But her eyes got glossy with tears as she continued.

"When you were young, he helped so much with you. I was so overwhelmed. I didn't really know how to do the whole parenting thing, and your father was never around to help. So, I started calling Sam," she said, taking a deep breath. "After a while, he was just… he was around all the time. Helping with you, with the cooking, my mental state. All of it."

She sighed, beginning again, "Spending time with a person like that, talking about everything—hopes, dreams—how could I not fall for him? He was my support system—my escape."

That was the most vulnerable I had ever seen my mother. Even at my father's funeral, she did a pretty good job of not letting too much show.

While I didn't understand the direct circumstances she had gone through to fall in love with another man while married, I could completely relate to the fact that she had gotten herself into a position to choose between two good men.

It was hard for me to think, let alone admit, that I was also a lot more like my mother than I had ever realized. Which was a very real fear of mine.

"Did Dad know?"

"That I was in love with Sam?" She paused and let out a sigh. "He never said as much, but I'm sure he did." She finished her glass of wine and then retrieved the bottle from the counter. She tipped it toward me in a gesture of sharing.

I nodded. I had never had a glass of wine with my mother. I had drunk wine *around* my mother on several occasions, but never together and never like that. Like two friends spending time together—it was nice. I didn't feel like I was being judged, and I wasn't judging her. Not in that moment anyway.

"Did Sam love you?" I asked, hoping the question didn't sound hurtful.

She smiled. "He did. But we both loved your father. He was a good man, despite his demons." She paused again. "Sam and I kissed once. But we felt so guilty afterward he didn't come around for a little while. We knew, if we had left your father unhappy, we wouldn't be able to be happy together anyway."

"Do you think you loved one of them more than the other? Like, if you weren't married, didn't have a kid already, would you have chosen differently?"

I knew I was searching for her to give me an answer to my own dilemma. I was trying to find an easy answer to a certain path to take.

"It doesn't matter. The past is the past, and I can't change it," she replied as tears formed in her eyes once again.

We both went silent. She downed her glass of wine, and I did my best to savor mine and not let it get the best of me.

"I didn't want to do the marriage thing," she began again. "Not so early anyway. But I got swept up in the love I had for your father."

I gave a light smile, but a smile never formed on her lips.

"Suddenly, I was married at 19, with a child at 20, and my life was planned out."

I could see the alcohol was pushing her to share. I had been around for that type of information dump a few times before, but the subject matter was never as heavy.

"Everything I had worked for," she began. "Everything I had wanted, the plans I had…"

I watched as she swallowed hard. "— was ruined. I gave up everything for him…" Her hands trembled as she poured herself another glass. "— and he left me anyway."

I felt my eyes grow heavy with tears as she stared at her glass of wine. I had fought for so many years to see my mother as a one-dimensional person and to never understand her. To never see her side of things and what she had gone through. My chest ached for her and the pain I could see she was in. I was trying to think of something to say but was struggling to find the right words.

She moved her chair back and picked up the empty bottle and her glass of wine. I watched her as she threw the bottle away and then stood in front of the sink and once again tipped back her glass until there was nothing left. She set the glass down and slowly turned toward me.

I assumed it was the wine that brought out the sadness in her eyes that she had always been repressing, but the haunted expression on her face made her breathtakingly beautiful.

"I'm sorry, too…" she said. "That we, uh, don't have a very good relationship."

I got up and walked over to her. She reached over and took the ends of my hair, twirling them for a moment with her fingers as she avoided my eyes. "I need to go to bed," she said, letting my hair fall back in place. "Lock up on your way out."

And before I could add in anything else, the lights in the hallway went off, and she disappeared into her bedroom.

***

I sat in my mother's driveway for a little while after she had gone to sleep—her words weighing heavily on my mind. As Sarah would say, there was so much to unpack there. She had shared more than I ever thought she would with me. More than I was sure I would get again—at least for a while.

My mother had married young. She had a baby before she was ready. She fell in love with two men. One who had swept her off her feet and then dropped her in a life she hadn't wanted. The other whose timing was just shy of a year too late. One that made her feel like she was different than the woman she had become.

She had said Sam and her couldn't be together because they couldn't leave my father miserable. That they wouldn't be happy if they had done that. But I got the feeling there was more than what she was saying. And knowing her, my feelings were spot on.

I think she didn't love Sam in the way she wanted to. I think she loved the idea of him and what he represented. I think she loved the different person she was when he was around. I think she loved just how uncomplicated of a person he was.

But loving those things didn't sever the love she had for my father. If it had, I was confident she would have left him long before he abandoned us.

Chapter Thirty-eight

I stood outside Jesse's door, contemplating my next move. Mike's bark grew louder as I saw him jump at the window. A rush of guilt ran through my stomach as I opened the screen door and tucked a note to Jesse inside.

Although my mother's words weren't said as a parable, they had given me some clarity on my situation. While I still had no idea what I wanted my future to hold, I knew that whatever I was going to decide to do, I wasn't willing to bring Jesse into it. I had messes to clean up. I had relationships to repair. I had myself to fix. I had no right to drag another person into my chaos.

As I turned around, headlights beamed into my eyes. My stomach dropped as Jesse's car pulled in the driveway next to mine.

"Well, this is a nice surprise," he said as he stepped out of his car.

I grinned and opened his screen door, taking the note back.

"What's that?" he asked as he stepped onto the deck.

"Nothing," I replied, tucking it into my back pocket.

He walked over and kissed me. I savored it for a little longer than I knew I should have—knowing it was the last time his lips would touch mine.

"Everything okay?"

"Yeah, uh, I thought you had to work tonight?"

"I did, but it was slow, so Jenna's closing up…" he answered hesitantly.

"Oh."

"If you thought I was working, why are you here?"

I stayed silent as I again contemplated what to do next.

"Gotcha…" he said as his tone shifted. "So, is that letter in your back pocket telling me you chose Caleb?"

"No, I don't know what's happening with me and Caleb."

"But you're done with me," he said, more as a statement than a question.

I nodded but then glanced at him. "You don't want to be with someone like me anyway. You're better off…"

"Well, thanks for making that decision for me," he responded, moving to his door to unlock it, and go inside.

"Jesse."

He paused and took a step back toward me.

"I didn't mean for this to happen."

He rolled his eyes and shook his head. "I know. I was just supposed to be a one-night stand. Sorry, I messed that up."

I thought that was all I was going to get, but I caught his eye line one more time. He sighed, shook his head, and stepped back on the porch.

My head was still reeling from my conversation with Jesse. My anxious thoughts turned to frustration as I saw Caleb's truck parked in front of my place when I returned. I wasn't confident in how I wanted to handle the two of us just yet. I wasn't even confident if there would *be* an us.

As I shifted my car into park, I glanced at him while he sat on the steps of my front porch. His eyes stayed on me.

I took a deep breath as I turned off my car and stepped out. I paused by it for a moment. I had had enough excitement for one day. I had had enough exhaustion over the past few weeks to cover a lifetime.

"Can we talk?" he finally asked.

"Uh, sure. What do you wanna talk about?" I asked as I approached him.

He didn't stand up, so I took a seat next to him. My body grew uneasy. I was unprepared once again for another conversation about my future with someone—a conversation that could very well at any point be the last.

"What are we doing?" he asked.

"What do you mean?"

He glanced over at me as he stayed silent.

I took a deep breath and stood up. I walked over to my door and unlocked it.

As I opened the door, I turned to him. "I don't know what we're doing, Caleb. I keep trying to figure out what's best, and I seem to keep coming up short."

He stood up and walked over to me. "Because you keep fighting what you really want."

He took my hands in his, but I pulled away and walked inside.

"I'm just trying to do the right thing for us," I replied, setting my purse down on the table.

"How is being apart the right thing?"

"Because we need to move on. We didn't work out. Why can't we just be friends?"

"Because I don't know how to be just friends with you, Harper!" he said. "And you don't know how to do that either."

"But at least *I'm* trying."

"How the fuck are *you* trying? I got a girlfriend… I started a life with someone…"

"So had I!"

"What, with Ben?" he asked and then exhaled as he shook his head.

"Is that why you're so pissed?"

"Of course it is!"

"But I broke up with him. It's over."

"That's not the point, Harper."

"Then what is?!"

"*I* told you I loved you, and you threw my key at me, disappeared out of my life, and then weeks later started seeing him?!"

"So?"

"So?! You would have rather been with a low-life manipulative piece of shit than be with me!"

His words stopped me in my tracks. I didn't look at it that way. I hadn't pieced together what it looked like from where he stood, the harm I had caused his insecurities by choosing the wrong person for myself.

"I mean, Jesse, I get. I don't like it, but I get it. But, fuck, Harper... am I really that bad?"

"No..." I began to say but felt a pain rush through my temple, so I paused to collect myself.

"Then what is it, Harper? Just tell me. Tell me so I can move on. If that's what you really want, just tell me now so we can stop doing this," he pleaded as if he was asking for me to take the kill shot and put him out of his misery.

But the words wouldn't be a hit on him. The words I had to say were my fears; they were my emotional shortcomings. The target for them rested solely on my head. So, without further hesitation, I aimed at myself and pulled the trigger.

"I'm scared to lose you."

"What?"

"I'm scared you'll leave me like everyone else has, and I... I don't want to lose you."

"I'm not the one who keeps leaving, Harper. That's your specialty," he replied, teetering between annoyance and sympathy.

"I know… we have so much baggage between the two of us… what if we date and it doesn't work out?"

He stepped closer, slowly as I was known to spook easily. "Harper, I love you. You could never lose me."

"You couldn't possibly know that. What if we break up and you hate me?"

Reaching me, he put his hands on my jawline and tilted my head to face him. "I could never hate you," he replied with a smile that reached his eyes.

I felt a tear fall down my cheek, and he wiped it off.

"I broke it off with Jesse tonight."

I let my eyes meet his. I could see a glimmer in his eyes behind his somber expression.

"What does that mean for us?" he asked.

I shook my head. "I don't know."

"Do you love me?"

I nodded.

"Do you want to be with me?"

I nodded again.

I watched as his lips curled into a smile once more. "Then do that. Be with me," he said like the world was just that easy.

"But what if—"

"Harper, the world is full of what-ifs and terrible things—we can't live in the what-ifs." He paused and then stepped back to look at me.

"You're terrified that I will hate you, that I will leave… but Harper, I am worried every time I am with you that you will do the same." He paused, exhaling as if the world was falling off his chest. "You said we have baggage, and you're right; we do. But so does everyone else; at least we know each other's baggage already."

I swallowed a lump as it was trying to form.

He thought I had told him everything, but I was just starting to learn what everything was. Would he feel the same way once it was all out? Once every irrational fear and subsequent damage was on display?

For a second, my mind drifted to Jesse and the last moments I had spent with him. His words of warning after he had stepped back onto his porch. I wanted to believe they were the words of a jealous man—angry about my choice. But part of me didn't believe that. Part of me was scared he was right.

I took a deep breath and let my nerves disappear along with the thought of him. I looked at Caleb, who stood silently, waiting for me to respond—waiting for me to say anything.

"You're right," I said in a moment of unusual hope. "Let's give this a shot."

***

I rolled my body off of Caleb's and moved to lie beside him. He ran his hand up along my upper arm as I snuggled in closer. I was excited to give us another chance. Excited to have him in my bed as a boyfriend instead of just another man dulling the lonely feeling.

I looked over at him, and he looked a million miles away.

"You okay?" I asked in some sort of weird role reversal.

He smiled. "Yeah, sorry."

"What are you thinking about?"

"Nothing," he said, rolling over towards me.

"Come on. If we're going to do this, we need to be honest with each other," I replied with a smile. However, I was in no way prepared for the two-way street that that sentiment implied.

"I was just thinking about us."

I smiled. "What specifically?" I asked, glancing up at him.

"Just our future. Stuff down the road."

"Like what?" I asked, in no way actually wanting the answer. But I felt not asking indicated that I was scared of hearing what he had to say. Something I didn't need to start off our relationship with him knowing.

"You as my wife, some kids, a dog, a house in the country…" he trailed off with a big goofy smile.

His body relaxed as mine grew tense.

The smile on his face had me mesmerized for a moment, and then my nerves took hold of the rest of my body. "I didn't realize you had your future planned out like that. I figured with your childhood…" I stopped, not wanting to ruin his pleasant thoughts on the future, even though he seemed to show little consideration for what mine might have been.

"It's *because* of my past that I want a future like that. I never got to have a family. Not like the ones you see on TV. The ones I've seen others have. I want that so badly."

His hopefulness in his future family life was refreshing to see in someone, but it also gave way to my fear of not being sure I even wanted that. I had spent so much of my adult life just trying to take care of myself. I hadn't given future Harper—potential *mother* Harper—much thought.

In the short time of knowing I was pregnant; I had decided to keep it. But as I talked things out with Sarah, I was starting to think maybe my logic behind doing so wasn't very healthy.

Keeping a baby so that I wasn't alone? I was sure our sessions were going to dive deeper into that.

But with that reasoning out of the picture, I couldn't think of a sound one to actually make me take that leap and want that future. I mean, for *Caleb*, I wanted it. I wanted him to have everything in life. He deserved the best. But was me having kids to please him just another trip down Trauma Lane? Wasn't I just taking a path towards another fear of mine?

I swallowed hard, feeling the lump in my throat grow bigger. I must have gone silent for too long—that or Caleb finally sensed the tension my body had created.

"Hey, I'm not expecting anything anytime soon," he said, starting to rub my shoulder again. "I don't want to freak you out. I know marriage and kids and all that is a ways off, but it's just nice to think of the *someday*."

I looked up at him and mustered up my best fake smile yet to date. "I know. And it *is* nice to think about."

He kissed me on the forehead as I rested my head on his chest and did my best to enjoy the moment. The moment of being next to the man I loved, the man I wanted a future with, the man I was terrified I would someday leave just as haunted and angry as my father had left my mother.

That was if he didn't leave me first.

Chapter Thirty-nine

The fire inched closer to me—I was ready. I was prepared to finish whatever it was my dream was trying to tell me—or possibly show me.

I heard the ping of my phone. I looked toward my nightstand as the fire took over that as well. I heard the sound once more as the fire reached my feet.

I shot up in bed, my body drenched in sweat as Caleb rolled over to face me.

"Still having those dreams?" he asked.

I nodded my head and turned toward my nightstand and grabbed my phone.

I had two texts from my mother. She wanted to see me. I was nervous to see her after our conversation the previous night, but I was also nervous about staying and chatting some more about Caleb's and my future children.

***

I pulled into my mother's and watched as she watered the plants on her front lawn. When I was a kid, she didn't like plants because they would always die. She said she just didn't have the green thumb they required. I think it was more she didn't have the energy to give to them.

She had her back to me when I got out of the car but said hello as I walked up. She looked less wrecked than I thought she would after finishing almost a whole bottle of wine by herself. But she had had plenty of years doing it to know how to keep herself looking together. A learned behavior I hoped to adopt someday.

She finished watering her plants and then ushered me inside.

"So, what did you need to talk about?" I asked, sitting at the kitchen island the same as I had the night before. I looked at her wine glasses, all washed and put away.

Leave it to her to have no trace that last night ever even happened.

"We didn't get a chance to discuss your interest in your grandmother's house," she said, washing her hands.

"Oh, yeah. So, what are your thoughts?"

"I discussed it with Bernard this morning, and he thinks it would be a good way to introduce us into renting properties. Starting out with a tenant we already know."

I smiled, but with Caleb's interest in our future, moving in with him wasn't probably far off.

"Don't tell me you're not interested anymore?"

"Oh, no, I am. Do you have thoughts on price or anything?"

While my mother went over the details that I should have been paying attention to; I did my best to calm my nerves—thinking about the future Caleb was wanting and hoping maybe it would be possible somewhere else.

Because having a man I loved at my side didn't change the woman I was. I was still the same person who had been through traumatic events. I was still the same person who coped with her anxiety and depression in unhealthy ways. Love didn't fix me. It didn't fix our problems. And it sure as hell didn't make our explosive personalities any more compatible.

***

When I got to Caleb's that night, I pulled out my phone and showed him the pictures from my grandma's place.

"That's really nice. Whose is it?"

"Mine," I responded with excitement. "Well, my mother's, but I'm going to be renting it from her and Bernard." I took my phone back and set it on the coffee table. "It was my grandma's. I talked to my mother this morning, and they thought it was a good idea to have a tenant that they knew."

Caleb didn't seem to share my enthusiasm. "That's great," he said with a deflated smile.

"You don't sound like it is," I replied, turning to face him.

He wrapped his arms around me and pulled me close to him. "I just thought now that we were together that we would live together."

I sighed.

While he had said the words to me the night before about marriage, kids, and the whole future of us was a ways off; I had suspected his timeline was much different than mine.

I was worried that moving too fast would push me to do the same thing I had done with Jacob—to get spooked and ruin things. To spend years regretting the life I had given up. How could I live with a man I couldn't even show my literal scars to?

He would start to wonder why I wasn't getting naked around him, why I refused to take off my shirt. Low self-esteem was only going to buy me so much time. My lying pushed him away before, and I was scared it would do it again if I wasn't careful.

***

When Sunday arrived, I got a text from Sarah for a group therapy meeting that was happening at a local church. While I wasn't stoked on the location, she said it wasn't affiliated with the church, that they were just able to use one of their rooms. She had gotten the location and time for the group from a co-worker of hers.

I wasn't planning on going. But something brought me to stare at the clock all day as I played through all the scenarios of what would happen if I did decide to go.

Finally, shortly before it began, I drove to the church.

As I parked, I felt sick to my stomach. I had to relive it all not even a week before when I told everything to Caleb, and it looked like I was going to have to do it all over again with strangers.

Sarah had said I didn't have to speak in the group, which I knew from when I had attended years ago. But I also felt like, without getting myself involved, it made it easier not to come back.

I saw two women about my age head in. Then, shortly after, a few more trailed behind. The youngest looked like she was barely in her twenties, and the others looked a few years younger than me. Finally, as the minutes counted closer to five, I got out of my car and headed inside.

I pulled on the door handle, but the weakness in my arms or possibly the heaviness in the door caused it to slam back shut. I took a second to breathe and tried to shake away the trembling in my hands. I was able to open it with my second attempt.

As I stepped in, a woman about my age stood outside of the main room directing people in. Her smile looked warm and inviting. She kindly asked if I was there for the meeting, though I was certain she only did it to be nice.

I passed through the doorway and took a seat in the circle in the middle of the room. I didn't make eye contact with anyone; instead, I allowed my eyes to venture aimlessly around the room. The air smelled stale like the sanctuary I had been at for my grandma's funeral. But one of the women clicked the brew on the coffee pot, almost instantly changing the smell of the air to cheap coffee.

I started to fidget with my fingers as the women talked amongst themselves. I tried to look unapproachable, hoping no one would feel obligated to come talk to me. But then I felt as if Sarah was scolding me for not trying harder.

When I finally got up the nerve to speak, the woman from the door with the warm smile took her seat in the circle. Everyone quieted down, turning their attention to her.

She looked at me and smiled again. I attempted a smile back but knew my discomfort was showing. I was nervous that the nausea that had swept in would overwhelm my ability to talk, causing me to focus on the fear of actually vomiting from my anxiety instead of just word vomiting like I was known to do.

"I'm glad everyone was able to make it tonight. I see we have a new face here. Do you *want* to share your name?" she asked.

"Yeah, uh, Harper."

Everyone gave a genuine smile.

"Welcome, Harper," she responded.

I didn't really know what I had expected. I had been to one before, but I wasn't really in the right state of mind to handle any of it at the time. But I wasn't sure what about my life told me that I was now.

The woman—Elizabeth, or Lizzy as she said to call her—had each girl say their names and reminded everyone that it was a safe space. While she seemed very comforting, she also seemed funny too, which I liked.

I started to lose myself in my own thoughts, as I always did when I wasn't the one talking. Then I realized everyone was looking at me.

"I'm sorry. What did you say?" I asked, looking toward Lizzy.

"Did you want to share anything tonight?" she asked.

I had been waiting for the question. I still wasn't sure if I wanted to talk about it in front of strangers. I had only just said it out loud to Caleb.

I felt my body grow uneasy as knots twisted inside my stomach. "Um, not today," I answered, immediately feeling disappointed in myself.

Lizzy smiled, reassured me that it was okay, and moved on.

***

I fell asleep in Caleb's arms that night. Hoping that maybe the nightmare would keep its distance if he was close because I didn't have the energy to deal with anything more. But I knew realistically it wasn't done with me yet.

The fire approached my feet as the people in my life continued to carry on with their light-hearted conversations. I again waited for the welcomed moment of being ripped from the universe I had created.

The fire stopped at the base of my feet. I felt the intensity of the heat on my skin. I thought for a moment that that was it. That I would finally be consumed by the flames—that I could end it all.

As I prepared myself for the end, I felt a hand grab my arm. I turned around as the heat continued on my body and came face-to-face with Caleb. His expression was full of confusion as his hand moved from my arm to lacing his fingers with mine.

I felt a light pull from him in his direction.

I glanced around his body and saw my family, my friends, my co-workers—all being able to see me. They were all staring at me as Caleb lightly tugged his hand, with mine in it, in their direction.

I stared at him for a moment. A moment that felt like it lasted forever. He was starting to sweat, too. I was worried for him. I was worried that the fire would burn him and that it would reach the people right outside my room as well. It was no longer just my safety I was concerned for—they were all in danger.

I wasn't sure why I wasn't letting him pull me away from the flames and toward my family—toward the people I loved.

Why wouldn't I want to go to them?

I looked up at Caleb, putting my lips to his. He looked at me sympathetically as he pulled his hand away from mine.

I was perplexed at his sudden change of heart. The love was seemingly disappearing from his eyes. He sighed, shook his head as if I had disappointed him, and walked towards the door, shutting it behind him. Leaving me to burn in the flames by myself.

For a moment, I felt relieved knowing he was safe, knowing he would not die along with me. But the moment I realized I could have gone with him, I felt remorse. I felt stupid for staying. I rushed towards the door as the flames burned white along the door frame.

I heard myself yell "Caleb!" as I gripped the door handle and pulled on it. An attempt that proved hopeless as it wouldn't budge. I felt tears well up in my eyes as I started to cough—a cough that overwhelmed my ability to breathe. I looked around, feeling helpless, not knowing what else to do.

I leaned my back on the door and slid down—losing any bit of fight I had in me.

I curled my knees to my chest and buried my head in my arms as the oxygen in the room was dwindling at a rapid pace.

I had missed my chance out of my own personal hell. I had stubbornly stayed—for what reason, I didn't know. And I had a feeling I wouldn't live long enough to find out.

The End

Made in United States
North Haven, CT
03 January 2022

14132888R00264